# BLOOD MUSE

# BLOOD MUSE

## TIMELESS TALES OF VAMPIRES IN THE ARTS

*edited by*

ESTHER M. FRIESNER AND
MARTIN H. GREENBERG

DONALD I. FINE, INC.

Library of Congress Catalogue Card Number: 95-060944

ISBN: 1-55611-470-2

Manufactured in the United States of America

10  9  8  7  6  5  4  3  2  1

Designed by Irving Perkins Associates

# Author Notes

P.D. CACEK's earliest memories are of the stories her Romanian grandfather told and the songs her Ukrainian grandfather sang, both of which appear in "Yrena." A successful short fiction writer for the last ten years, her work has appeared in numerous publications including: *Pulphouse, Grails: Visitations of the Night, Hotter Blood—The Seeds of Fear*, Peter Beagle's *The Immortal Unicorn*, and David Copperfield's *Tales of the Impossible*.

BENJAMIN ADAMS currently resides in Seattle with his wife, Erin Ward, and two cats of indeterminate intelligence. His stories appear in *100 Wicked Little Witch Stories, Midnight Journeys, 100 Vicious Little Vampire Stories* and *Miskatonic*. He is not a vegetarian.

THOMAS ROCHE is a San Francisco writer whose work has appeared in such anthologies as Katherine Kerr & Martin Greenberg's *Sorcery* and *Enchanted Forests* and Jeff Gelb and Michael Garrett's *Hot Blood* series, as well as several of White Wolf's fiction anthologies set in their *World of Darkness*. He recently edited the anthology *Noirotica* for Richard Kasek books.

COLIN RAFF, originally hailing from Seattle, studied literature for five years in Paris before returning to the United States. "The Transliteration of Infanta" is his second professional sale, the first being "The Wax Head Decanter," in the small press publication *Funeral Party*. Now living in Manhattan, he is currently working on finishing a novel and a translation for Alexandro Jodorowsky of his screenplay, "The Sons of El Tropo."

ALEXANDRA ELIZABETH HONIGSBERG's work has appeared in *Unique* and *Fresh Ink* magazines and the *Angels of Darkness* and *Dark Destiny* anthologies. She is a counselor, a scholar of comparative religions, a concert violist/

conductor, and a songwriter. She lives in New York City with her husband and two cats.

TERRY MCGARRY has been a street trader in Galway and a bartender on Wall Street; she is currently a full-time magazine copyeditor and freelances for several book publishers. Her fiction has appeared in *Amazing, Aboriginal,* and many anthologies, and more is forthcoming in *MZB's Fantasy Magazine, Terminal Fright,* and the anthology *The Resurrected Holmes;* her fantasy novel *Illumination* was the 1992 Gryphon Honor Book. She studies Irish traditional pennywhistle in New York, where a good session can be found nearly any night of the week.

CHRISTIE GOLDEN is the author of three bestselling novels, *Vampire of the Mists, Dance of the Dead,* and *The Enemy Within.* 1996 will see the publication of her Star Trek: Voyager novel, *The Murdered Sun,* as well as her first original fantasy novel, *Instrument of Fate.* Her short stories appear in the anthologies *Realms of Valor, Realms of Infamy, Realms of Magic, 100 Wicked Little Witch Stories, 100 Vicious Little Vampire Stories,* and *Miskatonic.*

MICHAEL SCOTT BRICKER is a graduate of the Clarion Workshop, and has sold stories to the anthologies *Young Blood, 100 Vicious Little Vampire Stories,* and *Eclipse of the Senses* and the magazines *Pulphouse* and *Midnight Zoo.* He lives in Santa Ana, California, where he spends his time writing, working at the nearby Bookstar, and collecting anything and everything.

SHIRA DAEMON has been writing fiction for several years. Her fiction has appeared in *Tomorrow* magazine and the anthologies *Splatterpunks II* and *Xanadu III.* She won the *Writers of the Future* contest in 1993, and appeared in *Writers of the Future,* volume 11. She also works as a reviewer of science fiction, and has directed a series of science fiction radio plays for WBAI's *Shelf-Life.*

CHUCK ROTHMAN has been writing science fiction for 14 years. His novel *Starover's Fate,* was published in 1986, and his short stories have appeared in *Realms of Fantasy, Aboriginal Science Fiction, Asimov's, Fantasy and Science Fiction, Galaxy,* and in the anthologies *Vampires* and *Swashbuckling Editor Stories,* among others. He works doing desktop publishing for an investment firm and lives in Schenectady, NY, with his wife, poet Susan Noe Rothman, and their daughter Lisa.

LAURA ANNE GILMAN sold her first story to *Amazing Stories* in 1994. Her most recent stories can be found in *The Day The Magic Stopped*, and the upcoming *Put on Your Spacesuit, Dear*. Ms. Gilman is currently working on a fantasy set in a small liberal arts college in upstate New York that bears absolutely no resemblance to the school she attended. She lived with her incredibly patient and decorative husband Peter, and the feline-in-control, Indiana.

MARK KREIGHBAUM has appeared in anthologies such as *Weird Tales from Shakespeare*, *100 Wicked Little Witch Tales*, *100 Vicious Little Vampire Stories*, and *Sorcery* (forthcoming). He is currently working on a science-fiction novel, *Palace*, with Katherine Kerr.

PAMELA D. HODGSON has sold short stories to *Amazing Stories* and *The Magazine of Fantasy and Science Fiction*, and is currently working on a novel based on one of my short stories. About her tale, she says, "The day after I completed "The Age of Maturity," I wandered into the Art Institute of Chicago and was confronted with a bronze of Rodin's "Jean d'Aire," at which point I knew I'd got the story right."

MARY ROSENBLUM began writing in 1988, with her first published story appearing in *Asimov's Science Fiction Magazine* in 1990. Since then she has published three novels and more than 35 short works. A hardcover collection of her short fiction, titled Synthesis and other Virtual Realities, will be released by Arkam House in 1996. She lives in Western Oregon with her two sons.

TERRY CAMPBELL lives and writes in Mesquite, TX. He seeks inspiration from old cemeteries and antique shops, preferably in rainy weather, and one such graveyard was the creative springboard for "The Porosity of Souls." His work has appeared in *Young Blood* and *100 Wicked Little Witch Stories*.

GREGORY NICOLL finds his muse in strong beers, rockin' music, and smell of gunsmoke. His short fiction has appeared in anthologies such as *Sex Macabre*, *It Came From the Drive-In*, *100 Vicious Little Vampire Stories*, *Cthulhu's Heirs*, *Freak Show*, and *Confederacy of the Dead*. Greg's tales have been reprinted three times in *The Year's Best Horror Stories*. When not writing, he can often be found tending his garden of vicious, man-eating chili pepper plants.

LISA LEPOVETSKY teaches writing, literature, and communication classes for the University of Pittsburgh. She has fiction, non-fiction pieces, and poetry appearing regularly in such publications as *Ellery Queen's Mystery Magazine, Cemetery Dance, Grue, Space & Time,* and many others. She also has work in such anthologies as *Grails, Air Fish, Dark Destiny, Dark Destiny II, 100 Vicious Little Vampire Stories,* and *100 Wicked Little Witch Stories.* Her poetry has been collected into chapbooks *As The Carny Goes By* and *Skeletal Remains.*

LYN NICHOLS is a logistics warplanner at Edwards Air Force Base, the mother of three rapidly growing boys, and is an admitted caffeine addict. Currently living on five acres of prime dirt in California's high desert, she is waiting patiently for a tornado to pick her up and drop her in Kansas so she can say, "We're not in Oz anymore, Toto."

DON D'AMMASSA has been a fan of horror fiction since he discovered Bram Stoker's *Dracula* when he was ten years old. He is the author of one novel, *Blood Beast,* and scores of science fiction, horror, and mystery short stories, as well as book reviewer for *Science Fiction Chronicle* for the past decade. Recent sales have included *Peter Straub's Ghosts, 100 Vicious Little Vampire Stories, Adventures in the Twilight Zone, Analog Magazine* and others.

DEL STONE JR. is a professional science fiction/horror writer. Known primarily for his work in the contemporary horror field, he has recently branched out into science fiction in both prose and comics. His first comic script was *Hellraiser,* by Marvel/Epic. Other fictions has appeared in *More Psychos, 100 Wicked Little Witch Tales,* and *Robert Bloch's Psychos.* His first novel, *Hitch,* is expected to be published in 1996.

DON WEBB has recently sold two books, *A Spell for the Fulfillment of Desire,* from Black Ice Books, and *Stealing My Rules,* from Cyber-Psychos press. He has also appeared in *Wheel of Fortune, War of the Worlds: Global Dispatches,* and *Forbidden Acts.* He lives in Austin, Texas.

World Fantasy Award winner JANE YOLEN has written well over 150 books for children and adults, and well over 200 short stories, most of them fantastical. She is a past president of the Science Fiction and Fantasy Writers of America as well as a 25-year veteran of the Board of Directors of the Society of Children's Book Writers & Illustrators. She lives with her husband in Hatfield, Mass. and St. Andrews, Scotland.

M. TURVILLE HEITZ is a science and environment writer/editor for the state of Wisconsin and part-time freelancer. Her short fiction has been published in the small press and received regional recognition. She is now working on a fifth novel. Her muse inspired this story.

RICHARD PARKS is a Mississippi storyteller. Atypical of the breed, he cannot tell a lie with a straight face and thus tries to overcome this handicap by writing everything down. Some of his better fibs are "Laying the Stones" (*Asimov's SF*), "Simple Souls" and The Ogre's Wife" (*Science Fiction Age*) and "What Power Holds" (*Dragon*). Parks lives with his wife and three cats who don't believe a word he says except on his birthday, and designated major holidays.

Nominated four times for the Nebula Award and once for the Hugo, the Edgar, and the World Fantasy Awards, SUSAN SHWARTZ is a frequent contributor to anthologies. She lives in New York, which is sufficient justification for writing fantasy and horror. Her historical fantasy *Shards of Empire* is forthcoming from TOR books and her anthology *Sisters in Fantasy* vol II. will be published by ROC books.

SUSAN L. WILLIAMS resides in Massachusetts. Her published works include the YA novelette "Medal of Horror" and "The Blue Path," a fantasy short story. Currently, she is collaborating on a heroic fantasy series and working on a YA novel. A licensed fortune teller, her life's ambition is to make a living at this writing thing, thus enabling her to abandon the mundane work altogether.

ADAM-TROY CASTRO's short stories range from comical science fiction to extreme supernatural horror. He's a regular in *Science Fiction Age, Magazine of Fantasy and Science Fiction*, and *Pulphouse*, and the author of the horror collection *Lost in Booth Nine*, published by Silver Salamander Press. He loudly claims he doesn't like vampires, but has managed to write a half dozen stories about them anyway.

RICHARD LEE BYERS holds a BA and MA in Psychology. He worked for over a decade in an emergency psychiatric facility, then left the mental health field to become a writer. A resident of the Tampa Bay area, the setting for much of his fiction, he is the author of the novels *On a Darkling Plain*, *Netherworld, Caravan of Shadows, Dark Fortune, Dead Time, The Vampire's Apprentice, Fright Line*, and *Deathward*, as well as the Young Adult books *Joy Ride, Warlock Games*, and *Party Till You Drop*. His short fiction has appeared in numerous anthologies, including *Confederacy of the Dead, Dark Destiny, Fear Itself, Grails: Visitations of the Night, Freak Show, Superheroes,* and *The Ultimate Spider-Man.*

TIM WAGGONER lives in Columbus, Ohio, writes both fantasy and horror, and teaches college writing classes to feed himself. His stories have appeared in the anthologies *Young Blood, 100 Vicious Little Vampire Stories,* and *100 Wicked Little Witch Stories,* as well as numerous small press magazines. His short story "Mr. Punch" received an honorable mention in the eighth annual collection of *The Year's Best Fantasy and Horror.* He's written over a dozen novels and hopes to eventually sell one.

BILLIE SUE MOSIMAN is the Edgar-nominated author of seven novels of suspense. Her latest novels are *Widow* and *Stiletto* from Berkley. She has written more than eighty-five short stories for various magazines and anthologies. She doesn't believe in vampires, but thinks perhaps they believe in her.

CYNTHIA WARD moved to Seattle after attending the 1992 Clarion West Writer's Workshop; previously she lived in the San Francisco Bay area, Maine, Germany, Spain and Oklahoma. She has sold fiction to *Asimov's SF, Tomorrow, Pulphouse, 100 Vicious Little Vampire Stories, Desire Burn, The Ultimate Dragon,* and other anthologies and magazines.

# CONTENTS

## The Gallery

| | |
|---|---|
| YRENA  *P.D. Cacek* | 1 |
| THE FRIEZE OF LIFE  *Benjamin Adams* | 14 |
| GALLERY OF DESPAIR  *Thomas S. Roche* | 25 |
| THE TRANSLITERATION OF INFANTA  *Colin Raff* | 33 |

## The Conservatory

| | |
|---|---|
| IDÉE FIXE  *Alexandra Elizabeth Honigsberg* | 45 |
| FLEADH DE DEUX  *Terry McGarry* | 56 |
| BREATHTAKING MUSIC  *Christie Golden* | 66 |
| SYMPHONY FOR THE QUIET ONES  *Michael Scott Bricker* | 74 |

## The Screening Room

| | |
|---|---|
| CRIMES OF FASHION  *Shira Daemon* | 91 |
| BELA  *Chuck Rothman* | 104 |
| EXPOSURE  *Laura Anne Gilman* | 111 |

## The Sculpture Garden

| | |
|---|---|
| ARS BREVIS  *Mark Kreighbaum* | 123 |
| THE AGE OF MATURITY  *Pamela D. Hodgson* | 131 |
| BLOODSTONE  *Mary Rosenblum* | 142 |
| THE POROSITY OF SOULS  *Terry Campbell* | 158 |
| CUT FROM THE HERD  *Gregory Nicoll* | 170 |

ALL FLESH IS CLAY   *Don D'Ammassa*                                   175
THE PARASITORIUM   *Del Stone, Jr.*                                   187

## The Dance Studio

PAS DU MORT   *Lisa Lepovetsky*                                       209
RHAPSODY   *Lyn D. Nichols*                                           217

## The Scriptorium

VAMPING THE MUSE   *Jane Yolen*                                       229
THIRTEEN LINES   *Don Webb*                                           232
SING HEAVENLY MUSE   *M. Turville-Heitz*                              240
NOTES FROM THE BRIDGE   *Richard Parks*                               254
DRAMATURGE   *Susan Shwartz*                                          262

## Special Exhibits

BLIND FAITH   *Susan L. Williams*                                     279
NIGHTWEAVER   *L.S. Silverthorne*                                     290
THE HAND INSIDE   *Adam-Troy Castro*                                  294
BLOOD AND LIMESTONE   *Richard Lee Byers*                             295
PRESERVER   *Tim Waggoner*                                            303
MAN OF THE DEAD   *Billie Sue Mosiman*                               313
BEAT SURRENDER   *Cynthia L. Ward*                                    326

# INTRODUCTION

It has been called seductive, beautiful, alluring, compelling, and all-consuming. It will devour your life if you let it, but if you let it, it may also grant you immortality. It is a riddle with a double answer: Some call it *vampire*; some call it *art*.

There is a strange but undeniable kinship between the vampire and the artist, between the vampire and art. Tales and legends of the undead frequently emphasize the vampire's view of common mortals as mere food to prolong its unnatural life. Then what is the artist who comes to see every experience and every other life surrounding him as just another potential source for a story, a painting, a composition, which in turn (in the best of all possible worlds) will be sold to provide him with the necessities of life?

As for art itself, the biographies of its more devoted followers are filled with instances where the thing they served demanded—and got—the sacrifice of their youth, their lovers, their families, their sanity, and sometimes their lives. In the same way, the histories of those who loved artists often contain similar stories.

The lure of the vampire, like the lure of art, is the promise of defying the power of death and cheating oblivion. Ordinary people seek to guarantee that after they die, their lives will endure through their children. For the vampire, this avenue is closed. He must resort to artificial means to procreate through those victims he turns vampire like himself. For the artist—though he may indeed create children of his flesh—there will always be those other "children" of his mind and hand to carry on his name and his memory. And how many times do the children of the artist's mind take precedence in his heart över the children of his body?

The interwoven kinship between art, artist, and vampire works on many levels, weaves together uncounted shades of what it truly means to create, to control, to live forever. In this collection you will read many explorations of this theme, each as unique as the art form it takes for illustration and as the writer who has chosen it. They touch the past, the present, and the future. Sometimes they speak of historical artists (And why not? One of the first authors in the genre, Dr. John Polidori, took the poet Lord Byron as his prototype for the seductive monster, Lord Ruthven, in his novel *The Vampyre*). They take you through the creative media of words, music, sculpture, painting, film, dance, and those arts that elude inclusion in the major catagories, but which for all that hold no less fascination, obsession, and passion for their devotees.

The galleries are open. The artists are waiting. Please come in.

—ESTHER M. FRIESNER

# YRENA

*P. D. Cacek*

She looked like a piece of trash someone had tossed to the side of the road. Tiny she was and pale . . . so, so pale that her skin seemed to glow in the darkness.

At first Konstantin Misurov thought she might not even be real, just some starving sculptor's joke crafted from the late winter snow and draped with rags. Not that it would have surprised him. Since the Great Revolution, Misurov had seen many sculptors starving in the streets of the newly renamed Leningrad. It was only by the greatest luck that he had not joined them; that, and the fact that even a society of equals needed signs to be painted. His talent, once renowned in the Imperial courts, was at least not going to waste.

Ah, she moved . . . slowly as if the cold had already worked its bony fingers into her, and Misurov blinked away the snowflakes building on his lashes. He'd almost forgotten the child was there and *that* worried him. It was not like him to indulge in his own misery such that he would let so tender a morsel get away.

Even if he could not paint, life still had its compensations.

The child moved again, drawing her stockinged legs closer to her chest as Misurov closed the distance between them. Her eyes, dark as the rags she wore and betraying the taint of gypsy blood in her veins, raised to the level of his face and stayed there. Even in the shadows Misurov could see that they held no fear—mistrust, yes . . . and something else, but not fear.

"Hello, little bird, have you fallen from your nest?"

The child nodded and a ragged seam slipped from her shoulder. Her flesh tone was a subtle mix of cerulean and ash. A less subtle heat filled Misurov's groin an instant before the wind snatched it away.

"You should not be out all alone," he said softly, his breath steaming in the cold. "Aren't you afraid?"

As he crouched on the hard-packed snow in front of her, Misurov was

1

aware of the others who shared the night with them. They were huddled forms . . . vague, faceless shadows . . . background images filling in an unfinished landscape. But one never knew in times like these what a mere shadow might remember, or a background image report to the wolfish authorities.

A lifetime ago, before the revolution, Misurov had relied upon his position in the old regime to make his "indiscretions" invisible. Now they would make him just another target for re-education.

"Where is your mother, little bird?" he asked gently, in a voice as soft as velvet.

Something glistened in the corner of her eye, just for a moment and then it was gone. A *tear?* Misurov wondered.

"Ah," he said, leaning forward over the woollen patches on the knees of his trousers, "you are alone."

She nodded again and an ebony lock slipped from beneath the shawl she wore over her head. Slowly, as if he were trying to pet a feral cat, Misurov reached out a gloved hand. He could feel the coldness of her cheek even through the layer of greased wool. Poor frozen little thing.

"I am Konstantin Ilyich Misurov," he said through the swirling steam of his breath, "I was once a great artist with many friends, but now I too am alone in this world."

She seemed unimpressed. Misurov sighed and watched his breath encircle the child's head like a holy aura. Almost immediately an image appeared on the empty canvas he kept behind his eyelids: a gypsy Madonna huddling before the Angel of the Lord.

A dirty, half-starved gypsy Madonna.

Misurov felt the ice in his beard crack as he smiled. *What a typical bourgeois thought,* he reminded himself. *But what a painting it would have made. Ah, well.*

"What is your name, child?"

The dark eyes left his face, glancing quickly to the left and right, a slight frown creasing the smoothness of her brow. Was his little Madonna looking for help or simply making sure that whatever proposition he was about to offer met no opposition? Bourgeois or not, Misurov prayed it was the latter. It would make things so much simpler if she knew the ways of the world and men. The innocent tended to scream and claw when he dragged them away.

"My name is Yrena."

Her voice was as brittle as the cold and just as numbing. No trace of her breath moved through the darkness. *She must be all but frozen.*

"My mother's name was Yrena," Misurov lied. Again. He had given his mother so many names throughout the years that he no longer remembered what it really was. Part of him hoped it had been Yrena.

"Are you hungry, Yrena?"

*Yes!* He could see it in her eyes, in the way her body tensed. Of course she was hungry, most of Russia . . . no, most of the Union of Soviet Socialist Republics was hungry.

Nodding, Misurov dropped his hand to her bare shoulder and squeezed gently. Her flesh was as hard and unyielding as polished marble.

"Come then," he said, pulling the child to her feet as he stood, "I don't live far."

They walked slowly, the loose rags covering the child's feet leaving serpentine tracks in the snow behind them, only Misurov's breath steaming the air.

Yrena was so quiet that he kept looking down the long, black line of his greatcoat sleeve to make sure she was still there. She was—a silent shadow at his side . . . his own tiny piece of night to caress and bury himself in.

The thought kept Misurov warm.

She had wrapped the scarf across her face so that only her dark eyes showed, twin holes punched into the white canvas of her flesh. And she never blinked, his little Yrena Vojvoda . . . his little girl who named herself for a village that might not even exist anymore. His little child of the night—never looking up at him, never questioning him about their destination. Silent and servile. The way he preferred them.

When another night traveler suddenly appeared in front of them, its gender and purpose disguised by the layers of snow and clothing it wore, Misurov tightened his grip on the child's shoulder. But only *he* trembled.

Yrena continued walking at his side, as indifferent to his touch as she was to the cold and darkness.

Two long blocks down and one across, and Misurov pointed to a narrow garret set above an empty stable. He was lucky to have found the place, with so many going without. The walls were thick and sturdy, the floors solid enough, and the one window faced north. Even the rats, poor thin things, were a source of comfort. They made him feel not so alone.

Misurov paused for a moment and studied the weathered lines of his current home, nodding. Whatever it had been before, it made a passable artist's studio.

Or at least it would have if he were still an artist.

The ice tugged at the hairs in Misurov's beard as he threw back his head and laughed, his breath a white plume billowing into the night sky. It was such a good joke, such a terrible good joke to play on a man who had once lived only to create worlds with pigment and brush. *Ah, God.*

A gentle tug on the hem of his sleeve brought Misurov back.

Looking down, he met Yrena's eyes and nodded.

"I am not as much a madman as I appear, little bird," he said, releasing his grip on her shoulder to take her hand. "Don't be afraid."

"I'm not," came the muffled reply.

Thanking whatever angel or saint it was that had managed to escape detection by the new government in order to place such a child in his hands, Misurov pulled her close and began walking them toward the narrow wooden staircase that led to the garret.

One of the other misplaced denizens of the area was singing, accompanied by a bandura—a sad song, probably gypsy or Ukrainian . . . definitely antirevolutionary. The rich baritone rolled through the frozen darkness, bringing with it memories of palace life—of golden children with satin skin and virgin canvases to fill with the finest Parisian tinctures, and where the light of a thousand candles was captured and reflected by snowflakes created by Fabergé instead of by God.

Misurov shook the frozen tears away from his eyes. *Foolish man,* he chided himself, *those things are gone forever. Dead.*

"Let's hurry and get inside," he whispered, half-tugging, half-carrying the child up the stair. "It's cold and you are hungry."

"Yes," she said, "starving."

Her voice was so pitiful it almost melted Misurov's heart. Almost. But not quite.

The brass hasp screeched as he opened the door, inciting a rolling tide of squeals from the rats as Misurov stepped inside. His palatial estate occupied a space no bigger than a pony stall in the Czar's stables and was as frigid as a grave. Another chorus of angry squeals met his blind fumblings for the wall shelf next to the door where he kept a tallow candle and matches. A thump followed by a high-pitched grunt let him know that the rats had again found a way up to the shelf.

Misurov felt a thumb-size strip gnawed out of the middle of the candle when he picked it up; the empty paint pot he kept the dozen or so matches in had been upended, the precious contents scattered or eaten. It took him another three pats along the shelf before the sodden fingers of his glove found a single match.

"Damn vermin," he growled, igniting the sulfur along the underside of the shelf. Shadows danced along the empty walls as he fought chills to light the candle. "If this new government of ours really wanted to do something, they would classify rats along with other political dissidents and send them all to Siberia. Bah . . . but enough of things we cannot change, isn't that so, Yrena?"

Silence and darkness answered him.

Misurov tottered slightly as he turned, the narrow, rat-chewed candle quivering. Shadows fled across the walls, solidifying finally into the tiny figure still standing in the open doorway. Perhaps fear had found her at last.

"Yrena."

She didn't move—*How many times had he told his models not to move?*—didn't lower her dark eyes from his, the pinprick of light they reflected the only things moving.

"What is it, Yrena?" Misurov asked softly, his voice a lullaby. "I won't hurt you. Come in, there is nothing of which to be afraid."

Her body started moving forward at the word *come*. And by the time the last echo of the last word died Misurov found himself being grasped around the waist in a surprisingly strong bear-hug.

Misurov's laughter clouded the air as he swung her up to his chest and slammed the door with a kick. She didn't seem to notice when he released his hold just long enough to slide the iron inner bolt shut. His quiet little bird didn't even seem to notice when he carried her to the tiny stone fireplace four paces away and set her before it.

A half-dozen thrusts with the fireiron into the bed of coals and a ruddy glow filled the room, exposing piles of dust-covered canvases propped up against the walls. In recent years they had proven to be a better source of fuel than a lasting monument to his genius.

To prove that, Misurov grabbed a painting from the stack nearest the hearth and set it on the embers. The portrait, showing one of the Czar's brood mares, sizzled into flames almost instantly, the heat from it sending shivers down Misurov's back.

"There now," he said, laying the poker aside to rub his hands vigorously in the warmth, "isn't that better?"

*Than what?* Yrena's dark eyes asked silently.

Another shiver raced through him. Sighing, Misurov pulled one of the only two chairs he owned over to the fire and let the wet coat slip from his shoulders. Wisps of steam that smelled like wet dogs curled up from the material.

"Come, then," he said, gently pulling the shawl away from her face and fingering one of the ebony locks it exposed, "off with those wet things before you catch your death."

Misurov felt his hands tremble, but not from the cold.

"We'll get you warm and dry first," he said, putting a promise into his voice, "and then food."

With that one word, Misurov saw more emotion in the child's face than he had since meeting her. Her need tore at his heart, but it didn't stop him from undressing her. If he could no longer paint, then life owed him *some* sort of compensation.

Without her shawl, dress, and stockings, Yrena was little more than blued flesh and knobby bones; barely a mouthful.

*But beggars cannot be choosers, Konstantin,* he reminded himself as he reached down to slip the child's gray undershift from her shoulders. *And you most certainly have become a beggar in this—*

Misurov was still chiding fate when Yrena lunged forward and sank her teeth into his wrist. The pain made him react without thinking, backhanding her to the floor, her shift coming away in his hand.

Blood dripped from the jagged wound at his wrist.

She lay naked at his feet, but for the first time in his life Misurov didn't care.

"You little bitch," he screamed, his right boot already cocked and waiting to spring, "why the hell did . . . you . . . do . . . ?"

Misurov's anger and shock transformed, scattered like ash borne before the winds as he gazed into Yrena's dark eyes. The hunger that lurked there was a living creature that reached out to him the way he had once reached out for the tender flesh of children. He felt it close around his soul. Pulling him. Luring him into its depths.

Without any effort on his part, Misurov kneeled before her and held out his bloodied arm. The dark eyes shifted to the wound, a sardonic grin slowly parting her lips. The light from the burning portrait reflecting off strong white fangs.

"Papa," she whispered, reaching up to take Misurov's hand. "Papa."

As Yrena's teeth pierced his flesh a second time an ecstasy Misurov had never found even in the arms of children exploded in his soul, creating images in his mind so real, so sublime that he began painting them on the invisible canvas of air around him.

*Yrena . . . his little bird . . . his little gypsy Madonna encircled by the ruby-red light of Heaven as she—*

The sound of retching shattered the illusion and Misurov collapsed, tumbling hard to the rough wooden floor.

"What the—?"

Yrena was curled into a ball, hunched over on her heels, the ridges of her backbone writhing snakelike beneath the thin layer of skin as she vomited. It took Misurov a moment to realize what she was throwing up was blood. *His* blood.

"God protect me," he prayed, forgetting that God had been declared dead as he scrambled away from her, stopping only when his own spine collided with the paintings lying against the wall behind him. "What *are* you?"

She looked up, his little bird, tears the color of garnets leaving tracks against her snow-colored cheeks—her fangs, like ivory scimitars, stained with his blood.

"You're not my Papa," she whimpered, "and I'm so hungry."

*His little bird. His little Madonna.*

A verdalak!

Misurov crossed himself quickly, forgetting again as he pressed his knuckles against the front of his teeth in place of the ceremonial kiss and watched the child slowly lower her head back to the blood-spattered floor.

No wonder she was alone. And starving. If the legends his Baba told him as a child were true, the verdalak was that form of vampire which could feed only on members of its own family.

"My God," he whispered, louder . . . and louder, pounding his fist against the floor. "My God. My God."

And God answered.

It was at that instant the frame within the fire cracked and spat out a smoldering piece of itself next to his hand. He could still see the intricate carving that had once decorated the wood, reduced now to charcoal . . . nothing . . . useless . . . a shadow of what it had been.

Like Yrena. Like his little bird.

Like himself . . . nothing . . . useless . . .

A painting appeared in his mind: Yrena lying there, cowering, night shadow and firelight playing over the contours of her naked body.

Yrena.

Misurov's fingers stung from the heat of the charcoal sliver as he sketched the outline. The floor was too rough for fine detail, too worn for the delicate features that soon appeared.

"Yrena. Lift your head and look at me . . . no, too much. Lower your chin. To the left, move your chin to the left, you're throwing a shadow across your arm. Yes . . . that's it. That's it."

A moment later two Yrenas stared questioningly back at him—one, the reanimated corpse, hunger filling its empty eyes; the other, a perfect Madonna surrounded by light.

*Yes.*

Nodding, Misurov stood and grabbed another canvas from the pile behind him. The painting was of a stately young woman in a flowing white gown—a lady of the court or perhaps even one of the Grand Duchesses themselves—walking along a spring path, golden sun dappling her amber hair, pink cherry blossoms cascading about her.

It was soulless. Dead. As imaginative as the signs he now painted.

A thin cloud of dust trailed across the room as he carried it to the long abandoned easel sitting beneath the room's window. The remains of a silken shirt, dust-stained and torn and yellowed with age, hung from the point of the skeletal frame like a decaying corpse. Misurov had placed it there in hopes of hiding one piece of the past with another. *Fool*, he chided himself as he tossed it over his shoulder, fitting the painted canvas into the frame.

A tube of gesso that had been in the tray for God knew how long fell when he moved the easel closer to the fire and shattered. Misurov crushed the hardened plaster flakes beneath his boots. It didn't matter. He could still paint her even without preparing the canvas. He could still *paint*.

Misurov looked at the monster-child over the edge of the canvas and felt something stir in his belly . . . his own buried dead rising from their coffins to feast on his life's blood.

*Like Yrena.*

The charcoal swept across the painting, obliterating one image as it created another. And Yrena watched, as complacent and silent as stone, only her dark eyes breaking the illusion as they darted left and right, following the blood on his wrist.

"Here," he said, bringing the wound to his face so her eyes would follow. "Look at me *here*."

"I'm hungry."

Misurov nodded and quickly sketched in the eyes before they broke contact.

"Of that I have no doubt, verdalak," he said, softening the shadows caressing the charcoal face with the side of his hand. "How long did it take you to kill your family? A month? Two? Not even wolves eat their own kind."

A garnet tear blossomed in the corner of one eye. Misurov copied it in charcoal, mentally keeping a list of the colors he'd have to buy to finish the painting.

"But I couldn't help it," she whined—a little girl being chastised for some minor misdoing. "My brother Oleg . . ."

"Ah, your brother," Misurov said, deepening the look of anguish in the thin lips. "Is he here in the city with you?"

"No."

Bold strokes—three, four, five—and ebony curls encircled her unpainted face.

"There is no one left then?"

The garnet tear fell. "No."

"So you decided to come to the big city, huh? Walked all the way from Vojvoda to see if there was some long-forgotten family member . . . like a wolf cub tracking lambs. But it wasn't that easy, was it, little bird?"

Misurov let the charcoal drop from his fingers as he took a step back to look at the sketch. Yrena, like the child Madonna, stared calmly back at him. Where there had been only need and hunger, there was now acceptance. Where there had been only shadow, there was now light.

"You came all that way and you found nothing." Misurov reached out and brushed his fingers lightly over the charcoaled shoulders. "Well, you are in good company . . . even the living have found nothing here."

"But I'm so hungry," the creature moaned, the points of her fangs digging into her colorless bottom lip.

Misurov nodded, understanding. "As I was."

Absently rubbing the charcoal into his beard, he walked back to her and kneeled—slowly pulled the blood-soaked cuff away from his wrist and held it out. Yrena yelped like a booted hound, covering her face with bloodied fingers.

"Go away," she whimpered, "leave me alone."

How many other children had told him that? Fifty? One hundred? And how many times had he heeded that plea? Not once.

Then or now.

"Shush, little bird," Misurov said as softly as he had every other time, "I'm not going to hurt you. Look, see what I have for you." Dark eyes lifted just enough to gaze at the wound. "Come, my Yrena, eat."

Caution, like black ice forming across the surface of a pond, momentarily replaced the hunger in her eyes. In the flickering light, Misurov watched the muscles in her narrow thighs and calves quiver.

"Why are you doing this?" she hissed. "Why aren't you afraid of me?"

*Why? Why wasn't he?*

The joints in his knees popped as he kneeled next to her. *Why?* Turning his head, Misurov studied the sketch he'd just done. It had been so long since anything had stirred him enough to go back to his easel . . . so very long since he'd felt truly alive.

"Because," Misurov said, on his knees now, moving his bloodied wrist closer even as she backed away, "I need you to model for me."

"But I *can't*," she whimpered, "I can only feed on . . . I can only . . ."

Her sobs sounded human enough.

"I know, I know," Misurov said, taking both her cold hands in his. "But listen to me, little bird, there is a way. I can adopt you. Do you understand? I *do* adopt you. That makes *me* your Papa now. Understand?"

The skin around Yrena's mouth tightened. She understood.

"My Papa."

"Yes."

"My *Papa*."

Misurov felt his body jerk as she darted forward, her fangs golden in the firelight and glistening with drool. It was all he could do to keep her at bay, the wound at his wrist held just out of reach.

"Yes, but listen to me, verdalak," he commanded, "I will be your Papa but you will not feed off of me. I have many cousins in this city, many more than any family needs, and each night I will tell you where to find one. You may drain that one to the dregs, I don't care, but then you will come back to me. Only to me, do you understand *that?*"

Yrena nodded, less child and more monster as she nuzzled the wound and whined.

"All right then, you may take just a little . . . to seal our bargain, so to speak. *Ah, God!*"

Light and fire coursed through Misurov when she reopened the wound and began to lap, her slug-white tongue making kitten sounds in the stillness. Closing his eyes, Misurov shuddered and saw colors swirl into a hundred paintings . . . masterpieces that had yet to be created. Hundreds? No . . . thousands, and all of Yrena. All of them of his little bird.

Misurov arched his back, groaning at the strength of the spasm that rocked through him.

*God, it was good to be painting again.*


He loved her.

Not the way he had once feigned love with living children, using their bodies to fill an emptiness he'd never even known existed until Yrena came into his life.

Because she had given him *back* his life and filled it the way her painted image filled the walls of his room. His little bird, gazing back at him regardless of where he looked—but always in shadows, features highlighted only by candlelight, the colors muted . . . dark.

She required so little of the spectrum: black, mulberry, lapis and cerulean, alabaster and ivory for her flesh, a touch of mustard and primrose for the candle's wan glow, and vermillion for her lips and cheeks.

It was sad in a way, Misurov mused as he swirled a drop of red into black, now that he had money enough to buy every hue ever imagined.

One of the benefits of Yrena's nightly "family visits" was the presents she brought home to her loving Papa. Sometimes rubles and sometimes things that could be more discreetly bartered for the supplies he needed. His lovely little bird.

Misurov felt no remorse. His morally superior family had kept their disapproval of him a secret as long as he was their link to court; but almost at the same moment the Czar and his family were falling beneath a summer rain of bullets, Misurovs were denouncing him to anyone who would listen as a pervert and Menshevik.

Bastards.

Rolling his shoulders against the cramp that had worked its way into them, Misurov stuck the sable-tipped brush between his teeth and took a step back . . . nodding at the Yrena who stared back at him from the finished canvas.

She was standing half hidden by the open door, looking back into the room over her right shoulder . . . the faintest hint of a smile playing at the corners of her mouth.

It was that smile which had driven Misurov back to the easel, the first *real* smile he had ever seen from her. The first, he prayed, of many more to come.


Misurov heard her light step on the stairs only a moment before she opened the door.

"I'm home, Papa," she said, closing the door and walking quickly to his side, her woollen cape fluttering behind her like angel wings.

Smiling around the brush, Misurov leaned forward to receive her offered kiss. And felt a shiver nettle his spine. Her lips were icicles against his flesh, her breath the wind from a slaughterhouse.

His little love.

"Did you remember to do as I told you, Yrena?" He asked as he took the brush from between his teeth, then tossed both it and the palette to the floor. He had asked that same question for twenty-six nights in a row.

"Yes, Papa."

"And there was no trouble?"

"No, Papa."

She was such a good child.

"Come then and tell your Papa all about it."

Misurov flexed the stiffness from his fingers as he walked to the hearth. The roaring fire he had started before beginning to paint had reduced itself to a fist-sized mound of rolling coals. *Where did the time go?* Picking up the wrought-iron poker he stabbed the embers and watched a million sparks fly to heaven.

When he turned around she was standing at his side, the knife blade laid out across both palms. Even though he didn't think the taint of the verdalak would extend to Yrena's adoptive family, Misurov didn't believe in taking chances. Instead of using her fangs, he had instructed his beloved child to slit throats or wrists to feed.

What news there'd been on the streets had been full of the ghastly murders. *The work of a madman,* it was thought, *or a Loyalist out to avenge the Empire.*

Fools, Misurov thought as he curled his fingers around the knife handle and brought it into the light. As usual it had been licked clean. Misurov nodded.

"Well, then," he said, listening to the rustle of her clothing whisper through the gloom behind him, "what have you brought your Papa tonight?"

There was no answer.

Misurov turned to find her staring at her newest portrait. There wasn't a trace of the earlier smile on her florid lips.

"Do you like it?" he asked.

"No, Papa."

"But why not, my little love?"

Her eyes traced the lines of the panting. "Because it's like a mirror," she said. "They all are. Do you hate me that much, Papa?"

"Hate you?" The knife slipped from Misurov's hand, clattering hollowly against the hearthstone as he stood. "How can you say such a thing? Just look around you, Yrena . . . these paintings . . ."

Misurov took a step toward her and spread his arms to the room. Smiled at each image he had made of her.

"These paintings tell how much I *love* you. Look here. And here, look." Misurov spun on the heels of his boots, stopping when he faced the first portrait he'd ever done of her, the night she had come into his life—lying naked before the fire, the soulless eyes glaring back at him. "You are my reason to live, Yrena, my reason to paint. How could I not love you? My God, how could you say such a thing?"

She shrugged. It was so human, so childlike an action that Misurov chuckled.

Until she turned and stared at him.

"What?" he asked. "What is it, my little bird?"

"That was the last one, wasn't it, Papa?"

Misurov made it all the way to his chair by the hearth before his legs gave out from under him.

Something scraped beneath the heel of his boot. Looking down he saw the knife blade gleam like blood in the embers' glow. Like blood. A grinding ache shot through Misurov's back and shoulders as he leaned forward to pick it up.

"I don't know what you mean, little bi—"

"You don't have any more family left. Do you, Papa?"

Misurov stared at his elongated features—*blood red*—in the blade.

"No. How did you know?"

"This one was so old and thin, not even much juice left, like the last apple in a barrel, Papa."

Misurov nodded, watched his reflection shimmer.

"Do you hate me, Yrena?"

"No," she answered from across the room. "Papa."

"Do you love me?"

"No, Papa."

"Are you going to leave me?"

"Yes, Papa."

Letting his eyes gaze at the portraits surrounding him, Misurov lifted the knife and pressed the point of the blade into the throbbing vein at the side of his neck. There was less pain than he had hoped for.

"Well, then," he said, "show your Papa what you have brought him before you go."

Misurov heard the rustle of her cape and the *tap, tap, tap* of her boots crossing the room toward him. But already she sounded so very far away.

"Here, Papa."

The goblet was exquisite, turned smoky quartz crystal with a reeded gold base, just the sort of thing his late spinster cousin would keep. A ghost from the past.

Like his paintings.

Like Yrena.

"How fitting," he said, holding the goblet up to catch the blood oozing from his throat.

She took the first brimming goblet full and drained it dry.

He filled it a second time. A third. It was getting harder to talk, to think.

"Will you love me when I'm dead, Yrena?"

"No," she said, licking her lips, "Papa."

Misurov heard glass break as Yrena climbed onto his lap and began kissing his neck. Closing his eyes, Misurov watched the colors fade from dull gray to black to . . . blood red.

# THE FRIEZE OF LIFE

*Benjamin Adams*

*I do not paint from nature—I take from it—or help myself generously
from its riches.
I do not paint what I see—but what I saw.
The camera cannot compete with the brush and palette—as long as it
cannot be used in heaven or hell.*

—EDVARD MUNCH, 1890

## PARIS, 1889

A series of sharp knocks at his door disturbed Emanuel Goldstein. He set
his pen aside and rubbed his eyes. Who could be here at this hour? His
modestly appointed room, lit only by one gas lamp on the desk, swam with
the shadows of deep night. A yawn overtook him as he stood, stretching.

The rapping came again, louder.

"Who's there?" Goldstein asked.

"Is this the residence of Emanuel Goldstein, the Dane?" asked a rough,
belligerent voice.

"Ah—yes. Yes, it is," sputtered Goldstein.

"This is the Sûretè. There is some question as to your residency here in
Paris. Have your passport ready."

"Wait—wait just a moment—"

Goldstein frantically rifled through his desk drawers. Ah, here—no, just
an empty wallet. Here was the volume of Baudelaire he thought he'd lost;
why on Earth was it in this drawer?

"Goldstein?" called the voice.

"Here it is!" gasped Goldstein. "I have it."

"Let me see it at once!"

Goldstein opened the door. Instead of the uniformed gendarme he expected, there stood a slim young man with an unruly mop of brown hair

14

and lush lips. His aquiline nose gave his face a taciturn appearance that not even the twinkle in his deep-set eyes could overcome.

"Edvard!" cried Goldstein. "You—you—I could strangle you, but I am too happy to see you." He took Munch's hand and pulled him close for a warm embrace.

"It's good to see you too, Emanuel," smiled Munch.

"Come in, come in!" Goldstein motioned his friend to a seat on the cot pushed against one dingy wall, then took for himself the wooden chair from the desk. "When did you return?"

"I returned from Åsgårdstrand just this afternoon," Munch said.

Goldstein blinked. "This afternoon? But it's nearly two in the morning. What have you been doing with yourself?"

"Wandering. Looking. Thinking. There was an exhibition by Gauguin which interested me; I spent some time there. Some of his work I found exciting, but he doesn't go far enough. Still, at least I think he's trying. I'll give him credit for that." Munch lapsed into silence, his dark eyes seemingly fixed on a spot somewhere over Goldstein's left shoulder.

Goldstein recognized his friend's abrupt segue to a foul mood. "I trust your summer was well spent?" he asked.

"Hm? Oh, yes. I rented a lovely cottage on the Oslo fjord. Someday I think I would like to own a home there, in Åsgårdstrand. My sister Inger came from Christiania to visit me; I painted her portrait, on the beach, by the rocks."

Still Munch did not meet Goldstein's eyes.

The Danish poet rubbed the bridge of his nose. "Edvard, something is bothering you. I know you didn't come to my apartment in the small hours just to exchange niceties."

"You're a wise man, Emanuel."

"No—I am a *tired* man, and beginning to feel quite cranky. Your little performance at my door is beginning to sink in."

Munch shrugged, a smile twitching the corner of his lips. "It was a sudden urge," he said. "And believe me, I needed the laugh."

"Tell me."

Edvard Munch groaned and lay back on Goldstein's bed. He covered his eyes with large, callused hands. The hands of an artist. They began shaking.

Goldstein realized his friend was weeping. He said nothing.

"I found myself by the Seine this evening," Munch finally said. "Strolling alone, keeping away from people. The Gauguin did me in. So many people there standing about—bowler hat to bowler hat—with a few women's hats in between! They became a whirlpool trying to drag me down, suck me in. I escaped. Out into the night.

"Ahead of me, on the riverbank, I saw a couple sitting on a bench. No one else in sight. I decided to stop and watch them from a distance. These two at the moment in which they are not themselves, but only a link in the chain of a thousand generations. The lights of the city twinkled on the water of the Seine, and soon they were making love."

Goldstein leaned forward, his curiosity piqued. How could the sight of lovemaking affect his friend so dramatically?

"She was red-tressed, he was blond. She was practically attacking him, Emanuel . . . riding him like an equestrienne. I—I have never seen anything like it. I found myself shocked . . ."

"You? The great Norwegian proponent of free love?" scoffed Goldstein. "Shocked? I doubt it greatly."

Munch raised himself off the bed to a sitting position, glaring at the Dane. "Yes. Shocked."

"Ah. Um. Yes," muttered Goldstein.

"She was an animal," continued the artist. "Primal. Savage. But what I saw after their lovemaking disturbed me even more. More than you could possibly imagine.

"She lowered her head to his neck, Emanuel. She lowered her head to his neck and drank, Emanuel."

"Surely not—"

Munch stood, nearly shouting. "And when she finished with him—finished drinking of him—she threw his body into the Seine!

"And then—Emanuel—

"*And then she looked at me and smiled—*

"And I plunged away. Lost myself in Paris again for hours on the blue boulevard—with the bright electric lamps and the dim gas lanterns—with the thousand strange faces glowing wraithlike in the electric light, until I found myself here, at your door."

Exhausted, Munch lay back on Goldstein's bed. A deep silence fell between them, until finally Goldstein knew from his friend's ragged, shallow breathing that he had finally fallen asleep.

"Edvard," the Dane whispered, folding his coat and preparing to lay it on the parquet floor of the apartment as a pillow. "May God help you."

*In the following three years I gathered together several drafts and pictures for a frieze, which was exhibited for the first time in Berlin in 1893. They were the pictures:* Scream, Kiss, Vampire, Loving Women, *and so on.*

*In the autumn of 1895 I exhibited at Blomquist's.—The pictures became the subject of considerable controversy. They wanted to boycott the premises—call the police.*

*These people need freshly slaughtered young painters for breakfast—a sort of sandwich paste.*

—Edvard Munch, 1918

## CHRISTIANIA, NORWAY, 1895

At times like these, Inger thought, I can truly believe my brother is mad.

The painting in front of which she stood pulsed with blood, a hemorrhaging sky glaring balefully over a terrified figure holding its head in its hands, mouth open wide in an eternal shriek. Inger felt violated by the image's intimacy. It reminded her of her older sister, Laura, who at times had to be confined. Seeing something like this, it wasn't hard for Inger to imagine Edvard the same way.

Behind her she heard, as if from a vast distance, the echoing comments of others viewing the exhibition.

"He is insane."

"Munch has gone too far."

"This isn't fit for the rubbish pile."

"A madman."

"What kind of foreign garbage did he pick up in Berlin?"

Inger turned her head from the tortured soul in the painting and looked out over the wide exhibition hall. Edvard's latest works, painted during his several-year stay in Germany, hung from each of the four walls of Blomquist's. To Inger it seemed as if each were a window into her brother's soul, and she felt disturbed by what she glimpsed through their dark glass.

In the center of the room stood Edvard, caught in a discussion with the darkly dangerous Hans Jaeger, leader of a loose circle of radical writers and artists. They were known as the Christiania Bohemia, after Jaeger's banned novel of the same name.

Edvard caught Inger's eye and excused himself from Jaeger.

"You look sad, little sister," Edvard said, approaching her.

"I cannot understand what you are attempting here," she said softly, casting her eyes from side to side, making sure they weren't overheard. "I look at your paintings and they make me feel strange. Polluted."

Edvard stood still for a moment. "Well," he finally said, "I apologize for having bothered you with them."

He turned to leave.

Inger plucked at his arm. "No! Edvard—I've offended you. I am sorry."

Edvard nodded acknowledgment of her words.

"Perhaps," she said, "perhaps . . . if you explain to me what you are trying to say with them."

He smiled and took Inger by her delicate hand, walking her around the exhibition hall.

"You see, I've had enough of interiors, and people reading, and women knitting. I want to paint real live people who breathe, feel, suffer, and love."

"But some of these don't even *look* like real live people," protested Inger. She shuddered, thinking of the shrieking figure that seemed so much like Laura.

"The form doesn't matter. It is the *impression* that matters."

"The . . . impression," Inger said dubiously.

"I paint picture after picture," Edvard continued, "after the impressions that my eye takes in at moments of emotion—painted lines and colors that show themselves on my inner eye. I paint only the memories, without adding anything—without details that I can no longer see. I paint impressions from my childhood—the blurred colors of days gone by."

"And what of this one?" asked Inger, drawing them to a halt. "Is this an impression from your childhood?"

The painting, in vibrant blood-reds, showed a crimson-tressed woman with transparent, pale skin, bending forward with her mouth on a passive man's neck.

Edvard sighed, and Inger thought she heard in his sigh the weight of an untold secret.

"While in Berlin," he said, "There was a woman. Dagny Juel—the fiancée of my friend Stanislaus Przybyszewski. We were all part of the same circle of intellectuals; Stanislaus is a Polish novelist. August Strindberg was there also.

"We—we all drank rather heavily, and would gather at a tavern to discuss Schopenhauer and Nietzsche, mysticism and psychology—"

"You slept with this woman?" Inger asked flatly.

A delicate shade of pink had begun creeping through Edvard's pale features.

"You fell in love with your friend's fiancée," she said in the same tone.

"And it ended badly. And this—" she gestured at the painting "—is how you view Dagny Juel now? As a vampire?"

Edvard nodded nervously.

"Oh, honestly, it is always the same with you! Dagny Juel, is it? I remember Millie Thaulow, too. Do you do this on purpose? Become involved with women who are already attached to someone else?"

"It's free love," he finally said. "There are no attachments, only friendship between everyone involved. With some significance, outside the bonds of marriage." But by his voice Inger knew he didn't believe it.

"Oh, Edvard! Don't you realize that there are *always* attachments in love? You underestimate the power of jealousy, and in the end you are hurt. Always—always *you* are hurt."

He looked at the painting once more, then back at her. He seemed about to speak. In his deep-set, shadowed eyes, Inger thought she saw something else. Something haunting him.

Hans Jaeger's boisterous voice interrupted them. "Munch!" he bellowed. "My good man! Come over here and meet Henrik Ibsen. He tells me he likes your work—"

Edvard took his leave, almost gratefully, it seemed to Inger. "I beg your pardon, little sister. I *must* meet Ibsen."

He strode away, to where Jaeger stood with the well-known dramatist.

Inger turned back toward the painting. *The Vampire,* read the small placard beneath it. She shook her head and decided to go home. She felt tired.

On her way out of the exhibition hall, Inger passed a red-haired woman who smiled at her and nodded as if she were a friend. Several paces onto Karl Johan Street, Inger stopped. She realized the woman reminded her of someone—

But when Inger turned back the woman was no longer in sight, lost in the crowd of people passing by, bundled against the cool evening. On their way home. Like she.

## COPENHAGEN, 1909

Dr. Daniel Jacobson pulled out his pocketwatch. Five minutes late! His new patient had already tried the limits of the doctor's patience. Perhaps he shouldn't have taken on this new case after all. Only the pleadings of Emanuel Goldstein had convinced him to see this man.

He rapped his fingers impatiently on the immense cherrywood desk which dominated the office like a standing stone. This kind of delay was absolutely intolerable—

A brief commotion sounded outside Jacobson's office door, the noise of two men's voices raised in conflict. Suddenly the door burst open, and there stood Goldstein with the doctor's new case, the mad Norwegian painter Munch.

"Good afternoon," Dr. Jacobson said curtly.

Munch stared at him with wary, paranoid eyes. His gaze left Jacobson's face and traveled over the wood-paneled walls of the office, passed the window facing onto a wide recreational lawn, scanned the rows of books on the doctor's shelves, then finally settled on a spot on the tip of his right shoe.

"I am here not entirely of my own volition," Munch finally said. "I want to return to Norway immediately."

"Oh, come now, Edvard!" cajoled Goldstein. "We agreed that a stay in Dr. Jacobson's clinic would be best for you. You're in no shape to travel." Goldstein turned to Jacobson. "His mood changes by the minute. I am afraid for his well-being. I am afraid he may try to—"

"What's that, Emanuel?" growled Munch. "Afraid I may try to *kill* myself? Fah! And what business is it of yours if I choose to do so?"

"I am your friend," Goldstein began tiredly, but Munch continued, waving his left hand in the air.

Two digits were gone from its fingers.

"Seven years ago I tried shooting myself, after an argument with Tulla Larsen; see how well I accomplished the deed? I cannot even kill myself properly."

"*Enough!*" snapped Dr. Jacobson, clapping his hands together sharply. The sound nearly made Munch jump out of his skin.

"I have no time for this," continued the doctor. "Herr Munch, I can tell you right now that you are not well, and I recommend a course of treatment which you can only receive at my clinic. Massage therapy and electrical impulses; the very latest in equipment, of course."

Munch nodded glumly. "I—I know that I need help. I feel that I am going mad. Everywhere I turn, I see her. From a distance I see her red hair, and I run to find her, but she is never there when I arrive—"

"So you will stay, then?" interrupted Jacobson.

"Yes. I will stay."

Goldstein clapped his friend on the back. "Good, Edvard, good. I'm proud of you."

"That will be all, Herr Goldstein," said the doctor. "I need to speak to my patient in private. Thank you, and please shut the door behind you."

Goldstein blushed. "Of course. Goodbye, Edvard—I shall be back to see you."

The door closed behind the retreating Goldstein. Jacobson motioned Munch to take a seat on the long sofa facing the cherrywood desk.

"So," said the doctor. "Where shall we begin?"

Munch shrugged.

"You mentioned seeing a woman. Why don't you tell me about her, why she is so important to you."

"*She* is the reason I am here!" Munch burst. "I see her, and my arms fill with lead. I see her, and my head pounds with fear and lust. She is everywhere."

"Who is she?"

"I do not know," Munch said, his voice breaking in torment. Tears streamed down his face. "I do not know. She is the pale one standing behind the trees. The full-blooded woman—the naked one. And she is always there."

Dr. Jacobson tapped his pen against his teeth. The case of Edvard Munch already seemed to be a most difficult one, he mused. But he was absolutely confident he could cure the man. Rid him of this delusion of persecution.

Suddenly Munch started in terror. His eyes widened as he stared at a spot somewhere over the doctor's shoulder. "It is she!" he screamed. *"It is she!"*

Jacobson twisted in his chair. There was nothing behind him but the window facing the darkening lawn. For a moment he fancied he saw something—the faintest hint of something pale and red quickly moving beyond the window frame.

But there was nothing. How could there be? This man Munch was mad.

*The Frieze is a poem on life, love, and death. The theme of the largest picture,* Man and Woman in the Forest, *showing the two figures, perhaps stands somewhat apart from the others, but it is as necessary to the Frieze as a whole as the buckle is to the belt. It is a picture of life as of death; of the forest, that sucks its nourishment from the dead; of the city that rises beyond the treetops. It is a portrayal of the powerful forces that support our lives.*

—Edvard Munch, 1918

\* \* \*

## EKELY, SKØYEN, NORWAY, 1944

Munch sat alone in his winter studio, wrapped in a stale-smelling woollen comforter.

He felt the end approaching, slow and inexorable. For nearly four years now, the Nazis had occupied his beloved Norway, and he refused to cooperate with them. Become a puppet, a showpiece. He was alone at his Ekely estate, alone with the fruits and vegetables he raised himself. No one came to see him any longer, not even Inger, and he didn't mind.

*She* was there, also.

In every shadowed corner of the room, she surrounded him. She looked down on him from the paintings of the *Frieze*, hungrily devouring him.

Consuming him.

"I am an old man," he whispered, just to hear his own voice. He could no longer see the pictures very well from where he sat; a burst blood vessel in his right eye some years before had almost destroyed his vision, and his left eye no longer worked in proper fashion, either.

He had to squint to see her in the *Frieze*, but he knew that she could still see him.

It had taken him several days, moving in slow, deliberate fashion, but once more the paintings of *The Frieze of Life* hung from his studio walls. The last time they were hung here was on his birthday in 1938, for a photographic portrait by Ragnvald Vaering. But then it was the younger, vital Vaering who had hung the *Frieze* in the space of an afternoon.

Many of the original paintings of the *Frieze* had been sold over the years, but Munch had replicated them in copies, vowing never to let his children go again.

His entire body ached. He sagged in the wing-backed chair in the studio, feeling his heart hammer in his chest. Odd that it refused to rest, now that he sat here, still and not expending any effort.

He sat under her gaze and remembered.

Remembered all the women who had been mere substitutes for her.

Millie Thaulow. Dagny Juel. The sophisticated Tulla Larsen, who he almost married, and over whom he almost destroyed his left hand and his life. The English violinist Eva Mudocci. Birgit Prestøe, his Gothic girl, with her cool, austere beauty. So many. So many women.

Had he loved them? At the time he believed he had. But all of them, even Millie, whom he had known before going to Paris, were but shadows, echoes of the voracious beauty for whom he truly longed.

Hard to believe that nearly forty years had passed since he sat in Dr. Jacobson's office and been pronounced cured. Had even painted the doctor's portrait! Placed him in the picture, big and strutting in a fire of color like all hell.

Cured. And though Munch saw her again, and again, and again afterwards, he took the visions calmly. After all, he was not insane. She was just as real as he. And if she ever desired, one day she would explain herself to him. Until that day, he was content.

The bleak January sun peeked through the skylights fringing the ceiling of the winter studio, and despite its rays he pulled the woollen comforter closer around himself. There was no more coal for Ekely's furnace; the Nazis had seen to that. Damnable German bastards, he thought, feeling his pulse quicken. Barbarous Huns, raping his homeland! His rage became something palpable. His vision swam with red—

And then something happened.

Munch felt something snap inside him, felt his heart give way. The pain lasted only a moment, replaced by a sudden rush of warmth. So this is how it ends, he thought, looking up at the skylight.

Day seemingly raced by, fading to twilight, and the room filled with darkness. And as the hours passed before his dying eyes, so also did the season change, from the dead of winter to something far deeper, far colder than any season he had ever known before.

And then he knew.

*She* was there with him. Not just an image of her, an impression slapped down wetly on canvas; but truly there, as real as himself.

From one of the shadowed corners of the studio she strode, her long red tresses flowing sinuously around her bare shoulders.

She stood before him, nude, her lush, proud body exactly as he remembered it from fifty-five years before. Her eyes were like two huge dark skies.

He saw her perfectly, with sight as clear as that of the twenty-six-year-old Munch who had first seen her on the banks of the Seine.

"Who are you?" he rasped. "Why have you haunted me these many years?"

"Call me Melpomene, if you must call me anything," she said.

Munch nodded in agreement. Melpomene was the Goddess Muse of tragedy, and she certainly had been that to him. "Yes. You choose your name well."

She bowed her head in acknowledgment. "In your art—in your suffering —I saw myself. You made me live again, real again, for everyone who sees your work. That is a very rare pleasure for one such as I, you know. Only through the eyes of others can we see ourselves."

"I know," said Munch. "Seeing one's own self is often the hardest act of sight."

Melpomene drew closer to him and took his withered, once proud right hand. The hand that had given her form and substance once again.

"Once you belonged to me," she whispered. "Now you belong to eternity."

She bent forward and kissed the old man gently on his parched lips. He smiled. "Love—" he said, then breathed his last.

*Art is the antithesis of nature.*
*A work of art can only come from within a man.*
*Art is the form of the picture that has come into being through the nerves*
     *—heart—brain, and eye of man.*
*Art is man's urge to crystallization.*
*Nature is the single, great realm upon which art feeds.*
*Nature is not only that which is visible to the eye—it also presents the*
     *inner pictures of the soul—the pictures on the reverse side of the eye.*

—EDVARD MUNCH, 1908

AUTHOR'S NOTE: Many of the phrases used in conversation by the Edvard Munch in this tale were written by the real Edvard Munch, who was far better suited to speak for himself than I. This story is dedicated to him, as well as Pam Hodgson and Mort Castle, who inspired.

—BENJAMIN ADAMS
February 27, 1995 1:30 AM
Chicago, Illinois

# GALLERY OF DESPAIR

*Thomas S. Roche*

Miriam wanders the top-story loft, bathing in the moonlight. Outside, the junkyard utters nightmare prayers of mechanical damnation. She whispers her own midnight liturgy as the hot wind blows through the open windows. She plays music by obscure Eastern European composers on a battered cassette deck. Her black lace dress blows wild in the wind and her black hair scatters about her pale face. Her eyes glow faintly red.

She regards the paintings which fill the room, dozens of reflections of the same woman. Each work is slightly different than its counterparts. One painting is unfinished. Miriam imagines what it will look like when completed. She knows that it will be beautiful, like its subject. More beautiful than any creature on Earth, alive or dead.

Lauren will be here soon.

Miriam smiles. She hears the flapping of wings, and a dark form appears in the skylight. The being is the size of a large bat, but its skin, normally sickly white, is flushed pink. Miriam notes that the sac under the creature's throat is swollen and bright red.

"Scythe," she chuckles. "You do your mistress justice." Miriam's familiar, the creature of her desire, has returned with its precious cargo.

A golden chalice appears in Miriam's hand. Miriam beckons to Scythe, and he flies to her in wide circles. The creature curls itself into her arms as Miriam lifts the chalice. The creature unfurls its proboscis and places the end into the chalice.

A spasm tears through Scythe's body.

"There, there," whispers Miriam soothingly, stroking Scythe's brow. "Mama loves you, bloodthirsty little fuck that you are."

Scythe's body contracts violently once more, and a stream of blood fills the chalice. Again, the creature writhes as Miriam strokes him. There is kindness in her touch, but Scythe is bound by the force of her desire, and cannot deny her. There is no question that Miriam's demands are unreasonable, but the creature has been brought into existence strictly to hunt for her. And again a spurt of blood; Miriam catches it. A single drop runs down onto her fingers.

Scythe heaves, breathing heavily, wheezing. Miriam waits to ensure the creature has given her its full cargo.

Then, with a gentle wave, she dismisses Scythe and considers her chalice.

It is not too much blood. But it should be enough.

Miriam is pleased. Lauren will be here soon.

Far above, in the night, Scythe howls in rage at his mistress and resumes his unending hunt.


She is perhaps the best-regarded local artist, and is growing in popularity. The eyes of her paintings are vivid, as if they could actually open up and swallow you whole. Her portraits live, as if the people portrayed have taken on a personality. Her work is animated by the blood of the living.

Lauren shows up precisely on time. Lauren is twenty-three and beautiful. Miriam is very much in love with her. There is more than a passing resemblance between the two women, but Lauren's hair is a very pale blonde whereas Miriam's is the color of coal. Miriam desperately wants to seduce Lauren, but she knows it is not yet time.

Lauren silently removes her clothes and resumes the pose she held earlier, stretched out on the black leather divan. Miriam begins to paint, continuing the work she started so many days ago.

Occasionally, she adds a drop or two from the chalice to her palette. Once in a while she seems to drift off into nothingness, seeing beyond the painting, perhaps considering the soul of the blood's previous owner.

Lauren is an excellent model. She does not move a muscle, and begins to resemble a very attractive corpse. She modeled for her uncle when she was a child, but she has never modeled nude before. It seems deliciously naughty to her, somehow evil. Miriam is very close to completing the portrait.

Miriam considers. She dips the chalice and adds a large amount of red to the deep blue-black, creating a sort of midnight purple. This seems the perfect shade for Lauren's hair, which has been edited for color to resemble Miriam's more closely.

Overhead, Miriam hears the flapping of wings. She laughs faintly. There is a howl, and Miriam shoots a warning glance skyward. Scythe, unable to disobey his mistress, disappears.

\*    \*    \*

Miriam paints late into the warm night. When the painting is finally completed, Miriam brings Lauren over to admire it.

"It's really something special," she tells Lauren, running her open palm across the flat belly. "It was always intended to be my masterpiece. *You* were intended to be my masterpiece." Miriam bends forward, and their lips meet. Tongues slide against each other as Lauren lets out a faint whimper.

"No," whispers Miriam, gently. A smile plays on her lips. "I am desperate to have you. But not until the world has seen our work. The opening is in two weeks at the Gallery of Despair . . . then you must come to me."

Lauren nods, smiling herself. Her heart pounds, and butterflies fill her stomach. The Gallery of Despair. The art world will be watching.

"But do one thing for me," whispers Miriam, nuzzling Lauren's ear. "Add your signature to the painting. But not with paint."

Lauren stares, uncomprehending.

Miriam slips a straight razor out of her pocket. She opens it and takes Lauren's hand. It does not even occur to Lauren to resist; she is completely in Miriam's power. Lauren watches, fascinated, as Miriam makes a small cut on her wrist. The pain is as nothing in the wash of Lauren's excitement and desire. Miriam repeats the cut on herself. The two women press their hands together, the fluid mingling in a sacred kind of blood prayer.

"Savor the fluid of life," whispers Miriam. "For blood is the essence of art."

Miriam gently turns Lauren's arm over, pressing her lips to her wrist. She begins to suckle, and Lauren watches, fascinated. As a rushing, ecstatic senation flows through Lauren, her eyes flutter closed and she whispers Miriam's name. Miriam is almost overcome, unable to stop herself from draining Lauren fully. But she stops without damaging the younger woman, and draws her head back, her lips slick with blood. A single bead of the deep red fluid runs down Miriam's chin and splatters onto her wrist.

Miriam then suckles at the cut on her own wrist, mingling her blood with Lauren's.

Continuing the ritual, Miriam kisses Lauren firmly, leaving her lips ruby-red. Then Miriam gently takes hold of Lauren's hand and guides her to the painting. Lauren, understanding Miriam's desire, kisses the bottom of the painting where the paint has already dried. The kiss forms a smudge at the bottom with their mingled blood, the shape of Lauren's kiss.

Lauren looks at the painting, unable to comprehend and yet understanding completely.

"Take the razor with you," Miriam says. "You will cut yourself again on our first night, when your image is given to the world. It will be our ritual at the opening, a sacrifice for the faithful to watch. The press will be scandalized, don't you think?" She leans very close to Lauren and whispers into her ear. "It is then, before my followers at the Gallery of Despair, that I shall drink your blood from this very chalice. Then our souls will be as one."

Lauren can scarcely comprehend what Miriam is telling her. But she wants nothing more than to be devoured by Miriam, her blood, as her soul, subsumed into the artist.

Miriam gets a first-aid kit from the closet and wraps Lauren's wrist in gauze. Miriam's own incision is left to clot on its own. Miriam licks the final traces of blood from Lauren's lips, whispering blood prayers in the near dark.

Silently, Lauren puts her clothes back on, bewildered but intrigued. She feels a heat all over her body as she tucks the blade into her handbag.

Miriam calls a cab for Lauren, and they kiss once as Lauren goes downstairs.

Scythe flutters meekly down to the table. Miriam stands there, unblinking, regarding the newly finished painting. She begins to laugh as she hears Scythe's mournful whimpering as he licks the empty chalice.

"I'm very sorry," sighs Miriam. "It was necessary that I use all of it. I'm afraid you'll have to go hunting again." She lets out a cruel laugh. "Though you must be weak from such hunger. Well, I've no more need for you. I've got what I want. The painting is almost completed, and Lauren was very impressed. . . . I'm sure she'll fall madly in love with me, if she hasn't already. I believe I'll seduce her when my art show opens at the Gallery of Despair. I hear Cooperman from the *Times* is going to be there."

Scythe wails angrily, deprived of his sustenance. He leaps at Miriam, driven mad by hunger, intent on devouring his mistress. But Miriam makes a casual sign with her left hand and Scythe is repelled. He spirals off into the air, his mirrored eyes shining with terror and rage. Scythe pauses, alighting on the jutting horn of a gargoyle, high above the studio. He has been released to return to the dark world where only bloodless ghosts wander.

"Thou art free, creature! Free to starve without your mistress to guide you. Perhaps when you return, upon my summoning, you will have learned some respect!"

Wailing, Scythe circles Miriam's studio. He regards the myriad paintings of myriad versions of Miriam's obsession. Each painting is different, as if it were of a different subject. But they are all somehow different versions of

Lauren—Laurens from many different decades, always reflecting the obsession of the artist—mixed with the soul of the person who paid in blood to make the portrait possible.

Scythe, wailing his rage, vanishes through the skylight. His mistress, who brought him into being, has banished him into the shadows until she has further needs. In the meantime, he must hunt desperately. Fight for survival. But her will has finally burst inside him, and now his hunger is clouded by rage.


The cab drops her off on Twentieth Street, near Dolores. She fumbles with her keys. The creature circles overhead, regarding the shadowy movements of the girl's leathered form.

Lauren climbs the stairs to her attic studio. It is a hot night. Slowly, she strips off her clothing. Pouring herself a cool iced coffee, she stretches out on the softness of her futon.

The cool drink is not enough. She rises and opens her window.

Delirious with her own kind of hunger, she stretches fully on the futon and revels in the play of the breeze on her body. She will be famous. And Miriam has become obsessed with her. Like all great artists for their models. . . .

Lauren begins to page through a biography of Frida Kahlo, becoming vaguely aroused. Such sadness . . .

She takes out the blade that Miriam gave her. She uses it to cut away the gauze around her wrist. She looks at the cut, and the smear of blood, on her palm. Fascinated with herself, she lets her tongue laze across her wrist.

Two weeks. She will bleed again for her artist, as all artists bleed for their art.

Lauren is buzzing with excitement, but eventually even the iced coffee must give way to exhaustion. She cuddles the razor under her pillow. Hot wind blows across her body. The black lace curtains part.


Lost in dreamlands, rolling in black silk sheets with Miriam. Encompassed by the hot flesh of the artist, finger-painting visions of ecstasy, and Lauren the willing canvas. Turned from blankness and nothing into a thing of beauty, radiating life and blood. The taste of the artist upon her lips.

Swallowing, working her tongue, suckling.

A piercing, deep inside her. Sudden choking. Lauren feels herself paralyzed, weakened, nailed to the futon as if to a cross. Her eyes open. She is unable to move.

The eyes are perhaps six inches across, shining convex mirrors. Lauren sees the expression of terror in her own eyes, reflected ten times actual size. Items in mirror are closer than they appear. Lauren tries to scream for help but her vocal cords have been frozen by the thick proboscis. Slowly, the appendage pulses, as fluids are drawn up through it. The creature makes a sucking noise as it feeds.

Lauren thrashes, begging for mercy with her eyes. But the plea is reflected back at her. Her heart pounds, and butterflies fill her stomach.

The only noise she can make is a faint, mournful whimper. Deep in her throat. But it is muffled by the creature's flesh. Her wrists are held by the insectile limbs. As the terror sets in, Lauren begins to lose consciousness. She weakens. Scythe reaches his capacity and begins to relax his grip on the unconscious body.

It is only then the girl is able, numbly, to find the razor underneath the pillow.


Miriam whispers the necessary prayers of summoning for the souls of her paintings. She can feel the life energy crawling through the canvases, the souls struggling inside the portraits. Every Lauren, as a creature reflected in a funhouse mirror, is Lauren mixed with the person who died. If Miriam listens closely she can hear their souls weeping in their oil prisons. She can feel her power over them.

It is a kind of possession, to give the girl all of these souls, to animate dozens of Laurens with the very beings of other people. It is that much more delicious that Lauren doesn't know how completely her soul will become one with Miriam's art. But she will, sometime soon . . . when she will finally appreciate all that Miriam has done for her and for her career.

Then Miriam and Lauren will be together forever, in the eternal blood shadows of the Gallery of Despair.

The flutter of wings. Scythe, flapping desperately overhead, barely able to stay in the air, hovers and eyes Miriam.

"I thought I told you to fuck off," she says.

It is then that Scythe alights near the chalice. Miriam sees the sliced wings, the razor slashes, the cuts across the belly. The mangled snout. His blood-sac is inflated far beyond capacity. It must have caused internal damage for Scythe to fill it so full. It is a great effort for Scythe to place his broken snout in the chalice and issue forth the seed he has borne to his mistress. It takes her a moment to comprehend.

"No . . . it's impossible . . ."

She stalks to the chalice and stares into the reflective chalice of blood. Groping for Scythe, Miriam takes hold and begins to twist. But the creature is already gone, and his dying act is to vomit the last of the blood over the front of Miriam's dress, with a sound approximating metallic laughter or the sound of breaking glass.

Miriam begins to wail, her rage exploding as she rends Scythe's flesh. That it went without its final meal to humiliate her so speaks volumes . . .

Miriam sinks to her knees, regarding the beauty of the dark fluid in the chalice. She doesn't have much time. There is only one course of action that will mean anything. . . .

Miriam sadly looks at her tubes of paint and searches for a fresh canvas.


The cruelty of fate in this case is, perhaps, accentuated by the fact that Scythe was normally unable to kill his victims. He simply did not have the capacity to drain all the blood from an adult human. A child, perhaps; a weakened person, maybe. But not Lauren. He simply would have taken his meal, as an insult to his mistress and her lover, and flown into the night, sated. But Lauren's razor sliced deep and he knew if he did not drain her to the point of death, she would kill him.

And it was thus that Scythe drained Lauren far beyond his capacity, and caused rupture of the abdominal ducts that allowed him to digest the blood. He would not have died from the razor-cuts Lauren inflicted, but the combined trauma was too much for him to survive. Knowing this, he offered his dying insult to the artist who had driven him into what passed for madness. And issued forth his own macabre composition.


Perhaps it is the exhaustion which finally causes Miriam to expire. It is also possible that she dies of a broken heart. Scythe may have been gambling on that, bringing the blood to her like this. If that's the case, then he was indeed a devious little fuck. In any event, there is a final painting which is, to collectors, many times more valuable than the others. The show goes on as planned at the Gallery of Despair, and the estate, per Miriam's executor, is donated to a scholarship program for young artists working in the medium of blood. It is a substantial sum, but goes unclaimed for several years until an impoverished SOMA artist named Alice discovers a notice about the scholarship in the public library and finds herself bewitched by Miriam Christian's work and the sad story of her life.

But that is, I'm afraid, another story, equally sad, and we must return to Miriam Christian. She becomes something of a legend, considered the godmother of the following century's Erotic Sanguinism. Years ahead of her time. Several lurid books are written about the artist's mysterious death. Strangely, the accompanying plates never achieve accurate color reproduction. In the darkened Galleries of Despair in Paris, San Francisco, and Luxembourg, there is the distant sound of weeping.

# THE TRANSLITERATION OF INFANTA

*Colin Raff*

Like the once-healthy blossoms preserved in epsom salts that she always wore in her hair, Infanta's beauty and radiance transcended her lack of vitality. Like them, too, she was treasured and revered in spite of her condition, since it was evident that she could not be replaced. She was never less than the focus of attention on those late afternoons of that summer, when the sky was honey and everything below was violet. At about five o'clock, everyone would gather at the bower—to eat olives from the Marchese da Ripoli's orchard, perhaps to hear Schumann or Beethoven in an impromptu quartet put together by Johannes, and, almost always, to listen to Infanta. The strength and clarity of her voice seemed undiminished by the ravages of her condition, and though no one could question her infirmity, many wondered if perhaps it had been misdiagnosed as consumption, for her coughing fits only came to her at the most convenient moments—never in the middle of sleep, never when she spoke, and certainly never when she sang. It was as though being an invalid was an affectation, a social code whose rules she chose to observe dutifully but unceremoniously.

She was a living illustration of beauty's battle with decay, and both sides had fought to a standstill. Eros preserved the canvas, but Thanatos controlled the palette, for her features—though Leonardo could not imagine more angelic contours—were earthen-colored; the sallow yellow of her cheeks highlighted by artificial dabs of rouge which made her head resemble a wax apple. Nonetheless, Gregorio went so far as to state that Eros now had the upper hand. "Surely she is more fascinating now than when she was younger and more robust," he said to Johannes behind the conservatory once, when the two were quite alone. "After all, we will always have plenty of fresh rosy cheeks, but there will only be one Infanta."

"But you're being cruel," Johannes replied. "You wish her illness upon her . . ."

"No! I wish nothing on her that she herself wouldn't want. She wishes to be an invalid because it adds to her persona. She could dispense with her illness at any time if she desired. Wake up cured tomorrow, as easily as if she were taking off a cloak. I know it."

Gregorio was emphatic. Johannes, knowing the intensity of his friend's strange convictions, let it drop at that. In fact, afterwards he himself would attempt, from time to time, to view Infanta through the eyes of his colleague. Though his conclusions were not exactly the same, he did perceive that Infanta, outward appearances aside, was always in control of those around her. Her suggestions were always scrupulously carried out, her smallest whims heeded without the slightest protest. The twin gifts of allure and pathos allowed her to have her way without appearing self-indulgent. It struck him that she was probably the gentlest diva there was.

She was the only one staying at the villa who was not a relative of the Marchese da Ripoli—aside from Johannes, who knew Gregorio, the Marchese's nephew, from Bologna, where the two studied together. When he asked the old man once how he knew her, da Ripoli replied, "I couldn't say I know her, really. I saw her as Aida in Milan three years ago and was enchanted, like everyone else who is exposed to her. I went backstage and barraged her with orchids. I didn't see her for a long time after that, but when I heard of her illness, I sent a letter to her saying she must come here for the summer and take in the seaside breezes. And here she is."

"And you know nothing of her past?"

"Why, her credentials are impeccable. Bayreuth, Maryinsky, the London Opera . . . but as for her personal history, no. One doesn't interrogate La Infanta. She hasn't offered any clues, and there it will have to stand. She speaks of Spain occasionally, but she seems to me about as Spanish as Sarah Bernhardt. We may never know."

As for Gregorio, he was less curious about Infanta than obsessed with her. Only Johannes, one who was more prone to live for art than to confuse art and life, felt any inclination to be nosy. But even he bore her no malice. He wanted only to inspect the peaks and valleys of her life history to determine for himself whether La Infanta had ever been tainted by scandal, or whether it fell away from her like water off the back of some aquatic creature. One lazy sunset, early in July, when he was leading her slowly by the arm around the luxuriant yellow rosebushes of which the Marchese was so proud, he made a small effort to unravel her mystery.

"What I would have given," he began, "to have heard you as Isolde at Bayreuth when I was there in 'eighty-seven."

"I am afraid you missed me by a year," she replied. "I can never stay in one place for too long. By that I mean no disrespect for your country. It is, after all, the home of Beethoven . . . but I could not have stayed there. Italy, too, will soon seem oppressive to me. Yes, I can feel it happening soon. Where next, I wonder?"

Johannes cleared his throat, then met the challenge: "Where did you *begin*?"

She did not turn her head, but her eyes looked up at him and her smile slanted coyly. "Singing? Why, Barcelona, of course. Where else?"

"You really are from Spain originally? You just don't look very . . ."

"My mother was Hungarian. But that was so long ago . . . Has the sun finally gone down? Look, the roses have closed their petals. I need to find a seat . . ." And she began to cough, in as elegant a manner as possible. He helped her to a nearby settee, noting to himself that the roses in her hair, almost grotesque in their beauty and for the fact that they had never known corruption, were still wide open.

He had tried, and she had won. Johannes was not adept enough in the social arts to pursue the matter further without seeming impudent. He decided he ought to tred in safer waters and seek his inspiration not in the diva herself, but in Gregorio's fixation with her.

And surely Gregorio, with his theatrics, was potent fodder for the imagination. Like opium or morphine, Infanta had taken over his life and his thoughts completely by midsummer. He would have done anything for her, and on several occasions confided in Johannes the most excessive masochistic fantasies of chivalric self-sacrifice in her name. It was true that she would acquire a hypnotic magnetism—like a serpent with the throat of a seraph—that spared no one when she sang. But Gregorio was triply affected, and did not seem to care who noticed when he would swoon in his seat, as if in the throes of passion, during her recitals on the lawn. He loved her the way she was then, but unlike some others who are obsessed with consumptives, he did not morbidly relish the idea of watching her waste away in front of his eyes. In fact, he seemed not to understand the realities of her alleged disease. He seemed to believe she would always remain in the same dying but beautiful state: static and unchanging, a summit of tragic perfection. To add to that, he was insanely possessive of her, despite the fact that she could not be possessed. "I sometimes think of her more as a force of nature than as a real woman," he proclaimed. "She is ubiquitous, like the sky. Still, I would die for her. Odd, isn't it?" It was comments of this sort that led Johannes to begin writing his operatic fragment.

He had intended to compose an entire short opera in one act, consisting

of seven numbers with a prelude. Titled *Die Herz-Blut,* it was to present
the story of two men, a painter and a poet, who kill each other in a
swordfight over a woman who loves them equally. The prelude culminates
with an aria by the object of the artists' attentions, a woman with long
trailing hair of seven hues of red—as many as can be seen on the horizon
as the sun sets behind her and her suitors prepare for their duel. They fight
not specifically for her love but for the right to depict her in the works that
she has driven them to create. Every time a duelist is wounded, a different
tint of blood spurts from the wound, and the opponent who has struck the
blow claims the right to use that color in his piece. Each of these ex-
changes (wine, ruby, vermilion, scarlet, damask, and crimson) make up a
number. At the finale, when each have been wounded thrice, they stab
each other fatally in the heart, unleashing the dark heart-blood of the title
and concluding the opera with moans of agony and selfless professions of
love.

Johannes never made it past the aria, claiming frustration with the li-
bretto. "It would just seem silly," he complained. "Surely I can find a
better vehicle for my discoveries in polytonality."

Infanta, on the other hand, declared herself enraptured by the score
after Johannes had allowed her to read it. Her lips moistened as she went
over the words, quietly humming to herself the saddened muse's declaration that she had been cursed with the colors of the sunset, which, she
knew, prefigured the blood of her lovers. The diva's eyes closed and she
held the sheet of music to her breast. "I must sing this at once!" she cried.

Johannes and Gregorio followed her into the music room. Johannes sat
down at the piano to play, and Infanta, to better read the notation, stood
behind him and began to sing. Gregorio, his back against the wall, fumed
with envy as he watched La Infanta, his sickly muse, immerse herself in the
work of his golden-haired friend; her white, dovelike hands, in gloves of
yellow silk, coiled gently around his collar, the forefinger of her right hand
rising occasionally to caress his neck. Still, Gregorio did not deny himself
the pleasure of appreciating Johannes's piece, which flowed marvelously,
even in this rough, unrehearsed rendition.

Gregorio was determined to overmaster his jealousy. He submerged it
with the genuine enthusiasm he felt for the music, and applauded loudly
at its conclusion. "Bravo!" he shouted. "A match of talents made in
heaven. Now I have a subject for my triptych."

"Your triptych?" asked Johannes.

"Yes, to be installed in this very room, after they tear out the paneling
on that end. Uncle has commissioned me to do it. It has to be a musical
theme, of course. I had thought of painting the death of Orpheus, but that

seems redundant after Moreau, don't you think? Johannes's opera will make the perfect tableau. It will seem fresh—an unfamiliar story, though the world will know of your masterpiece soon enough, Johannes. Surely I am only the first of many who will pay it homage."

"But that isn't . . . I told you I had decided not to . . ."

"Nonsense!" said Infanta. "You must finish what you've started. It isn't silly like you say: not at all. It is . . . sumptuous. All of Europe will know it. Through me."

"And my interpretation now will change your mind," Gregorio continued. "And I need to look no further than this room for my models. I will paint the ones who inspired the original work. I will paint the three of us!"

Johannes gave him a puzzled look, though he did understand how Gregorio could have misinterpreted things. But the trio standing in that room simply were not the living embodiments of the figures in Johannes's proposed opus. Only Gregorio—that is to say, the pining of Gregorio after Infanta—had provided Johannes with any impetus for his creation. But Gregorio—poor Gregorio, a melancholic art student who wouldn't (and probably couldn't) hurt a fly, was certainly not one of these fictive duelists, any more than Johannes felt himself to be. And as for Infanta her hair was an even auburn, not seven hues of red, and Johannes had envisioned a younger woman, as well—a fresh blossom, full of life.

Of course, there seemed no reason why the three could not, albeit in idealized form, function as the models for Gregorio's work anyway. But the idea of this, for reasons he found hard to articulate, upset Johannes greatly. This stemmed partly from Infanta's enthusiasm for the music. It seemed unnatural to him, somehow, that she should become so spirited all of a sudden; so untypically energetic in her desire to perform the opus. She had publicly announced her retirement the preceding winter, on account of the onslaught of tuberculosis, and Johannes did not believe that she truly intended to return to the stage. Instead, he could not help but suspect, against his reason, that some diabolical scheme was being concocted, one that could not be explained or rationalized by the conscious mind. Was Gregorio's passion placing him in danger? Was he becoming caught in the web of a predatory muse? Johannes felt that his own lack of romantic sensitivity was saving him from the same fate, but he still could not render with precision what that fate might be.

He looked to Infanta in an attempt to fathom her motives. She seemed to intuit his reservations about her. Her smile remained, but her eyes narrowed, and their gaze shifted to Gregorio. "*Cara mia*," she began, as if Johannes were not in the room, "Can you really see me as her?" Gregorio, noticing that he had won her undivided attention, nodded slowly, mesmerized. "Are you prepared," she continued, "to give yourself over to your craft—to sacrifice yourself, if necessary—to transform me into that vision? You must be ready to do this, if I am to be your model. La Infanta will accept nothing less."

These words lost much of their edge of cruelty and intimidation when Infanta spoke them, for she laced them with a narcotic caress, a gentle, soothing tone like that employed by nurses to those in great pain at the better hospitals. They were followed almost immediately by Gregorio's affirmations. "Then take me into the garden so that we may discuss this," she said, and, with a cursory nod in Johannes's direction, she offered Gregorio her arm.

Watching them leave, Johannes stood rigidly, trying to decipher Infanta's strange and frightening ultimatum. What could she have meant by saying that Gregorio may have to sacrifice himself for the painting? In what circumstances would this be necessary? If the diva wished to set in motion the conflict described in the story, Johannes would not allow it to follow through. He realized that, now that she had focused all of her infernal skills on Gregorio, there were no lingering doubts, no traces of her bewitchment left in his own soul. He no longer could see Infanta as intimidating or as pathetic. He could only feel concern for his friend.

A glass of cordial, provided by the ancient Duchess di Souza in return for small talk, did little to calm his nerves. He wandered aimlessly about the estate for what remained of that day with a tense stomach and a weary mind. He finally invoked enough common sense to tell himself that Gregorio was not in any tangible danger. With that, he bade the entourage a very early goodnight and slept soundly for eleven hours.

He did not see Gregorio again until the following evening. His friend was leaning against the glass wall of the conservatory with a handful of Infanta's embalmed flowers—a cluster of blue hyssops—and was bringing them to his nose and inhaling, as if the dead blossoms still possessed a scent. He appeared tired. His complexion was sallow, his eyes circled with dark rings. His clothing was more formal than necessary, with a starched raised collar and a satin cravat—strangely foppish for this normally ascetic bohemian, and impractical for the sultry weather, though he was not perspiring. He was obviously straining to maintain his posture and composure, affecting a vigor he did not possess. His newfound rapture, however, oddly disturbing though it may have been, was genuine. "I am the appointed vehicle of Infanta," he told Johannes excitedly. "I am the one who will breathe new life into her. Don't you see? She is more than we can perceive. Her turn as a singer was only a small phase of her career as an eternal muse, as a work of art. She was the deadly Siren described by Homer. She was the Lamia; she was Salomé. She was Judith, Ishtar, and Morgana. So will she be this sunset-haired angel of death. I will make it happen. I!"

Johannes stared at him for a moment, carefully putting the words together in his mind. Then: "Gregorio, listen to me. Do you remember what the painting is supposed to be about? There's the two of us to contend with. Not just Infanta. You should start doing some studies of me as well—"

"Oh, yes . . ." replied Gregorio, hazily. "The other two panels . . . but that is merely a matter of craft, Johannes. I need exert only my talent for that. Infanta requires much more. I must give of myself. You know, Johannes, that the most exalted moment for the artist is when he gives himself over completely to what he is doing, and loses his identity, loses himself completely . . ."

"You would die for your art."

"No! Only for Infanta." He sniffed at the dead flowers again and leaned back against the conservatory wall in a state of rapture. His glassy eyes turned upwards and a preverse smile played on his face. Johannes was appalled at this display. It did not make him think of anything noble, like self-sacrifice. It only brought troubling images to his mind of some of the more devious types of predator found in nature—the kinds that seduce their prey with their gaze and poison them gently with their intoxicating venom before devouring them. There was something about Infanta that made Gregorio want to die.

The predator herself was nowhere to be seen. "I have to go now. Goodnight, Johannes," Gregorio said, and ambled off toward the Villa da Ripoli. Johannes knew where he was going. The music room. He did not try to follow him. Instead, he waited for about ten minutes, then entered the building, approached the music room as quietly as possible, put his ear to the door, and listened.

He heard movement, but no speech, for a long while. Then a clattering sound (which Johannes interpreted as a brush hitting the floor), and Gregorio's voice, wearied and desperate: "Infanta, I can't go on. We've done enough for tonight. Take me . . ."

And her voice, more soothing than ever: "Yes, Gregorio, I need it as well. Just remember that time is of the essence for us . . . But I can see you've done a good day's work. Come to me, my love. You know how much I need you. Don't be afraid. It hasn't hurt yet, has it? Yesss . . . ."

He wanted to burst into the room, to stop whatever sick exchange was occurring inside. But he felt weak, nauseous, on the verge of fainting. Cowardly, trivial thoughts, not the kind that he was used to thinking, raced through his mind: *I am a guest in this house, a foreigner. I have no*

*right to interfere. Perhaps he would kill me if she told him to. I am so far
away from home . . . I don't belong here . . .* Fighting to stay conscious,
he staggered away, sliding against the walls, until he reached his room.
Drenching the sheets of his bed with his sweat, he tried to understand
what had come over him, as well as what was happening to Gregorio at
that moment while he lay helpless in the dark. Unable to come to terms
with the waking world, he finally drifted into a troubled sleep.

The following week, coming as it did in late August, was a golden one for
everyone, it seemed, but Johannes. No one else understood the gravity of
Gregorio's condition. They were all either too old or too naive to understand. He would appear infrequently, looking ever more dissipated, always
in that starched, raised collar and cravat, muttering something about Infanta, who was nowhere to be seen. He would usher the curious into the
music room and briefly show to them the easel with the unfinished center
panel—a canvas in oils of an idealized Infanta, looking no older than
eighteen, her face a muted pearl reflecting a sunset indistinguishable from
her flowing tresses. Then he would usher them out again and disappear
once more, and the relations of da Ripoli would make frivolous comments
about young love.

Johannes knew better, but could not find a way to elucidate the problem
with any rationality. Logically, Gregorio could not have been all that mori-
bund if he was so productive. To have related to the Marchese what he had
heard behind the door would have made Johannes appear mad. In fact, he
was sure that they all at this point considered him a jealous rival for
Infanta's attentions. His only recourse now would be to confront Gregorio
himself.

It was on one of those oppressively humid August nights, when the
landscape twists and slopes more than usual; when the vegetation seems to
have grown larger and more baroque; when heat and darkness are inter-
changeable concepts—it was on a night like this that Johannes waited for
pale Gregorio, prepared for the worst, when his friend sidled up to him and
began muttering. "I can see what you are up to, Johannes," said Gregorio.
"But you are too late. Tonight I will be finished, and Infanta will acquire
new life through me; through what I have done with my art. I will have
transcended all earthly passions, to have realized the highest of ambitions—"

" 'The highest of ambitions!' How can you talk like that!" Johannes
grabbed his friend roughly, tearing at the front of his shirt in an attempt to
expose his wasted body. This revealed more than Johannes had bargained

for. There were lesions on Gregorio's neck, dark red and inflamed, the veins beneath them blue against the yellowish flesh around the scabs. Johannes took these for indications of some foul social disease. "Look what she has done to you!" he cried. "And she has fooled us all into taking her for a consumptive. There's nothing noble about what you've been drawn into, Gregorio. You're only sharing the fate of a squalid whore—"

"Enough!" Gregorio gave Johannes a weak slap across the face. Tears streamed down his cheeks. "You've really no idea, have you? Yet you yourself wrote about the blood, the heart-blood . . . I'd assumed you understood . . ." He stood there, weeping wretchedly for a moment, and staring at Johannes, who said finally:

"Gregorio. Get away from her. There's still time; I'm sure of it. There are spas, sanitoriums. One I know of is not far from here, just outside of Rome. You could be cured there. Your uncle is rich . . . surely—"

Gregorio only shook his head. "Tonight Infanta will become another fragment of an eternal sequence. She will cease to be Infanta. The muse and the masterpiece will become indistinguishable. Then she will leave us. You should be proud, Johannes. After all, it was your idea." With these indecipherable phrases, he turned and staggered away.

Johannes felt that weakness return to him, and this time he was sure it was imposed on him from outside. The cold fingers of La Infanta seemed to creep around his skull, beneath the skin and behind the eyes, and deaden his joints. He fell to the ground. unable to cry out. No one saw him as he lay there behind a clump of azaleas, waiting for the spell to pass.

He did not know how much time had elapsed before he finally regained his strength. Only that the sky was dark as pitch, and the villa was silent with sleep. The songs of the thrushes had been replaced by crickets' chirping and the occasional derisive hoot from an owl. He rose unsteadily and made his way to the house.

Now that his body had recovered, it was his spirit that was weak. He had to struggle against himself in order to tread down that hallway, to that now-familiar door. He could not bring himself to look, yet looked anyway at the light and shadows that indicated movement behind the door, though there was no sound. Every fiber of his being combated his determination, but still he slammed his body against the bolted door, breaking it open. He tumbled violently into the room, and saw—

The center panel, finished, perched on an easel in the middle of the bare room. On its surface: a naked sylph with an idealized adolescent body and Infanta's face, sporting a dazzling halo of polychromatic crimson. Infanta, the real Infanta, real but transformed, standing next to the painting, mirroring its subject exactly; her hair now several shades of red, impossibly bountiful, coiled around her breasts and covering her thighs. Flowers, living flowers, impossibly beautiful, their stems woven into her locks. Her face, repulsive in its new youth; her beauty, frightening in its perfection; her eyes dark pools; her smile a ravenous blur. That smile, still on her lips, impossible to see in detail though it widened upon her seeing Johannes, numb and helpless once again—

And Gregorio's shriveled, lifeless body, utterly desiccated, the blood drained completely from the wounds in his neck, lying curled up at her feet.

# THE
# CONSERVATORY

# IDÉE FIXE

*Alexandra Elizabeth Honigsberg*

ELLE: I am the muse of Louis Hector and he is mine. We are each other's sustenance, each other's passion, each other's rage. And I am well pleased.

Once I was human, as he is. But that life was drained from me so long ago that it echoes only faintly in whatever realm where memory resides. And still my body held this spirit. I roamed the streets of Paris at night until someone desecrated my resting place in Montmartre and the sun turned that vessel to ashes.

Just as my doomed spirit felt the last silken thread near to snapping, I drew them close to me and reached out in one final, desperate attempt to feed and fill my horrible longings, terrible empty spaces where only hunger dwelt. That much humanity remained in me—the will to continue. And in consuming, I was consumed, taken in by her hunger as well, drawn down through a tight vortex and awakened to a riot of sights and sounds.

Then I looked through her eyes and saw him through the eyes of his own hunger and knew I was home . . .

BERLIOZ: Henriette, my beloved Henriette falls to swoon before me and I catch her by the arm lest she should come to her senses to find herself in the dirt with the vermin, her pink half-boots smudged—they remind me of Estelle, the unattainable. I fear it is the chill and damp of the night that brought this about on our walk from the Opéra, or perhaps I had been too generous with the potion, Paracelsus' draught, she shared with me from the vial in my vest pocket.

We lost track of time, floated through the night of fog and drank each other in, to find ourselves in the *cimetière* where Abelard and Heloïse sleep in peace together, just as the first, stark rays of the sun lance through the mists. Ah, Montmartre—that I might find some measure of that terrible peace.

I set Henriette, my morning star, on a bench nearby and we sit there, upheld by cherubs with marble wings outstretched, frozen in flight. For a moment, the air around her seems to thicken and spark, swirl in patterns like Alençon lace, but then is no more. She turns her face toward me and opens her eyes which shine with a light that is at once compelling and frightening. I gaze upon her awesome beauty and it pulls me in. We remain there, suspended in time, our souls in communion and at war, on the edge between devourment and oneness.

"Hector, darling," her voice comes as if from afar, "you must forget this phantom woman of your childhood, of your *fantastique*, who bedevils you. She sucks the life from you. I am all you need and you are mine."

She knows what I've been thinking and it shames me to be so disloyal, unfaithful. But I cannot help myself. It is Estelle, always Estelle. Even the things in Henriette that I love, I love for their echoes of Estelle—forever my tormentor, Florian's heroine come to life, and I am helpless but to play that hero, at first sight.

Through the movements of my *fantastique* I had lived, died, descended into Hell, and been reborn over and over again—all for Estelle, a twelve-year-old's damnation and redemption. Estelle of the pink boots. Estelle, who evaporated like Poe's Annabel Lee.

Henriette pulls me up from my awful reveries and inward spirals—patterns like my *fantastique*'s waltz-gone-mad.

"You're far away again, Hector. It's morning and I have to be at the *théâtre* for another *Hamlet*, by dusk. I need you. Take me home."

She needs me. Always. Would that I did not need her. And home—where is it? For us, home is where we plan life out of death, a sort of afterlife. We prepare to breathe life into our creations in the *théâtre*, before the eyes of many. Surely, even God and Adam had some measure of privacy when the spark leapt that infinitessimal space between two fingertips. And only now does the great He-She have to suffer the damnable critics.

Yes, it was the critics who had borne us apart, me and my Estelle.

But Henriette needs to prepare the death-birth-death cycle of her mad Ophelia. And I need to be off to the Conservatoire to kill a certain young Montague and fair Capulet again, in her honour. I'd written it for her. It seems that death woos my Henriette, my near-suicide before her what brought her that last step to cross over and stand by my side, to share the life-death dance.

But I am overtired and underfed. I vent my spleen, lose my good humour, and ramble. Henriette is beside me and I have good coin in my purse. That is sufficient.

ELLE: I see the morning. It is a miracle for a creature such as I am. But I am not even fully undead in this state. I crave the blood, but this body I inhabit cannot drink. In her, this Henriette, I drink of soul—her soul, his soul—and that is powerful, but it does not fulfill my nature. Still, to drink is Heaven in this Hell, whatever the draught. I might be in oblivion, taken by the Abyss, were it not for the nature of these two. I can wait. Her spirit is strong, thus I cannot seem to overcome it to make her what I was without the Devil's kiss. But when she is weakened, confused by Death's summons, then I shall have my chance to snatch this temple first, as the spirit flees.

Meanwhile, she is not so strong that she cannot be influenced. And Louis Hector is always in my thrall, my beloved supplicant.

Come to me, Louis Hector. Come and spin your sound-tales of the mad and impassioned, the demented and damned. Feed me. Fill me. Take me and make me your own. But we both know who really pays the piper, don't we, my love?

I will drive you to fame, send you visions, give you the frenzy that only the artiste really knows. Other souls who dream the dark will flock to you. Even now I see that rogue Wagner and the wild Liszt laud you. Drink, beloved. Drink.

BERLIOZ: My stick comes down and the drumrolls of death begin. Each time I perform this movement, this march to the scaffold, I know what I am capable of and want to run from my own self. It's all so simple, really—he loved her, she tormented him, he killed her and paid with his life, eternally.

The raucous trumpets scream their defiance in the face of the ultimate silence as the trombones blare and splat the grotesque imagery of what awaits the hero—the maw of Hell. That is the price for slaying the beloved. And through the chaos—his own, the raging mob's—he still hears, still feels the heartbeat of his love, her theme of life.

I experience the movement with the orchestra in a trance that only performance brings. We have already lived through the revelation of the beloved, the ball's waltz of hysteria, and the pastoral picnic ripped by the sinister storm-theme of the obsession. All of them forms of death, of thinking one is in the light and then discovering it is a sham as the darkness rolls over you.

Ah, but here we get to drive and drive, to chase and be chased by the things which eat away at men, alone. And only at the last are our frenzied posturings interrupted by the delicate reminder—like a wisp of perfume, a tiny strand of sunlight through the clouds—of the beloved, before the guillotine falls and sends us to our next destination. The brass blare in triumph. I tremble to face the witches' sabbath and all its horrors. It makes of my love and myself a caricature which Bosch would be proud to call his own. But that is as it should be.

ELLE: How does she stand it, this Henriette, night after night playing Ophelia, Juliet—doomed ladies of light and darkness? It does contain a certain allure that even now calls to me, I must admit. But it is . . . limited.

I was like her, once—a lady of some renown in my homeland, with a flair for the troubadour's art, even free for some travel 'round the lands of Provence. But then he took me and I became what I am. I despaired of my existence for a time, until I came to know that it offered me even greater freedom than my station and talents previously had, broad though they might have been for their era. The realm of the undead levels all and makes the roles of men and women irrelevent. Power, alone, prevails.

BERLIOZ: It is night and I am exhausted, that terrible exhaustion when the creative work has taken every last shred of strength from me and then a little more. Henriette is gone, gone early to the *théâtre*. I drove her away in a fit of pique. That's what the will to perfection does to me. It strips me of my reason and enflames my hunger for the truth that is only visible to me through my art. But my art is nourished by her. So I work, and go hungry, and feed the hunger.

This time, the culprit was Faust. He and his damnation may well be my ultimate creations, even more so than my *Symphonie fantastique*, perhaps. As I think back on my day's work, I marvel at its vulgar, utterly profane nature, mixed with the divine.

I dip my pen into the depths of the well, tap it against the side, and withdraw it. On the desk before me I face a most frightening thing—a large, totally empty sheet of score paper, awaiting my mark. Though parts of the piece are already written, each new page presents this unique moment of creating something out of nothing, sound from silence, silence from sound.

The tip of my pen—a glint of silver blackened by the ink—hovers for a moment above the staff. There is an attraction and it draws me closer, but still not touching. We wait.

I don't know when, but there is that moment there when time has no meaning. And then there is a spark and my hand feels as if it is pushed to the page and I begin to write what I hear in my head. The emptiness of the page pulls it from me as the pressure from inside forces me to release it and pour it out onto the paper, a tangled web of utter satisfaction and despair. I give birth. Some days I hemorrhage and bleed to death. The opium brings me back, dulls the pain and emptiness, and I rise up to try again.

Let the bloodletting begin.

ELLE: How curious to arrive home and find the composer crumpled, like a corpse, over his work. Night is usually his time and the sun is not even yet a hint on the distant horizon.

"Hector dear, it is Henriette. Please, wake up," I hear and feel the body I share say as she shakes his shoulder. But she is calm. Even her heartbeat is barely changed as she contemplates his slumped form. A sigh and she turns away, leaving him there to come to his senses while she undresses for bed.

Henriette turns once more to check on him when she notices the overturned vial amongst the scattered papers there on the writing desk. No drop left for her. Disappointment. And understanding. I feel her blood surge as she shakes her head and breathes the word *Fool*, before going back to her toilet and then to bed, alone.

It is hard to recall what it was like to take a man to my bed, or even to take a beloved victim into my arms and drink deeply, that sharp taste on my tongue, the thick fluid down my throat warming me as it progresses and flows through me, satisfies me. This woman's senses shroud my own, confuse my memories. They become enmeshed with hers. And she, unlike my once-self, seems forever unsated.

BERLIOZ: My body aches as I uncoil myself from an awkward position to discover that I must have fallen asleep at my desk. Not the first time, of course. I look down at the papers, my eyes refusing to focus, relieved to see that I had gotten some work done, at least, before oblivion had taken me.

But where is Henriette, I wonder? The candles have all burned down, the oil lamp empty and cold. A sliver of panic slips between my ribs. The sun is gone, but our bed's been occupied, the white gilded headboard draped in lace like a gravemarker with a shroud. Have I slept through the day and never a notion that Henriette has already come and gone? I have missed a day of work and her sweet face, and all for the demon of the vial?

Yes, that must be the story. Ah, me. But how can I face my work otherwise? How can I sustain myself through torment and Hell day after day without the wind beneath this dark angel's wings that is her voice and the fire in this imp's gut that is the potion? How to face the arrogant and incompetent orchestras, the snuff-wielding and pompous conductors, without some sustenance? Henriette, my divine muse. To overindulge and fail you makes me want to plunge myself back into that delirium.

I feel. I feel too much. The music once relieved those tensions, played them out. Now, I fear, there is no cure for what afflicts me.

To the *théâtre* to seek the redemption that only she can give.

ELLE: "A guiltless death I die . . . Nobody. I, myself. Farewell."

Desdemona was a fool. She wasted her strength, allowed it to be siphoned from her by a man drunk with jealousy, addicted to his own weakness. Othello doubted he deserved her. Those doubts, and not Iago's poisons, were his real undoing. Not even Iago, the predator, knew this. He was a fool, too.

But Henriette knows the Italian beauty only as one half of yet another pair of star-crossed lovers—the short sight of the shortlived. I see more. The dead always see more. And she feels vibrations of that knowing inside her and fears herself.

Louis Hector sees it and fears it, too. He awaits.

BERLIOZ: Her death was glorious agony, intensified by the adulation of the crowd. How pain can be so sweet and yet make me want to run from it I have not the capacity to understand. My body feels as if it does not belong to me, possessed and possessor. But woman is the cure, just as she is the disease. The divine mystery. Shakespeare knew this. My music knows this.

I do penance and stand with the multitudes outside her door. It opens and she is a vision in white, blinding. How did I ever win her? How can she have me, knowing my heart is split? Her love mocks me. I am but a poor supplicant before her, like so many others.

But she sees me, and smiles, lit by the afterglow of the stage. She beckons to me, the gesture a flow of white from her long, graceful arm and delicate hand. I reach toward her. My world is whole.

And then I see him—a man beside her, in proper evening clothes. I see the way he eyes me, wary, then looks back at my love with wolf's eyes. I see the way she defers to him and know what they are about.

My world is shattered. Only rage remains.

ELLE: "Hector, listen to me! He means nothing! Nothing at all! He was just a wealthy admirer I thought to attract to your work as a patron!"

How does she stand for this, this ranting? I saw the animal in his eyes at the *théâtre* and knew trouble would come. She knew it, too. Not even delaying her return for two hours with the excuse of a reception had been enough time for him to cool his anger. If anything, it had intensified.

He is insane. He throws things and rants about betrayals. The petty things the living call betrayals. Most of them haven't even begun to learn the meaning of the word. Obliteration is the only betrayal. The Almighty promised us more, even in damnation.

My Louis Hector tries to strike me and Henriette raises an arm to stop him. I lend her my strength. Focus. Resistance.

Ah yes, I see the surprise, even fear, in his eyes. He suspects. His frail beauty could not have done this. But he cannot compass the truth. Still, his spirit knows, as spirits always do. And that knowing, that fear, feeds me with nectar the likes of which I have not known since I could truly drink. Now he is even more mine.

He releases me, releases himself, and collapses on the bed.

BERLIOZ: Truly, truly I cannot live with myself. What have I done? I have driven her to him, that so-called patron, as surely as I have destroyed myself. Her heart is not true. But how can it be when mine own is forever yearning for Estelle?

Yet I saw it, the beast in her eyes. She held back my rage, hurled it back at me and I fell before it. This fierce creature—is this the Henriette of my affection, or some succubus come to dwell therein? No, that's a mad thought. Surely she has shown that and more on stage with every bravura performance. It is the drug's talk, no more.

I will leave her a note and go to the countryside for a day and a night to rejuvenate myself. A pastoral interlude should soothe me enough to bring me back to a proper gentleman's demeanor. Only then can I return and beg her forgiveness.

ELLE: Gone. He is gone. Just as well. Even alone I am not, within this body. I am grateful for the relative peace. Thinking has become so difficult in this state, so I let go and allow instinct to guide. Yet sometimes I know not if it is my instinct or hers on the reins, or some new creature growing out of a melding of the two, as a child grows in its mother's womb.

She is obsessed now with her next role of La dame aux camélias. Another role of death—a beauteous woman who is slowly consumed from within by the wasting cough. She dies well, this Henriette. Living seems to escape her. But she knows how to consume and drink their praises as I once drank blood—and the admiration of kings, long ago. In that, she feasts. Pity I never had the stages she commands.

BERLIOZ: "Come with me to the chapel at Montmartre, Henriette. The night is warm and we have not walked in too long a while."

I cannot read her expression. It is hard and not like her. But then it softens and I take her into my arms and her fragrance fills my senses as she yields to me, yields to our love.

We leave the *théâtre*. The streets are crowded with revelers of the night, under a moon that plays hide and seek with us amongst the clouds. I am reborn.

Her presence makes me giddy and I feel like a young Lelio with his Columbine beside him, the love he never hoped to have suddenly his. But she has always been mine, since that first time I saw her on the stage. And I have always been hers, even despite the specter of the perpetual Estelle. Henriette, my heroine who rises from death each night before their very eyes. And they do worship her, this phoenix, even as I do.

The chapel at Montmartre is small and dark, but no one ventures there late at night, save for the groundskeeper and a lone friar, on occasion. We approach quietly to find the door unbolted. It squeaks quietly in protest as we open it, no doubt happily at rest before our intrusion. Churches have souls of their own—not just of the patron saints they are named for, but of all the prayers that take wing within their walls and the vain hopes of the dead buried beneath their altars.

A rack of votive candles in the far corner provides enough light for us to make our way up the aisle to the front pews before the main altar and its vase full of flowers. The flames within the red glasses dance, make eerie merriment with the shadows about the space. They seem to make the figures in the stained-glass windows come to life. The trees outside, still not in full bloom, wave bent and bare limbs in the breeze that sometimes show through the sacred images—a hint here and there—and make a skeletal counterpoint to their outlines.

Henriette shudders against me, startled by every sound, it seems. The sight of her bosom's rise and fall with each breath enflames me to unseemly acts within these walls. Yet, is not love's expression also God's? Surely He could not decry the joining of hearts in His sanctuary. My brain is a riot of arguments, my body alive with sparks.

Full of passion, I bury my face in the valley between her breasts and feel her start. It urges me on. My wild Henriette, the white flower with the blood-red core that's mine alone to partake of. Can any other man be so blesst?

To consummate all we are on the altar of love—I nearly die with the thought of it. And yet, it is so, and her cries ring through the night. I drown in her presence and fall against her to hear her whisper her devotion to me in syllables which mean nothing, and everything. They do not matter. Only the feel of her breath, her heartbeat, her life, matters—

Until one word that is not of us slashes the night with its vileness.

"What did you say, my only one?" I can scarce choke out the words.

"Nothing. Only your name. Nothing more," she lies, and pulls herself away from me, tries to pull her shawl around her bare shoulders and clutches it to her breast.

"That will not protect you from the echoes of your guilty heart. Remember, you are in God's bedchamber."

"I said 'Louis,' is all. That is your name, is it not?"

Oh, the serpent has taken her! Sweet Jesu, how can this be so?

"Never in all our days have you called me by that name. Who is he! Tell me! God is listening!"

The darkness overtakes me. Oh, the rage, the rage. I want her still and I want to strip her of her life, as that one word has stripped me. She has emptied me, bled me.

I look into her face and see that face I have always known. Yet it is not. It changes and reforms with every expression, each moment, and I no longer recognize the one that was my beloved. All this time I'd sensed it, her duplicity, and I played but the fool all along. But I am the fool no longer. The lamb becomes the lion and asserts his claim.

I turn away to gather my wits and raise my arm to strike her down as the righteous are granted the power to do so, but she already flees from me in her guilt, a flurry of white, a ghost in the dim light. The chase begins.

I burst through the doors into the *cimetière*. The markers and monuments mimic the appearance of a small village, of sorts. A flash of white darts off to my left and I follow.

But my mind plays tricks on me. I try to reason through this fog of emotions and instead hear bits of my *dies irae* in my head. The drums pound and I can make sense of nothing. Away! Away! I've no time for that now! The storm, her storm, is taking me and I submit to it.

Round and round the paths we turn in this unholy dance. For all the times I have craved absolution from those lips, I would now have them voice repentence or she will know my wrath. That the waltz I wrote for her should turn to this—how could I know? I, who had courted death if not to gain her, now hunt her in the land of the dead where we once played the angels.

By our bench I see her, her head darting about this way and that in search of me. In a moment, I am behind her.

"It is I, beloved, come to claim you as mine own. Are you not pleased?" She turns at the sound of my voice and I take her.

But she cannot answer me. My hands are around her slender neck and it is such a delight that I can ignore the claws that rake at me. She cannot harm me now. I can feel the life under those hands, as I have so often

before—her breath, her pulse, the fire in her veins—and the muted sounds
she makes in our struggle, a lovemaking of another kind. I welcome the
stripes she gives me.

Her pulse quickens and I push on, harder. There is an abrupt shift and
we tumble to the ground together, spent. I look up at the headstone before
my face. It is delicate, a lady's headstone, no doubt. But I cannot read the
name.

All at once, the world caves in on me and I am thunderstruck, fallen. A
wave of dizziness hits me, I hear a shrill cry on the night's air, a spirit on
the wind, but it is gone.

I look down to behold my handiwork, the goblet that held what had
once been my Henriette crushed and empty. Still. So lost am I that I
cannot even feel, but move as one already dead. One hand, of its own
accord, reaches into a pocket. Two vials. Enough passage for a trip to join
my love, I hope. Never had I thought to follow my *fantastique*'s hero and
pray that I am more successful, if not far wiser, than he.

Let the Devil take me if it is to the arms of my Henriette.

ELLE: I feel her spirit slip its earthly bonds and hold on tight. There is a
moment of disorientation, a sickening wrenching that threatens to dis-
lodge me from my palace here. And then I am free, and blessedly alone. I
almost dare not open my eyes for fear that I might be mistaken.

The body is numb, lifeless, till I stretch myself and permeate its every
part. When I have filled its limits, it quickens with this new life that is so
very old—and I am nearly overwhelmed by the bloodlust. My arm shoots
out to grab any living thing that might have stumbled near my resting
place. I feel a smile stretch across my face, the incisors already grown to a
useful length against my bottom lip.

To awaken once again with my composer beside me is more than I could
have ever hoped for, though I would never have envisioned the transition
to occur as it had. I had my opportunity. I took it. To slay with a word is an
awesome thing—to slay and create with the same word, well, even I have
outdone myself.

Two empty vials lay on the ground and I laugh to see them. He is still
alive—gotten himself sick in the bargain. The sun is still just below the
hills, so I am safe for yet a time. And the bridal supper awaits. But he stirs
and opens an eye to find me looking back at him.

"Yes, my Hector, we are alive, you and I. It is a miracle, no?" I pin his
shoulders before he can roll away.

The whites of his eyes show like a crazed horse's, but he cannot bolt, does not. And now we see who is the dancemaster, at long last. Strength, glorious strength.

His horror is almost amusing. He will learn. The eyes focus on my mouth. "Yes, my love, it is true. I am so very hungry, after all this time, and I need you. They say that all composers are immortal.

"Shall we drink?"

My mind sings, remembers, and all times become one.

I am the muse of Louis Hector and he is mine. We are each other's sustenance, each other's passion, each other's rage. And I am well pleased.

# FLEADH DE DEUX

*Terry McGarry*

Cathal knew, halfway through the first tune the new whistler joined in on, that he would drink deeper of her music than she could imagine.

The slip jig was in A minor, and on the third repeat had crested to an orgasmic height. The fiddles wailed as if presaging death; the whistles keened, their upper octaves producing both shriek and sweet lament. The bodhran, in the hands of a steadfast but unimaginative man, kept the tempo from running away as the players threw themselves into the climax: Irish music, like sex, was most effective when the partners held back, directed the temptation of speed into intensity.

It was Cathal who made the tune three-dimensional—it was Cathal who had composed the tune, two centuries ago. The pale fingers of his left hand traced complex patterns on the fretboard as the long nails of his right, unbreakable as no plastic pick could ever be, drove hypnotic syncopation from the coiled threads of steel. Dark shapes flitted through his modal chords; like a descent into an underworld populated only by the masters of this art, the chords evoked the shades of music long gone. His playing defined and supported the melody; unnoticeable as breathing, it made the music live.

It gave Cathal, whose lungs processed no oxygen, whose arteries throbbed to no pulse—who could still taste the blood and smell the dying exhalation of his last kill—both breath and heartbeat.

Cathal's fingers missed the feel of harp strings. It was not the only other instrument he had played; over the centuries he had learned them all, and found in even the most modern its own unique echo of the old music. But a harp would come closest to remembering with him, and the guitar—grittier, less flexible, limited in range, yet portable, audible, acceptable—came the closest to the harp.

He appreciated an instrument he could drive hard—he who could play until the skin of his fingertips tore and bled, knowing they would heal themselves between chord changes. He could abuse the guitar in ways that would crush the soul of the ethereal harp. It was a process of continual exorcism, catharting the depths of his self through the lacquered wood and high-strung steel. Cathal would never again play any instrument of heaven. This conclusion was not based on religion; his existence predated Christianity, and if he loathed the Cross it was only for what its advent had done to his homeland, transforming it like disease, like necrotic rot. But he knew himself. He had been a demon for centuries, and the music of hell, however metaphorical, was all his legacy now.

When he looked into her eyes, burning in a face flushed with exertion, drink, exhilaration, he saw a reflection of what his own would look like if he could not conceal his nature. He had never seen such a combination of pagan light and darkness in a mortal's eyes. She resembled no one he had known; what she recalled for him was nothing individual, nothing human. And he harbored no illusions of creating a vampire queen from an extraordinary mortal. He sought nothing from her personally, neither her blood nor her allegiance. He knew the folly of love, the ashes all earthly bonds crumble into.

She had the bone structure and coloring of a Native American—unusual in this setting, but not unheard of, as people of many lands were drawn to Irish traditional. But she was, somehow, profoundly Celtic. In those eyes, in the tones of the silver Copeland whistle she played, he saw and heard the hillsides of his childhood. He smelled gorse along the dirt roads that Rome had not yet paved, heard wind soughing in trees that had not yet turned to bog, felt the heat of the fire in the center of his sept's roundhouse. In a world of steel and chrome and noxious fumes, a world that would never heed the call of battle pipes or hear a bard's tales—the new world that he had come to so that his people, the people among whom he would be ever an outsider, would be for a time outsiders themselves, and share at least that small bitterness with him—he had thought himself the only last remaining trace of the true Eire, whose history he embodied, whose soil he lay down on every dawn.

And yet, somehow, its soul had gotten into her, a ragtag session player in a seedy pub in an emigrants' city, as close to her ancestors' homeland as he was far from his.

He knew he must have her music—alone, uninterrupted, and unobserved—for one night. No audience, no recording devices. Just her flute and his guitar, the resurrection of the music of his youth—and the expression of all the tunes he held inside him.

*          *          *

He drew her to him easily enough. Her name was Jessie, and she was descended from an original tribe of this island; whatever ancient Hibernian spirit inhabited her was not genetic, but perhaps drawn into her, or from her, by her own native roots, as ancient and as mesmerizing as the music of his Celtic ones. It was not immune to his powers.

"Your eyes are so pale," she said, approaching him. "It's as if someone chipped off tiles of moonlight and made your irises a mosaic."

It was one of the odder lines he had ever heard. Perhaps she was mad, then, too; or perhaps, judging from the quirk of her mouth as she spoke, the unexpected was a tool she wielded as power of her own. He accommodated her by raising a brow, but he was not inclined to dally. "Tomorrow night," he said, "eight o'clock. I've rented this pub for a private session. Bring only your instrument, nothing electronic. It will be for just a few hours. I'll pay your cabfare home."

He gave a mental nudge to insure acquiescence, and smoothed over her suspicions. The compulsion would last only a day or so, but afterward he would purge her memory of it entire, leaving nothing to incriminate him.

The quirk of the mouth became a grin, showing teeth. It raised invisible hackles on his predator's neck. She must be a predator herself, among her own kind, he thought, and he couldn't help but wonder briefly whom she preyed on, and with what as the prize. Sex? Power? Or something more akin to what he himself sought? Perhaps she believed she was manipulating him. It would behoove him if it was so.

But for some reason he could not pin down, he got the impression that she was allowing his compulsion. Impossible; he had dealt with many a powerful mortal over the years, and the most strong-willed had never been capable of resisting him for long. He gave an extra push, staring right into her eyes, and she blinked, and nodded.

But the quirk never quite left the corner of her mouth, and her sculpted face never went entirely slack.

He made note of that. He would have to be prepared to make an extra effort, tomorrow night, to wipe her memory clean.

It was worth the trouble. As the music began again, he faded back into the group of players around the table, setting down his half-spilled-out pint of blood-dark stout, and became once again Cathal Horgan, reliable but not brilliant musician.

To play his best—to become a John Doyle, a Mark Simos, or more— would be to attract unwanted attention. So he must always hold back, let his technique shine only in increments, only at the height of a rousing tune. Then no one in the audience would be concentrating on the guitar, considered a backup instrument. The players would all believe it was their own contribution that lent the music the special flair. He planted his own compositions as those of others, or said he'd learned them from obscure elderly musicians in rural Clare or Donegal. He must always watch himself.

And he was weary of that watchfulness. The music was the long, green, vibrant vine of his long years, its roots in the earth of Tara; without it, the string of nights would become intolerable. But it could never safely blossom in a crowd, and until now, he had never found a player worthy of the risk of playing alone with.

He let the tunes coalesce around him, whiled away with moderate chordal invention the hours remaining until he could sleep, wake, feed, and make his way back here to a moment he had craved for all too long.


Cathal had owned O'Donnell's Pub for years. It was a dark, eerie place, considered dreary by those who came to play in the nightly sessions, spooky by some who came to listen; it had called to him the first night he himself had come to play. Something had happened here once: some musical connection, perhaps during a session, had been made to the ground it stood on. The shadows that collected in its corners, out of all proportion to the dim light that cast them and sometimes moving out of all relation to it, were an inverse reflection of a deeper, earthier darkness.

He had felt it hum in his bones the moment he walked in. For a while, he had let the bright and wistful Irish lives eddy around him, swirling in the pub life that centered them; he drank in their melancholy, the bright wit and camaraderie they fostered to keep it at bay. He had basked in their glow, as he had always done, as if in moonlight, the ghostly reflection of the cruel star he barely remembered.

Then, late in the evening, when drink would do more than any compulsion to erase the memory from their minds, he had sung a tune so ancient they thought it was new. The old-style singing they called *sean-nós* was, in the scope of his existence, in its infancy. His voice was pure, heartrending; he bent the notes in mourning, ornamented them with razors, dropped so low on the final, sustained tone that it became almost subliminal. The two nearest to him had shivered, though the pub was close and sweaty.

And he had known that he had tapped into something primal in this place; he had felt from their minds that he had conveyed it to them through the music, a supernatural conduit.

He had written to a solicitor that same night and arranged the sale quickly, through one of his many affluent identities; his ownership was anonymous. The place ran itself—the bartender, a Dubliner named Declan, had managed it for as long as anyone could remember, and he bagged up and deposited each night's take, paid himself honestly each Friday, and took care of the ordering and bills. Cathal had no need to watch him; even if the man had been stealing, it wouldn't have mattered, as long as the pub stayed solvent.

And as long as no one investigated the sealed basement storeroom in which Cathal slept off the sunlight, on his crate of stony Irish soil, taken with him when he joined the westward flood of emigrants, and never missed, in those years when all it grew was praties that rotted before they could be eaten. He would rise each dusk, slip out to feed, then gather his instrument and a change of clothes from a locker at the nearby ferry terminal, and return as the *seisiún* began.

The nightly kill had become as mundane as a human's morning ablution of brushing teeth. Like a drunk going out to take a piss, he would seek out a dark alleyway. There was always some urban predator or living corpse; he would paralyze it mentally as if it were a deer frozen in the headlights of an oncoming truck, then slit its throat or wrists with his razor nails and feed, casting it away like a fruit rind.

He had passed through the predictable stages. For centuries, the hunt had been a thrill, whether it took place at a glittering soirée or in the bog or gutter. He had preyed on the strongest because they were the most challenging. Then a mixture of guilt and ennui had prompted him to choose ethics, and he had preyed on predators. But even that had dulled, and now he made no distinction except in order to vary his routine, to conceal his tracks. He fed on whoever was most likely to be murdered or die anyway, or whoever was least visible—whoever mattered least to those who might threaten him. It made no difference, and was done quickly.

Only the music held his interest now. He had been both oppressor and oppressed, both rich and poor, landlord and tenant. He had lived one lifetime to the drumbeats of a hillfort, another to the sound of Druidic chanting, seen the comrades of still another die of starvation with lips stained green from eating grass. He had seen battle with iron swords, rebellion with guns. He had heard the music of war and the music of insurrection; he had been harper to kings and a king himself.

He knew the genesis of the music these people played as none of them could. He remembered the rough precursors of the bodhran; he remembered the *feadog*, the two-hole birdbone flute. He remembered the oldest of slow airs . . . and because of it, he was utterly alone, for no one had been where he had been or seen what he had seen, and even if he could summon up the words, there was no one he could say them to.

Now, only the music remained, and the dull ache of limited options: playing it alone or playing it badly. Tonight, for just a few hours, he would alleviate that ache, and then face the long stretch of nights that must pass before he dared do it again.

He felt on his cold skin the infinitesimal easing of pressure that meant the last rays of the sun had dripped down below the horizon, and rose to hunt.


She was precisely on time; he had opened the dark pub only minutes before, satisfied that Declan had not come to investigate why he'd gotten the night off.

She did not appear nervous, which made him wary, but he shook the feeling off; he would deal with her emotions and her memories when they were finished. He ignored her somewhat flippant attempts at small talk, as well. When his guitar was tuned to her whistle, he merely looked up and said, "Play. Play all the tunes you know, and play your best."

He was not disappointed. She warmed up with some swinging hornpipes, a few bright polkas—cheerful, rousing dance tunes, which he obliged with major chords and sprightly rhythm. They were part of the repertoire, after all. Soon enough they found their way into the tunes that moved him, the driving reels, the hypnotic jigs; she both led with her melody and followed with her ornamentation, feeling her way into his phrasing as he did into hers. The music ceased to be a combination of disparate styles and took on its own peculiar life.

He began to paint the tunes with darker chords, letting a little more of himself into the music as she played, unaware, a few of his own creations. And to his surprise, she followed, and expanded: her notes began to bend; her breathing and rhythm fit themselves to his increasingly archaic mode, and took it beyond itself. They began and ended tunes as one, even when he tried to lose her, experimenting with tempo and syncopation. When they exhausted all the tunes she knew, he played her the older ones, and she learned them on first listen.

And played them back to him. Tunes he had not heard in centuries, millennia; tunes O'Neill and the nineteenth-century scholars might have dismissed as fakes. Hearing them again, played their best, more than their best, felt like the warm infusion of blood after a kill: it permeated his every cell, made his epidermis glow, soaked into his internal organs, circulated into his fingers and through his brain.

He began to compose new tunes. He improvised, beginning a bit of melody here, a phrase there, and let her take them from him so that he could put harmonic flesh on their bones. All the music he had held inside in order to protect himself, he let out into the air. It filled the dank room with a burning light, echoed in the shadowed rafters, and made the shadows dance.

He had arranged this in order to release his pent-up talent and technique, to reminisce a little. He did not expect the sharp upwelling of emotion her playing engendered in the numb, dry husk of his soul. To feel again so strongly, to exult again, to *yearn* again—he let the guitar fall silent and looked up at her with an awe and gratitude far too profound for his margin of safety.

Was what they had done here so beautiful, so impossible, that he was going to have to kill her to preserve it?

"How old *are* you?" she asked. Her conversational tone set off a warning deep within him. She sensed what he was, and she was not afraid. She was the most dangerous mortal he had met in centuries—perhaps ever.

"Old," he said, his voice rough with disuse, no longer concealing that roughness, his true, unrecognizable accent. "As old as Ireland."

She nodded almost offhandedly. "I thought as much. Those tunes *feel* old. They feel as if you dipped down through the schist underneath us, reached under the Atlantic Ocean and across a thousand years, and pulled them up. Pretty cool."

He watched her carefully as she rose and went behind the bar. The gurgle of the soda gun was loud in the comparative quiet. Cathal felt the earth shift in its half-sleep far beneath him.

"Were you a bard?" She sipped Coke from a tumbler and regarded him over its rim with her old, dark eyes.

Could she be of his kind? Or something else? There had never been more than a handful of vampires in Ireland, not even enough for Irish mythology to have a vampiric figure in it. He had known selkies—he remembered feeding once, desperate enough to take carrion, from the flayed corpse of one of their victims—and he was well acquainted with the *bean sidhe*'s cry, which had nearly given him away before many a kill, alerting half the countryside. He had little truck with fairies, except that believing in them made the locals' beliefs suspect, protecting him from stray tales. No, she was none of those. She was nothing he had ever encountered before.

*What are you?* he wanted to whisper. He had expected release tonight, a modicum of pleasure, and that he had been granted joy had been surprise enough; he had never expected terror. It was a feeling so unfamiliar he wasn't sure he had correctly identified it.

"Yes," he answered, the truth escaping with a demonic hiss, as if he were some hellish punctured tube. "I was a bard once. A bard's son, a singer of tales, a keeper of history. Now I *am* history."

And that was the key, he realized. He was the keeper of his people's past, and unable to dispense it to them—cursed, instead, to take their present lives instead of returning their past ones to them. He was a closed archive, an oral tradition muted, a walking history book whose pages were glued shut. He was afraid that he would burn, like the library at Alexandria, and all his memories with him.

What was the use of being what he was, if he could not be what he was? *And what was the use of being shown this now?*

"You're not quite the original you think you are," she said with mild amusement, apparently having read his thoughts. "Oh, I believe that you were born to the bard of a high king of Tara. But you know yourself that your nature is nothing of Ireland. Who made you?"

Cathal had not thought about that for centuries. When he thought that far back, he thought of his human childhood, the dappling of sunlight on a bale of hay, the sound of lullabyes sung at day's end. Memories brittle as parchment, and more precious to him than he had ever admitted.

"A Roman," he replied at last. "A soldier. He must have found it easiest to feed in battle. But he was careless, and I lived through my death." He blinked, the memory rushing back. "I had played him a tune on my harp, a sad, sweet tune to make him homesick."

"Play me the tune, then," she said, returning to her seat and taking up her whistle again. "Let it be our session's last."

The memory was so strong that for a moment he had trouble fitting his hands to the small shape of the guitar, finding analogues for the ancient strings. String of the leading sinews, servant to the leading sinews, falling string, the string fallen . . . answering, response . . . *cronan ioch-dar-chanus . . . uach-dar-chanus . . .*

Slowly, painfully, the tune came to him: the saddest air, the forgotten air. The first air he had ever composed. He played the melody at first, mournful and solitary, then let it burst with chordal flavor, searching for the fullest expression of it, the version among all the versions that would make the heart crack.

When he found it, she took up the melody on her breathy flute, raised it to a piercing dominant height and then let it fall, gently as a dying leaf, to the tonic earth. Then, as the last vibration died away, she began it again: she took the oldest tune of all, and led it, and him, in a new direction, into a new song. She prompted him with her breath, her tonguing, and he felt himself pushed into variations, into elongations, and, at last, into an entirely new composition.

It became the most beautiful thing he had created in two thousand years. And because he believed that it was the last thing he would ever play, it was also the saddest, and full of more restrained terror than his music, even at its most hellish, had ever been. It was entirely his self— victim and hunter, child and demon—and every self he had ever been. It evoked every moment of cruelty and every hint of pathos, the howling loneliness and fear of abandonment and scorn of death. It was as human, and as supernatural, as he was; it was mortal love and immortal hell. He lingered long on the last suspended fourth, let it drift in the air, loath to allow it to subside back into the tonic. But he could not find another note to play; there simply was no more. The augmented chord faded slowly as the strings' vibration ceased, leaving the tune, and the moment, hanging.

"I have not lived this long to go down easily," he said into the flat silence, raising his pale eyes to meet hers, which were full of warm, dark, enfolding death. He thrust his mind out at hers, but his compulsion smashed against an unyielding wall and fell away in fragments.

"Must it be an ending?" she asked mildly, scratching her lower lip. "All you need is a reason to go on. Nothing more."

Reason he might or might not have, but he did still have a question, now that he had formulated an answer. "How did you get here? The Tuatha went into the earth long before I was born. Did you burrow in your long sleep and wake to find yourself across the sea in a native body?"

She smiled at his impertinence. "We are wherever our descendants are. We were the first, aside from the Firbolg we destroyed, but that does not make us immovable. In fact, you drew me yourself; the conduit was already here, opened by the incessant sessions, the music that spoke to the earth and woke it up. Your call merely pulled me through."

"You are not harbingers of death," he said.

"You, a legend, should know better than to believe in myths," she parried. "Come now, and bring your knowledge back with you, into the earth that spawned you. It's time, Cathal."

Her words sucked at him, a muddy, insidious version of his own compulsions. She said his given name with an inflection so old that it sounded as it had in his boyhood, before orthography and Anglicization, a name he had retained through the millennia, through hundreds of identities, hundreds of lives. All she did, all she was—the true incarnation of Ireland, when he was only its living history—recalled his roots. Perhaps he *had* drawn her out, made her tangible through the very intensity of his repressed longing.

But what was called up could be sent back—what sought to drink his soul could itself be drained away—and the time for nostalgia was over.

He sprang for her with every ounce of preternatural speed he possessed, before the impulse to do so had registered as something she could read in his mind. Her giant's spirit reacted sluggishly. The body she had assumed struggled in his iron grip, but it was, for all its authenticity, a human body, and as weaker than his own as turf was weaker than petrified wood.

Her blood was thin, made half of myth and more than a little of his own belief. He nearly gagged on it, but he forced himself to drink, sucking the opening his teeth had rended in the carotid artery until the flesh against his lips deflated, spent. Her eyes, in death, were still full of death themselves, but as a mirror in a dark room is full of darkness: a reflection of nothing.

He let the shell fall. Where had the spirit gone? Back into the earth through which it had come, most likely; he neither knew nor cared. Reduced to animal level, he had only two thoughts, unvoiced: The conduit must be closed, and he must go home.

He left the pub, found a gas station, felt dawn pressing on him from its birthplace below the horizon, like a vise tightening on his dead skin, as he returned with a canister of petrol. A subbasement next door connected to a lightless sewer; he dragged his crate of earth awkwardly through a steam pipe, then went back, doused the basement of the pub, lit it with a book of bar matches, and faded into the last shred of night.

The fire would take the body, his instrument, and this lifetime with it. When he woke, he would have to start anew, again. Again.                  ·

He settled into his crate. He was far enough from the flames and the light to be safe, but the sleep of death embraced him to the roar of conflagration.

When he awoke, he had a tune running through his head, an eerie tune that made him shiver as he had made the mortals shiver in the pub he had just destroyed; the flames themselves had composed it as he dreamed.

But when he awoke, he was not alone. And the melody of the tune had words:

*He was careless, and I survived my own death.*

The ancient spirit of the pagan race, briefly incarnate, now undead.

He had only moments to wonder what he had unleashed, unknowing, on the world.

# BREATHTAKING MUSIC

*Christie Golden*

Garage sales had been a Saturday morning ritual for as long as Anne and Eric had been together. Neither of them minded rising early for the best bargains, and they had a house full of knickknacks to prove it. Some were little more than worthless but appealing trinkets, but not all. As long as Anne could find something that she felt was a bargain, she was happy; and as long as Eric could find either an out-of-print favorite book or piece of furniture to refinish, he counted the morning a success. Of course, sometimes they found nothing, but the looking was half the fun.

It was a clear April morning and spring was in the air. Kids were out on their bikes, their parents busy planting gardens or working on the house. It was a typical suburban Saturday. Eric, a good-looking man in his late thirties, reached forward and rolled down the window of his little Escort and let his face be bathed by the freshness of a day that was still fairly new. Anne, grinning, pulled her hair back in a ponytail with a barrette she fished from her purse and imitated him.

"Beautiful day," Eric commented, inhaling deeply.

"Mmmm!" agreed Anne with a smile.

He spared a glance from the road in her direction. Anne looked like spring herself today. Her blonde hair shone like sunshine, and despite her attempt to secure it a few adventurous tendrils had escaped to fly merrily about her heart-shaped face. She was unaware of his scrutiny, her eyes, those beautiful china-blue eyes that had ensnared him four years ago on the road, a half-smile of anticipation on her pink lips. Anne wore no makeup. At a youthful-looking thirty-five, she didn't need to.

Eric turned his attention back to the road, but he reached over and squeezed her left hand, feeling the slight resistance of the gold band she wore around her left finger. Four years later, he still couldn't believe he'd won her. He counted himself among the luckiest of men.

"Oh, there's one," Anne called, pointing over to her left. Sure enough, there was a big yellow sign on a telephone pole that announced in black block letters ESTATE SALE TODAY.

"Great, an estate sale!" Eric's voice held a smile. There was a chance at getting something of real value at an estate sale. They'd found a gorgeous walnut coffee table at one such sale only three weeks earlier. He turned on his signal and took the next left, following the yellow signs until he pulled up in front of a largish colonial with a gorgeous lawn. Several other cars were there in front of him, and Anne pouted slightly.

"Not early enough, it would appear," she sighed.

"Ah, don't worry. It's only eight forty-five. It can't be picked over too drastically," Eric reassured her, swinging his long legs out of the car and getting out.

Anne did likewise, carefully locking the door behind her, walking around the car, and locking his door as well. Eric had, as usual, forgotten. She was much better at that than he was. Anne was the practical, cautious, wise one of the pair, the one who was always able to negotiate the price downward at these things. Eric had had to learn to work hard at his poker face. More than once they had not gotten the deal they should have because Eric had been too enthusiastic.

The front door was open and they wandered in. For all that estate sales meant better buys than regular garage or moving sales, Eric found them always rather depressing. There was no one living in those houses anymore. What was on sale were the dregs—what had been rejected by the survivors of the deceased as undesirable, impractical, or just not wanted. Sometimes Eric marveled at what people rejected. The old adage, "One man's junk is another man's treasure," seemed to apply in full force to estate sales.

There was the avocado-green refrigerator and stove in the kitchen, along with a mismatched collection of old china and chipped, coffee-grayed mugs that said "Grandmas Are for Loving" and other such sentiments. A rolled-up Persian rug in the library caught their interest, but someone had already beaten them to it. The word SOLD was etched across the very reasonable price of $100. Old furniture, heavy and dark, lined the foyer and huddled in the living room along with fragile china cherubs and flowers. A pretty crystal rose, its petals only slightly chipped, seemed out of place among the cheap trinkets. Anne picked it up, thought about it, placed it down again, and turned into the library.

There she lingered, searching through the dozens of titles to see if there were any of interest. He left her to it; she knew his tastes well enough to pull out any he might want. Eric went upstairs, thinking that the creaking of the stairs was a rather lonely sound, as if the house itself were voicing its displeasure at the death of its owner.

There was an old, water-stained bathroom with bits of bath salts available for a nickel apiece. A spare room was largely empty, its walls bare and the huddled pictures that had once adorned them propped up against the furniture. Eric wandered into the master bedroom, pretty much convinced that there was nothing in this forlorn old home that he would wish to buy, when he saw the flute.

It was propped up on the pillow, a gorgeous, sleek, silver instrument that caught the light and returned it a thousandfold. Eric was stunned. This was no secondhand instrument, picked up on a whim by an old man. This piece had surely sounded its sweet notes in an orchestra pit somewhere.

He couldn't believe it was still here. Even if one didn't play, the thing was clearly valuable. He walked to where it glistened invitingly, and peered down at the tag.

"Jesus," he breathed. Someone was asking only twenty bucks for the thing. Gingerly, almost ashamed to leave fingerprints to tarnish its silver gleam, he picked it up.

The flute felt both cool and warm in his hands. Eric knew nothing about flutes. His musical knowledge was limited to the ability to pick out "Jingle Bells" on someone's piano at Christmastime. But he knew how they ought to be held, and the flute fell easily into position as he brought the lovely thing to his lips. He inhaled deeply, pursed his mouth, and was about to breathe into the thing when Anne's sudden presence in the room startled him. She carried, he noticed, the crystal rose.

"Not another instrument!" Anne sighed, real annoyance on her pretty face.

Eric's breath tooted in a startled, unharmonic sound as it escaped from his lips into the flute. Anne's voice seemed harsh and unduly angry.

"It's beautiful, though," he said, defeated before he had begun to fight. He was just about to replace the instrument on the bed when the thought occurred to him: *What's she doing, telling you what you can and can't buy?*

"It's only twenty bucks," he said, firing the first volley.

Anne snorted—an unpleasant noise—and strode to stand beside him. "Eric, you don't have any musical ability. You can carry a tune all right, but we've been through this before." She began to tick off items on her slender, pink-painted fingers, cradling the crystal rose in her palm. "First there was the folk harp that you just *had* to get at that Renaissance fair we attended three years ago. Three hundred bucks. Then there was that beat-up guitar your brother sold you. Then the harmonica—"

"Maybe I just haven't found the right instrument." Eric didn't meet Anne's accusing gaze. He concentrated on the flute—good God, it was a pretty thing!—and found himself really, really wanting to take it home.

Anne babbled on. He ignored her. Suddenly he bent forward and snatched it up. "It's a concertworthy piece, Anne, and if I don't learn how to play it I can sell it for three times what they're asking for it, at least."

Anne's eyebrows crawled for her hairline. "That thing? Honey, the only concert it was ever at was some grade-school kid's Mother's Day bash. I mean, look at it!"

Eric did, and wondered how Anne could be so blind. This thing was gorgeous. "Look, it's twenty bucks. I won't buy anything else today, okay?" *Penny-pinching bitch, I earn every bit as much as she does and then some!*

"All right. Remember, you promised." She turned and stalked out of the room. As Eric watched her go, he wondered why he'd never before noticed the gray slithering through her long blonde locks, or the sag of her breasts and bottom.

He gripped the flute hard, and smiled.

The minute they got home, Eric collapsed into a chair in the living room and familiarized himself with the instrument. It was every bit as beautiful as it had been in the old house, when it had caught the sun and sparkled like a little sun itself. He ran his fingers over the keys, pressing them down and then letting them spring up again. So smooth and cool and friendly, he thought. He'd always had a sneaking suspicion that performers formed a sort of bond with their instruments, made them part of themselves. Now this lovely flute was part of him.

He lifted it to his lips, pursed, and blew.

The flute seemed to take his breath and return it with the sweetest sound Eric had ever heard. If water could sing, if sunlight could laugh, surely this was the sound it would utter. Eric closed his eyes. He'd never played a note on a flute before, but it didn't seem to matter. Oh, this was sweet.

"Jesus Christ, honey," came Anne's voice from the kitchen—shrill and harsh and ugly, he thought angrily—"do a few scales or something till you get the hang of it, all right?"

Eric stared, his jaw hanging open. Wasn't she listening? They'd been to concerts and musicals; up till now she'd always seemed to enjoy fine music when she heard it. He gazed through the open door at her moving around in the kitchen, preparing their lunch.

"I'm not hungry," he snapped. "I'm going upstairs to *practice.*" He rose and stomped up the stairs, not letting himself be moved by the puzzled hurt on Anne's face as she emerged from the kitchen to watch him go. Stupid bitch. What did she know about beauty, about the spirit suddenly being given voice?

For the rest of the afternoon, until his mouth hurt with the effort, Eric played the flute. He knew no songs, not really; he merely let the instrument voice its passion however it chose, using his breath to do so.

Anne avoided him for the rest of the day. She called him for dinner around six; he did not answer. Eric lay on the bed, flat on his back, the flute cradled in his arms. His eyes were closed. He was reliving the music that he had played, that the flute had held for so long in it slender silver length, the music that he, Eric, had breathed life into.

When he was up to it, he played some more.

Anne slept on the couch that night.


"How long has he had the flute?" Laura asked, expertly twirling her spaghetti into the spoon and popping the neatly wrapped pasta into her red-lipsticked mouth.

Anne stared at her own fettucine Alfredo. She hadn't touched it, nor the salad that had preceded it, but she'd drunk three glasses of robust Italian wine.

"Almost five weeks," she said softly. She wondered if she'd done the right thing, confiding in Laura. Laura was her best friend, but this whole thing with Eric was just so . . . so weird. "It's the damndest thing."

"Has he learned to play anything?"

Anne, her eyes ringed with purple shadows, shot Laura a look that was equal parts annoyance and hurt. "Sorry," Laura apologized sincerely. "Just thought a little humor might help, you know? C'mon, hon, eat some of that. You've lost at least ten pounds since I saw you last, and in all the wrong places, too."

Listlessly, Anne poked at the pasta. The fragrance of Parmesan almost made her sick.

"He just . . . blows into it. It's a horrible sound. The cat hates it, and so do I. He'll eat, but not much, and if he's half as preoccupied at his job as he is at home, well, then he's going to be looking for a new job soon. If he even bothers to look for a new job." She finally looked up, right into Laura's eyes. "I don't know how much longer I can take it. I mean, it would be one thing if he were a professional musician, or even a serious hobbyist. But this thing is so old and beat up, and he doesn't even *play* it, not really. I wonder if he's going crazy."

"Well, he might be undergoing a nervous breakdown. Do you think he'd be willing to see a counselor?"

Anne's reply was a short, harsh bark. Heads turned, and several other diners stared at her. She was past caring.

"Christ, no. He's . . . he's taken to locking himself in the bedroom and playing that thing all night. God, this is hard."

"Well," offered Laura, buttering her bread, "how about you? I could give you the name of my shrink. She did wonders in helping me get my head together after Tom and I got divorced."

"But I'm not the one with the problem!" Anne's denial was shrill, even in her own ears.

"I'm not saying that you are. But a professional might be able to offer some insight into what's going on. Might even be persuaded to make a house call, I don't know."

She wasn't going to cry, she told herself; wasn't going to break down right here, right now, in the middle of this stupid walking cliché of an Italian restaurant, but she did. Tears filled her blue eyes, the eyes that her husband oh-so-recently used to get lost in, the eyes that had watched her beloved best friend and lifemate turn into a stranger because of an obsession with a stupid musical instrument.

Laura's hand shot across the table and gripped Anne's limp fingers. "Hang on, honey. This is breaking you. Come on. You're moving in with me until Eric gets his head back on straight."

This time, the tears that blurred Anne's vision were tears of relief—and remorse. "God, I was praying you'd say that," she said thickly.


Eric heard the phone ring, but he didn't answer it. He was too busy playing the flute, breathing into it and being rewarded with sounds never heard this side of heaven. He heard the answering machine kick in, and then Anne's voice.

There was enough of his old self left that, when he heard the hitch in her voice, he put the flute down, even though it protested. He listened, heard the words that for just a moment sent anguish quivering through his body, the words *not coming home* and *separate* and *don't call me.*

"Anne," he whispered, and reached for the phone. She was still talking, crying now. He wanted to tell her he was sorry, that he loved her, that nothing was more important than—

Heat blazed through his left hand, the hand that still grasped the slender, smooth instrument. He gasped, but did not let go. Sanity returned almost at once. What had he been thinking? Give up the flute? Never, no, impossible! Not when it fitted his hands like a glove, when it gave and gave and gave, asking only his breath to animate it. Not when it even called now, called out for him to bring it to his lips, purse them, place them on the flute as if on the lips of a lover, and breathe, *breathe.*

There was no Anne anymore to nag him about going to bed, or eating, or going to work. He—they—were free now. Free to be everything to each other, the flute seemed to whisper silkily in Eric's fevered brain. This was the perfect union, far more intimate than sex, far more lasting than a marriage—the union of performer and instrument, breath and music.

Eric played.

He played until his fingers grew dead, the fingertips like wood. He played until the muscles in his lower arms cramped and screamed for rest. He played until his lungs grew hot, became not organs for the dispersal of oxygen to a living body, but merely a bellows to feed the flute. Eric played as the sun sank, and rose, and sank again, helpless to stop although now, now that it was too late, he wanted to stop, needed to stop, *prayed* to stop and tears flooded his face and coursed over the instrument.

Eric, helpless to resist the demands of the flute, played for many more hours. The thing drank greedily of his fear and despair, almost as greedily as it sucked out his very lifebreath.

Finally, as night crept toward dawn on the fourth day, Eric's fingers fell from the flute, and the instrument, sated for the moment, began to turn its thoughts toward new prey.


"Here's one," said Sandra, refolding the unruly newspaper as best she could. "Estate sale—furniture, household items, rugs, et cetera."

"Boy, I could use some et cetera in the dorm," joked Steve. Sandra giggled and punched him in the arm.

"Thanks for coming."

"Hey, I had to convince myself that you weren't sneaking off with some gorgeous hunk on your Saturday mornings," smiled Steve. "What's the address?"

"Fifteen thirty-six Lakeview Drive," read Sandra. "I know where that is. Turn left here, go two lights, then right."

They drove in a comfortable silence. Sandra still couldn't believe that Steve Matthews had taken such an interest in her. Even to the point of accompanying her when she went garage-sale hopping! And him a freshman in college, too. Sandra's mom had been a little leery about it at first ("Time enough for college boys when you're in college yourself," she'd said), but had put her worries aside once she'd met Steve. Handsome, courteous, Steve was the perfect date.

They pulled up at 1536 Lakeview Drive. There were already several cars there. "Hope it's not too picked over," worried Sandra as they got out.

Nearly everything in the house was for sale. They wandered, hand in hand, through the lovely townhouse.

"Kinda creepy," said Sandra, staring at a kitchen that had everything in it a normal kitchen would, with the exception that a price tag was on each item. She smiled awkwardly at the lady with the cash register, who had set up her station at the kitchen table.

"Wonder what happened to the owners," mused Steve. He went into the living room. "They had some nice stuff, man."

Sandra wasn't listening. She stared, captivated, at the exquisite flute that lay forlornly on a card table. Its companions were mostly cheap knick-knacks and broken china, the one exception being a still-pretty crystal rose. Amid the dross, the instrument shone like silver.

Her hand itched, and she reached to pick it up.

# SYMPHONY FOR THE QUIET ONES

*Michael Scott Bricker*

## I. EXPOSITION: THE FLYING DUTCHMAN

Preston Kingsbury would eventually learn that the man who was sitting next to him during the evening flight to Vienna was Richard Wagner, one of several immortal composers who had been presumed dead long ago. Kingsbury knew nothing of immortality, at least not yet, but he did know that he found the man to be annoying and pretentious from the moment he sat down. Wagner wore a purple beret with a matching silk cravat, a long leather overcoat with matching gloves, and a heavy gold watch chain which hung from his vest, catching the light until seconds before the crash, when the electrical systems on the plane would fail. He made demands of the stewardess in caustic German tones, constantly calling for her services until the oxygen masks came down. Kingsbury slipped on his headphones and clicked the tuning dial to a channel which featured classical music. The selection he heard was a piece called *Galway, 1936*. It helped to calm his nerves, and even though it had been decades since Kingsbury had composed it, the music still made him proud as well.

Wagner and Kingsbury had much in common. Both men were renowned and prolific composers, as well as being political radicals, music theorists, and designers of magnificent theaters. They were both generous to friends and ruthless to enemies, and both had lived well on borrowed money. Their births were separated in time by exactly one century (Wagner's in 1813, Kingsbury in 1913), as were their presumed deaths in 1883 and 1983 respectively. Neither of them would die, though, and despite reports of Wagner's demise at the Palazzo Vendramin on the Grand Canal in Venice, or of the plane crash over Vienna which had supposedly burned Kingsbury beyond recognition, they would both continue to exist, serving the Quiet Ones forever.

74

As it became clear that the crash was inevitable, after the lights went out and the inky blackness of night crept into the cabin, Wagner's tyrannical voice could still be heard above the screams of the other passengers. Kingsbury felt the German's strong, gloved hands on his face, tearing away his oxygen mask. He tried to resist but the man was too strong, and then he felt Wagner's arms slide around him, nearly crushing him as the plane spiraled. Wagner pulled Kingsbury *through* the cabin wall, into the open air, and they escaped from the plane shortly before it hit the ground. When the explosion came, as Kingsbury was carried over the wreckage, Wagner's sweaty face glistened in the firelight, and all he said was "*Der Fliegende Holländer*" before they flew off together into the moonless night.

## II. FIRST THEME: AWAKE, THE VOICE CALLS TO US

The cathedral ceiling was a baroque tangle of human bodies. When Kingsbury had first opened his eyes, he had believed that he was hallucinating, or perhaps mad. The chamber was lit by candles, thousands of them, and through the smoke and the haze of his muddled thoughts, he watched flying cherubim perform a perverse ballet around the gilded columns far above. Mortals clung to the walls, others melted into them, as angels and saints glided and spun through the dome of heaven, where the Romanesque architecture opened to reveal puffy white clouds glowing with golden rays of pure sunlight. Far above, obscured by cloud vapors, Christ hung from a tremendous cross. As Kingsbury watched the scene play out before him, he felt the first drop of blood touch his cheek.

It began as most rainstorms do, as a mild drizzle, only the drops left red stains upon the floor stones, and spots blossomed through the composer's suit as well. It seemed that the blood strengthened Kingsbury, helped to clear his mind, and he realized that he was lying on a long ebony table, surrounded by candles. He heard choral music, unmistakably that of J. S. Bach, similar to his "Osanna" from the Mass in B Minor, although the piece was unfamiliar to him. The rain fed upon the swelling music, and as the clouds above darkened, pregnant with blood, the cherubim began to descend. The candles burned out one by one as the downpour deluged the entire chamber, and Kingsbury tried to escape but found that he had no freedom of movement, as if he were part of the table, just as the mortals above fattened the walls. He watched as the cherubim flew closer, and he choked on the smell of blood and tallow as the rain washed over his body.

After the last candle was extinguished, Kingsbury felt the cherubim crawling over him, coating his body like ivory locusts, and the beating of their wings kept time with the strains of baroque music as they lifted him into the air, through the dome of heaven, toward Christ and the raining blood.

## III. BRIDGE: A WOODLAND PATH BY A POND

She might have been a nurse, if it wasn't for the dagger she carried. When Kingsbury awoke in the hospital bed, he found comfort in the notion that he had survived the plane crash, that the lunacy he had encountered (the flying German, the raining blood) were merely aberrations met in an unconscious state. When he saw the nurse's dagger and the doe drinking from the nearby pond, he realized that the madness had only begun. His mouth tasted of iron, and as he remembered the cherubs, their little hands, their flapping wings, he spat the blood away, then drew forth enough strength to speak. "What's this? Why? What do you want?"

"Immortality. Nothing more." The nurse appeared as though she had stepped from a World War One Red Cross poster (white apron, cap, and shoes), an image of purity shattered by that dagger of hers. "Would you like something to drink? Juice?"

"I'd like to know . . ."

"Of course. Lie still. Please." The room looked like a turn-of-the-century hospital ward. There were three beds, empty with the exception of the one which Kingsbury occupied, each beside a small, white enameled table topped with drinking glasses and various stoppered medicine bottles. The black-and-white-checkered marble floor, highly waxed, reflected gaslight from lamps along the walls. Twenty yards away, the walls, floor, and ceiling appeared to have crumbled away, revealing dense woods and a well-traveled path along the bank of a murky pond. An eerie, violet light rained from above, tinting the foliage in a way which suggested a stage set rather than natural woods.

Kingsbury heard opera. He tried to get up.

The nurse held her dagger against the composer's throat. "Lie down. You need juice." He offered no resistance, and then the nurse turned, took several steps, and a tree pushed through the floor tiles, maturing in seconds, sprouting branches, leaves, and heavy, ripening oranges as the nurse watched and waited. She lopped off one of the oranges with a quick turn of her dagger, and Kingsbury couldn't help but think about how Freudian it all seemed. She returned, then held out the orange for Kingsbury to take. "Drink this."

"I can't drink it. It's an orange, for Christ's sake. What do you want?"

"Sorry. I should have thought of that." The nurse slipped the dagger between her teeth, took a glass from the table beside his bed, and squeezed the orange in her meaty hands. It popped open, oozing seeds and pulp between her fingers, down her arm, and a stream of juice dripped from her elbow onto the floor. She handed Kingsbury the glass, and he was surprised to find that it was filled to the brim with fresh orange juice.

Kingsbury drank, and it seemed that his body craved the sugar. He emptied the glass in moments.

The nurse wiped her hands on her apron and removed the dagger from between her teeth. "That'll do you just fine."

Kingsbury returned the glass. "Explain. Please. For God's sake, what is this?"

"You should be familiar with it. After all, it's one of his old pieces."

The music began to build, and it seemed as if weird singing dripped from the twisted tree limbs. A tremendous red moon rose with little jerks and spasms. Kingsbury was reminded of a Chevy he once owned. It had vinyl seats, very similar to that moon in color and shine.

"Wozzeck will be here soon." The nurse slipped the blade of the dagger under her apron strings. "He's schizophrenic. I believe that's the term."

*Wozzeck.* Kingsbury knew the name. It was an opera by Alban Berg, one that he detested. Franz Wozzeck was a soldier, and a schizophrenic, certainly, who stabbed his unfaithful mistress, then drowned in a lake of blood. His mistress was named . . . Marie.

The nurse placed her hand over Kingsbury's forehead. "You know my name. I'm glad that your memory came through all right. It doesn't always go so well." As she removed her hand, he felt something slip across his forehead, and then it took hold.

Kingsbury found something wet there, something soft and awful, and he tore it away, then flung it onto the floor.

"You shouldn't have done that." She picked it up and slipped it between her breasts. "Good leeches are difficult to find."

A man dressed in a black Nazi SS uniform and crocodile boots approached from the woods. The music swelled.

Marie turned. "I see that Berg has made some changes again."

The *Wozzeck* that Kingsbury knew had been nothing like this. The scene was insane, surreal, much more so than Alban Berg's tragic opera had been. But then, if this was a delusion on Kingsbury's part, visions of a dagger-wielding nurse and a bizarre Nazi under a vinyl moon should have come as no surprise.

Marie slipped the dagger from her apron strings and held it in the air. In *Wozzeck*, Franz Wozzeck had killed Marie, not the other way around.

The Nazi (presumably the new Wozzeck) stood at Marie's mercy as the shadow of the dagger fell across his face. The music stopped suddenly, then began once again as three women dressed in frog suits danced a jig around the pond.

Marie brought the dagger down, plunging it into Wozzeck's chest. Blood sprayed across Kingsbury's sheets. He pushed himself out of bed, then moved toward the woods as quickly as his wobbly legs would carry him. He turned, looked behind him, and watched in horror as Marie plunged the dagger into Wozzeck's chest over and over again while the Nazi stood at attention, motionless, obedient.

As Kingsbury moved deeper into the woods, the music faded, the scenery dropped away, and he found himself walking in the emptiness of space with seven colossal planets to keep him company.

## IV. SECOND THEME: SATURN, THE BRINGER OF OLD AGE

It was an odd sensation. On television, Kingsbury had watched astronauts walk in space, and he remembered how clumsy their movements had seemed to him, how they were separated from the textures of space by those bulky suits of theirs. There were no such barriers for Kingsbury. He walked easily upon the nothingness, upon ribbons of time which took him on a tour of Gustav Holst's solar system. As he approached Mercury, he stopped and listened to the polite, graceful bitonality of the planet, watched the desolate surface vibrate with life as the brass cut in, and even in this fantastic, impossible environment, he found comfort in the familiarity of Holst's work. Kingsbury recognized the planets ahead (Venus, Mars, Jupiter, Saturn, Uranus, Neptune), and he knew that this place was a reflection of Gustav Holst's *The Planets*, just as the dark, eerie world of the dagger-wielding nurse had been a reflection of Berg's *Wozzeck*. As he passed by the planets and listened (the militant strains of Mars, the elephant walk of Jupiter), he found that the music was precisely how he remembered it, note for note. It hadn't been perverted into something *wrong*, like the Nazi Wozzeck or Bach's groping cherubim. It was truly the music of the spheres, powerful, elegant, perfect.

A man floated in space ahead, his suit obscured and speckled by the rings of Saturn. The music of the planet, deep and heavy, worked on both of them, pulling them together into its well of gravity. Kingsbury stared into the man's eyes, obscured behind his chipped spectacles, and he recognized him immediately. He was emaciated, pale, anemic-looking, with strands of thinning grey hair which rode the solar wind. "You're Gustav

Holst." Kingsbury's voice carried beautifully, washing through the surface gasses of Saturn, leaving bright bands of color behind.

"Of course. I'm pleased. Very pleased." Holst's smile didn't suit him, as if it was forced, as if worry had set and hardened upon his face.

Kingsbury remembered seeing late photographs of Holst, before his reported death in 1934, and although he was said to have lived only sixty years, his face, even in those photographs, portrayed a man at least a decade older. "Why?" That question again.

Holst grasped Kingsbury's shoulders, anchoring them together within the rings of Saturn. His touch was gentle, affirming, but Kingsbury could feel quakes passing through Holst's body. "It's because you're immortal."

"I don't understand." *Immortality. Nothing more.* That was what Marie had said.

"It's what you consist of."

More riddles.

"Your name is Preston Kingsbury." Holst wore a light gray double-breasted wool suit with a pocket handkerchief. The proper Englishman.

"How did you know?"

"I've enjoyed your work for a long while. They've let me listen to it on occasion. I particularly enjoyed *Galway, 1936.* Your *Suite for the Dark Side* had its merits as well, although I must admit that I prefer the more traditional pieces.

*Galway* was a musical reflection upon a walking tour of Ireland, composed when Kingsbury was only twenty-three years old. It was indeed traditional, reflecting elements of the Irish countryside, borrowed, perhaps, from the music of Debussy and Copland and perhaps even Gustav Holst himself. The *Suite* was written much later, after the death of Kingsbury's second wife, scored for an orchestra of jackhammers, leaf blowers, cymbals, and four harpsichords. It was a poor imitation of the music of John Cage, and it reflected Kingsbury's depression at the time of composition, as well as his addiction to painkillers. He considered the piece a failure, a representation of the darkest period in his life. "I'm honored."

"You've just arrived?"

"I don't know where we are. I don't know anything." Kingsbury paused. "I'm sorry. You're one of the greatest composers who ever lived, and I'm speaking with you. It doesn't make sense. It can't be happening."

"I'm not one of the greatest composers, Mr. Kingsbury, but I *am* immortal, just as you are. It's a blessing and a curse, I suppose."

"*I wish you would explain.* I wish somebody would. I'm sorry. I raised my voice. I . . . ."

"It's all right. Relax. Listen. I'll explain everything."

"Am I dead?"

"No. Not at all." Holst paused. "What's the last thing that you remember?"

"*Wozzeck*. I was trapped in *Wozzeck*, although the piece was different. Perverted."

"I'm afraid that Berg is losing his mind. It's very sad, and very common, I'm afraid." They floated in silence for a moment. "What happened before *Wozzeck*?"

"It was Bach, I believe. It was all extremely baroque. There were angels and men. I don't wish to talk about it."

"And before that?"

"The flight. I was taking a flight to Vienna. The plane went down, people were screaming, and then I began to hallucinate."

"How so?"

"I imagined that the man sitting next to me saved my life, that we flew above the city. My God. *We were flying*."

"It was no hallucination."

"Impossible."

"No."

"Then tell me."

"You *were* saved. You *did* fly."

"I still don't understand."

"You and I have left a body of work behind, Mr. Kingsbury. Our music will, I hope, provide entertainment, and perhaps even mental stimulation, for generations to come. Do you realize how rare that is?"

"There have been many composers . . ."

"That's true. Painters and sculptors and writers as well. Few of them are *immortal*, Mr. Kingsbury. Many are ignored, underrated. Many are simply bad at what they do. Once in a very great while, an artist will leave something behind. You and I have done this, though I feel compelled to say that your work far outshines my own."

Kingsbury could hear an awakened passion in Holst's voice, in his proper English accent, a passion which had been reflected in his *Mars* suite. "Are you saying that we're immortal because our work is?"

"Perhaps. In part. Of course, the Quiet Ones have a great deal to do with it as well."

"You've lost me again."

"I don't know much about them. Henry Purcell told me that the Quiet Ones were monks who had successfully communicated with God through Gregorian chant in the fourteenth century. God granted them immortality, and the power to bestow this immortality upon others, under the condition that they would spread the Black Death. These monks would bring outsiders into their monasteries, infect them with the plague, then release them so that they might infect others. Their monasteries were filthy, crawling with rats. They became known as the Black Monks or the Quiet Ones because it was said that their chants were supernatural in nature, that their words could be heard through the mind as well as the ears."

"Why would God instruct monks to kill people? That's ridiculous."

"Henry said that the Black Death made way for the Renaissance, that the people who didn't matter, those who would never leave something behind, were cleansed from the face of the Earth. Developments in technology, architecture, and music are rooted in the Black Death. It's not a notion that I feel comfortable with, to be honest, and it isn't one that I'm prepared to accept."

"Are you saying that this place is a monastery?" Kingsbury thought about the cathedral, the cherubim, and it made sense in an odd sort of way.

"I don't know exactly where we are. Reality is shaped through our music, and the Quiet Ones *do* exist here, listening, observing, *feeding* us. They bring renowned composers here and grant us eternal life in exchange for our services."

Kingsbury felt weak and ill. "*What* services?"

"We're expected to compose for them. They hope that we will eventually produce a work which is so wondrous and perfect that it will act as a vehicle of communication with God, just as the chant did in the fourteenth century."

"If they can communicate through chant . . ."

"It only happened once, Mr. Kingsbury. They've been trying to duplicate the episode for centuries. J. S. Bach came close with his Mass in B minor, but even then—"

"Bach was *alive* when he wrote that, I mean, he wasn't *immortal*. As I recall, the piece was assembled a couple of years before his death in seventeen fifty."

"His *reported* death. Besides, who do you think commissioned his religious works in the first place?"

"You don't mean to say that these Black Monks—"

"I don't know. The story is apocryphal at best. Henry told me that the Quiet Ones forced Bach to perform his Mass continuously for a full year before they gave up and allowed him to compose something new."

Kingsbury closed his eyes and felt the coldness of space embrace him. "What about you, Holst? Do you compose for the Quiet Ones?"

"I *must*, Mr. Kingsbury. It's part of what I am. Composing keeps me sane. One might say that I've kept my head while others about me have lost theirs. Besides, if I don't compose, the Quiet Ones will let me weaken. They'll leave me at death's door for an eternity, and I see no reason to experience that."

Kingsbury opened his eyes and steadied Holst's hold on him as they floated together. "You're losing me again."

"The Quiet Ones keep us strong by infusing us with spiritual energy, by sharing their blood with us."

"You're talking about *vampirism*."

"I suppose. Yes. I'm afraid so."

"I won't do it. I won't compose. It's *wrong*. I'll refuse."

"As I've said, if you refuse, the Quiet Ones will neglect you, leave you to die. But you'll never die, you'll merely become weaker, because the work you leave behind, your own *immortality*, will keep you alive. As long as people remember you, perform your music, you can never die." Holst paused. "Of course, I don't believe any of this, necessarily. I'm agnostic, after all."

"How do we get away?"

"Remember happier times. That's all you *can* do."

Kingsbury thought about his walking trip through Ireland in 1936, about the little cottage he had stayed at, and then he found himself there.

## V. CADENCE THEME: GALWAY, 1936

Leprechauns were beating his body with little shillelaghs. The cottage was just as it had been during Kingsbury's stay in 1936. Small, cozy, decorated with knickknacks and antique clocks. It had belonged to his uncle, who had been gracious enough to let him room there for a month while he was in London on business. His uncle's interests would compel him to sell the cottage and move to London a year later, where he would lose his life during a German aerial bombing in 1940. Of course, Kingsbury hadn't seen any leprechauns during his trip to Ireland, but he *did* imagine them while composing *Galway*, and perhaps that was why they appeared then, serving as a reminder that reality in this place was being shaped by the Quiet Ones, as well as by his own music.

The body was not truly his own, but rather a replica, a *doppelgänger*, which lay in bed on bloodstained sheets. Kingsbury watched from several yards away, near the door of the cottage, while the leprechauns continued their work, oblivious to his presence. He considered the beating to be a personal affront (the thing did *look* like him, after all), and the leprechauns looked puny enough to overcome without difficulty, so he searched for a weapon. His uncle had built a collection of antique agricultural implements, many of which hung from the walls. He had always thought that this collection was an odd one, but his uncle had claimed that it was a way to exhibit pride in their lineage, as the family was descended from farmers, and serfs before that. He removed an old planter's hoe from the wall and approached the leprechauns.

The little creatures continued their administrations until Kingsbury thunked one of them on the back, at which point they turned on him in unison and began to hiss. All nine of them wore short black capes and little pointy shoes, and they looked ancient, with deep wrinkles, long white beards, and tufts of hair which curled from their ears. As they pulled back their lips in a purely animalistic manner, Kingsbury could tell that they had filed their teeth.

He backed up, and then the leprechauns turned once again, tucked their shillelaghs under their arms, and lifted the body into the air. It *was* a precise replica of the composer, right down to its navy blue three-piece suit. Kingsbury looked at its face, *his* face, and for the first time, he noticed how much he resembled Gustav Holst. He was thin, frail, old beyond his years. Blood trickled from his double's mouth, and purple welts flowered on its forehead.

The leprechauns moved the body across the room, opened the door, and disappeared into the darkness beyond. They took the counterfeit Kingsbury with them, and the original was left alone in the cottage, confused, clutching the hoe. Bruises rapidly colored his arms, and then he felt a drop of warm blood slide down his cheek. This was more than just another trip through the weird realities of the Quiet Ones, it was a threat, a way of telling Kingsbury to cooperate or they would bash his brains in. He dropped the hoe, walked toward the open door, then stopped and stared through the darkness on the other side. There were no landmarks of any kind, no planets as in Holst's universe, only black nothingness. He looked behind him and saw that his shoes had left bloody footprints on the floor, felt his forehead and found that the warm trickle had become a steady stream, and he knew that he had no choice but to go after the leprechauns and stop them, or to somehow sever the bond between his double and himself. He realized that the Quiet Ones were stringing him along, playing a morbid game, but until he figured out exactly what he was dealing with, he knew that he had no choice but to play along despite the consequences.

So Kingsbury turned his head, took a deep breath, and stepped through the doorway into the darkness beyond.

## VI. DEVELOPMENT: REQUIEM AETERNAM

The Black Death might have still lingered behind the monastery walls. Kingsbury swam through the void as Latin hymns shaped the space around him, through pockets of density and freedom, toward the shining building beyond. It was impossible to tell how long it had been since he had left *Galway*, or how far the chant had led him, but it *was* pulling him in, offering him a destination, and for that he was grateful. Kingsbury might have been caught within a soundless void for an eternity, and he could think of no worse fate than to be deprived of music and learning and creation forever.

If Holst had been correct about the Quiet Ones, this had to be their monastery, because even from a distance Kingsbury could see the rats. The walls moved with them, and as the monastery seemed to shift in and out of reality, black as the void one moment, glowing with unholy light the next, the rats changed as well, becoming skeletal, then plump. Kingsbury touched down on a pad of human skulls before the arched monastery entrance and the chant grew louder, nearly deafening:

*"Requiem aeternam dona eis Domine: et lux perpetua luceat eis . . ."*

He had learned Latin as a schoolboy, and he recognized the Gregorian chant as well. *Rest eternal be granted to them, O Lord: and let eternal light shine upon them . . .* The skulls snapped beneath his feet in the darkness, then reassembled in the light. As the holy radiance bathed him, healing his wounds, he learned that his wristwatch was running backwards. Kingsbury might have gone back, reentered the void, resisted the tide which had brought him there, but what if he could never find *Galway* again? What if he met only an eternity of nothingness? He decided to move on, to pass under the archway as the rats lived and died within the shifting realities. The chanting continued, growing still louder:

*"In memoria aeterna erit iustus . . ."*

*The just man shall be remembered eternally . . .*

Rats flowed above his head, across the walls.

*". . . ab auditione mala . . ."*

*. . . ill tidings . . .*

He covered his ears, closed his eyes.

*". . . non timebit . . ."*

*. . . he shall not fear . . .*

Kingsbury found himself on a narrow stone bridge which spanned a cemetery to his left and a herb garden to his right. The chanting grew quieter once he had entered the monastery walls, and his reality solidified into a building which, for the most part, might have existed at the time of the Black Death. It was clearly a place of worship. Religious figures in wood and stone had been placed within the cemetery, offering prayers for the dead, guarding them, it seemed, should they live again. Passageways riddled the walls and the high ceiling was supported by a network of great, glowing arches. The herb garden was green, well tended, and the juxtaposition between the life found in that garden on one side of the bridge, and the cemetery on the other, represented the Black Monks as well. They had been, after all, givers of death as well as life.

Kingsbury moved on. He entered a long tunnel which emerged upon the cloister, an enormous covered garden surrounded by an enclosed walkway. A rat scurried past, then disappeared through one of the larger archways to his left. In the center of the garden, a man in black robes sat with his back against a stone well. There was something familiar about him, even from a distance, and when Kingsbury approached and saw the man's face, he dropped to his knees. It was his double, the *thing* that the leprechauns had carried off, sitting, smiling, drinking from a wooden bowl filled with what Kingsbury imagined to be blood. The thing wiped its teeth with its index finger then pointed toward the archway through which the rat had gone. Kingsbury stood, feeling weak, defeated, and returned to the walkway.

The arch began to glow, pulsing with Gregorian chant, and Kingsbury took a step toward it, then looked away. His wounds had healed completely, leaving only bits of scab in his hair, and he could think of no reason to proceed. His double was safe, after all, sitting, relaxing, *drinking*. Perhaps it was fear which held him back. The beating of his heart kept time with the pulse of that unholy light. He turned and went back the way he had come. It did him no good.

The tunnel had changed. It turned sharply, unpredictably, rising one moment, declining sharply the next. Black moss coated the walls, and Kingsbury's way was lighted only by an eerie light which seemed to follow him, drawing him forward. The chanting grew louder once again, nearly as loud as when he had passed under the first archway, and then he emerged within a chapel. Several monks began to approach the moment he entered. They chanted as they walked, and Kingsbury was stunned by the beauty and precision of their music. He felt little hands moving around his legs, up his back, and he screamed as he realized that the leprechauns were taking hold of him.

Kingsbury kicked at them, tried to shake them away as they rode his legs, then he punched one in the face, straight on, and the little bastard went flying. They made little guttural sounds as the leprechaun hit the floor, and then they began to bite him, to chew through his clothing. He screamed again, then turned and backed into a stone pillar, slamming a leprechaun which hung from his shoulders. It hit the floor as well, and just as Kingsbury was beginning to enjoy himself, the leprechauns scattered as the Black Monks drew near.

Kingsbury ran through the nearest archway, and he found himself moving through utter darkness, feeling the crumbling walls, descending so rapidly that he could barely keep his balance. He stopped to catch his breath, then noticed that he heard no chanting, only a dead silence, and he thought about how weak he felt, and whether or not the Quiet Ones would share their blood with him in order to make him strong again. Kingsbury tried to lean against the wall for support, and it seemed that his hand went *through* the wall, into something very cold, and very wet.

## VII. RETRANSITION: WITH THE DEAD IN A DEAD LANGUAGE

Bodies lined the walls, resting within long rectangular hollows. Kingsbury could see some of their faces under the weak flame of his cigarette lighter. They looked as if they were freshly dead, wearing the tattered peasant clothing of the Middle Ages. Their skin was a deep purple color, and Kingsbury knew that the condition represented the final symptom of the Black Death. If these were plague victims, preserved for centuries by the Quiet Ones, then he had surely been exposed to the disease. He frantically scratched his fingers along the wall, trying to scrape away the soft tissue which had lodged under his fingernails when he had touched the plague victim's face in the darkness. Kingsbury looked at the cigarette lighter in his hands, and realized only then that he didn't smoke, that he never carried a lighter, and that he had found it in his pocket only when he needed it. The Quiet Ones, it seemed, had anticipated his needs, and even then, they were still playing games with him. It was a good lighter, stylish, one he might have bought if he had ever needed one. They had even engraved his initials on it.

He continued his descent through the winding catacombs, through tunnels and rooms lined with bodies, and then he stopped for a moment and listened when he began to hear music once again. It wasn't Gregorian chant this time, but something much more recent in composition. Kingsbury recognized the piece immediately. It was the *Cum Mortuis in Lingua Mortua* from Maurice Ravel's instrumental reworking of Moussorgsky's *Pictures at an Exhibition*. As he continued his descent, the music grew louder, mixing with odd strains of Gregorian Chant and baroque opera, and he found himself deep under the monastery, standing before a great, glowing gate.

The light warmed him, renewed his strength, and as he watched, the age spots on his hands began to fade.

## VIII. RECAPITULATION: THE GREAT GATE OF KIEV

Johann Sebastian Bach was there, as well as Handel, Beethoven, and of course the young Modest Moussorgsky, nursing a bottle of something brown and alcoholic. The gate had drawn Kingsbury through, enticing him with utterly beautiful, nearly perfect music. He identified the composers through their compositions. They oozed with them, surrounded themselves with their own music, and Kingsbury was able to filter out the mingling sounds, to identify the composers one by one. The man who had sat next to him on the flight to Vienna stood in the beautiful, glowing chamber as well, enveloped by his *Die Walküre*, and Kingsbury realized only then that he was Richard Wagner.

The music floated through the chamber, lost within the impossibly high ceiling, and drops of light rained down from above, concentrating on a bare spot on the golden floor. Kingsbury was drawn to it, and as he stood within the radiance, feeding from it, letting the drops touch his tongue, he felt himself growing younger. The entire chamber glowed with light then, and he could see plague victims resting within the walls, the pillars, the floor, thousands upon thousands of them rising to the unfathomable height of that brilliant, shining ceiling.

Kingsbury was in ecstasy. Every muscle in his body tingled. He felt strong, young again, and although he saw the Quiet Ones approaching in their black robes, felt their hands upon his body, he would not move. They shared their blood with him, punctured his wrists and throat, and the wounds only strengthened him further, increasing his bliss even more. Kingsbury's entire body began to make music, and as the Quiet Ones backed off, his wounds healed over and he became whole once again. His own compositions issued from his fingers and toes, more beautifully arranged and performed than he thought possible, mingling with those of the greatest composers who ever lived.

He understood everything then. He pictured the Quiet Ones, the Black Monks, collecting plague victims during the fourteenth century. Holst had been mistaken, or he had deliberately lied to Kingsbury so that the composer might find the truth for himself. The Quiet Ones had never exposed anyone to the Black Death, they had merely collected the bodies, preserving them with their chants so that one day they might be revived with the most perfect music the world would ever know. Their communication with God had allowed them to grant immortality only to those who still lived, and even then, very rarely, and only to those who had already earned immortality through their own works.

Kingsbury embraced the music around him, within himself, and through tears of utter rapture, he watched as the dead began to stir.

# THE SCREENING ROOM

# CRIMES OF FASHION

*Shira Daemon*

"It's all about connections," Julie says. Her short bob fans out around her ears as she turns the steering wheel hard, to counteract the sudden up-swelling of the driveway. "Do the parties. Do the cruises. Cruise the men. Do the show." The red Geo Metro squeals to a halt, not quite running over the Filipino valet.

I let the boy open the door for me, knowing he already considers me a wimp or a faggot for letting my date do the driving, but Julie doesn't wait. Tossing away her keys, her miniskirt bouncing against tanned thighs, she rushes up the steps and into Juan's hacienda. More cautious about my own entrance, I am still near the convertible when the boy reaches down, re-trieving the keys from the gravel. His teeth glint rotten in the glow of the Chinese lanterns, and his poor dental work doesn't improve my mood. I follow Julie through the doorway.

Luckily, the booze is good. People who seem airbrushed drink plastic champagne and listen to sanitized jazz. It's the sort of night where I'm trapped in cocktail Hell, and the first person who spots me is Gladys. She's our local creeping magnolia. I can always scent her by the heavy perfume she douches with, it helps mask the ketosis from her latest diet.

"What's new?" Gladys warbles. She brushes nearer the pastel walls, blearily maneuvering me until I must either submit to her kiss or fall over the chrome-and-silk Japanese couch. Her lips leave dank prints on my cheek. I refrain from scrubbing my face, and instead suggest remembered intimacies by smoothing a permed lock from her brow. Gladys isn't much of a power at Fox, but every scrabbled inch helps.

"Nah, what could be new?" I murmur. "The show's overloaded with serial killers, and we've already done car chases to death. I'm looking to branch out. Anything up at Fox?"

She ignores my fishing. "Guess they've updated children's television since pizza-eating terrapins battled wrongdoers?"

I'm certain that Gladys hasn't been up before noon on Saturday since Nixon was impeached, but I chuckle.

"Turtles are passé, but I can sell you some live slime monsters, and a hot tuber who's running for office."

Gladys digs her fingers into my arm until flakes of skin lightly tan her red polish. I can't decide if this is her way of marking me for the evening, or if she has forgotten her own aerobicized strength.

"How's Julie's try at Disney?" she asks.

Ah, I think, the real reason for our little conversation.

"Naah," I say, lowering my voice. "Disney's not real interested in another spunky-girl-without-folks story, and they're not going to hire ole Jules on the basis of her animating skills." I can see I'm losing Gladys's interest. She only wants to know if Julie's turning up a winner.

"Besides," I add facetiously, "their animated morphing's coming along so fast that I think they're going to turn Mickey's ears into Cher's ass and sign a porno deal with it."

This gets a snicker, but Gladys's eyes are already wandering. Her nails leave half-moon scars as they retract from my bicep. I want to pump her for some dope on Spielberg, on pilots, on anything that'll get me out of the kiddie pool, but Danny-boy—the man with the candy—makes contact, and she and her bleary eyes leave me to my own devices. Which are rather negligible these days. I swipe a lace doily from the table and use it to scrub her lipstick off my face.

Picking a glass of plastic champagne up from the bar, I watch the shadowplay of silicone. Actresses court Actors. Actors leap at Agents. And Producers walk tall. I lurk near the potted plants, searching for a step up the ladder. Something in leather finds me in my corner.

"Come here often?" she asks.

"Only when somebody strokes me."

Surprisingly, she laughs. It's a nasal laugh, unusually high in such a large woman. The oriental cast to her features seems at odds with the hefty frame inhabiting the jumpsuit. Her blunt cut swings to an unwieldy length, well below her shoulderblades. I wonder how she dares to buck the current fashion forecast. There is something indefinably sexy about her, or maybe I just like the touch of incongruity she adds to an otherwise homogenized grouping.

"Rockumentaries?" I ask, trying to guess where the combination of insouciance and money comes from.

"No. Independent," she says. Her hair makes a satisfied sound as she tosses it around on her shoulders. The curve of her brow seems too delicate to bear the burden of manipulating such a muscular body, and her aroma is musky, if somewhat overripe. Her almond eyes are just below my nose, on a level where I could stare deeply into them, if I could pierce the arena behind her shades.

"I'm looking for other Independents," she says. "I have a private project I'm working on." She fingers the chest hair that juts out over the V-neck of my shirt. "I'm especially looking for a furry man who is seeking adventure."

This sounds like the beginning of a personal, but before I can reply Julie rushes over and drags me outside. In her white oxford-cloth shirt and loose miniskirt Julie looks like a Catholic girl on a bender. Hell, I got her the shirt last Christmas.

"What did you tell Gladys?" Julie asks. The hissing of the pool filters doesn't quite cover the sound of her annoyance. Julie isn't too swift, but even she must recognize my pitiful prevarications for the bad acting they are. I suspect my hopes of scoring even grudging sex with her are gone for the evening, and she'll probably take her mother with her when she sails tomorrow. Unless her soon-to-be-ex-husband catches up with her tonight and beats the cruise tickets out of her.

Spotting a Bakshi exec, she clutches her purse and flits off. Drawing kittens with swords has started wearing on her, and she'd rather ink nude fairies and gelled erections than stay in the kiddie ghetto. I wait for the executive to brush her off, and feel a momentary pulse of pleasure when she is humiliated.

Though she tries hard, Julie never has much heft. Even in bed she seems ethereal, always floating off the subject or lying, passively uninterested beneath my irresolute fumblings. Our affair didn't dissolve her marriage, it was just a symptom of its lack of cohesion. All her relationships seem to drift away; her husband is simply leaving a rockier wake.

I search for my leather Independent, but she's checking out a surfer dude in nylon and earthtones. He's got some interesting sideburns, but the Independent looks like she's finding his chest a disappointment. Still, I don't want to appear too eager, so I just remind her of my presence by brushing against her on my way to the pool. Her hand is colder than my drink, and I wonder if she's on something.

The outside speakers blare the house brand of pablum rock and I am trapped poolside by an actress dumb enough to think I'm worth shmoozing. She sways along with the artificial beat of a drum machine, but leaves when we get splashed by a balding agent. He is overly involved with the models and their trendy bikinis. While the bottoms of their suits are just thongs, the tops look like paired Victorian birdcages. A plastic Day-glo bubble tips each cage, covering the girl's nipples.

The models must realize that the suits were never designed for water, since the bubbles pop off when wet, but they splash and scream in a mechanical interpretation of coy modesty.

The agent dives. I watch as he resurfaces with canary yellow plastic trapped between his teeth. The plastic bubble is about the size of a cherry tomato, and the translucent yellow coats his lips with a bilious gloss. He splashes around, looking for a free nipple to stick the bubble on. Only the most naive of the swimmers allows him near.

She's so young I wonder whose little sister she is, or if she hitchhiked in from Minnesota. Eventually even she swats the agent away, staring sadly through her dampened coiffure at the shallow end of the pool, where all the pretty men are surreptitiously comparing their scars. There are fewer of them this year, and I worry about the longevity of sterile love, and how high the condom market can rise.

My Lady in Leather is there by the shallows, draped over an upholstered lawn chair. I suspect she has been checking out the glee club. Most producers won't hire them, for all the sadly obvious reasons. She readjusts her glasses. Her hand seems surprisingly white, a photonegative blot positioned against the shadowed sepia of her brow. Does she wink at me? It's hard to tell.

I try to join her, but Gladys lurches over and latches onto me, swaying. Her heels scrape the flagstones in a random pattern sure to completely destroy her expensive Italian shoes. Her presence cues the agent, and he stops chasing the pool bunnies.

"So what did you think of Sabrina?" shouts the agent. He squeezes a pink bubble in what I suppose is meant to be a suggestive manner, including me in his conspiratorial grin. "Ain't she a little honey? I think she'd be perfect as Redford's granddaughter."

I recall that the agent's name is Richard something or other. If Dick thinks I am going to help him convince Gladys that his latest acquisition is worth promoting, he's wrong. Gladys flicks ice cubes at him, and I silently applaud her when he paddles away. Then she leans against me until, in self-defense, I rub her back.

She's jittering so hard I don't think her synapses can fire a complete sentence. Even if she promised me an appointment with somebody useful, I doubt she'd remember it in the morning. I'm incredibly grateful when the Independent extricates me. Gladys's perfume lingers annoyingly on my hands as I match the odd beauty's purposeful stride. She finds us a quiet corner.

"What do you produce?" I ask. The Independent doesn't immediately answer, instead handing me some lukewarm Mexican beer from the pool bar, then pushing me into a lawn chair. Blunt nails taste the back of my neck, and her musk invades my senses, overpowering any civilized perfumes.

The scratching makes me shiver, and her hair falls over my shoulder. I reach up to remove a tangle from my face, receiving a shock of static as I do. The strand of hair crackles. She stares at it from behind dark glasses, as though searching for a portent in its brief and startling electric jump.

She considers my question in the light of her omens, finally answering. "Oh, I create pieces on sex, pieces on power. I get bored doing the same thing all the time. It's like wearing a garment that's worn out."

"Your leather fits you nicely," I say, a slight leer implied in my tone. I am dizzy with her aroma, and pleased that she has already mentioned sex.

"Ah, I always prefer wearing things that were once alive." She laughs. "I'm planning on going someplace cold just so I can wear fur again." She plucks a hair from my chest and puts it in her mouth. It is blatant grooming, stirring my taste for the primitive while revolting my stomach. I put down the beer.

"I like cold," I say.

Julie and Gladys run into each other, stop, begin a conversational circling doomed to lead nowhere.

"So, which one is yours?" the Independent queries. She motions to the women, then strokes icy fingers over the half-moon cuts Gladys has left on my arm.

I raise an eyebrow, an effect I perfected after watching too much sixties television. "I own neither," I say, trying to match her tone.

"Ah, but do they possess you?"

Now it's my turn to laugh, but to my overly trained ear it sounds brittle. I would reloop it if I could. Life, unfortunately, is not waiting for my artificiality to catch up with it. I am still near my physical peak, but I think that unless I catch this look on celluloid soon, I will be just another leading man who never made it to screen. Old models don't gain character, we just sag.

The Independent is waiting for an answer about possession, and I suppose devotion. I wonder if she is auditioning the echo of my laugh, her head cocked alertly to the side. One hand rests, limply chill, upon my neck. Julie leaves the pool area, apparently continuing her fruitless search for a material piece. Gladys and her perfume lurch by, filling me with a fleeting desire to gag.

"Why no," I finally say. "I guess I'm an Independent myself." This seems a code word to her. I don't understand the correlation, but she teasingly rubs the back of my neck. The short hairs behind my ears prickle, and I want to pierce this woman more surely than I want a decent part on next season's dramedy, or a hot new action flick come fall.

She kisses me. Her lips are hot and dry. My mind fills with her alien musk. When she purposefully strides away from the pool, I follow the gleam of her hair.

Somehow, I find myself locked in a chilly embrace in the spare bedroom, the one that holds the guest wraps and is free of candyheads. I don't recall undressing, but I am wearing nothing except my socks. Isn't this the way nightmares happen? Scenes shift and logic never completely bridges the gap. Still, the cedar-chest tang of the fur I fall into clears my head. It is a fresher, more subtle aroma than Gladys's eternal florals, or my Independent's alluring scent. How odd, I think, to be in Southern California and ready to fuck atop someone's dead chinchilla.

The Independent doesn't allow me to sit up. "Such nice fur," she says as her cold hands stroke my chest.

I still don't know her name, but she must adore hairy chests to risk sex in such surroundings. Goosebumps rise on my flesh. She runs a cool finger over the markings and then retrieves a tube from a pocket of her jumpsuit, squeezing red fluid from the tube onto her palm. I wonder if it's a new plague killer? A virulent spermicide? She coats my gonads with the crimson jelly.

A flush rises from my loins and hot flashes surge through my body. Yet my hands lie passive at my sides. I stare as she unzips her jumpsuit. The skin on her torso is surprisingly fair. There is a clean line of demarcation between pale and almond under her neck. Perhaps they are now making a Caucasian skin graft? Or an Asian color creme? In this business the possibilities are frightening. The portion of my mind not humming with sexual hunger is amazed by her ragged contrasts. With no preamble, she lowers herself onto me. The fluid makes her seem internally heated, although her ankles are as cold as her wrists. Her icy feet curl underneath my thighs.

I smell Gladys outside the window. It is impossible to hear what she's saying, the music from poolside is too loud, but even the hydrangea bushes can't hide that woman's proximity. I scent her clearly and feel the perverse desire to cry out that something is wrong, but the first roll of my lover's hips anesthetizes fear.

The Independent is so heavy on me. So very present. It is ecstasy just to know that someone wants me so fully, if only for the moment. I try to free my hands, try to touch her flesh, but she will accept our bond only at the prescribed point.

We roll. I am a demon leashed, my body trapped beneath hers. Her hair nibbles the soles of my feet. Tiny slashes of agony and pleasure hit me. Moisture wells like crimson kisses between my toes. Damp with scarlet jelly, her hands still clamp my wrists. Wondering at her agility, I look up. Her pale torso is framed before me, but I can't see her face, only her torso and then the ceiling. When she bucks, I close my eyes.

There is a sensual tasting, silken and warm, slipping along my chest and up toward my head. Her torso thrashes as my neck is caressed, enfolded. The strands of her hair encase my throat in fire, a living warmth I cannot feel from any part of her body, although it echoes the heat of the fluid on her hands, and on my groin. Inflamed by our affinity, I am stunned by the force of her need.

As her hair pulls taut around my throat, my brain almost re-engages. Yet I am too thrilled by our physical bond to care that her neck and head want me for their own. Lashing out under her, entirely wild, I feel the cords around my throat tighten, each strand a tiny whip of sensation. My tension has almost reached its climax.

The door opens. My rhythm is broken, yet I can't disconnect from what we've started, even though it's Julie who stumbles into the room. Someone has shattered her glasses, and she holds them clenched in her small, warm fist. I ignore the agony in her blue eyes as I cry out in spasm, desperate for sexual release, but Julie rushes over and grabs the Independent from behind.

A terrible tug of war ensues. I am jerked, forward and back, in motion with their catfight. Each time Julie yanks on the Independent's shoulders my entwined neck lashes upright, but Julie is not strong enough to pull her off. Then Julie changes tactics. The Independent's head looms nearer, the almond face stoic behind closed shades. Her head seems almost to hinge, dangling loosely on her neck, dropping away from her torso. The scent of musk becomes overpowering, completely masking the stench of my sweat. There is a sound like a rubber mat being ripped from a tub, and droplets of milky white, pink sheening their surface, splatter in a fine spray over my chest. Suddenly, the tendrils enclosing my throat uncurl, and my over-excited body chooses that moment to gush its release.

I am left, gasping and spent, on the bed. My oddly patchwork lover rises to face Julie. Tufts of black hair lash like cattails across the Independent's neck, and a thin trickle of strangely dilute blood dribbles down her back. The liquid fascinates me, as do the spongy suction cups that peer out from beneath the bottom of her neck, half hidden by the windshield-wiper action of her enraged hair. The cold body moves stiffly, and Julie pounds it with her fists. The Independent's dark hair smites Julie across the face. She falls backwards, hitting the plaster walls hard enough to raise powder. White dust ghosts around her.

I rise to save her, but I am slow, so agonizingly slow, as though I am fighting some sick desire to see what will happen, how the movie will end. It seems like some marvelous special effect and in my confused state I am having trouble taking it seriously. I can't seem to connect to the reality of the situation, and I keep waiting for the cut. As I move forward, each step taken as though MTV has pixilated my body, blunt, dark hair wraps itself around Julie's neck.

Then the cut comes and all I can do is whimper, "No, it's not fair," as Julie is garroted by the black cords of my lover's hair. Julie's head, blue eyes open and pleading, sails by me, landing on the bed. The white carpet and walls of the spare bedroom incarnadine into bloody Rorschach blots.

Adrenalin finally kicks in and I rush forward, cursing. Julie's blood showers the room. I now recognize the Independent for the monster she is. She turns slowly, wobbling between Julie's torso and me. Her head seems barely attached to her body. She wavers for a moment, a hungry gourmand unsure of which snack to pluck. The suckers on the underside of her neck are close together, octopoidal parasites ready to attach themselves to a new host. The proximity of Julie's blood seems to excite her in a way that our lovemaking didn't, and I can imagine the suckers closing off Julie's arteries, keeping her juices flowing and animate for a long time.

It is her hesitation which saves me. Even as she decides that I am the chosen victim, a warmer host than the freshly prepared one bleeding at her side, I wrap my hands around her throat. My thumbs slide along the rubbery slickness of her skin. Sickly fluid leaks onto my hands. I wonder if this thin trickle is all that's left of the gallons that once warmed a living body. As I strain, rocking the neck back, the almond skin continues its separation from the torso. Damp popping sounds accompany my steady pressure. Her hair whips me, raising welts across my hirsute chest.

The suckers open like fleshy flowers. In our struggle my hand slips between the head and body. A sucker attaches itself to my wrist. Its hungry greed raises fevered blisters. I jerk my arm out and wrestle desperately. With a final damp yank the head and neck come away, one discrete unit in my hands.

I throw the head across the room. The pale, muscular torso collapses into a bloody heap on the floor, sprawling over Julie's limp body. They lie together like discarded toys, dolls that have been played with too hard and then forgotten by their owners. I want to comfort Julie, hold her cooling hand, close her staring eyes, but the head rolls around in circles on a corner of the damaged carpet.

There is a roar and crash down the hallway. It sounds like Julie's husband on a rampage, and I wonder if that's why she came to me. Was she seeking sanctuary? I had assumed that Gladys's spiteful machinations were behind her entrance. Now it is too late to know.

I lock the door from the inside, tripping over Julie's handbag. Finding my pants, I grab the bag and climb out the window, into the bushes. What will I tell the police? There is blood on my feet. Some of it is mine. My socks are shredded. Fine scratches crosshatch my soles.

I am still dizzy with musk and shock, sticky with obscene juices. I smell the clean odor of chlorination. My head is too muzzy, the pool is too close. I know I must leave, run, but I cannot endure another moment coated in gore. I hope that a baptism in artificial waters will save me. I lope over to the pool, holding the jeans in front of my painted genitalia. When I drop my pants and dive into the water not even the pretty boys comment on my appearance.

I imagine that if the head were to come out and roll around everyone would consider it a special effect. A beach ball designed for a cocktail scene directed by Alfred Hitchcock. I no longer want to play ball and I dive underwater again and again, trying frantically to wash the blood from my scalp, drowning the memory of Julie's final moment in a frenzy of splashing.

Someone shrieks and I surface for air, wondering if they've already violated the sanctuary of a locked room. There's an unwritten rule that you don't force open a door, never know whom you might catch engaged in something garish.

There is a chilled laugh, and someone makes a frosty comment about California rats, but I catch sight of dark hair bruising the hydrangeas. The head is rolling through the bushes. As I open my mouth to scream, my groin sears and I feel my nuts being raked by probing teeth. I think that the head is achieving retribution. Even though it is rolling through the bushes I imagine that the monster is capable of destroying me, bite by bite, starting with my loins.

I backpedal and viciously beat the water. Dick surfaces, spluttering for his lawyer and clutching a broken nose. He has mistaken the vivid scarlet on my balls for one of the plastic bubbles.

A hired bouncer, somebody's personal trainer by day, drags me out of the pool. Hysteria has set in and I drop to the cement, screaming about almond heads and thrashing hair.

"Suckers, it's got suckers," I moan. He throws my pants at me and waits for me to shut up and put them on.

"I always knew about him, didn't you?" says a snide voice.

Dick continues calling for his lawyer while the young model fusses over him, visibly relieved that he is harmlessly emasculated with a bloody nose. The bouncer hangs Julie's purse over my neck. In my distraught condition I look kinky enough to wear one. He suggests, not terribly gently, that I take myself home. My painted groin looks like somebody's leftovers. I have lost sight of the monster.

Gladys lurches by. Even her disjointed presence seems like a lifeline, her cloying perfume a familiar nausea. I clutch her leg, babbling for help. The expensive leather on her shoes grazes my face. Somehow her lack of compassion, her utter lack of connection with my misery is so frightening that it shocks me into sanity. I manage to climb into my pants, and the trainer escorts me to the driveway.

When no one is looking he hands me his card and says meaningfully, "We should talk. I've got some friends who might be into having a party real soon. If you can control yourself."

I try one last time to warn him, going on about the danger, and the suckers, and the head, but he just laughs and says some head will have to wait.

The valet pulls up in Julie's convertible. His teeth seem as dark as the black Cadillac that sits, huge and rutting, on a lush patch of lawn. The Caddy is so familiar that I think it must belong to Julie's husband. Will the police blame him, at least long enough for me to get away? As I fumble in Julie's purse for the car keys, forgetting that the valet has them, I come across her cruise tickets. They are bracketed by wads of cash. There is enough here to make my escape. Enough for me to run away, over the sea.

Even though my body is bedecked with painful stains I'm as jubilant as Scrooge at Christmas. I vow that I will find some island where I can devote my life to serving people. As a bartender I will talk to customers, listen to them. Understand how to tell lovers from monsters, pearls from slime.

My legs are shaking, and the convertible gets off to a jerky start, spitting and backfiring when I release the clutch. Its gassy flatulence carries the taint of singed hair. My elation is shortlived, and I knock over the carphone in my haste to look behind me, not trusting a mirror to reflect my fears. There is nothing to be seen in the firefly flicker of the lanterns. No dark bruise swings after me down the drive.

The carphone has an annoying buzz; it seems louder than the breeze pouring over the car's open top. I stop the noise by recradling the receiver, but in the sudden quiet I can hear the engine's arrhythmic banging. It sounds like a matinee audience's lackadaisical applause. The steering wheel jerks under my hands as though pulled by some magnetic attraction toward a shifting north.

The car bucks, and it is almost a relief to see black tendrils reach up and lasso the hood ornament. At least they are not curling over the seat behind me. At least I have not already gone mad. There is a dropped-rubber sound, and the head bounces off the headlights and rolls onto the hood. Musk scents the breeze. The convertible skids and then stalls.

Why is she pursuing me? Surely by now I have become too expensive a habit. There must be easier bodies to take, lying stuporous and in deshabille on stained cushions. I can think of half a dozen actors who are hairier than I. Maybe she can change vacation plans, find someone to wear in a warm climate?

I explain this to the monster, using every vocal trick I can muster. She makes no comment about my lack of commitment, offering only a whistling condemnation. The dispassionate part of my mind, the fragment that is not frantically praying I haven't flooded the engine, sees that the suckers have closed. She inches her way nearer, sliding up the waxy paint in front of me.

Perhaps when she has taken possession of my lungs she'll learn how to create my hollow laugh, berating my dead body with a mockery of its former skills. How could I have guessed that she was auditioning my throat for such a purpose? She reminds me of the monsters by the pool, laughing, pawing, and then consuming all usable bits. Even Julie only wanted to use me as a shield, a physical barrier between herself and her ex.

I shift the car into neutral. It rolls down the inclined drive until the engine sparks, and then turns over. The head slides towards me until it is mashed against the outside of the windshield. The hair is just a tendril away from climbing over the open top and joining me at the wheel. The eyes are again stoic. I suspect that only the scent of blood will excite her.

In that instant I shift and floor it, flipping the wipers on high. Wheeling hard to the right, I jounce across the manicured lawn. The head flies off the windshield, dropping like uncooked steak onto the ground. A tire catches the hair, dragging it against the wheel rim. The convertible grinds, but I feel the head work loose. I will the car to become a huge meat tenderizer, hoping we can pummel the head between radial and frame, but the car shoots forward, plowing into a palm tree.

My head hits the dash. One of my bonded crowns shatters in my mouth. Crumbling enamel powders my lips, and the taste of old bone mixes with the dripping blood from my split forehead.

The car phone buzzes and in my concussed state I imagine that the disconnected whine is a call. It must be the police, I think, in that dreamy state where nothing quite connects. The police are calling me on the car phone. They want me to confess to Julie's murder.

I promise myself I won't answer the phone, and I want to ignore it, but the training of a lifetime spent waiting for a call, for a job, for an affirmation of my self-worth is just too great. My hand throbs as it moves toward the receiver. Blisters raised earlier by fevered tentacles sear with sudden heat.

Through the pain I think I've put the receiver to my ear, and hear nothing but the delicate caress of hair sliding across a line. I flinch from the sound wondering how she phoned? Did her hair pushbutton-dial? Her almond nose? I drown deeper in a smoky haze.

Then I am driving, and the highway is smooth beneath me. The convertible is an extension of my thoughts and we race swiftly, virtually flying between cliff and shore. The head rolls after me, but I put on a burst of speed and it's left far behind.

There is a boat. I push off from the beach and jump in, knowing that I'm safe, safe at sea. I stare placidly at the swelling ocean. The head will not be able to reach me here. Ghouls can't cross water. The sun beats down, and it is unimaginable that the head can attack by day. Such horrors cannot exist in the light, just as film cannot develop outside a darkened room.

The waves rock and crackle, boiling until they are the azure of Julie's eyes. Inside the eye's pupil I see the head. It is bouncing over a surrealistic plane, Daliesque in its points and spires. Dust rises in chalky spurts, and the shining hair whips along the peaks. It's hunting me, but I've outsmarted it.

Then the head enters the water. Its powerful hair combs the waves. Tendrils ask the breakers for directions. It's all just a dream I think as it climbs into the boat with me. The boat catches fire, and I open my mouth to scream, but there is no sound in dreams. Heat laps me, and I know that I'm still in the car, and the car is on fire.

I open my eyes, forcing my forehead away from the cracked windshield, and sink back against the bucket seat. Looking to my right, I seek an exit from the flames. Then I start to shake, for on the seat next to me are broken tendrils slick with a gloss of viscous fluids. Though the almond eyes are no longer properly aligned they both stare at me with a malevolence that I cannot, in my current state of distress, match. Through my haze I marvel at her stamina.

There is milky liquid all over the seats, bubbling in the heat of the fire, yet still she reaches for me. Her monstrous need to connect seems a parody of romantic desire. Tendrils shoot out and encircle my neck. Their rough embrace is an excruciating reminder of our once-sensual lovemaking. I feebly try to win free while flames lick the windshield, and black cords seem to jerk around my soul. When I realize that the engine is about to explode all I can feel is relief.

# BELA

*Chuck Rothman*

He woke up just after sunset, the hunger too strong to allow him his sleep. After all these years, he no longer hesitated; there was only one way to put an end to the gnawing pain.

He dragged himself upright and stumbled into the bathroom. The hypodermic was in the medicine cabinet, ready for him. With a sigh, he took it and, with a lack of squeamishness that came from long practice, injected the morphine into his vein.

Bela collapsed onto the toilet and waited for the rush of the drug to carry him away.

He hated his weakness. Sometimes he thought the best thing might be to overdose and put an end to it all. They would bury him and he'd have his last bit of fame. But he didn't have the courage. Despite everything, he wanted to keep on living.

Hollywood thought him a has-been, and the only acting opportunities were in wretched little films unworthy of his talent. But they gave him his only chance to do what he loved.

Slowly, his mood lightened as the drug began to work its wonders. In a few minutes, he felt the artificial elation begin to give him strength. It was almost like the feeling he had gotten when he was on stage, or in front of a camera, when he could ply his trade as an actor. The drug gave that back to him, if only for a little while, and he was grateful.

There was a loud tapping on the bathroom window.

Bela looked up, startled. Something the size of a robin fluttered outside, bumping into the window, its flight more like an insect than a bird.

Bela laughed. A bat. How appropriate.

Giddy from the morphine, Bela rose and threw the window open. "I bid you welcome," he said in his best Count Dracula voice, his tone only slightly weakened by age. "You may be an old friend of mine." He laughed.

The bat flew in the open window, then in a flash of darkness metamorphosed into a man.

"Yiiii!" Bela said, shrinking away.

"A fine way to greet an old friend," the man said, a smile twisting his lips upward, revealing sharp, pointed teeth. He was taller than Bela, and thin, with a long nose and dark eyes. He spoke with a slight accent that reminded Bela of his boyhood in Hungary.

"Who are you?" Bela demanded.

"I think you know."

Bela stared at the man, unwilling to voice what he was thinking. Finally, very softly, he said, "Are you Dracula?"

The other man laughed. "You may call me that, if you wish. Others have."

Bela wondered if he was going mad. The morphine had never given him a hallucination like this before. "You're not real."

"Bela, my friend, you know better."

How can he know me like that? Bela wondered. He had first learned about vampires from the stories he had heard as a child, drawing on those tales to create the character of Dracula. "What do you want from me?"

"Nothing," the vampire said. "I owe you much, my friend, and I have come to repay you."

"Repay me?"

"For portraying our kind in the movies. Once, we were reviled and hunted down. But no one wants to hunt down a movie star."

Bela looked dubiously at the stranger. "And how do you plan to repay me?"

Dracula smiled, showing his fangs all the more clearly. "I think you know."

Bela bolted out of the bathroom in terror. He needed something to defend against this. A cross? But he was not a religious man, and didn't keep anything like that around the house.

"You have nothing to fear from me, my friend," Dracula said as he emerged, his gait confident, as though he knew that he'd catch his quarry sooner or later. "I am offering the greatest gift anyone can grant."

"I warn you," Bela said. "I have garlic in the kitchen."

A look of concern crossed Dracula's brow for a moment, then he shook his head. "You are not a cook, my friend. You wouldn't have such a thing."

"I won't let you kill me!" Bela said.

Dracula laughed. "Kill you? Quite the opposite. I'm here to offer you eternal life."

"What?"

"I want to help you join us. Live forever as one of us."

Bela's mouth had turned dry. "I don't believe you."

"Why should I hurt our greatest benefactor?" Dracula stepped nearer.

"Why are you offering this to me? I haven't done anything for you!" Bela felt tired and older than ever. He collapsed into a chair by his desk, knocking it and nearly toppling the stack of the letters he kept on top.

"You underestimate yourself. You created a new image for us, one that recast us in the minds of humanity." He pointed at his cape, a close duplicate of the one that hung in Bela's closet. "I did not always dress like this. You showed us the way to respectability."

Bela felt oddly flattered. Despite himself, he found himself beginning to trust his visitor. "I was a monster," he murmured.

"Yes. But a charming and elegant one. You began the process of reducing people's fear of us. As time goes on, they will no longer run. One day, we will even be thought of as romantic."

"Nonsense," Bela said.

"Granted, it will take time, but we can take the long view." Dracula took a step forward; Bela was too tired and fascinated to try to move away. "But that's unimportant. What matters is that we have decided to honor you by bringing you into our ranks."

Bela was too close to death not to be tempted by immortality. But to prey on others? To drink their blood like a leech?

"You seem troubled, my friend. Yet I know deep down that you wish to join us."

"I . . ." But he was right. Bela had lived as Dracula for a long time, ever since he had first played the part on stage. In that time, he had thought about it, and had wondered. "What's it like?" he asked abruptly. "Drinking blood?"

Dracula's laugh was long and deep. "It's not merely the drinking; it's the hunt and the capture. The power you have over a mere mortal is like nothing you have ever experienced. No, wait. Perhaps there is something. You are an actor. Do you remember the first time they applauded you?"

Bela smiled.

"So vivid, even after all these years. And your walking across the stage, all eyes on you—isn't that a feeling you want to relive?"

"Yes," Bela whispered.

"And when you first saw yourself on that silver screen, and noticed the audience around you reacting to your image—do you remember that?"

God, yes, Bela thought. Sometimes the memories were all he had to keep himself going. They were still clear, relived a million times over the years. Sometimes, when he spent months between pictures, they were the only thing that kept him going.

"I can see by your eyes that you *do* remember," Dracula said. "The hunt is like that. It's like that and more. Join us and experience that feeling anew—and for always."

Bela realized he was trembling. "I don't know . . ."

"You've been trying to recapture that feeling, haven't you? Trying in ways you dare not admit."

Bela felt afraid. He didn't have any idea what the man knew, but did not want to tell a stranger about his habit. "No. No, I haven't."

"Come now, my friend," Dracula held up the empty morphine syringe. "Why else are you turning to this if not to recapture that feeling? Why do you make movies with that man in the woman's high-heeled shoes? You know they're no good and will be quickly forgotten."

"No. Eddie's a fine director."

Dracula shook his head. "Don't try to fool me. I know when a man lies."

Bela wanted to protest, but knew that Dracula was right. Eddie Wood was earnest and willing to help Bela any way he could, but he was not very good at his trade.

"You make the films to try to recapture what you felt. I *know* that hunger." He stepped nearer; now he was only a few feet away. "I can give that back to you. Stronger than you've ever felt it before."

So tempting . . .

"No," Bela said, not daring to believe. It was too good to be true. "You're lying to me. I know what you are—better than anyone. I know you're a monster."

"Do you want to know the truth?"

Bela hesitated. "How?"

"I'll let you experience it with me."

He felt his heart thumping. "What do you mean?"

"This," Dracula said. He leaned forward, his mouth approaching Bela's jugular vein like a lover planting a first kiss. Bela didn't have the strength—or desire—to fight him off.

The teeth tickled the side of his neck. "Watch," Dracula whispered.

There was no pain as the fangs bit into him, only a slight chill like an ice cube down his back.

And he was different. The room blurred away and he was back in his true element—the night. He flew through the warm black sky, finding his way unerringly using the echoes of his voice. All the ravages of age were gone; he was young and filled with life. Movement was no longer a chore, and flight was a part of him, something he did with total ease.

A window lay open for him. He entered.

The woman inside was very beautiful—with black hair and incarnadine lips, her pale face all the more striking because it was composed in sleep.

He approached her without making a sound, but she still awoke when he stood by her.

For a moment, she looked frightened, but when she saw his face she lit up with a smile. She sighed dreamily and, without a word, slid the collar of her nightgown aside to reveal her neck. Two puncture marks already marred the perfect skin. He paused, reveling in the power he had over her. She had surrendered to him totally; it was time to take the final draught of her.

Slowly he leaned over, then, satisfied she was completely his, he lovingly bit into her.

She gasped slightly as he punctured her skin. Her blood was sweet and delicious, ambrosia on his tongue. He drank deeply, savoring its bouquet and flavor.

The woman shuddered in pleasure several times as he fed. He ignored it, intent on his own hunger.

He didn't know how long it took to drain her; time didn't mean anything. But eventually the meal flowed sluggish and cold, and he knew she had left the world of the living. It was too bad she couldn't join his world, but she was not worthy of that.

He stepped back, licking drops of blood from his lips. She lay, looking peaceful, a smile on her face. They always smiled.

He was almost sated. One final pleasure.

With loving care, he opened the front of her nightgown. Then, powered by an intense desire that nothing human had ever experienced, he tore into her chest, his powerful fingers breaking through her rib cage, until he tore out her heart and held it in his hands. He savored its meaty aroma for several moments, then, with an almost sexual frenzy, bit into it, squeezing the last drops of her blood from it with his strong back teeth. The flavor was more intoxicating than the very best wine, a distillation of all the possible pleasures of the flesh and beyond. He could think of nothing finer. . . .

. . . And Bela lay blinking in the darkness, Dracula towering over him. He was surprised and embarrassed to discover that, for the first time in many years, he had an erection.

"That was only a taste of what you have to look forward to," said Dracula. "You felt the power. You felt the pleasure."

Bela nodded. The intensity of the sensation was overwhelmingly seductive. He felt himself longing for it as he did for his morphine, the degradation involving no more concern than did the degradation of his life. It was like a dream come true, to become what he had played at being. He wanted to live that dream. Forever an immortal.

His hand fell onto his desk, knocking the letters into his lap. He stared at them, startled by their fall, seeing his name on the envelopes. He remembered what was in those letters, the words he had reread and reread until they had lost their novelty. But not their importance.

My God, he thought. What have I come to?

He pointed at the monster in front of him. "You killed her. You ate her *heart*, for God's sake!"

"It doesn't matter. In the long run, she'd be dead anyway. But that isn't the issue. You *felt* what it was like. You know what the end of her useless life gave to you."

Bela found the strength to rise from the chair, taking the fallen letters in his hand. "She didn't deserve to die that way. To be devoured like a piece of meat."

"Mortals are merely food. You'll discover that once you become one of us." The monster smiled like a father talking to a naively rebellious son. "I had some of the same misgivings when I was first recruited. They quickly passed. You'll learn once you become immortal."

"No," Bela said. "No." He held up the envelopes. "You see these?"

"Letters. So?"

"Letters to me. From people who I've never met. They remember me. They remember what I was." He picked through the stack until he found one he recalled well. "This is from a boy fifteen years old. Fifteen! He wasn't even born when I played the Count. Yet he knows me. He remembers me. And when I die, people will still remember. My films—some of them—will continue to be played. And people will know I existed." The timbre of his voice was stronger than it had been in years. "I *am* an immortal already—an immortal of the screen. And one whose immortality is based on light, not darkness."

The monster seemed disconcerted by the outburst. "The light of a projector."

Bela nodded. "Yes. But I *am* light, while you have to remain skulking in the shadows. Like an animal. Like a subhuman." He understood finally what he was facing. "I know now why you want me so badly. You need me to join you so my presence—elegant, you called it—can let you justify yourself to the sick little remnants of your conscience." He shook his head. "You are pathetic. You are nothing." He stood up tall, and felt the years fall away for a moment. "*I am . . . Dracula!*"

The monster was quiet. He seemed smaller now, less fearsome. He no longer seemed important enough to frighten anyone.

"Now, get out," Bela said. "I don't want any part of you."

"You will change your mind," the monster said. "Once I finish."

"Over my dead body."

The monster giggled. "An unfortunate choice of words. You see, my friend, I have already begun the process. Your death—whether by your needle or just old age—will be only a deep sleep that will last several weeks before you finally succumb. I will visit you in the grave, old man, and finish giving you the honor you so richly deserve. You can't escape your destiny, my friend. Until then . . . farewell." He became a bat again.

"Destiny?" Bela said. "Never!"

The bat fluttered for a few moments before disappearing out the open window.

Bela shut the window. No more morphine, he decided, and knew he meant it this time. He'd get Eddie Wood to help him kick the habit. For all of Eddie's quirks, Bela knew he could depend on him.

As for the other threat, the solution soon came to him. He'd make sure everyone knew that he wanted to be buried in his Dracula cape. No one would deny him that last request.

But there was something else he needed.

The monster had been wrong. Bela found what he was looking for among the spices in the kitchen. He took his cape from his closet and began to rub the garlic into the collar.

# EXPOSURE

*Laura Anne Gilman*

The timer clicked, a cicada in the dark. Lifting the tongs off their rest, he swirled the paper gently; watching, deeming Good to go by the rules, better to work by instinct. Finally deeming it complete, he lifted the sheet out of its bath, placing it in another shallow tub and turning the water on, cold, over it.

The music played, one cd after another, continuous shuffle so that he never knew what would come up next: Melissa Etheridge, Vivaldi, the exotic noises of a rain forest. It suited his mood, prepped him for the evening's work. For now the lilting strains of *The Four Seasons* kept him company. Tugging at his ear where it itched, he studied the image floating face-up at him. Satisfied, he lifted it between two fingertips, shaking some of the wetness off. Turning off the water, he transferred the print to his right hand and reached out to flick the toggle switch on the wall next to the room's exit. Stepping into the revolving door, he pushed the heavy plastic with one shoulder and emerged from the darkroom.

Blinking in the sudden fluorescent lighting, he cast a glance over his shoulder to make sure that the warning light had gone off, then carried the print over to the line strung across the far end of the studio. Clipping it to the line, he stepped back to examine the other prints already there. Several, most notably the three shots of the hookers talking over coffee, leaning intently across the table to get in each others' faces, pleased him. Others were less successful, but overall he was satisfied. Checking his watch once again, he took off the stained apron he wore, hung it on a hook beside the door, shut off the stereo, and went to take a shower. Time to go to work.


"Hey, Westin!"

He slung the bag more comfortably over his shoulder, and stopped to wait for the overweight Latino cop who chugged up alongside him. "Going out again tonight, huh?"

"As I've done every night this week," Westin replied. "And the week before that."

"But not the week before that," the cop said.

"But the entire month before that I didn't miss a single night. So why are you asking now?"

The cop ignored the slight edge to Westin's voice. "There's some weirdo out there, past few nights. Scared the hell out of a couple slits Tuesday, cut into their business too. Guy's wearing Pampers and some kinda bonnet, according to reports. If you happen to run into him . . ."

"I should take his picture for your album?"

"The brass'd be thankful. And ya gotta know the *Post*'d pay for that picture. Anyway, keep your eyes out."

"I always do," Westin said, holding up his camera. He watched with detached affection as the cop loped back to his post, holding up a wall in the upper hall of the Port Authority. Swaddling and a bonnet. That was a new one. He could certainly understand johns keeping away, but why were the hookers afraid of him? Westin thought briefly about following up on it, then put those thoughts away. If he came into the viewfinder, then would be the time to wonder. For now, there was the rent to pay. He stepped into the men's room to moisten his contact lenses, darkened to protect his hypersensitive eyes. Another thing to bless technology for. Even he couldn't take photographs through sunglasses.

Leaving the bustling noise of the terminal, he exited into the sharp cold night of Eighth Avenue and paused. Where to go? Where were the pictures, the images waiting for him to capture? He turned in a slow half-circle, ignoring the line of dinner-hour cabs waiting in front of him, letting his instinct pick a direction. There. The hot white lights were calling him.

Walking briskly, he cut crosstown, one hand on his camera, the other hanging loosely by his side. The sidewalk hustlers and gutter sharks watched him pass, recognizing a stronger predator. But the hookers, ah, the hookers were another story. They swarmed to him, offered him deals, enticements. He did love women so, their softness hiding such strong, willful blood. But he was not feeding tonight. At least, not of that. Tonight was for a different passion. Bypassing Times Square itself, he wandered the side streets, catching the occasional sideways stare from well-dressed theatergoers on their way from dinner to their entertainment. Only the expensive Konica hanging by his side kept them from assuming he was a panhandler. The long trench had seen better decades, and not even the Salvation Army had been able to find anything nice to say about his boots except for the fact that they had once been sturdy. And the less said about his once-white turtleneck, the better. But he preferred these clothes, using them the same way wildlife photographers hid within camouflaged blinds. He was stalking wildlife as well, a form that was more easily spooked than any herd of gazelles or a solitary fox.

For the next seven hours he took shot after shot of the ebb and flow of humanity around him, occasionally moving to a new spot when people became too aware of him or, more accurately, of the camera. His choices satisfied him. The elderly woman in rags stepping over a crack in the sidewalk with graceful poise. The businesswoman striding along, topcoat open to the bracing wind. Two too-young figures doing a deal with brazen indifference to the mounted policeman just yards away, and the cop's equal indifference to their infractions. The hooker holding a Styrofoam cup in her hands, allowing the steam to rise to her face, taking delicate sips. He loved them all, carefully, surreptitiously, with each click of the shutter, every zoom of the lens to catch their expressions, the curve of their hands, the play of neon across their skin. He could feel the beat of their blood, pulling him all unwilling, and he blessed the cold which kept their scents from him. He couldn't afford the distractions.

Stopping in a Dunkin' Donuts to pick up a cup of coffee, he dug in his trench pocket for a crumpled dollar bill to pay for it. "Why can't you carry a wallet?" he could hear Sasha complain. "That way when someone finally puts you out of your misery I'll know to collect the body." Lovely, long-suffering Sasha. But she forgot her complaints when he had a show ready for her pale white walls, secure in her status as Michael Westin's only gallery. For three long, hungry years she had supported him, and for the last eleven he had returned the favor. He understood obligation, and need-ing, and the paying of debts.

Finally he came to the last roll of film he had prepared for the night. He took it out of the pouch hanging from his belt and looked at it, black plastic against the black of his thin leather gloves. High-speed black and white, perfect for catching moments silhouetted against the darkness, sud-den bursts of light and action. His trademark. One roll left. He still had time to shoot this roll before heading home, still subjects to capture.

Or he could try again, a little voice whispered inside his head. There was time.

Shaking his head to silence the unwanted voice, he removed the used film from the camera, marked it with the date, location, and an identifying number, then replaced it in the pouch. Still the unused film sat in his palm. He could reload the camera, finish the evening out. Or he could save it for the next trip, cutting the session short and going home. At the thought his lips curled in a faint smile. Home to where Danielle slept in their bed, her hair fanned out against the flannel sheets. She would be surprised to see him, surprised and pleased, if he knew his Dani.

Or you could try again.

"Damnit, enough!" He would be a fool to listen to that voice, a fool to even consider it. Hadn't the three attempts been enough to teach him that? If the third time wasn't a charm, then certainly the fourth was for fools. And his kind didn't survive by being fools.

But still the thought lingered, caressing his ego, his artist's conceit. He could picture the shot, frame it perfectly in his mind. The conditions were ideal tonight, the location tailor-made. It would be the perfect finish to this show, the final page of the book he knew Sasha would want to do.

Stuffing the thought back into the darkness of his mind, he deftly inserted the black cartridge, advancing the shutter until the camera was primed. He cast one practiced eye skyward. Four A.M., give or take fifteen minutes. He had another hour, at most, before he would have to head home, wrap his head under a pillow, and get the few hours of sleep he still required before locking himself in the darkroom to develop this night's work. Then dinner with Dani, and perhaps he would take tomorrow night off. Fridays were too busy to get really good photos. Better to spend it at home, in front of a roaring fire, and his smooth-necked, sweet-smelling wife and a bottle of her favorite wine.

*You work too hard,* she had fussed at him just last month, rubbing a minty-smelling oil into his aching muscles after a particularly grueling night hunched over the lightboard, choosing negatives. *Always pushing, always proving. You don't have anything to prove.* But he did. Had to take better photos, find the most haunting expressions, the perfect lighting. All to prove to himself that he was the photographer his press made him out to be, and not just some freak from a family of freaks, that his work was the result of talent and dedication, not some genetic mutation, a parasite on human existence.

*Shh, my love,* he could hear Dani whisper. *I'm here, and I love you.* She would whisper that, baring her neck so that he might graze along that smooth dark column, feel the pulsing of her blood . . .

He swore, cutting off those thoughts before his body reacted to the thought of her strength, her warmth. Jamming his hands into the pockets of his trench, he watched the street theater, looking for something that would finish the evening on a positive note, leave him anxious to see the proof page. But the street was empty for the moment, leaving him with the little voice, which had crept back the moment his attention was distracted. *The perfect photograph,* it coaxed him. *Something so heartbreakingly perfect that only you could create. Otherwise this exhibit is going to end on a downer, and there's enough of that in this world, isn't there?*

Cursing under his breath, he scared off a ragged teen who had sidled up next to him. Westin watched the kid's disappearing backside with wry amusement. It had been a long time since anyone had tried to mug him, and he would have given the boy the twenty or so bucks he had in his pocket, just to reward such *chutzpa*.

Checking the street one last time, he sighed and gave up. Time to call it a good haul, and head on home. *To bed, perchance to screw, and then to sleep.* Hanging the camera strap around his shoulder, he adjusted the nylon webbing until the shoulder patch fit snugly against his coat. *There's still film left,* the little voice said, sliding and seducing like a televangelist. *Can't go home with film left.*

"I'll take shots of some of New York's Finest," he told himself. Fragile humans, holding back the night. It would be a good image, and it would please Miguel to be included. And Tonio, his partner. Kid was so green his uniform squeaked when he walked. Veteran and rook, side by side, against the squalor of the bus terminal. Maybe he'd catch them in an argument. He could see that, frame it in his head. The possibilities grew, flicking across the screen in his head fast enough to wipe all thoughts of That Shot out of his head. By the time he reached the corner of Seventh Avenue, he had it all planned out. Stopping to look up at the still-dark sky, he thought he could see just the faintest hint of light creeping skyward from the east. False dawn. At home, he would be watching the deer come down from the wooded area to eat his bushes. He had done an essay on them for National Wildlife which paid well enough to replace the rosebushes the hoofed terrorists had devoured the spring before.

Waiting at the light on the corner of Forty-first and Eighth, something made him tilt his head to the right. There. By the chain-link fence protecting an empty lot. A shadow that wasn't a shadow. His soothing thoughts broke like mirror shards, and he turned his head to stare straight across the street. Live and let live. The fact that he chose not to hunt—did not, in fact, have to—did not mean others might not. Only once had he made it his concern, when a kinswoman had gotten messy, leaving corpses over the city—*his city.* His mouth tightened as he remembered the confrontation that had followed. He hadn't wanted to destroy her—but he wasn't ready to end his existence yet either. And letting her continue was out of the question. Only fools saw humans as fodder. They were kin, higher in some ways, lesser in others, but in the balance of time, equal. He believed that, as his father had believed that, raising his children to live alongside the daylight-driven world as best they could, encouraging them to build support groups, humans—companions—that would offer so that they need not take. It was possible, his father had lectured them, to exist without violence. And so they had. And the daylight world had given him good friends, a loving wife—and the means to express the visions which only his eyes could see.

With that thought in mind, he turned slowly, looking up at the sky behind him. False dawn. It was almost upon him.

*The perfect photograph. It would only take one shot. One exposure, and then it's done.*

A scrap of memory came over him. "If 't were done, 't were best done quickly . . ." *Damn. Damn damn damn damn.*

It seemed almost as though another person took control; moved his body across the street, dodged the overanxious cabs turning corners to pick up the last fare of the night. Someone else walked across the bare floor of the terminal that even at this hour still hosted a number of grubby souls wandering, some slumped over knapsacks, asleep, some reading newspapers or staring down into their coffee as though it held some terrible answer. His hand powered by someone else reached for the camera, holding it like a talisman, a fetish. Standing on the escalator, he watched out of habit, his mind already on what he was going to do. He could feel it pulling him, a siren's song, and he cursed himself. But he couldn't stop, no more than the first three times he had tried. Tried, and failed.

Crossing over to the next level of escalators, he paused at the first step, willing his body to stop, turn around, get on the bus that would take him home. Only a fool would continue, only a madman. Looking down, he saw first one boot, then the other, move on to the metal steps, his left hand grasping the railing. With his right hand he fingered the camera's casing, stroking his thumb over the shutter button.

At the end of this escalator he stopped, hitting his free hand against the sign that thanked him in Spanish and English for not giving money to panhandlers. The pain made him wince. At least in that they were equal, humans and he. Pain was a bitch. He hit his hand again, then gave up. The siren call, as strong as blood, had him again, and he had no choice but to give in. If it was to be done, it had to be done fast. Get in, get out, go home. Punching the up button, he waited for the elevator that would take him to the rooftop parking lot.

*He adjusted the camera in his hand, barely aware of the sweat that ran down the back of his neck and down the front of his shirt. Shifting closer to the roof edge, he leaned against the ornate masonry, bracing himself. A glint of light caught his attention and he squinted, the hair along his arm rising in protest. "One minute more," he told himself. "Just one damn more minute,*

*you bitch, and I'll have you. Come on, come on, do it for me!"* He swallowed
with difficulty, wishing for the water bottle at arms' reach, as impossible as if
it were on another planet.

Another flicker of light caught the first building, fracturing against the
wall of windows. *"Come on,"* he said under his breath, unaware of anything
except the oncoming moment. *He could feel it, a sexual thrill waiting to shoot
through his body, better than anything, even the flush of the first draw of
blood. This was why he was alive. This was it, this was the perfect moment
. . . He drew the camera to his face, focusing on primal instinct. The light
rose a fraction higher, and he was dropping the camera, running for the
maintenance door, aware only of the screaming animal need to hide, survive,
get away from that damn mocking bitch. The camera lay where it fell: abandoned, broken.*

"Goddamn," Westin swore, shaking himself free of the memory. "Go
home, Westin. It's a fucking picture. Not worth dying for." The woman
exiting the elevator glanced at him, pulling her coat closer around her body
as she swept past him, eyes forward in a ten-point exhibition of New York
street sense. The first rule: never let them see you seeing them. He moved
past her on instinct, not realizing until the doors had closed that he passed
the Rubicon. "Well goddamn," he said again, but he was grinning. A
predator's flash of too-white teeth, a grin of hungry anticipation. His fangs
tingled, the veins underneath them widening in response to the rush of
adrenaline coursing through his body.

The parking lot was mostly deserted—the late-night partiers having
headed home, and the Jersey commuters not yet in. There were a handful
of cars parked in the back for monthly storage, and one beat-up blue Dart
pulled in as he stood there. He waited in the shadows until the driver, a
heavy-set man wearing workboots and carrying a leather briefcase, passed
by him into the elevator.

Going to the edge of the lot, he sat on the cold metal railing, hooking
one foot under the longest rung to keep himself from slipping five stories
to the pavement waiting below. The air was noticeably colder here, the
wind coming at him without buffer. Dawn was coming, damn her. He
could feel it in every sinew of his body, every instinct-driven muscle
screaming for him to find a dark cave in which to wait the daylight hours
out.

Forcing himself to breathe evenly, he took control of those instincts,
forcing them back under the layers of civilization and experience. There
would be plenty of time to find a bolthole somewhere in the massive bulk
of the Port Authority. He had done it before, here and elsewhere. It was all
timing. Timing, he reminded himself, and not panicking.

Squinting against the wind, he swung his body into better position, facing eastward, toward the East River. Toward the rising sun.

*Idiot,* a new, more rational voice said in tones of foreboding. *Do the words crispy critter mean anything to you?* He shrugged off the voice, lifting the camera to his eye. There was only the moment, and the shot. His entire universe narrowed down to that one instant, his entire existence nothing more than the diameter of the lens. His fingers moved with a sure steadiness, adjusting the focus minutely, his body tense.

A particularly aggressive gust of wind shook the rooftop, making him lose the frame. Swearing, he fought to regain it, all the while conscious of seconds ticking by, each moment more deadly than the last. A taloned claw clenched in his gut, and sweat ran along his hairline and down under his collar. "Damn, damn, damn," he chanted under his breath, a mantra. The muscles in his back tightened, his legs spasming. But his arms, his hands, remained still, the muscles cording from the strain.

The first ray of light touched the rooftops, glinting deadly against empty windows. He swore again, his finger hovering over the shutter button.

"Come on, baby," he coaxed it, a tentative lover. "Come here. That's it, you're so perfect."

Another ray joined the first, the faintest hint of yellow in the pure light. The hairs along his arms stirred underneath the turtleneck, his heart agitating with the screaming in his head to *get out get away you dumb fuck get OUT.* His hands remained steady, his eyes frozen, unblinking: waiting, just waiting. He could smell it now, that perfect moment, with more certainty than he'd ever known. Everything slowed, his breathing louder than the wind still pushing the building beneath him, his body quivering under the need for release.

A third ray sprang across the sky, then a fourth and fifth too fast to discern. Suddenly the rooftops were lit by a glorious burst of prism-scattered light, heart-stopping, agonizing, indelible. A ray flashed toward him, reflected by a wall of glass, and glanced off the brick barely a foot to the left. His forefinger oh so slowly pressed toward the shutter button while every muscle twisted in imagined agony. "Come on come on come on . . ." he whispered, holding himself back for the perfect second.

The smooth metal was underneath his fingertip when the first light caught him, slashing against his cheek, his chest, reaching through the skin into his vital organs.

He screamed, falling backwards in a desperate attempt to keep the deadly light from him, slamming to the cold cement floor even as his finger pushed, even as his ears heard the click of the shutter closing underneath the sound of his own primal voice.

His skin was burning, the blood seeping from the pores of his face and arms. The pain was everywhere, searing him, branding him. Tears tinctured with red washed a track down his narrow nose.

Crawling to his feet, Westin barely retained the presence of mind to shove the camera back into its padded carry-bag before dragging himself to the elevator and slamming his fist against the Down button. Blood dripped down his arm and onto the fabric.

The elevator opened in front of him. Westin pushed himself into the empty space, shaking. He leaned against the back wall and drew a deep breath, knowledge of his own stupidity battling with the sheer exhilaration of a different sort of hunt.

All too soon, the rush was over, and he was himself again, drenched in sweat and drying blood. In his memory, the sun rose like some killer angel, and he knew his actions for what they were—vanity.

But he would do it again.

# THE SCULPTURE
# GARDEN

# ARS BREVIS

*Mark Kreighbaum*

The afternoon light wriggled like a thief through crosshatched iron bars and down into the dankness of Suzanne's basement apartment. It was slashed to ribbons instantly by a jumble of iron chessmen on the windowsill, all angles and mutated limbs. What remained of the light, a few slivers and sighs, crawled through the hundreds of other sculptures jammed together in the darkened apartment like a close-grown forest. The walls were hidden behind masks of aluminum and gold, many hung in front of others, so that even the masks had masks. The ceiling supported rank upon rank of devices, gadgets for the building of nightmares. The light bled the last of its life down numberless edges.

Most of the sculptures were simply hammered metal, uncontrolled, jagged, an invitation to a severing. A few were joined together by rough welds into an unholy intercourse. The welds were obvious, extravagant, deliberate, the sutures of an angry child with the fires of hell sleeping in her fingers. Here and there, however, were objects that hinted at some larger design. Ten lumps of bronze, worked into skinny twists, lay like broken fingers caught in the springs of a naked bedframe. They reached toward a sheet of iron that could have been a page torn from the book of some god of blacksmiths. The page drew the eye to a trio of severely curved white gold vines coiled around an obelisk of jet that glinted with touches of some dark green gem melted down the sides like candle wax. In one corner loomed a steel cross, filigreed and ornate, buffed and polished to a sheen. The cross was suspended upside down in a vast complex of gears and pulleys. In another corner stood a brass shadow of a running man, deformed as if traced through melted glass. The running man's elongated form stretched to the ceiling, his cattail limbs whipped out into the air, full of the promise of pain. Crude, roughly etched, the man's only graceful features were his eyes, with holes for pupils. The eyes were beautiful, nuanced to an astonishing degree, the brows curved up in some mysterious dismay.

Her bare feet tucked up under her, Suzanne sat in an ancient over-stuffed armchair far back in the darkest shadows of the basement, where no light had hope of purchase. She was thin, a stick figure almost, wearing army fatigues and a T-shirt with a silhouette of a crescent moon crudely stitched on it. Her long hair was lank and unwashed. Suzanne squinted at the faint glimmers of light, shading her eyes with one hand. Despite this, her small eyes, agate dark, sparkled with tears and she blinked rapidly. Still, she stared at the light for a long time, studying its movements. Finally, she donned a pair of dark glasses and fell to a stillness more complete than her sculptures.

When the afternoon light died into dusk, starved to darkness by the hungry metal in the old room, Suzanne removed her dark glasses. After a few minutes, she picked up a long knife, a replica of a kris, and made a long slash with the grain along her pale thin wrist. Blood, black and viscous, welled up and where it touched the metal of the knife, it gave off an acrid smoke, like burning rubber, or a dung fire. She lapped up the blood, crying out as it blistered her tongue and scalded the inner flesh of her throat. Her whimpers echoed in the room. Yet she drank deep and long, until the blood ceased to flow. Her hand fell away, raglike, to the side of the chair. The wrist cut faded to a white line that disappeared in moments.

Suzanne tipped her head back, exposing her neck to the darkness. She remained thus for a long time. At last, many hours later, she leaned forward, made a small space on the floor in front of her armchair, and carved a sigil into the wood of the floor with the blade of her kris. There were other sigils driven into the wood, too, many of them, dense signatures scrawled into the floor in no discernible design. She whispered a word that burned in her throat a thousand times more painfully than the acid of her own blood.

Silence fell in the shadowed room, then deeper silence still, then deeper again and again, until deafness would have been a relief.

"Do you make, or are you made, little sculptor?" taunted a resonant voice, breaking the stillness. It was the brass running man, whose pupils suddenly brimmed with fire. The flames failed to relieve the darkness. "What hope of inspiration, feeding alone?"

The running man flowed out of the corner of the room, his movements hesitant, powerful. He did not approach Suzanne, but rather moved among the other sculptures, fire sinking further, further into the holes of his eyes. He craned his neck to stare at the masks on the walls. He paused to take up the monstrous chessmen and turn them in his hand. He walked atop the sculptures. Even he could find no space among them.

"Hello, Master," murmured Suzanne, speaking to the kris, pitted and streaked, that she lifted to her lips to kiss, lightly, like some knight playing at chivalry. In a low voice, she added, "I knew you would choose the running man."

"Why do you drink your own blood, child? You can own any man or woman, yet you masturbate yourself at the edge of light?"

"Every artist loves her own blood, even when the taste is bitter." Suzanne raised her head and watched the deformed man-thing lurch around the room, never touching the floor. The corner of her mouth lifted into a sweet smile, but her agate eyes were cold and dark. She offered her wrist. "Care for a taste, Master?"

The running man paused, flaming eyes riveted to the frail woman.

"I gave you the gift of eternal blood and you promised me art. Pay me now, my blood price, or I will taste you true for seven times the centuries you've lived. And you know the lesson of my teeth that you have delivered to so many others for so long." The running man wavered. His movements were still ungainly, but they were becoming fluid, also. The great long whips of his arms flailed the air, always somehow missing the other sculptures, though the limbs moved with uncommon speed and seeming randomness. His hands, flayed spurs of steel, flexed. His mouth, previously no more than a chiseled slash, lip-synched the voice that really came from the darkly burning eyes. He gestured to the room full of sculptures. "These are poor whispers. Where is the scream?"

"Soon, my lord," murmured Suzanne, in a distracted voice. She lifted the kris and turned it before her eyes. "Art pays all debts."

Suddenly, she leapt out of the chair and into the musty air, transforming herself into an arrow of gray smoke that smelled like an acre of tires smoldering in a daylong fire. The rags of clothing fell burning to the floor. She arced through the window and up into a clouded night sky. Her mind, trained by centuries of study, hammered away at the smoke, until it took on a form, a wave cresting; she had long ago discarded the echoes of flying things, the ships of air, the remnants of little winged myths, and now moved above Earth in stranger guise, in uncommon grace. The running man moved beside her, melting through the darkness, cutting the night with his dark spurs of steel. The sky exhaled soft screams every time the Master dug a jagged metal foot into the substance of night. Suzanne shuddered at the sound.

"Do we hunt?" asked the running man.

"In a sense," Suzanne replied.

She paused in her flight and descended to a rooftop garden. Her companion followed; his breathing had become the screams of wounded air he had caused. He was learning the business of substance again. It was clear that the shape of the brass man pleased him. Suzanne drew flesh over the smoke of her soul. She walked, naked and unchilled, to the garden, perhaps fifty feet square, that filled the rooftop of a tenement in the city of night.

"Behold," said the sculptor.

The garden was not living vegetation at all, but a marvelous simulacrum of verdigris metal. Each plant was cunningly crafted down to the drop of bronze masquerading as dew on a leaf. The garden itself seemed a riot of color, though only in the uncertain glance of starlight. Each row was planted with immense care to suggest careless life.

"A garden. The lifeless pretending to life. How droll." The running man bent at his fingerwidth waist down to the ground. He brushed blunt steel fingers over the sculptures, but caused no harm. "Is this your hope of redemption? If so, you are not the artist I imagined."

"No," murmured Suzanne. She still held the kris. With it, she levered a perfect rose off the frame of the sculpture. She handed it to the running man. "Teach it to die in the sun, to give off its song of sweetness. You've often claimed to be the equal of God and you must have learned how to be an artist by now, right?"

The eyes of the running man flared into white hot arcs, which gradually died to a smolder of gold. He crushed the mock rose in one hand. The metal became rust and fell to the earth like a fall of bloody snow.

"No, I am no artist. Why do you suppose I give the gift of endless life, of blood and change, to you children of the sun? I recall the great symphony of the Romanian, yet unfinished, always changing, played with instruments of flesh. And the dark canvas of that strange child, numberless reds in his palette, the paintings that only I could see. There was also that mad dancer who presumed to make others of his kind, to play at being the Master. But it was a grand ballet. It was true art.

"No, I am the source of your metal, little sculptor, but I do not breathe the sun into you, nor do I guide your hand. I am the Master of the Night Way, the endless dark. Yet, for you, I am merely a patron of the arts." He bowed low to her.

"Yeah. I know." She tilted her head up, looking into the starry night sky, sieved by clouds. She seemed to search the sky for something, some movement, or sign. "This isn't my offering, Master, just a taste of what I know, what I've learned. Come."

Again she ascended, and they flew.

Next, they descended to stride through a cemetery, filled with numberless graves, some of them marked by immense stone angels, most headed only by a mossy gray block of granite, or white quartz.

"Is your creation buried here?"

"You're too impatient, Master. Look more carefully.'

The running man's black limbs were losing their metallic cast, shifting to something closer to human skin, yet not quite—perhaps scales, or leather. His movements had gained grace, but the original chaotic force seemed always present. The whips of his hands moved restlessly, drifting close to Suzanne, as if eager to caress her with edges. He moved among the graves, examining them with his fiery gaze.

"These gravestones . . . the names of the dead are missing and the dates go back to before this city existed." He paused, then laughed, a sound like tearing metal. "I see. These commemorate your victims. So the entire graveyard is your work?"

"And more," said Suzanne, but she didn't elaborate.

"Clever. A bit self-indulgent, perhaps even maudlin, but audacious for all that. A fine journeyman piece. I have seen its better at Dachau and Treblinka, in the midst of creation. It does not suffice to pay your debt to me."

"I know," said Suzanne. "But maybe it'll help me explain my art to you. You once said that if I could teach you the essence of sculpture, you would consider my debt paid."

The running man, so tall that he resembled a skeletal tree looming over the frail naked woman, seated himself in the lap of a stone angel and assumed an attitude of contemplation.

"Very well. Instruct me, child. But I have been the student of thousands of your kind and none yet has kindled the divine spark."

Suzanne didn't speak at once. She spent a moment or two wandering among the graves, pausing occasionally to crouch down and read a stone set flat in the earth. Finally, she faced the Master, holding the kris between them.

"Is this a sculpture?" she asked.

"It is an object, a knife. Its intent lives in its shape, but it fails of art, by lack of context. Without context, there is no art. Or so that delightful mistress of Rodin's claimed. Do you remember her, little one, her taste?"

Suzanne ignore the jibe. "But what if you just don't *know* the context? What if I had stolen the kris from a diorama? Wouldn't it simply be a sculpture separated by space, divided by time?"

"Do you suggest that provenance confers context? I could as well claim that the empty canvas is art that is sleeping, waiting for the hand that will wake it."

"Isn't it?"

Suzanne crouched down below the angel's feet and used the tip of the kris to cut something into the stone. The brass man leapt lithely to the earth and studied the name she had scratched there.

"*Suzanne?*" His voice, supple and deep, filled the air. "So. You alter one piece of art with another to recast the context. It is an interesting exercise, perhaps even a kind of art. But it is not sculpture."

"It wasn't meant to be. I'm just showing you that context is fluid. If sculpture is about form, then what's form about? You saw my garden, but you didn't really see it. You saw a work in progress, just as this angel was unfinished, until now. You'll never understand art until you understand that no work is ever done until the artist says it is."

"Sophistry. But I grant you the point. I gave you eternal life so that you would have time to finish a work that would teach me a new thing. Do not claim now that there is no conclusion. Art must always have boundaries."

"Like life," said Suzanne. "Art is mortality in miniature."

"An obvious epigram." The running man reached out a splayed steel hand and let the edge of one finger brush her cheek, leaving behind a curve of dark blood. "You owe me a masterpiece, child, or a lesson in art that is more illuminating than these assumptions. Your time is short. When the dawn comes, so shall I, and you know the conclusion of such an orgasm."

Suzanne bowed her head in submission, bringing her hands together in an attitude of mock prayer.

"Patience, Master. For an immortal, you're terribly hasty."

"An hour more, little one. I have other concerns. Show me your great work, or inspire me."

"I will do both."

Suzanne lifted into the air as a dark flash of starlight. The running man followed and did not notice that the stone angel's eyes were identical to his own.

Finally, they came to the shore of a lake that shimmered beneath the stars. The running man moved over black sand, eyes flashing, red and gold.

"Is this body of water the body of your art?"

"It's been a kind of communion, yeah, the only one I'm allowed." Suzanne bent down occasionally to draw the kris through the sand, leaving behind designs. She never strayed far from the running man, so that he became the hub to the wheel of her movements.

" 'A touch, a touch. I do confess 't.' " The Master bent down to pick up a rock from the beach. He studied it closely. It was a sculpture of a stone, so intricately crafted that only a careful examination revealed its true nature. "You have some intent to teach me again, I perceive. Here is my stone of regret, unmarred." He offered it to her in his palm.

Suzanne glanced at him, surprised into a genuine smile. In the moment, it was possible to see how she had been seduced by him so many centuries ago. But this time she refused the gift. He shrugged, marvelous eyes wide and unconcerned. He flung the stone out into the water, where it sank without a sound, out almost beyond the limits of sight.

"Sculpture is at least as much about what presses against the shape as the shape itself, true?" Suzanne asked.

"So I have heard."

"Let's say that the air is the sculpture and the lake the medium that defines it. Where is the art?"

"In the definition, I presume." He laughed.

"What's shaped by human hands is sculpture, what's shaped by divine hands is life itself. But both are defined by what they reveal and disguise, yes?"

The running man was now clearly annoyed. A prickling of maroon light appeared on the horizon.

"Dawn is almost upon us, divine or not. Where is your great work of art?" His razor limbs wandered the air between them, like tongues of black fire. His eyes were losing their fire, becoming merely crimson pools. He regarded her with something resembling affection. "I am inclined to grant you another century or so, if you wish. You have been amusing this night."

Suzanne sat down beside the Master. She drove the kris into the sand hilt-deep, so it became a cross.

"I am the chisel," said Suzanne, gazing at the horizon, eyes watering already from the merest echo of dawn's light. "My sculpture is begun, the great work you demanded."

The Master frowned, his fabulous eyes so intricately carved that the expression gained subtlety. "Ah. You intend to serve up your pretense of flesh to the dawn, then? You disappoint me. Mere suicide is not art, but the failure of will."

"Always you've seen the grain in the wood, but not the structure," said Suzanne. "Once I knew that, I knew what to build."

False dawn cut away at the gray night revealing the pink flesh beneath. It also sent a weak river of light into the design Suzanne had trailed into the beach around the two of them. It was a sigil, the same as the many designs carved into her floor over too many years to count.

The running man grasped this in almost the same moment that the sun came to true dawn. He snapped a vicious limb at the delicate woman seated at his feet, but not before she spoke the word that must summon him to the circle.

In the same breath of agony, the sun's light tore apart her mockery of flesh and burned away the dirty smoke of her soul, leaving the running man summoned but alone. Summoned and unable to conclude his pact. Summoned and caught in the sculpture that he had transformed over the night into flesh and was now frozen once again into metal.

And so the brass man remains to this day, there on the beach, to greet each dawn, a bit of art offered to the sun.

# THE AGE OF MATURITY

*Pamela D. Hodgson*

*Of the dream which was my life, this is the nightmare.*

—CAMILLE CLAUDEL

Most of all I miss the smells of the atelier, the wet, earthy aroma of the clay, the dusty tang of the plaster . . . that and the click click click of the chisel against marble, its repercussion jangling the flesh of my hand with each mottled gray chip that comes away to reveal the figure within. Yes, I have asked again, just as you suggested, and again they have told me that I will not be permitted to work, even as therapy. When a scrap of dirty paper comes into my hands, I find myself rolling it between my fingers like a bullet of damp clay, molding it with my fingers into whatever shape feels right.

Then they take it away from me, and sit me down once again between the flat-featured old woman who babbles into the sleeve of her robe about heroes of the Great War and the sour-smelling one with the knifelike cheekbones who sits passively, blank-faced, until another fit overtakes her and foam spews from her mouth like an angry ocean battering against the jagged rocks of her face. I am told she is here because she lost a child. I have lost that too, but so much more.

Three children, actually, I will confess to you, because as a woman you might understand. Two are away in the care of the nuns, thanks to the pockets (generosity would be the wrong word) of their father Auguste Rodin. The third was never born. I was very young then, and he had not yet agreed to marry me. He never did marry me, despite the promises he made—always he returned to the old slattern Rose and her useless son to whom he never gave his name. And I ended up here, imprisoned amongst the madwomen, sequestered from the world lest it learn the bloody truth.

And so I set it down here for you and perhaps your readers, in hope that you will trust my word and I will be remembered. I remain amazed that you troubled to find me, and befriend me through your letters. Your motive is of course only to eulogize the *maître*, but your kind letters and attention warm me nonetheless. I am moved to trust you. Of course, what have I to lose?

I was only eighteen when I met Auguste Rodin, in 1882, and he became my tutor because I showed promise as a sculptress. I was taken with the passion of his work; he poured his very soul into the figures, and I wanted to be just like him. I wanted my figures to live and breathe and speak, just as clearly as his *Porte d'Infer*, always in progress, affords a peek into the lurid fantasies only the boldest of us dare to enact. Just as clearly as his *Nez Cassé* reeks of working-class nobility under a neoclassical headdress, his stare scorning the Salon that scorned Rodin.

Later, I met the man who modeled for that bust, and for others. He was a coal hauler when Rodin first offered him a few francs to pose; by the time Rodin used him to portray the body of his *Saint Jean-Baptiste prêchant*, the poor fellow was as pale and ragged as the Baptist living in the wild. Later, he stood for one of the damned on the *Porte d'Infer*, and one of the *Bourgeois de Calais*. By the time of that last, he was thin and haggard, used up. Rodin ended up returning the figure to the clay pot, and starting with a new model. The man with the bent nose died cold, drunk and penniless not long after.

He was hardly the first or last to suffer such an end in Paris in the latter half of the century. You English have been so mercifully free of revolution. Do you know enough to be grateful?

The young woman who sleeps in the blood-scented cot next to mine has come to ask for my hairbrush. I give it to her. She is as sane as I; her husband committed her owing to the malaise and discomfort she experiences with the cycles of the moon. Being a hard-handed country woman of little education, she believed herself insane. Her husband feared she would turn to animal with the full moon, and must be put away to keep their children from harm. Her eyes still widen with fear when the full white circle peeps through the tiny barred window at the top of our wall. I have explained to her about woman's time, but still she inspects her fingers and gropes at her face for the telltale signs of change. I wish that I could make a bust of her, all broad marble-smooth cheeks and frightened eyes, mouth parted slightly as she runs a trembling finger over the serrated edges of her teeth . . .

If only she knew.

I had seen Rose Beuret, the mistress who was closest to wife to Rodin. She helped at Rodin's atelier like a servant when I first met him, carefully draping wet cloths over the clay, fetching him tools, sweeping up around him. At first I could not understand what he saw in her tiny cowering figure, her illiterate talk and country accent—she looked like a servant. Once her breasts had been large and full—he had sculpted her figure a dozen years earlier, no doubt pinching her nipple like a pellet of clay and then caressing the clay as if it were a woman—but now, now with the weight of age and childbearing they sagged like homespun sacks. Too, the light had gone out from her eyes—had it been there in the first; I can only judge by the heads she modeled for, and I could not know then if the light and energy came from her or from the *maître*'s hand.

It seemed no surprise when he took me to his bed. He could never love any woman as much as his work, I knew, but he professed to love me nearly that much. I buried myself in his long reddish beard, I stroked and touched his middle-aged body as if it were my own creation, molding it to a form which pleased me. Some days he was pliable, like clay; some he was cold and solid as bronze; some he was fragile as a plaster cast from life. When I tired of his *humeur changeante* and left for England, he implored in letters that I must return, that he needed me badly.

It was true. His work suffered in that year. He produced nothing of note except a series of excuses for the delays with his commissions.

Why did I leave him, you ask? Because he drained me, he tired me, he took everything from me. I do not mean this figuratively. This is not why my brother had me incarcerated all these years later in this ward full of filthy human stench—it was rather that a sister who does not feel constrained by convention is an embarrassment to a rapidly rising diplomat— but had he known my story then, my fate would have been sealed much sooner. The seal is no less sturdy. My life might as well be frozen in bronze.

Now you think me mad as well. You think you have wasted the minutes you have invested so far in this narrative, that your sympathy over the last several weeks has been ill-spent. But please, spare me a moment more of your time, no more, and let me tell you how I have come to know the truth. Then you may judge.

Perhaps you have heard rumors of Rodin and Victor Hugo in 1884. The great poet had been disappointed in previous busts of himself, and so would not sit for Rodin. Instead, he invited Rodin into his home to observe him, to take meals, and do his *moulage* out of the great man's sight. Hugo's home at the time flowed with the crackle of conversation; he hosted dozens of artists and poets every day. But his mistress and hostess Juliette Drouet grew frail with a cancer that chewed away at her intestines. The visitors drifted away, leaving Hugo to his place at Juliette's bedside. The great man would not leave her. And yet, Rodin came every day to observe. He came into the sick room and sat amidst the stale odor of sweat-soaked linens and the subtle rot of Juliette's failing body. He peered nearsightedly as Hugo leaned close to Juliette to hear her faltering voice, so that one might think he was also listening, and then surreptitiously sketched the poet's profile, his expressions, on a bit of used tissue, images to sculpt from later. It is said that he did his best work on the Hugo bust the day he watched the poet at Juliette's deathbed.

By that time Rodin maintained a household with me in the Boulevard d'Italie and we shared studio space there and at the Dépôt des Marbres. That day, the day Juliette died, I ran my fingers over the pocked mass of clay that was the Hugo bust. A chill ran through me, as if the wings of the angel of death had brushed lightly against my spine. For a moment too short to measure, I saw Juliette dying through Victor Hugo's eyes, and I felt his sorrow as if a part of myself had been cut away and replaced with an aching, black pit of emptiness. In the space of a breath the sensation had passed, but it had left its mark in my recollection. I could never look upon the Hugo sculpture again.

I was horrified at that first transcendent moment. But I came to envy it. That Auguste Rodin could transfigure the very clay into a glimpse inside the soul of a man—what greater aspiration is there for an artist? What greater desire?

The following morning I skulked around his workspace at the Dépôt des Marbres looking for opportunity to touch his works in progress when he wasn't looking. He was engrossed in one of the figures of the *Bourgeois de Calais*, the one with tearful head in hands, and I longed to finger it and see what it brought me. Of course he was not modeling from life—the leading citizens of Calais had offered their lives in return for the safety of their city five hundred years earlier—but it is a powerful work, and I wondered from whence it derived its soul. From whence *he* derived it.

After a while Rose came, wiping her hands on a threadbare skirt while she chattered at him about household expenses, and how long it had been since he had been to their home. She smelled of flour and grease. He nodded absently at her through most of the chatter, not turning away from the clay his fingers pummeled. When she burst into tears and flung herself at him he spun away from his work as if noticing her for the first time. He collected her into his arms and held her, leaving clay-colored handprints on the back of her blouse. When she looked up at him again, I could see in the silhouette of her brow that she had indeed once been beautiful. He muttered comforting sounds into her hair as he guided her out of the studio and across the marble block–filled courtyard to the street. She glared at me with such fervor as they passed that had he not been there, I think she would have spat in my eye.

He strode back in but did not return to the tearful man of Calais as I had thought he would, but rather seized a fresh hunk of clay and began anew, forming a small, crumpled woman in his hands. Satisfied, he set the tiny maquette aside, and went back to the bourgeois. I too returned to my own atelier and my own work. In the face of a woman, I tried to evoke Rose, her bitterness toward me (and my own toward the hag). What came forth instead was the rumpled brow of confusion and the slack jaw of ignorance.

I forgot about the small female figure until I saw it again, larger, in plaster, waiting outside the Dépôt des Marbres to be taken to the foundry and cast in bronze. *The Fallen Caryatid*, you will know it as; he added a base below and stone above, as if the weight of the building it held had crushed the life out of it. I touched the plaster and waited; I felt the energy pour out of me as if an artery had been sliced cleanly and its contents pumped out into the work in front of me. But all of it was not Rose . . . I saw in my mind as well the image of Eugénie Robert, the *praticienne* who made the plaster from Rodin's clay model, and knew her exhaustion at the end of a long day, felt the quiver of her empty growling stomach and the hopeless droop of her shoulders. I shook plaster dust off my hand as I stepped away. A tear ran unbidden down my face. I had a few francs in my purse; I dropped them into the pocket of Eugénie's smock hanging on the back of the door.

In fact the sense of Rose Beuret in that work was feeble, weak. I wondered if perhaps he had had his fill of her, and there was nothing left. My heart leapt inside me at that thought; if he was through with Rose, and only maintained a seldom-visited house with her out of aging loyalty, then perhaps he would commit himself to me at last.

We wrote a letter together—he was never so good with words as he was with his hands; I frequently found for him the phrases he was seeking, as I knew him intimately enough to know what he meant to say even when he said nothing—in which he promised to marry me. We even planned my wedding photo. Some say the letter was written by me, but anyone who knows his hand can tell that it is his pen that wrote it. And he truly did love me, at least at that moment.

He had finished *Le Baiser*. My brother called it vulgar and unchaste, the intertwined marble nudes, their open lips joining. But to me, it spoke of summer afternoons, long walks in the Bois de Boulogne with a handful of jonquils tucked in the band of my hat, the heat of a hand pressed possessively against the small of my back. It spoke of summer evenings, the marble smoothness of flesh against flesh, the coolness of the evening breeze against passion-soaked skin. Of course it spoke to me . . . it was his work, but it came from me.

I knew this for certain—and knew what it was that drew him to me—as he finished the *Bourgeois de Calais*. I worked closely with him on the six life-sized figures as the pressure to complete a project so long in the making, one for which he had collected the bulk of the payment years earlier, became intense. He always believed hands were the most expressive of parts. Of his own it was certainly true. Even in conversation, the flex and dance of his hands in the air spoke with more fervor and truth than his thin, soft voice. He seldom permitted anyone to work upon the hands of one of his sculptures, but he always let me.

He gave me the hands of Jean d'Aire, the holder of the key amongst the doomed men of Calais, to complete. Jean's iron-straight back and defiant scowl had been set by the master's hand. It was left to me to determine whether he would dangle the giant city key or clutch it, hold it with fondness or with fear.

When I touched the hardening clay as Rodin had left it, I braced myself for the rush of emotion, the snatches of catharsis that I had come to expect, and even ignore, from his work. But this time, there was none. I felt again, thinking perhaps I had become jaded or protective of myself, oblivious to what was there to be experienced. I ran my open hands over the folds of the cloak, traced the downward curve of the mouth, even the rope that hung in grim promise around the neck. I felt only the pinprick bumps in the cool surface tingling my fingertips. I pressed my cheek against the man's back, held the figure like a lover. Still I felt no more than the lines of its shape.

"It's not finished," he said from behind me. Pink light from the setting sun outside the window glinted off his pince-nez, clashing with the graying orange of his beard and hair. He wound his pale fingers around my forearms and lifted me up and away from the figure with the gentle force one uses on a child. "You have work of your own. Let me touch this one up some more." A cloud of dust from his smock tickled my nostrils as he slid between me and the Jean d'Aire.

"You gave me the hands! I want to do the hands!" I protested, my voice rising and breaking like a boy's despite my best efforts at controlling it.

"You can do the hands," he said distractedly. He did not turn to acknowledge me. He had already taken his modeling tool to the figure's left shoulder. "Not now."

I shook the dust from my apron, blinked it from my eyes. I stretched my fingers toward the sleeve of his smock, but he followed the curve he was shaping just out of my reach.

I went back to my own studio and sunk my hands deep into a bust of Rodin. I closed my eyes tight, not wanting to look upon the man, but let the fabric of his being flow from me into the mass of wet clay at the ends of my arms. The clay fought me, becoming stiff and reticent no matter how much I wet it with water and spit. At last, I let it go. I would take it up again another day.

He asked me back to help with Jean d'Aire exactly a week after. I remember, because I had heard from a local gossip that he had gone with Rose to Meudon, and I counted the days in which we were apart, wondering at what number I must consider him lost to me.

Not lost. He may have spent time with Rose, but his soul was with me. I knew that when I entered the atelier and looked upon the figure of Jean d'Aire. He had the same stern features and strong stance, but his eyes radiated as much pain as passion. He stood tall, but one could see the tension as his shoulders fought off a defeated slump.

I knew in him my own fight to deny the truth of my defeat.

It was more than I wanted to know. I started to leave then, to go away, to save what strength I had in me for my own work, not for this man's, nor for a losing battle to win his love. I edged backward toward the street door, brushing clumsily past maquettes and half-finished bricks of marble, figures still partially trapped in stone. I was nearly outside, nearly free of him when he stopped me with a word. "Camille," he whispered into the silence cut only by the hammering of a woodpecker outside, "his hands." He splayed his own huge, callused palms open toward me. "You must help me with his hands."

I gazed down to the place where the figure's arms ended in ugly clumps as if sadly deformed. I saw the useless defiance of a helpless cripple, and could not abandon something that was so . . . so much *myself* in such a piteous state. I thought to escape, to leave this monstrous thing that confronted me and run, run back to my own workspace and create something as unlike it as possible, to deny the truth by remaking it. But that was not possible. The only thing to do was give the *whole* story. To finish the hands.

I perfected them. I don't mean fine detail of cuticle and crosshatch line of palms. I perfected the shape, the posture of the hands so that they were not wretched and impotent, but rather grasped the key to Calais with strength and firmness of purpose. Even in defeat, these hands would not tremble or quake. These hands were noble. Powerful. Strong.

And when I returned to my own atelier, leaving behind the sweat-smell of the hard-working crowd of assistants, students, and acolytes as well as the crackle of activity and anticipation that surrounded everything the *maître* did, there was nothing left in me but silence. I stroked the pile of clay on my worktable. I plied it, I poked and squeezed it, but it took on no more form than sand under a child's hand. I pounded at it, beat it, brutalized it. Before long I had lost control and pummeled the hunk of drying clay with my fists like a prisoner begging to be let free. I gasped and grunted with the effort, hammering the sides of my hands murderously into the shape. My voice rose from gasps of pain into the wet wail of an abandoned child.

And still, within, there was silence. There was nothing left of me. I was drained.

And so I left him again. I said nothing; I simply moved my home and my work to another address, not too far removed from the one we had shared. I worked on *The Conversation*, a tiny group of gossips executed in green onyx, as unlike anything of the *maître*'s as I had ever done. And it lived! Yes, it had life, a soul of its own, more spirit and warmth than anything I had done in the ten or twelve years under Rodin's tutelage. At last, I felt free.

Still, I loved the man. He had taught me so much. For a long time I was bitter; he would write to me, or to my English friend Jessie, inquiring about my health. I would tear up the letters into tiny snowflakes, then set them in a pile and burn them. He would help my career by mentioning my name for a state commission, suggesting I be included in an exhibition. Whenever I learned it had come from him, had been a product of what he had siphoned from me rather than from the merit of my own work and my own soul, I rejected it, angry. No doubt I did myself much harm in those years—leaving many to be unsurprised when at last I was sent away—but what he had taken from me had left an empty space, a dark cavern inside me, as sore as if he had gored it out with a dull-edged modeling knife.

And at last that emptiness, like the vacuum nature abhors, sought to fill itself. After not leaving my home for perhaps as much as three months, I attended an exhibition of new works with my friend Mathias Morhardt. Rodin sent the marble *Je Suis Belle*. At first, from a distance, I saw nothing in this strange work depicting a man, upright, with a woman, compact and fetal, balanced on his head and chest. His usual vibrant contortions of the human form, certainly, but I could see no meaning in it. I felt icy satisfaction. I drew Mathias closer so that he too could see the nothingness of it and vindicate me.

We pressed past a bosomy auburn-haired woman whose potent perfume made me sneeze. She giggled and fluttered at her companion, loosing a cloud of powder from her face as she protested how *much* she adored

Monet because he *so* captured her *adored* Nature. One could hear the capital N in her enunciation of it. I snorted to Mathias, who darted a quick look at the woman's companion, then drew me stiffly away. I resisted his tug on my arm and looked back. Next to the fussy woman, gazing deeply into the painting while his hand, as if with a separate mind, roved along the woman's arm and shoulder, was Rodin. His beard had grayed a touch more in the months since I had seen him, and his spiky military-style haircut had grown out a bit. I felt hellish heat in the pit of my stomach while icy tentacles danced along my spine.

There was nothing I could say to him, had I been able to summon breath to speak. After a moment frozen to the spot, I let Mathias lead me away. Within two steps, we were confronted with Rodin's statue, much as if we were caught in a house of mirrors, with no escape from some manifestation of the man.

It took me a moment to recognize the posture of the woman as yet another edition of the crumpled woman, the one he had sketched in clay in miniature the day Rose was in the atelier. I reached upward, letting my fingertips graze her shin, bracing myself for whatever might come in the hope that I could experience it without embarrassing myself in public.

There was nothing.

I circled like a predator and prodded gently with my finger, then stroked with my full hand, every side of the woman. And still she had no soul.

I felt the warmth of a body standing too close to my left elbow. When I turned I found myself face to face, almost chest to breast, with the *maître*. Mathias sputtered behind me, but I relegated him to the crowd noise and traffic—Rodin and I became the center, the only part that mattered, the part of the stone that is the figure, needing only the rest to be chipped away to free it. Rodin took my wrist in his rough hand and pressed my palm not to the woman, but to the male figure. Actually, he let go just a fraction of an inch before I made contact, letting the momentum take me the rest of the way.

I closed my eyes and viewed through the eyes of another. I saw the world only as fleeting souls needing to be captured and sealed in shapes of plaster, marble, bronze, that must be made solid and permanent to save them from their mortal fate. I felt the *maître*'s love for every one of them, his passion, but overall his need to seize the spirits of the living and make as many immortal as he could before they escaped into oblivion.

And last, I felt his defeat. I felt the ache of remorse at his knowing that in order to capture life he had drained away life, from me, from Victor Hugo and Juliette Drouet, but most of all from Rose. He had taken her spirit, and had nothing left to give.

I broke loose from the cool touch of the marble, my hand trembling and brow damp. The tang of my own perspiration drifted around me; I closed my arms tight around my chest. "Do you see?" he whispered, his voice as soft and pleading as when he first took me to him. I did not answer.

But I saw. And in desperation I attempted to do the impossible, those next several years. I tried to re-create genius such as his by myself stealing the souls of those around me to capture in clay and stone. I did not care about making them immortal, however; I cared only about myself, that *I* should be remembered for my work, for something more than my liaison with Rodin.

First there was Debussy, then there were others, so many others that I can barely name them. I took them to my bed, into my life. I loved them as best I could, then taunted them and stole from them, both their hearts (if they had offered them to me) and their spirits. But at the last, I lacked the soul of a *maître*. I didn't care enough for my lovers, and so they could not give enough to me.

And of course there was my prudish brother, virgin into his middle thirties, busy building his career as a famous diplomat. To him, the elder sister who had taught him in childhood what it was to have passion for one's work had become simply an embarrassment, an aging whore passing as an artist, so he called me.

By that time there was nothing left in me that I could give him, that might rekindle our youthful love for one another and bring us back together. When he visited me, no doubt all he saw was my frantic, consuming passion to survive beyond this life, and the terror that coursed through me like electric jolts as I tried to enliven the clay and stone, and failed. Perhaps he felt something more than horror and pity; perhaps there was still an element of love that caused him to have me locked away from the work that I so adored, the work that was my life. Perhaps he thought to save me.

And now Rodin has died, and he will be remembered. Not just by journalists like you. Generations to come, years hence, will graze his plasters and his bronzes, and be seized with a momentary glimpse into a soul long dead. At least mine is one of those souls.

Looking back, I must say that I produced my finest work in 1894, the year our relationship ended. It is called *The Age of Maturity*. It portrays a man, Rodin, being led off into old age by a woman, not unlike Rose, while the figure of youth—myself—pines its loss. Or so the critics have described it. They miss the point. It is not about age overtaking youth, or a lover scorned. It is about Rodin breaking free.

Would that I had done the same.

*All this humanity in Rodin's work isn't really human. These beings who twist and turn hysterically seem to be moved by a sort of electricity of death; the soul is absent.*

—ODILON REDON, 1897

# BLOODSTONE

## Mary Rosenblum

It was easy to spend the last of her money. Rho had meant to buy food—a last meal to commemorate failure. Instead she zipped her debit card through the Rue d'Hiver Gallery's entry slot. Titania Drovnika's Stones were showing. It wasn't a choice really. The reader clucked at her in disapproving tones—warning her that her account was now empty. Rho tossed it into the street as the door opened.

If she was going to starve, she would at least experience Drovnika's Stones first. Bow to the winner of a contest that Drovnika would never know had existed, she thought bitterly.

The gallery building had been a warehouse once. Scabby concrete, metal beams, and exposed electrical conduits gave the huge space a grimy twentieth-century ambience. The Stones had been mounted on simple pedestals of real wood, subtly lighted. Alien asteroids, drinkers of the human soul, they filled the gallery with silent music; muted notes of love and sorrow, the half-heard whisper of a sob, the icy tickle of raindrops on sunhot skin. Eyes half closed, Rho drifted among them, drunk on the currents of emotion and sensation radiating from the Stones.

Only a sculptor with a sculptor's inborn gift could wake a Stone. Once wakened, the asteroids absorbed the emotions and sensory perceptions of nearby humans—until the sculptor let it sink into slumber again. Layered into the Stone over many years, those emotions could be woven into a complex tapestry of human emotion.

Titania's weaving was a dark one.

Rho came to rest on a shore of brooding contemplation, piqued by the sting of campfire sparks on naked skin. These immediate sensations floated on a depthless sea of emotion. Drowning in it, her skin shivering with a million instants of pleasure and pain, she focused on the Stone itself. Small—less than a meter in diameter—it shimmered with soft grays and greens, swirled through with streaks of rusty red. The color of dried blood, she thought dizzily.

"You like this one?" a woman asked from behind her.

"It's so . . . rich. How could she get this much depth in . . ." She peered at the small plaque on the pedestal. ". . . in only thirty years? The depths of despair, slow pain—human darkness."

"You are a sculptor?" the woman asked in softly accented syllables.

"No." Rho tore her eyes from the Stone and faced the woman. She was small, petite, with a Semitic face and very dark skin. "I can waken a Stone, but I am not a sculptor." Spoken out loud like this, the words became a declaration. Closure. It was time to go. She started to walk away, halted abruptly as the woman's fingers closed around her arm.

"Very few *sculptors* would have perceived what you have noticed." The woman's eyes seemed to pierce Rho. "Take me to your Stone."

"What makes you think I have one?" Rho tried to pull her arm free, trying for affront, because this woman had guessed a lot more than Rho had intended.

"Show it to me." The woman's eyes burned into hers, draining Rho's strength.

"Who are you?" Rho whispered.

"You have already guessed." Her captor slid an arm around her waist, guiding Rho toward the entry. "Do we need a cab, or is your studio nearby?"

Studio? Rho laughed bitterly and tossed her unruly hair back over her shoulder. "I'm dreaming. Sure, Ms. Drovnika, come view the ruins. Let's see if I wake up before we get to the studio."

"I will tell you if it is a ruin," Titania Drovnika said. She did not smile.


She sat on the concrete floor of the shitty basement apartment, elbows propped on her knees. It was chilly down here and Rho began to shiver as she sat on the futon that was her only furniture. She had tossed away her empty card, so the heat remained off. Titania Drovnika was the best. The critics loved her, raved about the dark power of her Stones. There were rumors of suicides after her shows.

I was going to be better than you, Rho told her silently. And the old feelings seized her, fierce as lust or hate or maybe love. She had thought that they had died.

"It is not a ruin." Titania stretched and got gracefully to her feet. "You have relied too heavily on anger." She looked down at Rho, her eyes full of dark fire. "Anger is a childish emotion. It is too shrill a note for what you attempt, but there is brilliance here, too. You are very young." She smiled finally, and her face softened into such unexpected beauty that Rho's breath caught in her throat. "You will come to understand. And now you are cold." She reached down for Rho's hands, pulled her to her feet. "I will take you on as apprentice." She nodded at the Stone. "You will finish this," she said. "What do you call it?"

Finish this . . . Rho stumbled over to her Stone. Grey, mottled with silver, and streaked with subtle hints of turquoise, it began to wake as she pressed her cheek against it. The texture of the Stone was neither stone nor flesh, and it gave the illusion of warmth in this freezing basement. "I call it . . . Bloodstone," she whispered. And then she fainted, sliding down the smooth hard flesh of the Stone to the floor. As the darkness closed in she felt Titania's arms around her, felt the touch of her lips like ice against her own.

Titania called a crew that very night to move Bloodstone to her studio. It was in an upscale city arcology—a self-contained environment sealed away from the dirty city air. It was an inside unit, with windows to the garden core of the tower rather than to the outside. A large kitchen-living area gave access to a bedroom and a huge, windowless studio. The crew that Titania had hired moved the blanketed Bloodstone into the studio and set it onto a vacant pedestal. "Open some wine," Titania said and followed the three men into the hall.

Still stunned, Rho looked around. The handwoven carpet, huge floor cushions, and the low wooden table increased her sense of unreality. She had spent her life surrounded by plastics and synthetics. Real wool and wood were the stuff of dreams. Numbly she went to the door. In the carpeted hall, Titania leaned against the wall, hip cocked, talking to the youngest member of the crew. He had a shaved scalp and a thin tail of blond hair. Rho watched him smile, bright-eyed and lustful, watched Titania sway toward him, her spread fingers planted lightly on his chest.

She turned, as if Rho had spoken.

"I . . . couldn't find any wine." Rho blushed.

"It's in the rack beside the counter." Titania's tone was cool. "He will come model for my Remembrance Stone." She nodded at the departing youth, smiled slowly, and touched Rho's jaw lightly with one fingertip. "Jealous already?"

"No . . ." Rho jerked her head back, her blush deepening. "I just couldn't find the wine."

Titania laughed and swept past her into the apartment. "He is no sculptor." She bent over the wooden wine rack that stood in plain sight beside the kitchen counter. "He does not matter, except in how he may add to a Stone."

There was something . . . predatory about those words. Rho shivered and took the glass Titania handed her. "I should go get my stuff," she said. "Maybe tomorrow."

"Leave it." Titania touched the rim of her glass to Rho's and her lips revealed the tips of her very white teeth. "Whatever you need we will buy. To your talent." She lifted her glass. "May you one day be better than me."

"Yes," Rho whispered. "What is the price? And the rules?"

"The price is that you become the best." Titania's eyes burned into hers, fever-bright although she had barely sipped her wine. "As to rules—when I lock a door, you may not enter. Other than that . . ." She shrugged. "I do not care for rules." She set her wineglass down and held out a hand to Rho. "It's not late. Come into the studio and we will listen to your Bloodstone together."

Subtle light filled the studio, making the Stones glow with rich color. Their dark music overwhelmed her, and Rho swayed, drunk on the wine and their voices. So much darkness. She struggled for breath. You could drown in this bottomless sea.

"Who taught you?" Titania walked over to lay her hand on a large smooth Stone.

"Zwaire-Bennet." Rho straightened, revived by old anger. "He sold one of my Minor Stones and said it was his." Her voice shook. "Nobody believed me when I said it was mine."

"Zwaire-Bennet is a technician." Titania's lip curled. "I would ask him to be a model," she said in a cold silky voice. "But he has nothing to offer my Stones. Our pretty boy from the crew can at least offer honest lust." She lifted an eyebrow at Rho. "Come here and tell me what I am doing."

In a daze, Rho walked up to the Stone, laid her hand on it. It wakened, responding to her empathic focus. Human love, anguish, pain, remorse . . . its layered voice swept her away. Rho trembled, caught a glimpse of a woman's glazed, dying eyes, felt tears on her cheek, pressed her lips together as grief pierced her, cradled the still, cold body of an infant in her arms. "Death," she whispered. "You have captured human death here."

"Death, yes," Titania breathed. She twisted long fingers into Rho's tangled hair, her touch sensual and hurtful. "Death is what makes you human, child. Death is your soul. Never underestimate Death. Never fear it. Now." She released Rho to touch the Stone into slumber once more. "Waken Bloodstone for me. I wish you to listen to your use of anger here. I want you to focus on the resonance, hear how it jars with the more profound notes in the Stone's song."

Rho started toward it, found herself veering toward a corner of the room. Something tugged at her—a clear pure note that wasn't dark the way that the Stone Titania had wakened was dark. This darkness had the quality of *depth*—the way a thousand layers of clear blue lacquer would create a dark surface. The Stone stood in a corner, as if it had been pushed aside. Nearly as small as a Minor, its surface was etched and pitted. It looked as if it had been burned—as if it had fallen to Earth instead of being harvested by an asteroid miner.

She faltered to a halt, drowning in a sea of faces, touch, the gleam of candlelight on tarnished silver, the chill breath of damp night on her skin. Loneliness, the Stone sang. Eternity of one. Rho stretched out a trembling hand to touch it.

"No." Titania's grip on her wrist startled her from her daze. "You may not waken it," she said coldly. "That door is locked to you."

"I . . . I'm sorry." Rho retreated a step, rubbing at the darkening bruises on her wrist. "I won't touch it."

"Make sure you do not." Titania brushed the hair back from Rho's face, full of warmth again. "Waken your Bloodstone now."

Rho did so. Nuance by nuance they picked their way through her composition, discussing each model, each whisper of emotion or sensation and its role. Yes, the anger she had layered in was too shrill. She winced at its brassy, juvenile note. But Titania made her see Bloodstone's strengths, too. "Talent," Titania said, her eyes glowing in her stark face. "This Stone will be a masterwork if you can fulfill what you have laid down." Fine beads of sweat glistened beneath the fringe of her short hair, and her whole body seemed to quiver with tension.

Her scent filled Rho's nostrils—musky but unfamiliar—pungent in a way that was spicy and almost . . . animal. It made Rho uneasy, or maybe it was the way Titania kept touching her. Hungrily.

Everything had a price, no matter what Titania might say. To be the best, she would pay.

"Listen." Titania snapped her fingers impatiently. "That note of despair you wove in—focus on it. You must isolate it if you are to temper it in your next model."

That thread was so deeply buried . . . it slipped from her focus, and Bloodstone began to slide back into slumber.

"No!" Titania's slap jolted her. Rho shrank back from the glittering rage in her eyes. "Never let go like that. If you are working with a model, the break could muddy the entire Stone." Her face was inches from Rho's, lips parted.

Her teeth had been sculpted to points and inlaid with tiny glittering diamonds. It was a popular style, but Rho recoiled, briefly envisioning a wolf's grinning fangs.

Titania turned abruptly away. "You are tired." She touched the now-sleeping Bloodstone lightly. "I work at night, so I am used to the hour." She strode across the room and opened the studio door. "There is bedding in the closet. You may sleep on the futon out here in the main room. Find whatever you need. I am going out." She closed the studio door behind Rho. "I will not be back until very late." Titania took a black real-leather jacket from the closet and swept out the door. "You need not wait up for me."

That last sentence had the sound of an order. Rho listened to the door lock click behind Titania. Slowly she crossed the room and touched the palm-plate. The door didn't open. Neither did the studio door when she tried that. Or the bedroom door. Hugging herself although the room was warm, she retrieved the bottle of wine from the kitchen counter. The closet shelf yielded a pillow as well as a crimson velvet comforter. Wrapping herself in the comforter, she settled onto the futon to wait for Titania to return. Drinking from the bottle, she wondered how high the price was going to be.

She woke to darkness and disorientation. The sound that had wakened her came again, a thin, hopeless cry that raised the hair on the back of her neck. Blinking, she struggled onto one elbow, knocking over the empty wine bottle beside her as memory returned. Light glowed beneath the studio door, and she thought she heard a faint moan from within. She struggled to get up, to speak, but her body refused to obey. I didn't drink that much, she thought in confusion, but already she was sinking back into smothering dreams.

Rho woke late and with a headache. She stumbled into the kitchen and got coffee from the kitchen-wall beverage dispenser. The single window-wall that opened onto the arcology's garden core admitted only a soft jungle twilight. As Rho folded the comforter and picked up the empty wine bottle, her eyes returned again and again to the studio door. Dream, she told herself. Caused by the wine and the Stones' dark voices. The apartment felt cramped, suffocatingly small, and she yearned to run along the city waterfront, or stroll down the sidewalk eating crab rolls purchased from a street vendor. Titania's bedroom door was closed. She didn't even check to see if it was locked.

Someone knocked on the main door about noon. "Who's there?" Rho asked, glancing at the closed bedroom door.

"I'm supposed to come model." The door-mounted security screen showed her a woman with purple hair and a hooker's dramatic dress. "For somebody named Rho. Weird name." She took a small inhaler from her pocket, stuck it into one nostril. "So you gonna let me in?"

Rho touched the palm-plate. This time the door opened. She stared at the small, skinny woman, half tempted to walk past her and take the elevator down.

Bloodstone was in the studio. And Titania Drovnika, whatever her appetites and weirdnesses might turn out to be, was the best.

For now.

"Come in. What's your name?" Rho closed the door behind her.

"Celadon." The woman followed Rho to the studio door, inventorying the room with a few sharp glances. "What do I do, huh? You gonna give me chemicals?" she asked hopefully.

Despair. It rolled from her like the chill from an iceberg. It was what they had talked about last night—the kind of addition that would strengthen the thin anger she had layered into Bloodstone. "I'll give you something to relax you, yes." Rho said, and palmed the studio door with absolute confidence. It opened, just as the front door had, and Rho ushered the woman inside.

The sedative she used on her models relaxed the woman almost to unconsciousness. She sat loose-limbed on the floor, head tilted back against the Stone, mumbling answers to Rho's gentle questions about her life.

And Bloodstone drank her despair.


When the woman left, the door locked behind her. Fancy programming, Rho decided, but she didn't care. She returned to the studio, woke Bloodstone and listened to her Stone's new voice.

It was good.

The small ugly Stone in the corner poured quiet power into the atmosphere, disturbing Rho, tugging at her. She got to her feet and stood over it, staring down at the ugly pitted surface, her head full of that rich dark sense of *time*. She stretched out her hand, her fingertips almost brushing it. Then she took her hand away and went over to listen to Bloodstone again and marvel at how much the hooker's despair had increased its power.

When Titania woke in the early hours of the evening, she listened to

Bloodstone also, and approved. And then she showed Rho how she could have added even more strength and complexity than she had done. "I know another good model," she said as she wakened Remembrance. "I'll send him up to you. Now tell me what I did here."

Thin fragile notes of pain and fear segued into a fading echo of ecstasy and sorrow. The new addition strengthened Remembrance Stone, but Rho shivered, remembering the sounds that had waked her. She raised her head, found Titania's eyes on her face. "He's dying." She held Titania's eyes, found neither confirmation nor denial in those black depths. "It counterpoints the emotional harmonies of your main theme. It added . . . a lot," she said softly.

For a long moment Titania regarded her silently. Then she nodded. "I think you may become the best." Her smile revealed the tips of her diamond-studded teeth. "Except for me, of course." She leaned forward and kissed Rho slowly, sensuously, on the mouth.

For an instant Rho stiffened. Titania's strange scent made her want to recoil, but her muscles refused to obey her. She closed her eyes and shivered as Titania's long fingers curled across the nape of her neck.

"You have three visitors," the door security system announced.

Titania straightened with a jerk. "Models." She gave Rho a quick brooding glance. "Which is a good thing," she said and strode out of the room.

Rho looked after her, shaken by the sense that she had just been saved . . . from what?

In the main room, a man shepherded a pair of young girls through the door. He had the facial twitching of someone who had used illegal neurotransmitters once too often. Rho eyed the two girls uneasily. Asian blood gave them tilted dark eyes, but their skin was darker than Rho's. Twelve and ten, she guessed, and suppressed a shiver of apprehension.

"He says you won't hurt us." The older of the two looked up at Titania. "But he lies like shit."

The man growled and raised a hand.

"You." Titania's voice cracked like a whip. "Wait outside." The man flinched and shuffled obediently into the hall, glowering and sullen.

"It won't hurt." Titania ushered them into the studio. "I only want you to remember." She glanced at Rho. "Tonight we will begin a new Minor Stone together."

Together. Excitement mixed with unease as Rho followed them into the studio. Minor Stones only absorbed sensual memory. Emotions weren't retained. Titania wakened a small turquoise-streaked Minor after the girls were sedated and relaxed. It was a new Stone. Titania began to query the girls about their play—chasing the feral cats in the urban alleys, stealing vegetables from the rooftop gardens, playing in illicit water tapped from a city pipe. Together they wove the moments of sensory memory—hot sun, chill water, the heady scent of overripe strawberries—onto the blank canvas of the Stone.

"Enough," Titania said at last, and they stood back to let the Stone slumber. "You may go," she said to the girls, and gave them each a cash card. "Don't tell him."

Their eyes lighted up, groggy as they still were, and they scurried out unsteadily. "You're tired," Titania said gently.

"I am." Exhaustion overwhelmed her suddenly, and Rho put a hand against the wall as she swayed. Titania leaned briefly toward her, and Rho waited for her to put her arms around her, pull her close, and finally name the price for her apprenticeship.

It would be a relief.

"Go to bed." Titania walked abruptly into the other room. "I'm going out, and I won't be back until late. Don't wait up for me."

Again, a command. Rho leaned against the studio doorway as Titania collected her coat and went out.

Hugging herself as if she were cold, Rho went into the studio. The small, old Stone in the corner beckoned her, enticing, tugging at her. *Come hear me, listen to me, I can show you secrets that she isn't willing to share . . .*

"No," she said out loud. As she turned to leave, a faint stain on the studio's soft gray carpeting in front of *Remembrance Stone* caught her eye. Rho walked over and stared down, seeing where several spots had been scrubbed from the fibers. They were faintly brown and very slightly damp.

They were the color of old blood.

From the corner, the ancient Stone mocked her. Shivering, Rho fled the studio. She slapped her hand on the main door's palm-plate, pounded on the unyielding panel when it didn't open. *Fool*, voices shrieked in her head. *You know you are a fool.*

No, no, no, she answered the voices, but they merely laughed. Finally she fled to the kitchen and opened a bottle of the pale wine. She curled up in the corner with all the lights on and drank from the bottle until she passed out.


She woke at noon with a hangover. She was on the futon, covered with the crimson comforter. It had been tucked around her lovingly, like a mother might tuck it. Rho flung it aside and scrambled to her feet. For a moment she stood swaying, wondering if she was going to throw up. Then her stomach settled, leaving her with a pounding headache. Stumbling across the floor, she looked into the studio. It was empty. There were no new stains on the carpet in front of Remembrance Stone.

Slowly, unsteadily, she went to the front door and laid her palm on the plate. The door opened. Rho blinked into the yawning emptiness of the hallway. She took a single step, halting in the doorway. If the door closed behind her, it would never reopen. She knew it as surely as if Titania had whispered it in her ear. *He's dying, isn't he?* she had asked. And she had accepted it. Because that nameless death had added so much power to Remembrance Stone.

"What *am* I?" Rho whispered.

*The best . . .* The words echoed soundlessly in her head. *You will become the best.*

Rho groaned and buried her face in her hands. Pierced by grief. For nameless man who had died in front of Remembrance?

Or for herself?

Turning, she stumbled back into the main room. The door whispered closed behind her. It didn't lock. She spent the afternoon sitting cross-legged in front of the apartment's inner wall, staring down into the green leaves of the core garden, watching the blue and yellow flicker of macaws in the leaf shadows. In the afternoon she lay back down on the futon and went to sleep. So that she would be ready for the night's work.


Their lives together fell into a pattern. They would work all night—sometimes on their own Stones, sometimes together on a Minor. Titania taught, and Rho absorbed it all, greedy for every new skill, every new understanding Titania had to offer.

She would be the best. The certainty burned like fire inside her. The best. Except for Titania.

That fire helped drive the chill away when Titania told her to sleep and took a model into the studio alone. Rho would drink the crisp white wine on those nights and try not to hear the sounds from the studio. To be the best, you did what your art required, she told herself. But sometimes the hunger seemed to be Titania's and not the Stones'. Some nights she dreamed of Titania's fingers on her neck, dreamed she lay helpless, her eyes on the glinting diamonds in Titania's wolf teeth. But when she woke, the dreams were just that. And she reveled in the new skills that Titania showed her.

The apartment door was never locked to her anymore. Neither was the studio door.

The bedroom door was never open.

One morning, just after dawn, Rho woke and stumbled into the bathroom. Titania was there, washing her shirt in the sink. Light glowed on her youthful torso, the dark aurioles of her small breasts, and on the flecks of blood that speckled her arms. The water in the basin was red. She wrung out the shirt and let the water swirl down the drain, into the recycle filters. Rho clung to the doorframe, her heart thudding in her ears, unable to tear her eyes from Titania's calm face.

"It's just blood," Titania said. The tips of her teeth glinted in the yellow light. "Go back to bed, dear. You're half asleep."

"What are you?" Rho blurted.

"A Stone sculptor." Titania bared her teeth in another smile. "Or have you given me another name?"

"You could do so much," Rho whispered, thinking of the old Stone's dark translucence. "You'd have time."

"Could I?" Titania touched her cheek with one fingertip. "I am going to bed, Rho. Goodnight."

"Will you die in the sun?" Rho asked in an ecstasy of boldness. "Does it really burn you?"

Titania paused in the doorway of her room, took a step toward Rho. "Do not listen to silly stories." Her hand shot out and her fingers closed on Rho's chin, nails digging into her flesh, forcing her to meet Titania's glittering stare. "Silly stories may betray you. You do not want that to happen," she hissed. Then she let go of Rho's chin, turned, and vanished into the bedroom. The door closed with a click behind her.

Rubbing the marks Titania's nails had left, Rho went on into the studio. The light grew slowly as morning seeped into the tower core, and the Stones seemed to glow with their own radiance. Stones. Asteroids. Vampire drinkers of the human soul. Who better to sculpt a soul? Rho asked herself and laughed, wincing at the echo of hysteria in her voice.

You could be the best forever.

For the next two nights, Titania rose and went out immediately. They didn't work together. Rho tried to stay up until she got back, but she never managed it, even though she drank no wine. It was as if Titania had laid a spell on her. She thought about hunting for the next model for Bloodstone, but she didn't. Bloodstone teetered on the brink of greatness—even she could feel it. She had to find the perfect note to push it over.

On the third night she woke in darkness, knowing without even looking at the clock that it was almost dawn. And that Titania had come back. She eased the comforter back and got up, skin ridging to goosebumps in the nighttime cool. Thick silence filled the apartment, broken only by an occasional drip from the kitchen tap.

A soft groan came from the studio. Agony or ecstasy? The hair rose on the back of Rho's neck as she tiptoed barefoot across the carpeted floor, dressed only in her sleepshirt. The studio door was partly open, lit only by the moonlight that seeped into the tower's core through the domed roof. Its colorless glow drenched Remembrance Stone and burnished Titania's powerful, naked shoulders. It shone on the body of the naked youth in her arms. She recognized his pale braid—the kid from the crew who had moved Bloodstone. Titania had wanted his lust for Remembrance. She had wanted . . . something.

He writhed in her embrace, their mouths locked together in a seemingly passionate kiss. His wrists were tied behind him, and Rho sucked in a quick breath as she realized that the dark shadows on his chest and shoulders were streaks and smears of blood. His back arched, bare feet scrabbling on the carpet. Titania bent over him, arms around him like a lover, muscles cording on her back and shoulders.

The song of his dying whispered at the edges of Rho's mind—ecstasy and pain twisted together into a brief dark climax, then fading, fading, dissolving into . . .

. . . nothing.

Titania lowered his limp body to the carpet. Tenderly, she released his bound wrists, crossed his arms on his naked chest, and reached up to stroke Remembrance's surface. Her own face was streaked with fresh blood.

Stone of death, sculpture of humanity's mortal soul.

Masterwork. Better than anything Rho could do for at least a hundred years. Or a thousand. Rho took one last look at the youth's body. She could make out the small cuts on his chest, but his throat was hidden by the curve of Titania's arm. She was staring at her Stone, her face radiant in the moonlight, without emotion.

Rho withdrew as silently as she had come. Shivering, she looked around for a weapon—any weapon—seized a paring knife from the counter. Pathetic, but she slipped it into her pocket and lay quickly down on the futon, pulling the comforter over her just as the studio door opened. She was carrying him. Rho could tell by her footsteps. She kept her eyes closed, forced herself to breathe slowly, regularly. Her heart skipped a beat as Titania paused beside the futon, and for a terrible instant she wondered if Titania could read her thoughts. Then the sculptor moved on to the door, her steps heavy and slow with her burden.

The door whispered open. Closed again. Rho leaped to her feet, pulled on a pair of tights and hurried to the door. It was locked for the first time in a long time. Again her heart skipped a beat, but there was nothing to do now except to wait. The studio door gaped open and the old pitted Stone in the corner whispered to her in a thousand voices.

Slowly, step by step, Rho crossed the room. Dark new stains showed on the carpet in front of Remembrance Stone. Come to me, the old burned Stone whispered, and its dark forever voice closed around her. Her hand trembled as it reached out. The Stone felt almost flesh-warm beneath her palm, its surface rough as scabby skin. Illusion, she told herself, but she gasped as the Stone began to waken.

Images, touch, the scent of mold and damp earth, cool water dripping musically, the dry musky scent of rodents and dead insects . . . "Remember." Titania's face shimmered against the screen of her eyelids. "Remember me? Remember me? Not too much, but you need to remember how to live . . ."

This alone was genius—to inlay an image so clearly and so independently of the rest of the Stone's layered song. Titania's face shimmered and dissolved, becoming a thousand vivid almost surreal instants: log cabins in a sere plain where men and women in heavy fur-trimmed clothes chopped wood and hoed weedy gardens. A city with onion-shaped domes and horse-drawn carriages in the crowded streets.

Ancient Russia? Rho thought vaguely. Turkey? Somewhere like that. A horse's hooves pounded, and the animal heat of its ribs burned her thighs, hot counterpoint to the icy terror that squeezed her throat. Dogs bayed death, and then she was looking at a distant forest from a stone-framed window. Cold bit her and her fingers traced paths in the frost.

Vision after vision swept over her, washing her away as waves wash across a sandy beach. How to live—how to live among those you hunt, and survive. How to be invisible, and the penalties if you were not. Her life, Rho thought dimly. Or was it *my* life . . . ? *Remember*, Titania whispered in her ears, her face wavering at the edge of vision. *Life feeds on life. All this is necessary.* Rho felt the smooth curve of a small boy's throat beneath her frozen fingers, felt the orgasmic shudders of the woman who lay dying beneath her terrible hunger. And that orgasm of dying ran through her, thawing her frozen flesh, making her come, making her laugh out loud.

"Enough." A hand grabbed her wrist, shattering the visions, spinning her away from the Stone.

Rho heard bone snap with the sound of a brittle twig breaking, felt nothing but the echoes of these wonderful terrible visions. "Life feeds on life," she whispered, her vision beginning to clear.

"I told you." With almost casual ease, Titania flung her against the wall, so hard that Rho fell stunned to the floor. "Why did you have to pry?" Her eyes blazed. "You are so good. I could have talked to you. I could have . . . loved you." She turned her face away. "You're just another animal."

Her wrist had begun to throb with pain. Rho struggled to her knees, gasped as Titania seized her by the throat. Struggling to breathe, she stared into the black-pit eyes inches from her own. "I want to . . . be the best. So do it." She turned her face aside, exposing her throat. "Make me one of you," she gasped. "I need forever. I need to be what you are." She sagged in Titania's grip, her vision tunneling. "Do it," she cried.

Titania let go of her and Rho fell to the floor. "I told you that silly stories would get you in trouble." She laughed softly, bitterly. "What do you think? That there is a secret society of immortals? Blood-sucking demigods? One bite and you get your union card?" She knelt beside Rho and pressed her thumbs lightly against the veins in Rho's throat, filling her head with instant pressure. "There is only *me*. And I don't know what I am, because before I found the Stone I forgot. *You* experienced it. Didn't you understand?"

"No," Rho croaked. Death whispered from the blackness at the edge of her vision. She struggled, but Titania was so strong. "Don't," she sighed with the last of her consciousness. "I am so close . . . don't . . . end it now."

The pressure on her throat eased slightly. "I have killed hundreds of people," Titania whispered. "Probably thousands. Sometimes they plead for life. And sometimes it is death they ask for. If you are not terrified by death, you are obsessed with it." She stroked Rho's face gently, but her face was utterly cold. "I understand neither response. I am not one of you, ransomed from Death. I am . . . other. And I am . . . the only one."

"Yes," Rho sighed. "I . . . heard it . . . in your Stones." And now she understood. "How can that be?"

"Do you know how many times I have asked myself that question?" Titania's fingers tightened briefly on Rho's throat. "I have screamed it until my throat bled. You are insane."

"I . . . I'm sorry," Rho gasped as the killing pressure relaxed.

"I have searched the entire globe." Titania's face was devoid of emotion. "I have had all of your history to do it."

"All . . . of it?"

"Most of what matters." Titania shrugged impatiently. "I forgot much —until I found the Stone—" Her face softened as she turned to look at it. "One day, in the middle of the Mongolian plain, I found it. It had fallen to Earth a generation before. A primitive tribe used it as an altar. It spoke to me of blood and death and pain and I was intrigued." Her smile was not at all human. "It took me six months to kill them all. I was not hungry for that time, although they almost killed me. Later, I recognized the first Stone that was sent down by the asteroid miners."

Rho shuddered.

"Put your blood-drinking fairy-tales out of your head." Titania looked as if she wanted to spit. "Would you drink the blood of a cow?" She looked at the stained carpet. "Sometimes I need pain, but I take life bloodlessly. As you may yet find out." Her grin was a wolf's grin again. "Only you have ever come close to understanding what it is that I put into my Stones. Only you." She touched Rho's face again. "My models feel themselves dying, and that is a dark energy of its own. Almost . . . I wish that I could experience it. Death."

"You . . . can be killed?"

"I do not think that I can die." Her brooding gaze fastened on Rho's face. "Do you know why I didn't kill you just now?"

Rho shook her head, chill walking up her spine.

"You didn't plead for life or for death. You pleaded to become the best." For a moment a wistful look filled her face, vanishing almost instantly. "I cannot talk to an animal, I cannot love one. But I could talk to another artist. You . . . could have been that one. But I have not lived here for four thousand years without learning caution, animal." Titania's eyes were small holes into the emptiness between the stars. "You are a risk to me."

"No." Rho stared up into her face, found no hope there. "I want to be what you are," she whispered. "I would never give you away. I only want to be the best."

"And you will never be as good as I because you do not have the time to mature your skill. You pass so quickly." A spasm of pain crossed Titania's face as she reached for Rho. "One day you will realize that you will never equal me, and then you may try to destroy me."

"No," Rho whispered, and put her good arm around Titania's neck, hiding her desperation. "I love you," she whispered, and kissed her. She felt Titania flinch, then her arms tightened around Rho.

"I could have loved you," Titania picked her up as easily as if Rho were a child. "Or perhaps not. Perhaps in my loneliness I delude myself."

Rho nearly cried out with the pain in her wrist, helpless in that powerful embrace. She gasped as Titania pressed her back against Remembrance Stone's frozen flesh. "I can still love you," she whispered as the Stone began to wake. "If you kill me you will be alone again. Forever."

And for an instant, Titania's face filled with pain. "No," she whispered, and her grip relaxed. "I cannot . . ."

With a sob, Rho snatched the paring knife from her pocket and drove it into Titania's face.

With only the slightest resistance it penetrated softness, plunged deep. Titania gave a single shivering cry, her body spasming violently. Rho crumpled to the floor with a cry.

The plastic handle of the knife jutted from Titania's left eye. Tears and blood gleamed on her cheek and for a moment she stared at the Stone, her hands twitching. Then she fell forward, arms going around Remembrance so that the Stone rocked precariously on its base. Slowly she slid to the floor, shuddered once, and lay still.

For a moment nothing happened. Then she burst into flames. The yellow tongues licked the ceiling and the heat scorched Rho. She rolled desperately away from the conflagration, slapping out the small flames that had already caught on her clothing. Staggering to her feet, she ran. Already the fire alarm was going off and the door popped open as all the electronic locks were disarmed. She stumbled down the tower stairs and out into the street where she collapsed in the blessed dawn as the first of the firecopters dropped from the sky.

The Stones weren't damaged by the fire. The streaks of soot were easily removed. There was no sign of a body in the ruins of the studio. The police searched carefully. They filed a recommendation against Rho for therapy at a public clinic. They would have liked to file an arson charge, too, but they could find no evidence of that, either. Finally they went away.

Rho dutifully went to the clinic and agreed with the technician that she was suffering from abandonment delusions after a breakup with her artist lover. No one came to claim Remembrance or any of Titania's other Stones. Sitting in the small sunlit apartment she had bought with the proceeds from her first showing of Bloodstone, Rho listened to the old Stone's whispering voice and shivered at the thousand years of utter loneliness embedded in it. Drinker of human souls. Diary of forever.

It was . . . waiting. For Titania to waken it.

Rho was the best. *The* best. Titania had been right about Rho, in the end. And some nights found herself lying awake, listening to the old Stone's voice and waiting, too.

Because only one of them could be the best.

# THE POROSITY OF SOULS

*Terry Campbell*

Maria gazed up at the finely crafted piece of statuary standing among the many tombstones that dotted the rolling hills of Mount Zion Cemetery. She had never seen anything quite like it. The statue depicted a young boy of perhaps ten years of age collapsed across the stone that bore the information of one person's forgotten existence on earth. The artistry was exquisite, from the torture and pain in the boy's eyes and the total exhaustion portrayed by his slumping posture, to the beautiful pink hue of the material from which it was fashioned. Maria could not tell if the piece had been molded or carved, but the obvious beauty of the stone and the intricate detail led her to believe that it was a one-of-a-kind sculpture, and not a replica cast and mass produced. Maria stepped back to further drink in the statue's beauty, pausing to pull her coat tighter to her body in an effort to shut out the chilly winter winds, and made up her mind; she wanted something like this for her grandmother's grave.

The purpose of visiting her grandmother Natalie's grave was what had brought Maria to Mount Zion in the first place. Natalie Salboni had passed away six years earlier and, until today, Maria had not visited her gravesite. She had attended her grandmother's funeral, but at the time, Maria could not bear to see her laid to rest in the cold, hard earth.

Maria knelt at the base of the statue. The words on the stone were worn, but she could see that the occupant of the grave had died in 1889. She rose and inspected the statue front and back, hoping to find the artist's signature. But if it had been there, it had worn off long ago. It did not matter; the sculptor would certainly be dead by now.

The sound of a car door closing drew Maria's attention away from the tombstone. Toward the front of the cemetery, a man was entering the grounds office. Perhaps the man would know more about the artist who created the statue. It was such a beautiful piece of work, surely visitors had inquired about it on more than one occasion.

Maria took a final look at the magnificent sculpture and turned, crunching piles of brilliantly colored leaves under her feet as she made her way toward the office.

The man in the office had been very helpful. Evidently, the creator of the statue that had initially caught Maria's eye had passed his talent and expertise on to his son. According to the cemetery director, statues such as the one at Mount Zion were still being crafted by a man who resided in upstate New York, not far at all from Mount Zion.

Maria steered her Mitsubishi Eclipse into the parking lot and stopped under a sign that read Rose Hill Cemetery. There were more of the family's works of art here.

Maria stepped from the car, inhaling the fresh aroma of fallen autumn leaves, and peered through the cemetery's wrought-iron fence. She could already see several of the pink-hued creations sticking up among the many moss-covered, nondescript markers. Excitedly, Maria pushed open the rusted gate and walked quickly to the nearest statue.

It almost made her weep. The statue depicted a sleeping infant curled up in a blanket atop a bed of roses. She could not see the eyes, but the overall visage, as it did in the piece at Mount Zion, seemed incredibly lifelike. The child interred in the grave had died in 1976. This piece was evidently the work of the original artist's offspring. But the style and attention to detail was as evident here as it had been in the other statue. Either the original sculptor was an excellent teacher, or his child an apt pupil. Nothing had been lost in the transference of knowledge and talent.

Maria inspected the other statues in the cemetery. It was easy to spot them; they all had the same pink coloring. There were a total of six statues in the graveyard, each one as breathtakingly unique as the one before.

Maria thought of her grandmother's small, square marker, blending in with all the other nameless, faceless tombstones at Mount Zion, with nothing to set it apart, nothing to show that she was remembered. Maria wiped tears from her cheeks. Whatever the cost, her grandmother would have one of these beautiful works of art on her grave.

Maria nervously picked up the telephone and looked down once again at the business card the man at Mount Zion Cemetery had given her. The card bore the artist's name, Letharius, the words *Cemetery Art and Monuments*, and an address and phone number.

Maria glanced at the clock above her dining room table. Her errands had taken longer than she had anticipated. At eleven o'clock, it was likely this man was already in bed. But she had had no luck in attempting to reach him earlier in the day, and her many attempts at contacting him during the past week had gone unrewarded as well.

Maria had checked her financial situation and figured that she could afford whatever the statue would cost. With the obvious effort and sheer blood, sweat, and tears that went into this man's creations, she was expecting the price to hover around the five-grand mark. She assumed the payment would be half up front, the rest on completion and acceptance of the final product.

Maria glanced at the clock once again and dialed. She was surprised to hear the other end picked up on the second ring.

"Hello?" a deep, groggy-sounding voice answered.

Stunned at the quick response, Maria was momentarily silenced.

"Hello?" the voice repeated.

"Hello, hi," Maria finally answered. "I hope I didn't wake you."

"No, I was working," Letharius said.

"Working? At this hour?"

The man chuckled, a deep, throaty laugh that seemed to rattle the receiver. "I always work at night. And you are?"

"Oh, I beg your pardon. My name is Maria. I picked up one of your business cards at a cemetery about twenty miles from where I live. I saw some of your works and was very impressed."

"Thank you. That's very nice."

"Well, you do excellent work. In fact, I'd like to commission you to create a piece for my grandmother's grave."

There was a pause. "Are you certain?" Letharius asked.

"Yes. Well, at least I'm certain I want to check on it. You know, prices and all."

"My prices vary greatly, depending on the size and subject matter. What were you envisioning?"

"Well, I was thinking a girl about my age. Mid-twenties or so."

"Okay, that gives me an idea. But I'm not sure I can create a piece at the moment."

"What do you mean?"

"The materials I use can be difficult to obtain. I must make certain they are available."

"I understand," Maria said.

"I tell you what, Miss . . ."

"Balroni. Maria Balroni, call me Maria."

"Maria, where is your grandmother resting?"

"At Mount Zion, just outside of Black River," Maria said.

"Yes, I know where that is. Meet me there two days from now around midnight—"

"Midnight?" Maria interrupted. "You mean, in the dark? In a graveyard?"

"I always work at night."

Maria sighed. "Can't I meet you at your studio, or a coffee shop maybe? Anywhere but a graveyard."

He laughed again. "It's all right, Maria. I just want to see your grandmother's grave so I can get an idea of what will be needed."

Maria sighed. "Okay, I'll meet you there."

She hung up the phone and stared at it for a long moment. A *midnight rendezvous with a total stranger in a graveyard*. What in the hell was she thinking?


Maria pulled into the Mount Zion Cemetery and parked her car next to a black Jeep Cherokee. She assumed the vehicle belonged to the sculptor. *No, it belongs to graverobbers, and you're going to stumble across them and they're going to throw you in an empty grave and bury you alive*. Stop it, she told herself. Maria opened the car door and stepped into the frigid night air. It was very cold, but at least the wind was still. Maria closed the door and peered into the dark cemetery.

"You're a damned fool," she whispered to herself.

Not only were there carjackings, gang warfare, whatever else New York had to offer, but there was a report on the radio of a young woman being abducted a few days earlier.

But this guy was okay. Letharius was an artist, and Maria had dated enough artists in her day to know they could be an idiosyncratic lot. They had their own unique personalities, their weird little ways of doing things, and this guy just liked to conduct business in a cemetery. That wasn't so odd actually, considering the type of art he did. It was his choice of working hours that was strange.

Maria paused to push open the swinging gate, noticing the unclasped padlock hanging from a chain. The light emanating from the offices faded as she moved farther into the cemetery, and Maria switched on her small flashlight. The beam illuminated the frame of a man standing in front of the statue of the little boy. Maria approached him.

It was evident that this artist was a third-generation talent, for he was young, not much older than she. Maria shined the light across his face as he turned to greet her. He was tall and thin, and the combination of the weak light and his black attire made him appear extremely pale. His hair was long, black and shiny; a crucifix earring dangled from his left lobe. And his eyes—was it a trick of the light?—were pale violet. Maria had never seen anything like them. *Hypnotic,* she mused.

"Maria Balroni?" he said in his deep voice.

Maria extended her hand. "You must be Letharius."

He took her hand, and Maria was surprised at how cold his fingers were. He must've been waiting for a while.

"You have a key to the front gate," she said.

"I have a key to all the cemeteries that contain my work. I insist they be locked up at night. I don't want my creations vandalized."

Letharius turned and redirected his attention to the statue.

"It's a beautiful piece of work," she said.

"Yes, I'd almost forgotten it. One of my finest weepers."

"You mean your grandfather's," she corrected.

He looked at her momentarily, then turned back to the statue. "Yes, my grandfather's." His voice was distant, detached.

"Do you want to see my grandmother's grave?" she asked.

"Yes, of course. That's why we're here."

Maria turned and led the artist toward her grandmother's final resting spot. Letharius seemed nice enough. A bit distracted, a little morbid perhaps, but that was to be expected in his line of work. He was certainly nothing to be feared, and was even attractive in a tragic, Gothic sort of way. What did they call those kids obsessed by death? Deathers?

Maria stopped in front of the woefully small marker at her grandmother's grave. "Well, this is it. Not much to look at, is it?"

"Every tombstone is special in its own way. Every one is marked by great sadness. Stone is porous, much like the human soul."

"You're speaking metaphorically, right?"

"A sponge is lifeless, yet it absorbs that which it contacts. The soul absorbs emotions in much the same way. But, unlike a sponge, it cannot be wrung out, it cannot be cleansed of the dirt and filth it acquires. It keeps it forever. A tombstone absorbs the sadness that it witnesses, the tragedy that surrounds it, and holds it for all of eternity. It's sad for me to remove an original, even for the sake of my work." His eyes scanned the cemetery, following the flashlight beam that sliced through the black night. "There is much history in a tombstone."

"It doesn't do much for me," Maria said. "That's why I want you to make a better one."

"A young woman, you said. Correct?" Letharius said.

"Yeah, about my age."

"A weeper?"

"Yes, very sad. I want it to move people," she said.

"Okay, I believe I have the correct materials at hand. I can start tomorrow. How does that sound?"

"Sounds great," Maria said. "I'm sure you'll do a wonderful job."

"Indeed," Letharius said. He turned to face her. His eyes still shone brightly even in the cloaking darkness; it was as if there were light behind them. "But Maria, I must ask you. Is this really what you want? Do you really want to disturb your grandmother's surroundings? To take away from the unique originality of her grave?"

"You're not much of a salesman, are you? If I didn't know any better, I'd think you were trying to talk me out of it."

"No," Letharius said. He looked back at the statue of the little boy. "I must create again. I need to create. It's just that sometimes it troubles me so. I just want you to be sure."

"Yeah," Maria said. She wasn't sure what he meant by that, but she didn't really care to attempt to understand an artist's mind. "Yeah, I'm sure."

Maria pulled her scarf closer to her chin and returned her hands to her coat pockets. The smell of sour dirt, an acrid odor of decay and earth long denied the light of day, found her senses. A new grave had been dug since her last visit; perhaps tomorrow the tombstones of Mount Zion would have a new round of emotions to absorb. Maria turned her attention from the freshly dug grave to the glorious work of art that now graced her grandmother's grave. Letharius had done a wonderful job. The piece had turned out greater than she expected.

The young woman, clad in a long, flowing gown, leaned across the new tombstone, her head turned skyward, one hand resting on the marker, the other on her forehead. Her hair fell across part of the tombstone, skillfully done in a type of bas-relief so that it appeared her hair blew in the wind, the strands cleverly dissecting the dates carved into the pink stone. It was so real, so disturbingly lifelike. As with the boy's statue, there was great suffering portrayed in the eyes. It was as if the woman felt the very sadness Maria had experienced when her grandmother passed away, that she was *still* feeling the pain and sorrow. Letharius had captured that essence, the despair of that day, perfectly. The thought saddened Maria. It was an incredibly powerful piece.

Now, when people visited Mount Zion Cemetery to pay a brief visit to deceased loved ones, they would not pass over the grave of Natalie Salboni.

They would stop, they would know the woman existed, they would know she was loved, and they would be moved by the artistry of a man named Letharius.


Maria knocked on the door of Letharius's studio. Winter moths swarmed around her head, drawn to the light hanging to the side. Maria listened as the sound of heavy boots on hardwood flooring drifted to her ears. Tumblers clicked loudly in the silence, and the door swung open.

It was only the second time Maria saw Letharius, and the first time under adequate lighting. He stood before her, streaks of drying, reddish mud gracing his bare, hairless chest. His long hair fell across his shoulders, and once again, Maria was taken aback by his violet eyes.

"Maria, what a surprise," Letharius said. "Come in, please."

"Thank you," Maria said, stepping into the warmth of his studio-apartment. The pleasing aroma of wet clay greeted her, and she paused to remove her coat. Letharius took it and draped the garment over a hardback chair near the door.

"You saw my creation?" he asked.

"Yes," Maria answered. "Earlier today."

"And?"

"What can I say? It was perfect. Incredibly beautiful. Even more so than I imagined."

"I'm pleased you liked it."

"I never doubted that I would. I've come to pay my balance."

"Ah, a prompt payer of debts," Letharius said. "I like that." It was the closest thing to a sense of humor he had yet to display. "Can I get you a drink?"

"Please, anything warm," Maria said, her body still numbed by the northeast winter.

"Coffee?"

Maria nodded and watched as Letharius moved with the grace of a cat across the floor of the one room apartment. A refrigerator, stove, and sink in one corner served as a kitchen. There was a large addition built outward from the kitchen which Maria assumed housed the massive kiln needed to fire Letharius's creations. A bed and one bookcase graced another corner. The rest of the spacious area was devoted to his craft. A large, splattered canvas covered what was apparently a work in progress.

Maria slowly made her way closer to the work area as Letharius busied himself preparing their drinks. He had given her a brief explanation of how he molded his creations. He used a large armature constructed of a flexible metal wire around which he molded a fire clay mixed with fine sands and certain local earths. He worked the wet clay around the armature with his delicate fingers and various detailing tools, and when the sculpture was complete, he fired it in a large kiln. The entire process fascinated Maria to no end. She was always drawn to artistic types and their creations, though she had no skills in the area herself.

Maria stopped before the large canvas tarp. Haphazard splatters of wet clay and dark splotches stained the hardwood floor around the area. A big container of wet mud sat near the covered statue, a smaller bucket of clear water next to it. She longed to see what lay beneath the tarp. Appreciating the finished product was one thing, but to view the work in progress, to see how it was created step by step would be a joy to behold.

Maria smelled the brewing coffee, heard the jangle of cups from across the apartment, and she glanced toward the sound. Letharius's back was still turned to her. She looked back at the tarp, then again at Letharius. A fold of loose canvas hung halfway between the top of the statue and the floor. She could lift it briefly, take a quick peek. Letharius would never know.

Her hand shaking, one eye watching the sculptor, Maria gripped the canvas and lifted it. What she saw baffled her. There was a smooth, finely detailed foot at the base of the sculpture, but the clay line began just above the ankle. There was a marked difference in the color and texture of the two materials utilized. If Letharius used wire armament, then she should be seeing some sort of metal below the ankle rather than a completed foot. Perhaps he molded the work in wax or plastic first, then built up the fire-clay mixture around this mold.

The creative process intrigued Maria; she had to see more. She didn't know how Letharius would react to someone viewing an unfinished work, but if he was like most artists she had met, he would not be pleased. But Maria couldn't help herself. She lifted the canvas a little more, but pulled too hard.

Maria heard a quiet moan as the canvas became heavy in her hand and the tarp slid to the floor.

"What are you doing?" Letharius shouted.

Maria screamed and stumbled backwards, knocking over a table covered with rags and small tools. The work of art in progress was not a statue, but a young girl of about twelve being covered in clay. The girl's head did not move, but Maria could see her blue, watery eyes, could see the tear roll down the girl's cheek, mixing with a streak of dried clay and turning it into pink mud.

"Maria, what have you done?" Letharius said, moving up behind her. "You are not to view a work in progress."

Maria felt as if she could not breath. She gulped dust-filled air in an attempt to regain her senses. She tried to speak, but only gasps escaped her lips. Finally, she managed to sputter, "You . . . you . . . she's not a statue . . . a little girl—"

"Maria," Letharius said, taking her arms. "Let me explain."

Maria looked into his violet eyes and for a moment was lost in their tragic depths. "No!" she screamed, jerking away. "Get away from me!"

She turned back to face Letharius. "How could you? Is this how you create all your works? My God, is this what's on my grandmother's grave now? Did you kill someone to make my grandmother's statue?"

"Maria, please," Letharius begged. "You must let me explain. I killed no one. Not really. You . . . you just don't understand. I merely offer them a choice."

"No!" Maria shouted. "I don't want to hear this! There can be no explanation for this. There can be no art in this. There is nothing beautiful or creative or artistic that ends with a little girl suffocating to death!" Maria turned and headed quickly for the front door. She grabbed her coat, reached into the pocket for the check she had written for the amount of the balance, and ripped it to shreds.

"Maria, she's not suffocating. You weren't meant to see this. But now that you have, you must let me explain."

"There's nothing to explain," Maria said, gripping the doorknob. She expected it to be locked, found it wasn't. "Goodbye, Letharius."


Maria stood before the statue that now graced her grandmother Natalie's grave, a statue that had once inspired her with its grace and beauty and tragedy. In Maria's hand was an aluminum baseball bat she carried in her car for defensive purposes if needed. Now it would be used on the offensive.

She would not go to the police. Too many questions, too much time involved. But if she destroyed the clay surrounding the dead girl that was obviously encased inside, the groundskeeper would find what lay beneath the next morning, and then the police would certainly become involved.

Maria brought the bat over her head and wept. How had all this happened in such a short time? She had wanted something unique and beautiful to grace her grandmother's grave, but she had succeeded only in desecrating her final resting spot.

Maria closed her eyes and swung the bat hard, connecting with the left shoulder of the weeping girl. The clay cracked, sending tiny crevices shooting across the surface of the statue like a tiny earthquake on an alien world. Maria brought the bat down again, and again, until bits of the hardened pink clay flew through the air. Finally, she felt the bat hit something soft, heard something slump to the ground.

Maria could not bear to open her eyes and witness the gruesome sight that certainly lay before her. The girl would've been missing for several weeks now.

Maria moved, her eyes still closed, toward what she thought would be the cemetery entrance. That's when she heard something shuffling behind her.

Maria turned to see the nude woman crouched over her grandmother's grave, the moon shining alabaster across her bare back, her feet crunching broken bits of clay. The girl's head turned upward, looking at Maria with an intense gaze.

*No, that's impossible,* Maria's frightened mind rationalized. *She's been in there at least two weeks. It can't be.*

Her gaze locked into the girl's violet eyes, just as vivid as Letharius's, and the freed woman's lips curled into a grinning sneer, revealing white, sharpened fangs. The girl hissed loudly once, and before Maria could even realize what was happening, pounced on her.

The woman's strength was unbelievable. Maria pounded at her cold body, but the attack was relentless. Maria could feel the girl's nails digging into her flesh, clawing and scratching. She tried to push away but was no match for her assailant. There was a cold wetness on Maria's neck a second before the terrible fangs ripped into her throat.

Maria awakened to find Letharius staring down at her. Her vision blurred around the sculptor a few moments before clearing. She was weak and very cold, but she could feel a warm stickiness on her neck. Her numb fingers went to the spot and came back bloody. It was then that Maria remembered the night's events.

Letharius took Maria's ravaged body in his arms. "Maria, dear, sweet child. Why did you have to do it? Why didn't you let me explain?"

Maria looked up at him, and in the frigid cold of the night air, realized something about Letharius that she should've noticed on their first meeting: his breath created no steam in the chilly air.

"What are you?" she asked weakly.

Letharius held her gently in his arms. "I am a vampire."

"B-b-but the girl—" Maria stuttered.

"A vampire as well," he said. "One of my victims."

Maria coughed and spat. She tasted copper in her mouth. "I . . . I don't understand."

"I did murder the girl, Maria. This girl, the one in my apartment, the boy many years ago. I am a vampire, an immortal, an undead.

"I don't enjoy killing innocent people, Maria, but I must if I am to exist. I must drink the blood of my victims, or die."

Maria looked up into Letharius's violet eyes, so full of sadness and tragedy. She reached out and touched his pale cheek.

"I live with what I do every day. It's a curse. But do you know what's worse than the killing?" Maria slowly shook her head. "It's having to live with the fact that with each victim I take, I create another such as myself. I force the tragedy that is being a vampire upon others. If they were to just die and cease to exist, then perhaps over the centuries, one could grow accustomed to the bloodshed. But no, I must turn them into me. I must make them hunt, make them take human lives, make them feel the guilt of murder, and the guilt of creating others such as themselves. It's a never-ending cycle."

"But . . . the statues," Maria choked.

"That's what I wanted to tell you in my studio. The offer I make toward my victims. The statues, all of them, were created by me, throughout centuries. Encasing their souls in a mixture of fire clay, sand, and their own native soil, combined with their blood, puts them in a state of suspended animation, where they remain alive and undead, but incapable of murder, for all of eternity."

He looked down at Maria, stroking her dark hair in his porcelain-smooth fingers. "You are dying, Maria. Angela chose to be contained in her own soil. I always thought my victims could feel no pain, no emotions. But Angela still hungered, I suppose. I don't know, maybe the pain is worse that way. She is the only one who has been freed after being suspended. Perhaps the confinement, the anguish of the hunger consumed her. When you freed her, she attacked.

"Don't you see, Maria? I'm not really an artist. I'm a judge, jury, and executioner . . . and I'm also the criminal. But most of all, I try to be a savior. I try to help as best I can in a terrible situation. It may be wrong, but it must be one way or the other. Either way, I lose."

"What will happen to me after I die?" Maria asked, her voice weakening.

"In a week, you will rise," he said. "And then you will have a choice to make."

Dark storm clouds rolled overhead. A few flurries began to waft in and out of the bare branches of the graveyard trees. Brittle leaves chased one another in the cold wind, crashing into and bouncing off tombstones. The air grew colder, the snow fell harder.

Maria looked out across the cemetery, her view limited only to what she could see directly in front of her. Tombstones, scraggly trees, a barren landscape. *Sadness.* Letharius was wrong. She *could* feel; she *could* hurt. Her eyes cried, but no tears fell forth. She hungered for sustenance, but her pangs went unanswered. Passing in front of Maria's vision, an elderly man shuffled toward his car through the light dusting of snow. Perhaps, if the weather were not so frightful, he would stay longer. Perhaps he would pass by her. Perhaps he would revel in her beauty, and the exquisite craftsmanship evident in her creation, and maybe he would inquire as to where he could commission such a stunning piece of art to adorn his loved one's final resting place.

Perhaps, if the weather weren't so terrible.

But it was, and the elderly gentleman started his car's engine and drove away, leaving Maria alone in the barren land of death and sadness.

She could feel the pain. She could feel the hunger. She could feel the anguish.

And in a state of porosity unmatched by even the most absorbant sponge, a tiny crack formed in her soul, and the sadness, the loneliness, and the terrible, bitter cold began to seep in.

# CUT FROM THE HERD

*Gregory Nicoll*

"That was a little too bloody for me," said Susan, setting down the knife.

Alice raised her glass to her lips and sipped the dark red liquid slowly. "The wine's excellent, though. I haven't had any this good since the reception on the night the Finster exhibit opened."

Susan motioned for a waiter. "You and your damn art. Oh—please forgive me, Alice, but I just *know* if you'd stuck it out another couple years with the company it would've been *you* sitting here with the gold card, about to pick up the tab."

Alice shrugged. It was late and they were the only diners left in the warm little downtown restaurant. The honey-scented candle in the crystal bowl had almost burned itself out. "I don't regret it," she said quietly, finishing her wine. "I'm happy, Sue. I know that's hard for you to accept, but I *am.* Besides, remember I sold two of my pieces last year. Who knows? Maybe in another year or so it'll be *me* buying the steaks."

The waiter presented them with a brown leather portfolio branded with Dante's logo. The end of the check protruded from its edge like a dead white tongue. Susan crowned it with her AmEx card, and the waiter vanished.

She leaned forward and raised an eyebrow at Alice. "Listen, I've got a stock option meeting in the morning at eight, so we'll have to continue this argument another time." She paused, letting out a short breath. "Alice, I want you to think about something. How much did you really earn from those two little chiseled slabs you sold? And another thing—just think about how *long* it took you to produce them. How many of those things *could* you produce, even if you had the orders?"

Alice shook her head. "Art doesn't work like that, Sue. It's not like the company—you don't have *orders* for your work. And you don't *produce* it like some assembly-line product. You create it. At your own pace. Over time."

"Well, you know what I mean, Alice. It's just—oh, never mind. But tell

170

me this, how many have you, uh, *created* lately? It's been a while since you've talked about any new projects . . ."

Alice shrugged. "Art's like that. Sometimes the Muse is with you, sometimes she's busy inspiring somebody else."

They walked together out to the parking lot, the restaurant door snapping locked behind them. It had rained briefly while they were inside, and the cool dark pavement now glistened. The air had the watery smell of heavy humidity. Scattered lights from the windows of the tall, silent skyscrapers reflected in puddled rainwater.

Alice had arrived early that evening, parking her white VW Rabbit only a few spaces from the door. Susan had been late leaving the office. Her four-door Lexus was a dim silhouette in the distance.

The security lights winked off, casting the entire lot in shadows.

"Didn't realize how late it was," Sue whispered.

"Get in," Alice offered. "I'll drive you over there."

Sue climbed into the little car, shaking her head as she appraised it. She settled awkwardly on its torn vinyl seat, wincing as Alice fired up its noisy diesel engine. "How can you stand this thing?"

Alice smiled. "It's practical. Only cost me sixteen hundred bucks—and gets forty-eight miles to the gallon."

Its tiny engine rattling, the Rabbit chugged across the lot and rolled up alongside Sue's long, sleek import. The rain and the dim light made the new car shine like a jewel.

Sue smiled. "I ordered this one in the same color as my AmEx card." Her smile wilted. "Uh-oh! *Christ!* Back there in the restaurant I signed the tab—but they didn't return my card."

Alice turned and glanced back at Dante's door. "The inside lights just went off. Better drop back in the morning to pick it up."

Susan nodded. "When I get home to the condo, I'll call them. There's got to be a supervisor in there, somebody doing their books. It's a shame I haven't had my car phone installed yet."

She climbed out, brushed her skirt, and waved as she slammed the Rabbit's door.

The diesel rattled impatiently while Alice waited for Sue to fumble for her keys and get into the Lexus. Only when Susan switched on her car's headlights did Alice wave and accelerate slowly away.

Alice pulled out on the street and started south toward the warehouse district. At the intersection she glanced back in her rearview mirror.

The headlights of Sue's car were moving up behind her, but suddenly they swerved and cut a wide U-turn in the center of the street. Red taillights glowed as the gold sedan glided back toward the restaurant.

Alice let out a short breath. *She's going back for that damn card . . .
doesn't she have any idea how dangerous this part of town can be at night?*
Alice remembered hearing on the radio about the cops finding another
victim of the Midtown Butcher, some local sicko who was making Jack the
Ripper look like Doogie Howser, M.D.

She turned her Rabbit around and set off after Susan. Alice was almost
all the way back to Dante's lot when her car listed to one side, the steering
wheel turning with a mind of its own. Alice let the car pull itself to the side
of the dark avenue, coasting to stop in a pool of yellow streetlight glare.

*Great . . . now I'm worse off than Sue . . .*

She got out of the Rabbit and glowered at the bald, flat tire. *Shit . . .
and me running without a spare . . .*

She locked the door and began walking briskly back toward Dante's. *If I
can just catch Sue while she's still there . . .*

Susan's Lexus was pulled up to the front of the restaurant, its driver's
door hanging open. But its lights were off—and there was no sign of Susan
anywhere nearby.

Puzzled, Alice walked up to the car. She felt her pulse quickening, and
her mouth was dry. "Sue? Where are you? *Sue?*"

Then it came to her. *Of course—she's still inside Dante's, getting that
damn card back.*

Alice slipped into the Lexus, settling comfortably into the front passen-
ger seat to wait. She noticed its key protruding from the ignition switch, a
gold chain joining it to the keys of Sue's office, condo, and safe-deposit
box. The car smelled of leather and marbled walnut, its seats like fine
recliners. She leaned back.

*I can get the Rabbit fixed tomorrow . . . let Sue drive me home to-
night . . .*

*Where the hell is she?*

She looked at the dashboard clock, watching the seconds tick by slowly.
*How long does it take to get back a credit card around here?*

*Sure hope she's all right . . .*

There was a sound from the alley beside Dante's—a thump of metal on
concrete. Then a muffled shout. And another.

Something metal rattled again, and a sharp *smack* cut the air.

Alice eased herself slowly out of the car, leaving the door open. She
made her way around to the side of the restaurant, grateful for the silence
of her soft-soled shoes. Her pulse quickened, her heart surging in her chest.

Behind a discreet wooden stockade was the huge garbage dumpster. In
the dark beyond it, something moved.

Alice slipped up alongside the dumpster, blending herself with its shadow. The stink of the restaurant's moldering discards was overwhelming. The thought crossed her mind briefly that she'd probably never think of Dante's in quite the same way again.

The alley yawned open before her.

There were five of them—big cowboys dressed entirely in black like Zorro, their entire faces masked. A row of five weird, sleek black motorcycles lined the alley wall. One of these machines had somehow fallen on its side—probably accounting for some of the noise Alice had heard. The dark men moved as smoothly as liquid as they gathered around Susan.

She'd been stripped naked and was now splayed out over the fallen motorcycle. Her ankles were lashed to the rear wheel, her wrists secured to the spokes of the front one. Her breasts had not flattened, her implants clearly showing.

The dark man knelt down between Susan's forcibly splayed legs, displaying a gleaming silver butcher knife.

"Why?" Susan whimpered. "T-tell me why—"

His dark voice was deep as a canyon in hell. "Because," he said, "you're a cow."

Another voice spoke, this one identical to the first man's. "You just run with the herd. You don't produce, don't contribute anythin' useful. You're just a consumer, an overly greedy grazer in these crowded fields."

The third dark figure leaned more closely over her. "You don't make music, don't make art, don't write any words worth rememberin'."

The fourth one added, "No science. No new ideas, concepts. Nothin' original. Nothin' profound. You've got no purpose—*you just take up space.*"

The fifth reached out a black-gloved hand and ran it slowly down her hysterectomy scar. "You can't even breed."

"You're a *cow,*" repeated the one with the knife. "Not a dairy cow. Not breedin' stock. Nothin' worth keepin' alive. Just—*a cow.*" He paused, moving the knife like a pendulum back and forth across her face. "And us— we're the farmers, the harvesters. There's cowboys like us in every town 'cross the land. 'Round here, it's us five that're charged with maintainin' the herd. And tonight, your number's up."

Susan squirmed helplessly against her bonds. She gasped for breath, her lungs constricted by fear.

"You," said the man with the knife once more, "are a *cow.*"

Then each of them spoke in turn.

"And."

"We."

"Are."

"The."

"Butchers."

The man with the blade pressed it to Susan's flesh.

Alice slipped slowly, numbly, back around the dumpster. She took careful steps, again grateful for the quiet, soft soles of her shoes. Without a sound she made it back to the parking lot.

She reached the parked Lexus, released its handbrake, and moved its stick from Park to Neutral. Straining as she pushed hard against the doorsill, she felt the car begin to drift forward. When at last it reached the street, Alice hopped inside and dared to start the engine.

She drove immediately back to her loft on the southside and abandoned the car, unlocked, on the sidestreet outside the parking deck.

High above the streets in her fourteenth-floor studio, Alice flicked on the spotlights. Their hot white beams glared down at the huge block of marble.

It towered before her, a giant gray tombstone. The monolith stood on an altar of dusty canvas, a tiny part of one corner sculpted away. Otherwise the stone was as raw as the day it had been delivered—eight and a half months ago.

Alice took off her clothes and knelt down on the edge of the canvas. She held up the chisel and the mallet, a priest with wafer and wine.

Outside in the night a transit bus rumbled by, its brakes squealing. Motorcycles *bratt-bratted* in the distance.

Alice waited, trembling, hoping that her Muse, her Inspiration, would come.

And fearing and knowing that, if it did not, someday *they* would.

# ALL FLESH IS CLAY

## Don D'Ammassa

"Nikki tells me you've been stealing mud from the cemetery again." Laura Merriam poured herself a glass of wine and seated herself with exaggerated dignity in Greg Clark's favorite chair.

"Clay, not mud." He continued to work the material with his hands, not even glancing in her direction, still searching for the shape he knew existed within it. "Use artificial media and your results are shaped by the falseness. That's why we moved here, you know. Managansett has some of the best natural clay in North America. It works with you instead of against you; you can almost feel it responding. And it fires as well or better than anything you can get at Block Artists Supply."

Laura's tabby ambled in from the patio, jumped up onto her lap, butting its head against her breast, demanding attention. "All right, but why the cemetery? You could pick up as much as you want down along Scituate Road and no one would mind at all. I know for a fact that the police have been receiving complaints about vandalism in the cemetery, and if they catch you in there some night with your shovel and wheelbarrow . . ."

Greg sighed, his hands frozen in position, and he willed the muscles at the back of his neck to relax. "The texture and color are better, that's why. I'm not robbing graves, Laura, I'm just taking some clay. I know there's been some trouble, disturbed headstones and the like, but it's been going on for years. Give it a rest, will you?"

Laura switched gears easily, spoke next with genuine concern. "Not going well?"

He shrugged, gestured toward the clay. "It's a bust, I think, probably a man, judging by the size, a big man, powerful. But I just can't see the details yet. Sometimes I almost think I have it, and then something feels wrong."

She pushed the cat off her lap and leaned forward. "Looks too big for just a head."

"Well, I'll be taking a lot off once I know what's hidden there, but you're right. I think these are shoulders," he traced two symmetrical lines with his fingers, "and part of the chest will have to be modeled as well, if for no other reason than to give the composition some stability. It wouldn't do for it to fall over in the middle of a showing."

Laura laughed politely and stood up. "Well, I'll leave you to it. I just came over to remind the two of you about dinner tonight."

"We'll be there."


Greg worked for another half hour after his neighbor left, but with no more progress than before. Frustrated, he wrapped the amorphous shape with damp cloths and went upstairs to shower, rapping on his daughter's door on the way.

"Don't forget we're eating at Mrs. Merriam's tonight."

Nikki muttered something unintelligible that Greg chose to interpret as assent.

Nikki troubled him, though he was reluctant to admit it, even to himself. She'd never been a fast learner, and her graduation this past year from high school had been more an act of mercy on the part of her teachers than proof of any achievement on her part. Her guidance counselor had made noises about Nikki being "socially challenged," but Greg was undisturbed by his daughter's reluctance to date regularly. On the other hand, she had difficulty retaining even the simplest of information, and drifted off into reveries from which it often took considerable effort to rouse her. She needed focus, he believed, something that would capture her imagination completely.

As he showered, he traced shapes where the steam condensed on the walls, human heads and shoulders.


The clay remained perfectly malleable the following morning, moved obediently under his probing fingers. For the first time since he'd started, he felt a degree of confidence, drawing inspiration from a dream he'd had the night before. It was a static sort of image, but remarkably clear in his memory, a foursome for dinner, himself, Nikki, Laura Merriam, and the fourth, a man, a very big man, powerful, commanding, dominating the entire conversation without saying a word.

Greg's fingers found the forehead in the clay, smoothed the brow, worked up over the crest of the head, tracing the outline of the hair. Thick hair, straight lines, long and full. It fell to the shoulders, which were massive. He stripped clay away and discarded it to one side or the other, littering the floor of his studio with divots that slowly dried and crumbled.

Thick muscles from shoulder to the neck, a strong chin though somewhat pointed, long aquiline nose above a full, sensuous mouth that was just a bit too wide for the face. Greg hesitated, started to smooth off the corners, but that seemed wrong somehow, so he left them the way they were. The eyes then, fairly large but set close together and deeply recessed. High cheekbones but not rounded, angular. A face almost craggy, not entirely handsome but infused with raw power.

Greg stepped back only when his fingers were cramping from the exertion. Fully a quarter of the original material had been discarded now, and what remained was undeniably the bust of a man, though the features were still too rough to suggest more than an identity.

He was startled to notice that he'd worked for four straight hours.

Although he burned with the need to return to the sculpture, Greg forced himself to drive into town and complete his scheduled errands. The post office box yielded two royalty checks, three bills, and four pieces of junk mail that he discarded in the lobby trashcan. Then the dry cleaning, some groceries, and a brief stop at the hardware store for a better shovel.

Except for one bag of perishables, he left his purchases in the car when he arrived back at the house, put those away quickly, and returned to the studio. Laura's tabby was on the patio, batting at the glass door with one paw. Greg ignored the cat, instead removed the wraps from his sculpture. The clay remained soft and workable and the underlying shape seemed to have acquired more clarity during his absence.

In fact, something had definitely changed, though even to Greg's trained eye, the difference was subtle. After fifteen minutes of intense study, he decided that the lips were fuller than he'd intended, and the left side of the mouth was slightly distorted, suggesting a sneer. The angle of the eyes seemed wrong. Maybe the clay was too soft, wouldn't hold its form. He raised one hand, planning to erase the changes, but then let it drop. For some reason, it seemed inappropriate to interfere. If that was the true shape concealed in the clay, then he would liberate it, not fight it.

He spent the remainder of the afternoon working on the half torso, quitting only when the sun dropped abruptly behind the horizon.

"You shouldn't work so hard, Dad. It's not like, you know, we need the money or anything."

Greg regarded his daughter solemnly across the breakfast table. "A real artist doesn't work for the money, Nikki. He does it for the art itself."

"Oh, right," she rolled her eyes, "like you'd give it all to charity if that meant you could work in peace."

He shook his head. "No, I'm not that altruistic. But art isn't just something I do, Nikki. It's what I'm all about. It helps me to define myself, recognize who I am. I put my heart and soul into my work because in a way it's all a part of me, an extension of my mind, if not my body. Some day you'll find something you care about the same way, and then you'll understand."


There were more changes. Greg walked around the emerging bust several times, rubbing his chin thoughtfully. The mouth was more distorted than ever, the cheeks had receded, losing the fullness he'd originally given them, and the hair was longer, as though the clay had stretched. There was an odd smell as well, faint, almost undetectable, but it persisted until midmorning. It smelled like liquid copper.

But as soon as he put his hands on the clay, he knew that things were going to go well. The thick material almost seemed to anticipate his thoughts, moving of its own accord, flowing in harmony with the emerging face. Greg skipped lunch and worked on into the afternoon, stopping only when he staggered with exhaustion and his hand slipped through the clay, making a ragged line across one ear. He repaired the damage slowly and carefully, then collapsed onto the sofa.

The face had a definite personality now; the eyes seemed to positively glower across the room. The mouth, even the tilt of the chin, implied superiority and contempt. Greg decided that he didn't particularly like the man he'd found hidden in the clay, but he'd never before had a sculpture go so quickly, so easily.


When Greg entered his studio the following morning, he froze for several long minutes, then returned to the kitchen, his face as dark as that of his creation.

"Nikki! Have you been fooling around in my studio?"

She glanced up from her poached eggs, clearly startled. "What do you mean?"

"If this is some kind of joke, I don't appreciate it." His voice was barely under control, trembling with rage. "I've put my heart into this project and I won't tolerate anyone messing with it, do you understand?"

"Are you accusing me of doing something to your old statue?" Nikki pushed back her chair and glared at him. "Don't you think I have better things to do with my time than play in the mud?"

"It's not mud!" He caught his breath. "Look, maybe you just went to look and bumped into it or something and then tried to fix things. I did the same myself, as a matter of fact. Just try to be careful from now on, all right?"

He spun on his heel and left before she could answer, went to assess the damage.

The changes were too radical to explain away as problems with the consistency of the media. Both sides of the mouth were misshapen, almost as though something had been concealed within and had recently emerged. Air bubbles? No, he'd worked the clay too thoroughly to miss even one this size, let alone two. And the brow lines had been drawn together across the gap, a solid bar over the nose. The cheeks had sunk even deeper, flat planes under the high ridge. And the forehead was slanted farther forward, or perhaps the eyes had sunk deeper. The overall result was an almost canine cast to the features. This was no longer the face of a man; it was the visage of some preternatural beast.

The clay resisted his efforts, slowly hardening with exposure to the air, and it took most of the day to reclaim the lost ground. When he was satisfied that he'd done all that was necessary, Greg checked to make sure the patio door was secured, then locked the studio door when he left.

Nikki's door was closed, but she didn't answer when he knocked. Probably sulking. Greg felt a passing regret; in retrospect he'd probably accused her unjustly. Nikki lacked the talent to make the alterations he'd just reversed. Nor could he believe that someone had broken into the house just to bedevil him. It had to be some idiosyncrasy of the clay, some reaction he'd never encountered before.

He showered and lay down on his bed, falling asleep almost immediately despite the early hour.

Greg Clark's dreams were dark and crowded. It was the same as before, the four of them sitting around a small supper table, but the unknown fourth was even more dominant, his face darkly furrowed, features distorted and lupine, eyes glowing embers. Their unknown host lifted a covered pan and removed the lid with a flourish, revealing three still-beating human hearts.

Greg woke in the darkness.

It was a hot August night, the air thick and moist. They were far enough from downtown that there were no traffic noises, although in his experience, there wasn't much traffic anywhere in Managansett after ten o'clock.

A faint hint of music drifted in from somewhere in the night. Perhaps Nikki was playing her radio.

His throat was dry. Greg slid off the bed and padded barefoot out to the kitchen to get a drink. The music was louder here, a single human voice, but it wasn't coming from Nikki's room. It originated on the opposite side of the house, from his studio.

Greg moved silently through the unlit rooms.

The studio door was ajar. He slipped his hand into his pocket. The key was still there and, insofar as he knew, there existed no copy. He closed the distance carefully and peered through the opening.

There was a woman in his studio, a naked woman in fact, humming to herself. He could see her body clearly as she stood in front of the patio window, outlined against the nearly full moon. At first he thought it must be Laura Merriam. She'd lived here for years, knew the Talbots before they'd moved away. Presumably they'd given her a key for some reason and she'd never returned it. The coppery smell was back as well, stronger than ever.

But then he realized that it couldn't be Laura. His mysterious guest was considerably shorter, her figure less ample, and her hair waist-length. Laura's barely brushed her shoulders. Greg opened the door slightly, then gasped with recognition. It was his daughter.

Just as he recognized her, she moved closer to the bust, touching it with her body, wrapping her arms around the clay statue. He opened the door wide then, afraid she was going to lift it from the workbench and throw it to the floor, but instead she used the leverage to climb up onto the table-top, straddling the lump of clay, wrapping her legs around the torso.

Greg gasped out a protest. What was she trying to do? She could destroy several days of work in a moment if she wasn't careful. But Nikki neither saw nor heard him, even after he'd entered the room fully and moved to stand close enough that he could have reached out and touched her shoulder.

She was making love to the statue, rubbing her breasts and thighs over the worked clay. Dark streaks crisscrossed her body where it had touched the moist medium. Her head was thrown back in a bizarre parody of ecstasy as she raised and lowered herself rhythmically. Greg felt himself growing aroused, and shock at that discovery spurred him to move.

She reacted to his touch as though a switch had been thrown, collapsing so abruptly that he barely caught her head before it struck the floor. He carried Nikki back to her bed, assured himself that she was breathing normally, covered her with a blanket, then poured a brandy before returning to the studio to see how much damage she'd done.

The bust was back the way it had been that morning, before he'd erased all the distortions he'd discovered. The eyes seemed to be watching him thoughtfully as he paced back and forth. Experimentally he placed his hands on the clay. It was unusually moist, perhaps augmented by his daughter's perspiration. That thought was enough to send him half running from the room. The agency that allowed for such clearly nonrandom changes in the clay was something about which he chose not to think at all.

Nikki was using the garbage disposal when he entered the kitchen the following morning. She greeted him cheerfully and pointed to a full coffeepot. As far as he could tell, she had no recollection of the events of the preceding evening, and Greg couldn't imagine how he could ever bring the subject up. But something had to be done, hadn't it? Even if it was simply a complex form of sleepwalking, an expression of her unfulfilled sexual drive, it was potentially dangerous. What if she'd left the house? What if someone had seen her?

"How're you feeling this morning, honey?"

"Um, me? Fine, I guess. A little stiff and sore. Guess I slept the wrong way. You working again today, you know, on it?" She inclined her head toward the studio. Greg regarded her thoughtfully before answering.

"Maybe later. I thought I'd go up to the mall and walk around for a while. Feel like coming?"

"Nah, I'll pass, thanks. Think I'll just go get some rays down by the pond."

Greg pointedly did not unlock the studio, but on the other hand he had absolutely no desire to go to the mall without Nikki. There was something else that had just occurred to him, something he needed to do right now.

He was on his way out the door when the phone rang. It was Laura Merriam.

"Hi, Laura. What's doing?" Greg wasn't sure in what direction his relationship with their attractive, unmarried neighbor was moving, and was even less sure about his preferences in the matter. He hadn't remained celibate since his wife's death six years earlier, but neither had he ever wished for another close relationship.

"Oh, nothing much. I was wondering if you'd seen Gingham."

"Gingham? Your cat?"

"Got it in one. Seriously, is he hanging around there looking for a handout? He went outside yesterday afternoon and never came back."

"Has he been fixed?"

"No, I've been meaning to, but I just never got around to it."

"Well then, he's probably out having a very good time. He'll come back when his libido has been drained away."


Greg parked in the small lot behind the Managansett Police Station and walked into the lobby. The desk sergeant glanced up incuriously. "Can I help you, sir?"

"Is Chief Dowdell in?"

"Yes, he is, but he's quite busy today. Can someone else help you?"

"Would you just tell him that Greg Clark is here and would like a moment of his time, if possible? It's personal."

Five minutes later, he was sitting in a small office whose walls were completely covered by layers of paperwork, wanted notices, circulars, correspondence, even advertisements.

"Never had much use for filing cabinets. Out of sight, out of mind, I always say. What can I do for you, Greg?"

Greg's late father had been Dowdell's college roommate, and the two men had remained close friends up until the elder Clark died of leukemia in 1980. It was Dowdell who first told Greg about the abundance of natural clay in the area, and although the two men spoke only once or twice a year, they considered themselves friends.

"You know I live out near the cemetery?"

"Sure do. I know where pretty much everyone lives in this town. Know about your late-night requisitioning habits too." He winked.

"I understand there's been some trouble out there lately. Gravestones overturned, things like that. I was wondering if there was any, well, danger I should be aware of. Nikki wanders around there on her own sometimes."

Dowdell shrugged. "The world seems a lot less safe a place these days, although statistically I guess we're no worse off than our grandparents. If you're asking me if you should keep her out of the graveyard, I'd say no, she's as safe there as anywhere during the day. After dark, well, that's another story. You might bear that in mind yourself as well."

"What exactly is going on out there?"

Dowdell shifted his weight. "I don't exactly know. Lots of disturbed graves, but no real damage. The bodies aren't being stolen. No one's spray-painting obscenities on the burial vaults, and as far as we can tell they're not smoking pot behind the mausoleum anymore. But there's lots of little things. Like all the dead birds . . ."

Greg raised an eyebrow.

"Yeah, dead birds. I even sent one over to a vet to check out, but he couldn't find anything. And some of the neighborhood pets have died as well. I thought this all ended back ten years ago."

"Ended? You mean this has happened before?"

Dowdell nodded. "It's bad ground, according to the town records. That's the exact phrase—*bad ground*. There used to be a farmhouse there, young couple just starting out, but they both died within a month of one another. The next owner kept losing livestock and moved out less than a year after buying the place. About a dozen other people tried to use the land before they all just gave up and the town took over the land to use as a cemetery."

"Have you tried the EPA? Maybe there's some kind of toxic chemical in the soil."

"Had some fellas from Brown University up here a few years ago. They couldn't find anything, and one of them had a stroke and died while he was walking around the graveyard. I'm not a superstitious man, Greg, but I'm not a stupid one either. I stay away from there, and suggest you do the same."

He spent the afternoon in the town library, but other than confirming what Dowdell had told him, he learned nothing new. It was late afternoon by the time he started home, and when he had parked in the driveway, he walked next door, wondering if there was some way he could bring up the subject without having Laura Merriam decide he had a screw loose. But he was spared solving the problem because no one answered the door. Her car was in the garage so apparently she'd gone for another of her frequent walks, probably searching for the elusive Gingham.

He unlocked the studio door and stepped inside, then gasped. Even from a distance, he could see the changes in the bust. The eyes were darker and more menacing than ever, the cheeks so sunken they seemed cadaverous, and the hair had flared wide into a mantle around the head. But most obvious of all was the mouth, because the two discontinuities at either side had altered more radically. Two indistinct but easily identifiable fangs protruded from the clay.

Greg stepped outside, closed the door, and locked it with shaking hands.


"Nikki? Are you in there?"

Her door was closed but not locked. He turned the handle, hesitated, then opened the door. There was chaos inside, but it was familiar chaos—film magazines, CDs, junk food bags, discarded clothing—the comfortable debris of a teenager's life. The bed was unmade and empty, though cluttered with stuffed animals.

The pond! She'd said something about going down to sunbathe by the pond. Greg half ran from the house, trying to remember exactly how to get there. It was somewhere beyond the maze of gardens gone wild behind the Sheffield Library, he remembered. There was an access road somewhere, but he'd be better off traveling by foot.

He ran most of the way.

It was nearly dusk when he returned to the house. There'd been a handful of teenagers at the pond, and they'd been sulky and resentful of his intrusion. They admitted knowing Nikki by sight but insisted she hadn't been there.

The house was quiet.

Greg stripped off his dripping shirt and dried himself with a towel, then went to the kitchen for a beer only to discover that he'd finished the last. Frustrated, he grabbed a glass and ran cold water at the sink, grunting with annoyance when the water backed up from the drain. Something must be clogging the garbage disposal. He leaned close, got a whiff of the familiar coppery smell.

There was a muffled thump from the studio.

He used the key to unlock the door, moving as silently as possible, then edged it open. Nothing seemed to have been disturbed, but the wheelbarrow had been drawn up much closer to the workbench. Someone had been inside.

Greg opened the door all the way and stepped across the hearth. There was a sound to his right. He turned, started to raise an arm as the shovel arced toward the side of his head, but he was much too late.

"I'm sorry, Daddy. But I was afraid you'd stop me before I was done."

Greg blinked, trying to bring the room into focus. His body felt wrong, uncomfortable, but it was a few seconds before he realized why. He'd been tied into a chair.

"Nikki? What the hell . . . let me out of this." He twisted and turned, but the rope held him easily.

His daughter was awake this time, and to his relief, fully clothed. But her eyes were unusually animated, almost feverish, and she wouldn't meet his gaze. Instead she kept glancing around the room.

"I think I know how you feel now, you know? I mean, when you talk all the time about having something really important to do with your life, and getting lost in your work, and really like putting your heart into what you do. I know I kind of messed up what you were planning, but it was important, you know, and like I think made something real, didn't I?"

She turned to face the sculpture, and Greg followed her eyes. And gasped. Twice, in fact. First he was shocked by the latest alteration in the bust. All of the fine detail work he had expected to do over a period of weeks seemed to have been accomplished in a single day. The bust was finished except for the glazing and firing. The subject matter might not be the most pleasant, for the beast man was even more menacing than before, but there was no question that someone—Nikki?—had turned his rough work into a masterpiece.

That was the first gasp. The second was because he saw what Nikki had been doing all day. Judging by the size of the new sculpture, she'd brought at least four wheelbarrows of fresh clay up from the cemetery. The legs were massive columns, the powerful arms and hands were tipped with clawlike nails, and the chest was broad and full. The figure lacked head and shoulders, of course, because those had already been done.

"What . . . ?"

Nikki ignored him. "The blood was the secret, you know. I couldn't figure out what I was doing wrong until I cut myself with the trowel and bled a little. The clay works a lot easier when you mix some of it in. I'm really sorry about Mrs. Merriam's cat, but I couldn't think of any other way to get some more right away and it needed to be done. There was just enough to finish the head."

"How did you do the body so quickly, Nikki?"

"Well," Nikki dropped her head, "I'm really sorry about that too."

That's when Greg noticed that there was someone tied in one of the other studio chairs, someone not moving. Laura Merriam.

Greg closed his eyes and struggled to remain calm. "Nikki, you have to untie me now. Your work is done."

"No. There's something missing still." She sounded suddenly like a little girl, petulant, frustrated, self-concerned. "It's not, you know, complete. Remember how you told me you like to think you breathe life into your work? Well, I want to do the same thing, but I don't, like, know how. Help me, Daddy, please. Tell me what to do next."

"Honey, it looks fine to me. Maybe if I could look at it more closely. Why don't you just untie me . . ."

But Nikki was no longer listening. She was, in fact, shedding her clothing. Greg tried to look away, afraid to see, afraid not to.

Naked, she picked up a trowel, bent over the wheelbarrow, dipped into her last load of clay, then moved to face the statue.

Greg closed his eyes to hold back the tears he knew were coming, tried to ignore the sounds of his daughter making passionate love to a body made of earth and blood.

The sounds stopped and he opened his eyes.

Nikki had fallen away from the statue, lay on the studio floor staring sightlessly up at the ceiling. The left side of her chest was a ruin from which the blood was still spurting. Greg's immediate feeling of great loss was subsumed by absolute terror when he noticed that bust and body were no longer separate, that the thing he and his daughter had made together was now whole.

It stood up, its dark, striated body naked but no longer made of simple clay. Absently it rubbed at its own chest, where a fresh wound was fading visibly.

"What?" Greg stared into that malevolent face, not expecting an answer, but just before those now-too-solid fangs tore the life from his body, he had an answer.

"Nikki finally found something she could put her heart into," it said.

# THE PARASITORIUM

## Del Stone, Jr.

It was three o'clock in the morning when the call came.

They always come in the early morning, those calls, when it is still dark, when the subconscious mind is only beginning to unclench, when the soul is quietly reclaiming the body. The telephone emits a sound that rasps against the spine like the toothy blade of a hand saw. There is a disbelieving and reluctant groping for the handset, a mumbled hello, a moment of silence, a shocked intake of breath.

Always, always, it is some calamity that must be understood and responded to: a crib death, a car accident, a flat line on a cardiac monitor.

Always.

But not this time.

Because Barthel was calling.

And Katy wanted to go.

Ancient brick buildings. Burned-out factories. Empty warehouses. Gantries like storks dead on their feet.

An abandoned industrial district—a wall around the dark that cut off the stars and sucked the oxygen from the air to feed its decay, scoured by a mournful wind that hooted and wailed through the desolate canyons of sooty brick and rusted iron.

And Katy, driving amidst all this, wondering how she had come to be here and asking herself over and over again: Am I doing it again? Am I? Am I doing it again?

She did not want to be here, could not believe she was here, peered over the steering wheel as the hulks that refused to be illuminated moved past her car, and saw *things* out there, in the dark. Movement. Shapes. Hiding or scuttling or retreating from the headlights. She felt cool eyes following her, cool intellects measuring the distance to her car, weighing their chances of getting inside and stopping the car and dragging her out and—

Am I doing it again?

No.

And yes, she admitted, allowing herself a shiver that was equal parts apprehension and delight.

No, I will be on my toes this time, I will be careful, I will not let what happened with Robert and Andrew and Patrick happen again. And yes, I am . . .

In love?

She did not want to be in love, could not believe she was in love, and as she peered into the future she saw furtive *things* her mind refused to focus on, which made them more frightening than the horrors she imagined lurked in the boneyard of buildings around her. Reflections of memories, mostly, of Robert—

—his fist flying toward her face and a neck-snapping impact and a moment of paralyzed realization (He hit me my God he hit me) and the physical pain by no means atoning for the guilt (I did something wrong. What? What?)—

—and Andrew—

—he isn't speaking again today; something has gone wrong and he isn't speaking and the days will become a week, then two weeks, and finally he will speak and then she will know what she did wrong and she will never make that mistake again—

—and Patrick—

—she is a sexual idiot, a total dumbfuck, and how could she have failed him in bed so miserably and why can't she satisfy him and it's all her fault, her fault, but he'll fix it, he'll make it right for her and she'll owe him and he'll own her—

Even the memories left her drained and exhausted. She could imagine herself at the time, a pale, shriveled creature, sucked dry by some invisible parasite but still grimly clinging to life, unaware that she had ever lived any other way.

But not this time.

She'd walked away—*escaped* was a better word—from Andrew and Patrick, and afterwards had rebuilt her strength and tried again with Robert and failed. She'd fully expected the recovery period to last the rest of her life. The therapy that followed, the catechisms from self-help books ("Only through utter defeat are we able to take our first steps toward liberation and strength. Our admissions of personal powerlessness finally turn out to be firm bedrock upon which happy and purposeful lives may be built"), the support groups and tearful discussions with her friends—none of it had done very much for her.

And then Barthel, whose studio lay somewhere out here, in these labyrinthine ruins.

Barthel, whom she had met at a downtown gallery, one of those trendy places that served calamari and sweetened water to its patrons as they strolled the corridors making futile attempts to interpret the incomprehensible and subtle and very private longings of the painter or sculptor. She had had little appreciation for contemporary art, but had gone anyway and had seen Barthel haunting the corridors. *Haunting* was the most descriptive way of putting it. He had roamed the aisles with a hungry, hunted look, and something about him seemed to strengthen the tiny bit of hope still kicking around inside her, so that without having met him she felt grateful. Later, she would wonder what, exactly, it was about Barthel that had caught her eye. Something about his appearance, maybe, his thinness or the pallor that gave him the affect of a needy child, those two qualities conspiring to play on her maternal instincts? Or was it something less definable? His intensity, or the focused concentration in his eyes?

Katy peered uncertainly into the dark, slowing the car. She looked for the weird trestle of iron girders Barthel had described in his directions, but saw nothing like that. She wondered if she had gone too far, and a part of her shivered at the idea of becoming lost out here in these industrial barrens.

She had met Barthel that night . . . well, to be honest (and you *must* be honest, Katy), she had put herself in a position to meet him. But nothing he said or did gave her any reason to feel cautious. In fact, the opposite had been the case. His voice was quiet. His manner was deferential (Patrick had been that way at first, she'd warned herself). And he seemed genuinely awed by everything around him, exuding a kind of childlike wonder and enthusiasm Katy found herself enjoying, and even emulating.

Still . . . and still.

She had bumped into him at a reception, and later they'd gone for coffee, where she learned he was an artist himself and was working on some grand piece that nobody would see until it was complete. Katy had come away from that encounter (date? Hardly a date) with a multitude of impressions: his frailty, trust, naiveté, vulnerability . . . because Barthel had talked about feelings. He spoke of things she believed no man would ever speak of, and he showed his hurt (her name had been Judith and she had cut him to the bone with her betrayal, as badly as Robert and Patrick and Andrew had hurt Katy, and with that they shared a similar wound and a mutual need to heal). She began to see that beneath the innocence lay a thick welt of scar, and *that* she could trust. She knew it so well.

So they'd met at restaurants and coffee shops and he never so much as kissed her or held her hand.

Until tonight.

His piece was nearly complete. He'd invited her to be there for the . . . denouement? The unveiling? And as she'd hurried to the car, a part of her mind had played with the many interpretations of that invitation.

She found the trestle and drove beneath it, bearing to the right. His studio was nestled in the back, a one-story warehouse affair that sat next to an empty freight station. The warehouse-studio was low, like a pillbox, and looked solid and formidable. Banks of angled skylights marched across the roof. Miraculously, none of the panes were broken, and no light showed through them. Maybe they'd been painted. The only evidence of human habitation was a single, dim light hanging over the front door.

Katy stopped her car in front of the door. She debated leaving it unlocked, but locked it anyway. The wind blew freely across this place, and it produced odd sounds, at times a soft moaning, or a subliminal whispering that seemed to echo through the gullies of ironworks and crumbling brick edifices. She peered with a sense of wonder at her surroundings. Never, ever would she have believed she'd find herself in a place like this at this hour of the morning. Was she insane? the rational part of her mind asked sternly.

Her heart flared with warmth.

No, not insane. She felt herself beginning to smile.

She pushed the door open and stepped inside.

The wind blew it shut behind her.


Within.

A single room, long as the building was long, dark and not dark, the ceiling hanging low like a descending bank of fog. Hooded light fixtures swayed from a gridwork of bare trusses, shedding cones of sulfuric light, while shadows crowded the edges and the corners. The sound of water dripping, and somewhere, a set of chimes tinkling, though Katy could feel no movement in the heavy air. Smells of earth and musty decay.

And almost filling the room was . . . Katy didn't know how to describe it. A structure of some sort, vaguely circular in shape, with an entrance that faced the wall to her left. It was roughly twice her height and was made of a material she couldn't identify, smoothly textured and nonreflective so that the lights hanging overhead didn't illuminate it but instead brought everything around it into stark, shocking contrast, as if she were staring at a black-and-white photograph of a crime scene, shot with a strobe. A webwork of scaffolds rose from the center, suggesting some work there remained to be done—an odd juxtaposition to the structure's overall sense of . . . antiquity? Yes, she decided. It seemed old somehow, and . . . what was the word . . . *corrupt?*

"I'm here," a voice spoke from the gloom, and Katy jerked around, her heart thumping in her ears. She hadn't realized she was so nervous.

Barthel was standing in the dark, down the room a short distance. She could see only a shape, blacker against the gloom, but the voice was definitely his, rich with a blend of wonder and sacrifice and unknown passions. She started to walk to him and he held up a shadowy hand.

"No, no," he said quickly. "Thanks for coming, Katy, but I'd rather you didn't see me this way."

She stopped, a stab of fear shooting through her. What had he done to himself?

"I've been working many nights now. I work that way—in fits and starts and streaks—and I'll go nights without sleep, without food or distraction until I've finished. That's the way I work, and during those periods I neglect myself, and I wouldn't want you to see me this way. Does that make sense? I hope it does."

She started to say something mundane and simplistic—"Let me cook you a meal; you can use my shower"—and was instantly ashamed. He had invited her here for a higher purpose than a can of soup and a bath. Much as she wanted to see him, to see the things in him that had brought her here, she told herself to wait and respect what was important to him. So she turned back to the structure and gazed at it. She could feel him watching her.

Finally he said quietly, "It is my finest work." Somewhere water plinked, counterpointing the sound of his words. Katy dared not speak. She would have asked him what it was, what it meant, or if he had finished it—any number of questions that might have hurt his feelings. So she said nothing.

She heard him take a scraping step. "The entrance is over here," he said, and she allowed her gaze to travel along the edges until it rested on the opening. Inside she could see nothing. It was very dark, despite the lights overhead. She wondered if he wanted her to go inside.

But she did manage to ask a question. "What do you call it?"

He offered a tired, mirthless chuckle. "I call it the Parasitorium. It is my autobiography, my explanation to the world."

He receded farther into the dark, talking all the while. "It is a participatory art form. The viewer doesn't look at it so much as experience it, and in a way it is shaped by the viewer's perceptions. Actually, that's why I asked you to come here."

He was moving to the far wall, careful to avoid the light.

"I need you to do something for me, something that's very important to me.

"I need you to go into the Parasitorium and give me your impressions."

Oh.

Katy felt a flush of some very strong emotion, maybe gratitude, rise to the surface of her flesh and set it to tingling. Her throat tightened. Her eyes felt watery and hot. She dared not speak for fear of strangling on her excitement.

He was asking that she help *shape* his creation—an utterly private act that could take place only between two people who trusted one another and shared feelings of . . .

Love?

He continued to move along the fringes of the room. Katy strained to see him, but the darkness masked even a suggestion of his form. So she tested her voice by clearing her throat, then shouted in his direction, "Thank you. I'd be happy to. But why me? Surely your other friends know more about this—"

"I want you to," his voice trickled across the room, now from behind the structure. She heard him mumbling other things she couldn't make out, the words dissolving into the sound of dripping water and tinkling chimes and the creaks and groans of the building as the wind outside sighed. Suddenly, he shouted, "You've been hurt by people. You know what it means to suffer," and her heart became a liquid thing as her mind's eye filled with images of passion built upon a foundation of common pain. "That has galvanized you for the Parasitorium."

Yes. True.

She walked to the entrance, her footsteps sounding loud in the dark, and stopped at the opening. She took a deep breath. She didn't want to screw this up. Maybe later they would laugh about this, an odd way that two people should cement a relationship, a story to tell their children and grandchildren. And then she chuckled quietly and chided herself. She could be foolish sometimes. Girlish and foolish, which was kind of fun. She hadn't had this kind of fun since the first few weeks with Robert. And Patrick. And Andrew.

She sighed heavily, saddened that those memories still held such power over her.

I will not do it again, she told herself, squaring her shoulders.

I'll be careful. I promise.
She stepped inside.


Somehow, the wall closed behind her, and at first that bothered Katy. She was not claustrophobic but she liked to know where the exits were, just in case.

"Thank you," he called softly from somewhere within the studio, his voice apparently coming from every direction at once.

She looked around. It was very warm. She seemed to be standing in a tunnel. She moved closer to the wall. It curved upward and arched over her, not quite meeting the receiving arch so that a little light filtered in. The walls radiated moist heat, as if steam pipes were buried inside. She ran her fingers across the surface. It was pliant, and slimy with a kind of viscous fluid. Beneath the slime she could see a filigree of thin, pulsing lines that resembled the traceries of capillaries on an X-ray negative.

The light began to improve. The walls brightened to a dull gray finish. She began to hear a sound, a swishing or a thrashing that at first seemed far away. Maybe the wind outside had picked up, she thought. She glanced upward, at the skylights, and saw that they seemed lighter. But the sound was all around her.

Something was moving inside the walls.

Katy peered into the grayness. It was like staring into the murky waters of a decorative pond, hoping that the cloudiness would part to reveal garibaldis swimming below. She could see nothing at first, but as she leaned closer, vague movement became apparent. Shapes wiggled and squirmed beneath the surface. She pushed against the wall experimentally and it sank beneath her touch, like a balloon filled with scum. Several of the moving things clustered around the spot she had touched, wiggling insistently against the surface.

"This is unbelievable," she called out to Barthel. "Like fish in an aquarium. How did you do this?"

She giggled and pressed her finger to the spot again. "This is amazing—"

Something bit her.

She yanked her hand away, purely out of reflex. The wall somehow parted to admit the thing—it was still fastened to her finger—then sealed shut behind it as she screamed and flung the thing off her. Her heart was slamming in her chest and she couldn't seem to catch her breath. The thing squirmed sluggishly on the floor, slowly edging toward the swath of light that crossed the path. It resembled a pale tadpole, about six inches long, with a raylike tail that whipped back and forth. She had never seen anything like it. More of the things were gathering at the spot on the wall. They had lamprey mouths ringed with needlelike teeth, and somehow she knew if she touched the wall again they would be all over her. She took in a huge lungful of air and felt her stomach turn itself over with nauseating languor. The thing on the floor heaved itself a final time and landed squarely within the light, where it began to shrivel. In moments, it had dried to a lump of curled flakes.

Katy backed away from the thing. Her finger had begun to throb. Without thinking, she wiped it across her slacks and saw a dark smear, the color of old motor oil. Fresh blood welled around a circlet of bite marks.

"What do you see?" Barthel said tonelessly from some unseen distance. Katy stared at her finger.

"I see blood," she answered.


Shock.

A fragment of time, suspended, as the brain attempts to reconcile expectations with reality, and the stunning realization that the two are irreconcilable—

An unwashed coffee cup in the kitchen sink. She'd known Robert was a neatness freak. She'd known it, had teased him about it, had recited to him in a playful singsong: A *place for everything, and everything in its place.* He'd tried to make her into a neatness freak, too, along with all the other things he'd tried to make her change about herself.

But a part of her resisted.

So she'd screwed up and left a damn coffee cup in the kitchen sink.

(Robert's fist connecting with her nose, her skull banging against the refrigerator door but the pain she feels does not transcend the greater hurt of amazement because Robert has never done this before and how does this fit in with everything she expected of him, his gentle aspect and his quiet discipline, and now all those things have been smashed by this violent contradiction of who she thought he was, and it is utterly, disbelievingly shocking—)

How could Barthel have done this to her?

Katy moved through a narrow opening toward the next chamber, then stopped. A gleam of ochre light shone from ahead. Her finger sent out pulses of raw pain, as if the nerves had been stripped of their sheaths and dipped in scalding oil. The finger had already swelled, and the bite marks had the look of something gangrenous and infected.

"Barthel," she called, hearing her voice spread across the room amidst the drips and hisses. "What was that—that thing?"

A sigh. Then, "It was part of the Parasitorium."

"It bit me," she shouted angrily.

"I'm sorry," he said, and she thought she heard true remorse in his voice. "It's part of the experience. The moment of revelation can be painful."

She sucked in a breath, suddenly cold. "This isn't going to happen again, is it?" she asked, waiting a moment and hearing only silence before adding, "I want to know because it hurt me, Barthel. That thing hurt me."

"There are no more of them," he answered. She thought his voice had come from a different spot, as if he were moving around the Parasitorium, perhaps within its walls, though she didn't understand how he could do that.

"Listen, Katy, I can't explain it to you now," he went on, almost pleading with her. "But trust me, okay? It's part of the experience. If I explain it to you now, I destroy the purpose. The moment of revelation can be painful, but it's essential. That's the point of all this."

Somehow, somewhere, she had heard this before, a part of her warned, and just as quickly an answering voice dismissed her caution as cynicism. She did not know what to say or do, and could only think of her admonition to herself that she would be careful. She would not repeat the mistakes of the past.

"I'm sorry," he whispered.

She sighed and cursed silently. Already, her anger was beginning to cool. It was a predictable and irresistible process, this wavering, this willingness to believe. She could feel the explanations segregating themselves into an argument: okay, okay. Maybe she was judging him too quickly. After all, she barely knew him, and wasn't it true she had come here almost expecting trouble? The past had taught her to be careful, but there was such a thing as overcaution. Obsessive overcaution, Katy, she scolded herself. Maybe she should just give the man a chance.

"Well," she found herself caving in, "all right, then. But no more creepy things jumping out of the walls. You promise?"

He answered quickly, "Yes!"

She nodded to herself. She would try to put this business out of her thoughts. "Then apology accepted," she said, and her relief was almost a palpable thing. "Where do I go next?"

"Oh, thank you," he gushed, an entirely childlike response to forgiveness. "The next chamber is up ahead. Follow the light."

She moved along the corridor, toward the ruddy glow, telling herself to be patient, be patient, and give the man a chance. But she knew she'd heard that line before, too. It would be a long time before the factions within her would know peace, she sighed.

The hallway opened into another chamber. Katy glanced over her shoulder and saw that the door behind her had closed, and she wondered briefly how Barthel was able to do these things with such subtlety. It was an engineering marvel, and an image formed in her mind of the Pirates of the Caribbean ride at Disney World, and the animated buccaneers who swung their fiberglass swords and leered at the gawkers on the trams. The Parasitorium could rival anything the Disney folks offered, she decided.

The room ahead was very wide and nearly empty. A dais at the center was all she could see.

Something lay atop the dais.

It moved.

She strained to make it out, but the light was dim. So she edged closer —slowly this time, half-expecting something to lunge at her.

Whatever lay atop the dais stopped moving. Had it heard her enter the room?

She willed herself to be quiet. She took careful steps, and did not remove her gaze from the dais. A muffled silence hung over the room, the way a thick fog will blot out faraway sounds.

The thing on the dais turned its head toward her.

A child, an infant, Katy realized, and for a heart-stopping moment she had the crazy impression that it was real, and a sleetstorm of horrifying images fell into her thoughts: Barthel had kidnapped somebody's baby and was using it as a display in his work and what kind of horrible monster would do such a thing and even more sickening, if he would do this to an infant, what would he do to her?

She clenched her jaw and told herself to stop. "It's not real," she whispered, remembering the fat pirate with the cutlass that perpetually chopped at the dark, cool air inside the Disney World ride. "It's a puppet. It's an animated mannequin."

The baby opened its mouth and arched its head back, as if to scream.

No sound came out.

Katy let slip with a nervous giggle. "See?" she said under her breath, "Not real."

She leaned close to the baby. Its skin was a rubbery gray and coated with a layer of condensation, like a jar of pickled eggs somebody had forgotten to put back in the refrigerator. She prodded it with a finger. Cold. She picked it up, careful to hold it at arm's length. It was heavier than she'd have guessed.

She hefted it a couple of times.

Its eyes tracked her eyes.

They can do that with computers now, she thought uneasily. They hook up a computer to tiny motors, and that allows the mannequin to move the way a living thing moves. The whole thing is battery-powered, and . . . and . . .

She felt a finger of unease rub against the knobs of her spine. It was unnerving, the way the thing seemed to watch her.

It held out its arms, exactly the way a baby that wanted to be held would reach out with its arms. Its mouth opened and silently implored that she bring it closer to her.

Katy felt her lip curling into a grimace. This thing had an ugliness to it, made more grotesque by its resemblance to a human baby. But something about it was clearly not human, and she didn't want to hold it. She set it down on the dais and started to back away.

Something trailed from the baby's navel. She hadn't noticed it before.

A thin, segmented umbilicus, nearly transparent.

It swayed in the humid air, between the baby and . . . she looked down in numb fascination.

Bulges of bright, arterial red fluid moved down its length and into the baby, as if it were swallowing . . .

And at her wrist, at the other end of the umbilicus . . .

An eyeless, faceless mouth chewed at the vein, burrowing painlessly into the soft flesh to get at the blood, like a child using a straw to suck up the sweet, juicy slush from the bottom of a snowcone.

Katy's stomach bolted. She snatched the thing out of her and it writhed angrily and sprayed blood, and Katy heard herself utter a low, despairing moan as dozens of the wormlike things erupted from the baby's skin and began probing and testing and feeling the air for her, like some monstrous undersea creature slithering out of the dark to seize its prey.

She stumbled back, her head shaking, the air coating her throat with a layer of mucus.

An opening in the wall lay before her and she stumbled through it, senseless to anything but escape.

It closed behind her, shutting away the chittering, gyrating thing on the dais.

She knelt to the floor, her knees coming unhinged.

And began to sob.

*          *          *

Pain.

A gigantic spike of pain that divided Katy's perceptions into a small and distant awareness of rationality, crowded out by a towering, throbbing lobe of hurt, all of this occurring in stark, ear-ringing silence, like the periods with Andrew when he would not speak to her—

She had done something wrong. She had put herself before Andrew somehow, had hurt his feelings, had offended him, and now he was not speaking to her and wouldn't speak until the days of torturous pain had taught her . . . what?

(She should have told him she was stopping off for a drink with Laurie; she should have known he'd worry. But she was like that, always doing some spur-of-the-moment, spontaneous thing and she couldn't do that anymore because Andrew would worry and his fear would be transmuted into anger, an anger she had earned because she never stopped to think about anyone but herself.)

The pain of silence. Why hadn't Barthel told her?

"Barthel," she called.

"Barthel, I don't want to see anymore."

Dripping. A sliding hiss.

"Barthel, this is not art. This is torture."

He spoke from the innards of the Parasitorium. "The moment of revelation can be painful."

"Okay," Katy stifled a hitch in her voice. "You've made your point. Now show me the way out of here."

A weary, timeworn reply. "There is only one way out."

Katy planted her hands on her hips and shouted, "I want to be let out of here!"

"Trust me," he said.

"You're toying with me, and I don't appreciate it. I won't play this stupid game anymore."

"Trust me," he whispered.

"I'll go back the way I came," she threatened.

"There is no going back."

"Then I'll tear a hole in the side," she shouted, but she knew she would be unsuccessful. Her fear went from slush to ice.

A sigh drifted down the corridor of the Parisitorium. "I told you, Katy. It's part of the experience. Trust me."

*Trust me*, she thought, a tear blurring her vision.

*Trust me.*

How many times had she been told to do that?

She stared at the ceiling. The skylights marched across the roof. The panes were definitely lighter, and she wondered if the sun had risen. She thought she heard the wind hooting outside.

She wanted very much to be home.

She started walking. When she finished here she would say her goodbyes and go home and shower away this horrible experience and sleep. Yes. And never again would she make this mistake. Never. *Trust me,* she thought sneeringly.

She stopped at the entrance to the next chamber. It was hot and musky and dark. She glanced inside, then backed away, her skin seeming to harden into a waxy shell. She wondered how she would get through this.

The walls were alive with intertwined phalluses and pulsing testicles that throbbed and slid across and around one another like blind snakes probing the moist warmth. Milky slime drooled from the ceiling, hanging in slick ropes that sagged and fell to the floor where they dehydrated into fly ash. And at the far end . . . Katy could only stand and stare.

The room converged into a vertical slit that lay within fleshy, labial flaps. A phallic knob dangled from the top of the slit. The entire structure pulsated, the slit opening and closing like a mouth.

This is beyond insanity, she thought, simultaneously marveling and shrinking from the crazed genius that had gone into the construction of the thing. She tiptoed down the walkway, dodging sudden gouts of slime, and approached the opening. She could see another room beyond. It seemed a much larger room, perhaps the center of the Parasitorium.

And escape.

She swallowed and balled her fists. She would force herself through this final indignity, she told herself in as firm a mental voice as she could compose. Outside lay the sun and the wind and the real world, and that would be her reward.

She approached the slit. Again, it struck her as a giant mouth, the bulbous clitoris an obscene parody of a tongue, waiting to gulp her down. But she moved forward. She grabbed the lips of the opening and forced them aside. The opening contracted spasmodically, forcing her to crawl on her belly.

Something she hadn't noticed before: a thin membrane covered the opening. She would have to break that to get through.

The sides closed in around her, gripping her with a muscular heat that reeked of pungent secretions. She pushed herself farther into the tunnel and struggled to breathe. For a panicky moment she thought she might suffocate. Slime oozed from the walls and coated her body, slicking her hair to her cheeks and neck. It formed a sticky mask over her face that threatened to cover her nose and mouth, and her stomach heaved in response. Her hands and knees were beginning to sink into the spongy, slimy mass, and a brief mental image of her body being absorbed into the walls of this tunnel, to be digested and spread throughout the Parasitorium, blinded her to any thought but escape.

She scrambled forward and clawed at the membrane. It bulged but did not break. She punched at it.

A sharp, stabbing pain drove into her midriff. Another bored into her thigh. Then others, across her arms, her feet, her breasts, until she felt hundreds of small wounds erupting across her body.

In front of her, from the walls of the tunnel, fangs slid out of the slime like knife blades cutting through their sheaths. They arched toward her.

Katy made a fist and drove it into the membrane.

It gave for a moment. She did not think it would break, and hit it again, letting fly with an animal scream of rage.

It tore.

Blood was geysering in a red, choking flood that blinded her and the walls were expanding and contracting like a throat and Katy was forced through and swallowed onto the floor of what lay beyond.

Dimly, in some faraway place, as the flood swirled around her, she heard Barthel say, "The moment of revelation can be painful."

She could only think of sleep.


Her eyes snapped open. For a moment, she didn't know this place or how she had come to be here. She blinked and sat up, then almost fell back as the pain crashed over her, blackening the edges of her vision. She could not separate waking reality from dream reality.

Dream reality . . . she had been dreaming of Patrick.

A multitude of impressions. Patrick had been her first and she would always remember him for that, but the other memories were not so kind. She could not please him, and he beat her up with words, a reality drawn from a nightmare of guilt and fear. His impotence had been her doing, and he'd never hesitated to let her know, up to the last, futile twitch of their time together.

(Patrick. Andrew. Robert. How is it that these men knew more about right and wrong, good and bad, or goddamned to be or not to be, than I did?)

And then she remembered Barthel.

She was in a large, open space, surrounded by the interior walls of the

Parasitorium. Multiple pathways wandered in an apparent random pattern. Some were lined with low, thorny bushes; others were fenced in with borders topped by stakes; yet others were enclosed by jumbled heaps of scrap metal, sharp edges pointed outward. Mounds of pale, bloodless bodies lay between the paths, their faces contorted into expressions of agony. Pools of dark, stinking liquid steamed in low spots. Things moved just beneath the surface of the pools, or squirmed amidst the corpses.

The paths converged on the center of the room, where a gazebolike structure stood. It was circular in shape, supported by chalk-white columns. A lattice of bars studded with glittering spikes formed the roof and rose to the warehouse ceiling, where it surrounded a skylight. Katy remembered an earlier, more comforting moment when she'd mistaken the latticework for scaffolding. She wished she could go back to that moment.

A figure was seated in a thronelike chair at the center of the structure. A forest of tubes ran from the chair to the floor, where they covered it entirely. Katy had the impression there was no real floor, that the entire structure had simply arisen from the slow accretion of this bizarre plumbing, like the base of an ancient tree forced out of the ground by a thousand years' accumulation of roots.

Katy struggled to her feet and gazed across the heaps of bodies at the figure in the chair.

"Yes," she heard someone say. A corpse lying next to the pathway was gazing up at her with marbled eyes. "I am Barthel," it said, and somehow she knew it spoke for the being in the chair.

"I am all of this," other corpses said, their creaky voices rising in a rickety, grating babble around her. "The walls. The biting things. The man who called you here."

She followed the pathway through the carnage. As she drew closer, she was able to make out the figure. Incredibly, he did resemble Barthel, though he was older than any age she thought a human being might live to be. His skin was the color of tanned leather and wrapped tightly around twiglike bones, drawn in around the cheeks and jaw, and sunken between the picket fence of his ribcage—giving his eyes and teeth a preternatural hugeness that suggested an active and insane mind, alive with crazed hunger. He drew his mouth back. Yellowed fangs slid out.

"I am grief," he said in a papery-thin voice. "I am pain and fear and anger. But more than anything else, I am grief. And this," he waved a skeletal arm at the Parasitorium, "is my explanation to the world, nearly finished now. Do you understand?"

Katy shook her head dumbly.

"She hurt me. She did this to me," he said darkly, and Katy remembered Barthel's wrenching confession at the coffee shop.

"She was my first, my only, and on a night I will never forget, she bit me and left me this way—she called it an act of love, but I know better. It was an expression of her own, selfish conceit. And now I am this—her creation," the corpses moaned.

Katy continued along the path. Everything around her had taken on a surreal quality. She simply rode with it, as if she might endure a bad dream.

"The years give you time to think," he went on, "and the weight of those years compresses your thoughts into a single, driving need. Do you know what that need is?"

The path straightened out. It led directly to Barthel's throne. The figure there grinned at her.

"It is the need to explain yourself to the world—your pain, your fear, your anger, and more than anything else, your grief."

She could see no path that led away from the structure. She could see no way out at all.

"I will never forgive her." His lizardlike tongue flicked across the words. "I can't hurt her, but I can hurt the memory of her."

Katy jerked her gaze back to him. Much of what she was seeing did not make any kind of sense, but that last statement settled into her thoughts like a murder victim tossed into a dark pool.

"This is my greatest work," Barthel said, sweeping his hand across all that lay before him. "The Parasitorium. Isn't it grand? My heart, for all the world to see." The corpses began to untangle themselves, to rise and stand in the bloody murk.

"Your journey through the Parasitorium has brought you closer to my pain and fear and anger. All that remains now is the moment of revelation.

"When that moment arrives," the corpses uttered in husky whispers, "you will take my place in this chair, and become the completion of the Parasitorium—my heart, you see. My explanation to the world."

The structure rotated slightly. Tubes surrounding the chair were tipped with needles.

Katy saw herself bound to the Parasitorium, pierced in a hundred different places, her mind still alive and filled with a blinding terror as she fed this horrible monument to pain.

The corpses shambled from their pools, splashing blood across the walkway. Blades and spikes ripped at their flesh.

Her throat burned. She felt the old pain and wondered how she had gone so wrong, and how she had brought this upon herself. She remembered something Andrew had said, toward the end: "Look, dumbass! You're the one who wanted a *commitment*, for Christ's sake! Well, here I am, warts and all!" and she was crying, "God, if I'd known it would be like this I never would have—I'm just going to walk away—" and he was screaming back at her, "You goddamn idiot! You think you can just walk away? You'll be back before I can wipe your lipstick off my dick! You know why? 'Cause you like it! You like being treated like shit—"

The memory was like one of the Parasitorium's fangs going through her. It provoked a single reflex.

She ran.


She threw herself onto the first rung of the latticework. Spikes sank into her thigh and scraped bloody tracks across her arms and legs. The pain was a blinding flash that nearly knocked her unconscious, but she forced herself to go on.

"What are you doing?" Barthel croaked from somewhere below, his voice rising from all over the Parasitorium.

She grabbed the next rung, planting her fingers between the spikes, and hoisted her other leg. It was impossible to wrap it around the bar without stabbing herself. Below, she saw the mob of corpses. Other things—long, slippery ropes that looked vaguely reptilian—were gathering at the base of the columns to come after her. She planted her leg on the rung and screamed when the pain crashed in over her.

"Are you trying to escape?" Barthel trilled.

She climbed higher.

"You won't," the words floated across the warehouse. "The pain will be too great."

Something grabbed her ankle. She stomped at it and drove a spike through the sole of her shoe, into her foot. A dazzling bolt of pain shot through her leg, up her spine, to explode in her skull. Her hands were slick with blood and she nearly lost her grip as she reached for the next rung.

"How disappointed you will be when you discover that you don't have the strength to escape," Barthel crooned. "It will sweeten the moment of revelation."

The hanging lamps began to sway, strobing across the Parasitorium, bringing the body of it into and out of view so that she couldn't see it in its entirety. She averted her eyes.

She scaled the final rung and bumped her head against the skylight frame. For a moment she simply lay there, her chest heaving, the mob of hurts roaring in her ears. She wondered if she would have the strength to haul herself over the edge of the window, assuming she could open it at all. She slitted her eyes and stared at the things below her that were drawing closer. How easy it would be to simply give herself to them, let them carry her down, let whatever was to happen run its course. She would never again wonder how she had gone wrong, or worry about her mistakes. She would become a part of the Parasitorium.

She would become Barthel's creation, a work of art. A monument to pain.

She could not fathom such an existence.

The window was opened by a simple crank. She grabbed the rusty handle and jerked.

It broke off in her hand.

She heard snickering laughter bubble out of the Parasitorium, and she felt exactly as Barthel had said she would feel, overcome with despair so complete it forced her to her feet, where she wobbled on the bar, her head bent against the painted-over skylight panes. Cables of pebbled, reptilian flesh slid over the hand she used to grip the latticework.

She stared down at the Parasitorium. The lights had stopped swinging, and finally she could see it as a single entity.

A human heart. Divided into four chambers.

Worm-eaten with the mazes she had traveled, the whole thing pulsing in slow, languid contractions and expansions of ancient muscle, like a tumor endowed with a sickening life of its own.

She realized then that there was no way out, the hopelessness taking over her completely. No way . . . except one.

"I'll walk away," she announced to the Parasitorium as she prepared to jump. "Do you hear me, Barthel?" And a reservoir of anger ignited. "Robert? Do you hear me? And Patrick, and Andrew?

"I'll walk away."

She let go of the latticework.

But the snake thing had her and would not let her fall. And someone was grabbing her around the waist—the young Barthel, the Barthel she had met and had given magical abilities to bring happiness into her life.

He held her close to his coldness. "The moment of revelation can be painful," he tittered.

The wind rustled against the skylight panes.

She balled her free hand into a bloody fist and punched through the skylight. The pane smashed and an avalanche of glittering slivers broke down on them.

And sunlight exploded through the opening.

It cut across the Parasitorium like an arc welder's torch, scorching and blackening everything it touched. A howl of refined agony warbled out of the depths as smoke began to rise, obscuring the wan illumination from the lamps. The younger Barthel flinched away in agony and began to shrivel. The snake that was knotted around her wrist went rigid and fell away from the latticework.

Katy giggled and punched out another pane and felt the bones in her hand shatter, but the light burned a new swath of destruction across the Parasitorium. The howl below went skittering up the scale of octaves until she thought her eardrums might explode, but she found herself screaming with laughter. She used her elbow to break out more glass. The wind blew through and she sucked in chestfuls of the cool air as the younger Barthel groaned and fell away from the latticework like a dead stone.

She held her face in the sunlight and let it burn into her skin. The latticework trembled under the weight of the light.

Something had come loose inside her, something that went deeper than the pain of memory, and as she stood there, gathering the light around her and drawing strength from it, she thought she might have found something she'd been looking for.

Something within.


Later, on the roof.

The sun very high in the sky. A hole in the skylight where she'd kicked out the frame.

Lying there, collecting her energy, savoring her life. A fire escape awaited her.

But there was something else she needed to do.

Because to walk away would not be enough. This time, there would be resolution.

She got herself up. She found a metal pipe amid a scattering of scrap. She hefted it, like a baseball bat.

"I am not yours to create," she muttered. She would remember that.

Rows of skylights marched across the roof.

Scraps of paper floated by on the wind, light as souls.

She started breaking glass.

# THE DANCE
# STUDIO

# PAS DU MORT

*Lisa Lepovetsky*

*The dance. The dance was everything—her work, her blood, her life. And now they were going to take her life away, give her place of honor to a younger dancer, the wispy, blond Donna Chai, a simpering child who scampered across the stage like an overgrown grasshopper. Moira's world was suddenly unfamiliar, threatening—nameless evils waited in the dark corners for her. All her signposts were turned upside down. She would have to find her way home alone.*

Moira's first idea for the vampire dance came as she toured the New Orleans cemeteries. St. Louis Number One, the oldest cemetery in the city, seemed to crumble around her even as she wandered the hot narrow walks between crypts with a little group of tourists. Jason Sitare, her dance company's director and choreographer, was spending the first few days in New Orleans auditioning new dancers—and retraining at least one dancer for Moira's solo, her *pas seul*. That gave the rest of the company time to tour the city before rehearsals started. On a whim, Moira had decided to take the two-hour city tour, which included a walk through the cemeteries.

Martin, the bearded tour guide, indicated points of interest in a bored sing-song voice as his charges huddled together in the steamy late-afternoon drizzle. The damp air seemed to swallow sounds, and his voice had a flat, distant quality, though he stood less than ten feet from her.

"And behind you," he sighed, flipping his dark ponytail over his shoulder, "is the crypt of the famous voodoo queen Marie Laveau. As you see, people leave trinkets and gifts of food for her, and write coded messages on the walls. You might call it voodoo graffiti."

Martin's little joke fell flat, but he didn't seem to notice or care. He turned toward the back of the cemetery, his black umbrella obscuring his next few words, and the tourists hurried forward so they wouldn't miss anything. Moira hung back. She wanted more time to examine Marie

Laveau's tomb. She walked slowly around the small building, trying to decipher the patterns of crosses and circles chalked on the sides. All she could make out was some message about the birth of anarchy.

Returning to the front, Moira noticed a brass plaque set in the cement wall. As she bent to read it, her eye caught a dark movement around the corner of the small stone crypt. Moira glanced up, but saw nothing. A shudder passed through her as she remembered the warnings she'd heard about muggers lurking in the New Orleans cemeteries, waiting to prey on solitary tourists. She couldn't hear the guide anymore, or see her group.

She straightened, trying to remember which way they'd gone. They couldn't have gone far—the cemetery was only a block or two deep. She should be able to find them easily, but her heart thudded deafeningly in her ears as she listened for them. Moira had a terror of becoming lost ever since she'd wandered away from her mother in a large department store when she was six. Her mother had finally found her cowering beneath a rack of long black fur capes. Moira had been praying the big people wouldn't notice her and take her to the dark places her mother had warned her about. Then she'd never find her way home.

She'd thought she conquered the old fears, but those horrors crowded in on her again like vultures around a dying doe.

"Mama, Mama, please find me," she whispered, feeling her childhood terror plucking at her nerves. But she was on her own. Not only was Mama not in New Orleans, but she'd been in her grave for seven years now.

Moira tried to draw deep, calming breaths, but the air seemed too dense to drag into her aching lungs. She heard a soft rustling noise behind her and whirled, hoping the guide had found her. Nobody was there. The air was empty, except for that sense of something moving just beyond her field of vision again, something dark and feathery that she'd just missed seeing. She thought she heard someone laugh softly—or was it the faraway call of a bird?

Moira looked up toward the gray skies, as though she'd find some message written in the clouds, some map showing her where to go. Of course, there was nothing up there but a lone black bird drifting slowly above the cemetery. But she suddenly heard Martin's voice off to the left.

"And if you'll just step this way, ladies and gentlemen . . ."

With tears of relief filling her eyes, Moira hurried in that direction, finding the group behind a long row of what the guide was describing as "oven crypts," because their curved openings in the brick wall looked like nothing more than bread ovens. It was when Moira glanced up over Martin's head, looking for the bird she'd recently watched, that she saw the weeping statue. High on a pedestal, a gray silhouette against grayer clouds, a woman knelt, her head bent in sorrow, a granite cape drifting around her in pale, unmoving waves.

There was something familiar about the delicate features, nearly hidden by the folds of the cloak. After a moment, Moira realized with a cold start that the statue had Donna Chai's face. Well, the nose was a bit more aquiline, the lips a bit fuller, but the resemblance was striking. On closer inspection, Moira thought the woman's face didn't quite mirror grief—the hint of a dark smile seemed to tug at the corners of the stone lips.

At the same moment, Martin was discussing the popular theory that vampires roamed the streets and cemeteries of New Orleans.

"Of course," he said, "I can't say whether or not there are such things as vampires, in New Orleans or anywhere else." However, his rehearsed smile and raised eyebrows spoke loudly, saying, We both know there are no such things, but let's play the game, okay? Then we can all go home.

"Several popular fiction writers from the area have stirred interest in vampires, those evil, undead creatures who travel only by dark and prey on the living by drinking their blood."

Moira stopped listening to Martin's droning voice as he described books and films about vampires along the bayou. Her attention was riveted on the stone woman who seemed to float in the air above the cemetery—the delicate positioning of her arms, the curve of her spine, the way her bowed head tilted ever so slightly to one side, as though listening for a healthy heartbeat.

And suddenly she could see herself spotlighted on stage, dressed in black —no, deep, bloody crimson, her dark hair loose and liquid down her back, dancing her way through the life of a vampire in the City of the Dead, New Orleans. The director had complained only last week of being tired of Moira's Saint Joan number. She needed something new, something to make them remember how good she was, to make them forget about the golden girl Donna Chai. Her vampire number was the perfect solution, Moira's gift to the city of New Orleans and her rebirth as premier danseuse.

Moira fairly trembled with anticipation. She couldn't wait to get back to the theater and start working on it. She would use the "Totentanz," the Death Dance from Berlioz's Symphony Fantastique, letting the haunting dark notes fly around her, clothe her in their sensual, dangerous rhythms. And she would dance as no one before her had ever danced, creating a world that would at once fascinate and terrify her audience.

As soon as the bus driver dropped her off at her hotel, she grabbed her dance clothes and took a cab to the rehearsal hall. She searched the practice rooms until she found the music director. He said he had the music she wanted, and she changed into her leotard while he cued it up for her.

She found an empty mirrored room, and pressed the play button on the tape recorder . . .


Six hours later, Moira collapsed onto a metal folding chair near the door, panting and dripping with sweat. Her lungs ached and every muscle in her body trembled with the strain of her nonstop effort. But she'd finished the overall design of her vampire number, her *Pas du Mort*—and it was good, very good. She could feel it.

Moira's legs and arms had seemed to know where they should be with very little input from her brain. She had felt the Berlioz clutch her like strong fingers from the first chords, bending her body in serpentine rhythms, arching her back and neck until the sinews felt as though they would snap. Moira had seen the music swirling around her like dark grave-yard mists. It was as though her body had directed her thoughts, rather than the other way around. She still had a few steps to fill in, transition movements mostly, where the music changed, but the dance was essentially complete now. If she had to perform it tomorrow, she could.

Still, Moira couldn't rest. This was the most important dance of her life, and it had to be perfect. She couldn't afford the tiniest wobble, the least shift in balance. Though her whole body screamed for her to stop, her brain ordered her to continue practicing until her movements were flawless. Moira knew if she sat any longer, her muscles would begin to stiffen and the rest of the night would be lost. With tears in her eyes, she rose, rewound the tape, and began again.


By Thursday, she was ready. The next night was the company's last night in the city, and Moira approached the director with her proposal.

"I have a surprise for you, Jason," she said coyly. "I've designed a new number for the show tomorrow."

He sighed and didn't look up from the papers on his desk. "Not another *Saint Joan?*"

Moira cringed, but breathed deeply before answering. "No, this is something special, inspired by New Orleans itself. I call it *La Pas du Mort.*"

"Dance of the Dead?" Jason glanced up, a skeptical frown on his face. "Sounds a little melodramatic. How long have you been working on it?"

"Nearly a week," she lied, knowing he'd never believe the dance was finished if she told him she'd been working on it less than three days.

His frown deepened. "Are you sure you're up to a new solo? You look kind of pale, tired."

Moira realized she was tired—exhausted, in fact. She hadn't slept more than four hours a night since she'd toured the cemetery. All her free time had been focused on her new dance. But she straightened her shoulders and tried to look as energetic as possible.

"I'm fine," she said. "Never better. Wait till you see this number—you'll love it. It won't take much preparation: I'll make my own costume, and I'll just need a simple set of some Styrofoam tombstones and dead trees. The fog machine will take care of any imperfections."

Moira hated the pleading note behind her voice. She'd never had to beg for a dance before.

"What about music? Lighting?"

"I've already set it up—no problem. There's just one catch."

Jason sat back in his chair and laced his fingers behind his head. "Catch? I don't like the sound of that."

"I don't want anybody to see the dance before Friday."

"Not even me?"

"Not even you."

"I don't know, Moira . . ." Jason was shaking his head.

"Jason, have I ever let you down?" Moira held her breath as Jason seemed to take forever to answer. In the end, he didn't.

"All right," he said, bending over his papers again. "But it'd better be as good as you say." He glanced up once as she turned to go, and spoke very quietly. "Don't let me down."


The next night, the house was full. Jason had made up a huge poster advertising Moira's vampire dance as the company's "gift to the good people of New Orleans." The management had even set up a row of folding chairs in the back of the theater, to accommodate their accidental oversell.

Donna Chai opened the show with her homage to the life of Isadora Duncan. In her green gossamer shift, she fluttered between vine-laden pedestals like a damsel-fly. Watching from the wings, Moira grudgingly admitted to herself that the girl had talent. She felt fear cramp her belly at the thought. Her eyes shifted to the audience, and her gaze was caught by a copper-haired woman and two men—one dark, one blond—sitting in the front row. There was nothing unusual about them; they were dressed in evening clothes like everyone else, and they weren't more or less beautiful than those around them. But they were very pale, and the reflected spotlight made their skin look almost translucent.

And they weren't looking at Donna Chai, or even the stage. All three were looking straight at Moira. Their eyes held an intensity that seemed to bore into her, to merge with her soul as she stood rooted to the spot. Moira felt her legs tremble. She wanted to run both from them and to them at the same time.

Suddenly Donna's dance ended, and the dancers for the next number pushed past Moira, jostling her farther backstage. The spell was broken, and she returned to her dressing room to await her call. To his credit, Jason had scheduled *La Pas du Mort* last, as the crowning glory of the night's performances. The significance of this position was not lost on Moira—if she was anything less than perfect, she was through.

The evening dragged on endlessly until the stage manager tapped on her dressing room door and, without opening it, called, "One more number and you're on."

Moira's blood froze in her veins. She rose slowly from the dressing table, and watched herself in the long mirror as she drew on her black leotard. Her movements were graceful and sure, but she noticed a tremble in her hands as she wrapped the burgundy satin cloak around her shoulders. Long black feathers fluttered at the hem, and danced around the edges of the hood.

Moira had covered her hands and face in the palest foundation she could find, accenting the hollows of her cheeks and eyes with blue-gray shadow. She nodded with satisfaction at the woman who watched her from the mirror. She looked beautiful and gaunt, without being skeletal, and her dark eyes glittered almost feverishly from the pale depths of her face.

She whirled away from the mirror and headed upstairs to the wings. The Civil War number had just ended, and Moira watched the stagehands move the wood-and-Styrofoam cemetery into place. Despite the last-minute construction, the tombs and crypts looked amazingly realistic. Anticipation tingled along the edges of Moira's nerves and she drew a deep, shuddering breath. As the lights dimmed to blue, one long black light breathed ghostly life into the fog being pumped from the wings.

The first haunting strains of Berlioz's "Totentanz" rippled from the speakers, and Moira felt herself drawn toward the stage. She crept between the crumbling makeshift crypts, hunched into herself until she found the center of the stage, where light caught on the fog swirling around like a phantom almost ready to materialize. Then she crossed her hands beneath her face, staring into the audience, frozen for a long moment.

She heard a combined gasp as the black light turned her flesh purple and rippled along her cape. In that moment, her gaze found the three people she'd seen earlier. Their eyes were riveted on hers, and she felt something pass between them, some almost-painful thrill of electricity.

The jolt passed into her brain and coursed down her spine, settling like hot mercury in some deep recess she'd never known existed.

Then she was moving again—gliding, whirling, drifting in the whiteness, her body moving in ways even she couldn't believe. One moment her arms wrapped around themselves like hungry snakes, the next they flew out and up to become the branches of long-dead, long-forgotten trees. Her legs stretched tighter and leapt farther than she could have imagined, and she could sense the audience holding its collective breath at every arabesque. They were hers, and she was in love with her power. She dared not look at the two men and one woman sitting in the center of the front row, however, or she knew somehow she'd be lost.

All too soon the dance ended, and the last strains of the insane music faded into the rafters. All the lights dimmed, leaving only the black light illuminating Moira's upturned face and clenched hands. Then, suddenly, that too disappeared. For a long breathless moment, the night lay in complete silence. Moira's ragged breathing sounded like a tornado in her ears.

Then the applause began and the lights came up. The pale trio were standing front row center, and soon others rose behind them until the entire audience was on its feet, applauding wildly and cheering. Moira saw tears streaking the cheeks of many. She sank into a low curtsy, her head down and arms outstretched as though gathering the adulation of her public. Three dark red roses landed at her feet, and she knew immediately where they'd come from. She grabbed them and curtsied once more, then ran into the wings.

Jason bowed as Moira ran past, and Donna Chai reached out to hug her. But Moira pushed her away and flew down the steps. She slammed the door of her dressing room behind her, and collapsed onto the floor, her stomach heaving drily and all her muscles cramping violently. She felt as though she were in the throes of a virulent flu. Her skin hurt and her head seemed to wobble heavily on her neck. Moira tried to weep, but was unable to manage even a tear.

Then someone was lifting her from the floor, standing her on her trembling legs. Cold hands grasped her upper arms firmly but tenderly, and a deep male voice spoke.

"You were magnificent tonight. We knew you would be."

The voice seemed to come from inside her as well as from outside. She lifted her face and saw before her one of the two men who'd been sitting front row center. His eyes seemed to have a life of their own. As she gazed into them, Moira thought she saw something move in their depths, like a small creature trying to escape. After a long time, he blinked.

She glanced around them, and saw his two companions standing on the other side of the room, their arms around one another. The blond man licked his lips.

Moira's voice croaked painfully through her throat. "What are you doing here?"

"We've come for you," the dark man before her said, his lips barely moving.

The woman brushed her red curls from her face and smiled. "We've known you were ours from the moment we found you in the cemetery."

"The cemetery? You were there?" Moira recalled the whispered laughter and the sense of being watched. She shook her head, trying to make sense of it all.

"We were there," the dark man said, "and now we're here. You called us, and we came."

"I didn't call you. I don't even know you." Moira tried feebly to pull away, but the thin cold fingers gripped her tighter.

"You called us with your dance," he said. "Your body speaks more clearly than your voice, don't you know that? You've always known us. You've waited your whole life for us to come take you with us."

He bent his face to hers, biting hard into her lower lip. Blood poured into her mouth.

The pain was excruciating, and yet exquisitely beautiful. She felt her own blood stream down her chin, both from the front of the wound where his long wet tongue flicked out to catch it, and from the overflow inside her mouth. She swallowed, tasting the salty copper flavor of her own blood —and something else, something bitter that seared the delicate lining of her mouth.

She gasped from the pain and tried to jerk her head away, but his tongue hooked behind her front teeth and held her. His hands flew to the sides of her head and pulled her lips against his. The thick tongue snaked into the back of her mouth, choking her and coating her throat with something that seemed to freeze and burn her flesh at the same time.

But suddenly, Moira didn't want him to stop. She wrapped her arms around him and drew him close to her, aching for the icy chill of him inside her. She heard soft laughter from across the room, and ignored the small voice deep in her brain warning her one last time that she'd never known until now what it really meant to be lost.

# RHAPSODY

*Lyn D. Nichols*

The blue light shining on the stage dimmed as the last chords of the music faded. The stripper held her final pose—hips thrust forward, legs spread wide, head tossed back, arms reaching skyward—until the last of the light and music trailed into darkness, then, grabbing up her discarded costumery, she slipped off the stage.

Desultory applause followed her exit. Grant clapped his hands a few times then signaled for the waitress to bring him another bourbon and Coke. It had been a waste of time to come here, he thought as he fished a five out of his pocket and set it on the table. John had said there were a few terrific dancers here—dancers that could do justice to his music. He hadn't seen any he'd let near his stuff, and doubted he would. Not here. Not tonight.

The stage lights flashed through a rainbow of colors and then went completely dark, casting the stage in deep shadow. Grant looked up, his weary attention caught by the momentary shimmer, curious despite himself. Slowly, a red light bled onto the stage, spotlighting a shapeless black form standing still at center stage.

The form remained motionless as the red light pulsed, each strobe slightly brighter than the last. The dancer, draped head to foot in a flowing black robe, seemed to pulse with the light. Grant was startled to realize that a deep bass beat—like a heart throbbing—accompanied the pulsing light.

As the beat of the music became louder and the dancer's movements more pronounced, the background chatter within the nightclub died away. Grant sat up, intrigued, as the dancer's robe slipped from her head to her shoulders to her waist. Long white hair swirled around her body as a flute wove itself into the heartthrob bass. Her long, lean back swayed and Grant recognized the tenor call of a clarinet.

As more instruments found their way into the music, more of the dancer's body was revealed until the robe lay like a black puddle on the stage floor around her feet. And still, she only swayed, her hair writhing around her hips and waist as the tension in the music, in the room, rose.

A crash of drums, a blaze of flashing lights. The music and the dancer came to life. Grant was transfixed. Every sound, every movement was joined; never had he seen music brought to life so well. He was seeing the music, hearing the dance, feeling both in the deep heartbeat that continued to throb at the core of the composition.

With an effort, Grant pulled himself from the hypnotizing effects of the music, lights, and dance to concentrate on the dancer. He reached for his drink, surprised to find the waitress had brought his refill without his noticing. He looked back at the stage, sipping. The dancer was almost completely naked, only a G-string covering her mons.

The music teased him, hauntingly familiar and yet not. *What was it? Who was the composer?* The notes took unexpected turns, racing up the scale when he would have expected them to hold, flats and sharps sneaking in where they shouldn't have fit, and yet did, perfectly. Interesting. Compelling. Maddening. And the dancer matched the music perfectly.

He forced himself to ignore the music and look at her.

She was tall and lean, and so very, very pale. Milk white, bone white, death white. She moved with the boneless grace of a predator, sliding through the music as an owl slips through the night or a shark slides through water. Her sinuous movements threatened to pull him into the music's spell once more and he blinked, narrowing his vision only to her face as it appeared and disappeared again under the flowing mass of her white hair. The only colors on her were her lips and her eyes and her fingernails. Lips and nails so very red, eyes so very black.

Grant studied her, watching her movements, measuring her against the music without allowing himself to be swept away by their mating. Long, long legs. Narrow hips. Breasts that he would have thought too small for a stripper. Everything about her suggested strength and frailty, heat and ice. Life and death.

Without warning, lights and music vanished, leaving the stage a dim cave once more. Only the throbbing beat and the pulsing white of the dancer remained. Grant grabbed the table edge as she seemed to collapse upon herself, then disappeared into the inky black.

*I have to meet her,* he thought. *She's perfect. She's the one to dance my "Impulsion." The only possible one. No one else could possibly bring its every nuance to life. She has to agree. She has to.*

Grant stood, almost upsetting the small cocktail table in his haste. He ignored the two burly bouncers who watched him as he pushed his way to the bar. He was used to their reactions. Big men were an occupational hazard for them, and Grant was bigger than most men. He reached the bar and signaled, catching the bartender's attention.

"That girl, the dancer with the white hair. Who is she? What's her name?" he asked.

"The last one?" the bartender asked, pouring a shot of tequila into a glass. Grant nodded. "That was Silka. She's something else, isn't she?"

"Yes. Fantastic," Grant agreed, nodding. "I need to meet her. I have to talk to her."

"Not likely," the bartender laughed, pouring orange juice over the tequila. "Our girls are off limits." He dribbled grenadine into the juice and handed it to a waiting waitress.

"No," Grant said. "It's not like that. I need to talk to her."

"Sure, pal. That's what they all say."

The bartender moved down the bar to tend to another customer, dismissing Grant with a laugh. Grant suppressed the urge to slam his fist into the bar and muttered a curse under his breath.

"Hey." A female voice and a hand on his arm. Grant turned toward the source of both. "Dancers don't mess with the customers," a short brunette in cocktail-waitress uniform said, her faded blue eyes desperately searching his face. Grant noticed needle marks on her arm. Her name badge said Brenda. "But I'll be off in an hour." She smiled a promise and exposed crooked teeth. Grant started to pull away, and checked himself, leaned toward her instead.

"Can you take a message to Silka for me?" he asked. She pouted and started to turn away. Grant caught her wrist. "I'll pay you ten bucks to take my card to her."

The little brunette eyed him over her shoulder before turning back and leaning against him, pressing her tits into his arm. "Silka's a cold bitch," she whispered. "Not like me. I'll treat you really good." She slid a hand down toward his crotch.

Grant caught her hand and folded a twenty into it. "Listen. All I want is for you to take this card to her." He paused and scribbled a note on the back of the card and held it out to her. "Please."

Brenda took the card and read it. "You're a composer?" She looked at him again. This time her eyes held dollar signs. "I can dance, too."

"Fine," Grant said, pulling another card from his pocket. "Call me tomorrow, and we'll set up an audition for you." He handed her the second card. "Now. Will you take my card to Silka?"

She stared at the card for a moment, then shrugged, accepting defeat. "Sure," she said. "I'll take it."

Grant watched as she threaded her way through the crowded club and into a hallway leading backstage. He glanced at the stage where a dark-haired dancer was up, peeling her glittery costume off to a recording of Santana's "Black Magic Woman." Grant sighed and returned to his table.

He watched two more dancers and finished his drink while a third undulated to the Eagles' "Hotel California." He was trying to decide whether to order another drink or just leave when a hand touched him on the shoulder. He turned toward it hoping, no, expecting to see the dancer, Silka, standing behind him. Brenda shrugged apologetically and handed him his card back. He looked at it. *I'm flattered, but no,* was written in old-fashioned script across the bottom.

"I'm still available," Brenda purred into his ear. "And I'm off work now."

*What the hell and why not?* Grant thought, standing and swaying slightly. He pulled Brenda close and aimed for the door. *Right now, the dancing he was interested in didn't take a lot of talent, and Brenda would suit as well as anyone.* He could enjoy Aerosmith if he couldn't have Vivaldi.


For the next three nights Grant sat in the bar watching Silka dance. Each night she danced to something new and different—a blues tune one night, hard rock the next, a reggae song the following night—and each night he was more convinced that she *had* to dance to his composition.

"Impulsion" was perfect for her. *She* was perfect for it.

Each night he sent his card backstage, begging her to at least listen to his music. Each night she refused him. And each night he took what solace he could find in the eager warmth of Brenda's well-used body.

On the fourth night, he didn't send his card backstage. When Silka finished her number, he left the club. He didn't go far; just around the corner where he could watch the stage door. He leaned against the side of the building and prepared to wait. *If I can just talk to her,* he reasoned, *she'll change her mind.*

An hour passed, and then another. Grant toyed with the idea that she had become an obsession. He laughed at the thought. No, his only obsession was his music, and finding someone who could make his music come to life was an extension of that.

Another half-hour ticked past and finally the stage door opened. Several people exited. Most of them turned toward the parking lot at the rear of the building, but Silka went the opposite direction. She wore tight blue-jeans tucked into ankle length high-heeled boots, and a lightweight white jacket.

She walked quickly, her high heels clicking on the concrete sidewalk.

Grant waited until she had reached the corner and turned before pushing away from the wall and following.

He followed her for twenty minutes as she moved steadily toward the downtown area. *Not a safe place for a lady,* he thought. Silka walked confidently, passing drunks and young punks without seeming to notice them. Grant was sure the only reason they didn't bother him was because of his size. At six and a half feet and two-eighty, not many people were brave enough—or stupid enough—to challenge him. Why they didn't bother her, Grant couldn't imagine.

Silka turned another corner and Grant walked faster, afraid of losing her. He reached the corner and almost fell in his haste to stop. Silka stood half a block down, talking to a man. Casually, Grant crossed to the other side of the street and slowly ambled toward them, watching.

The man Silka spoke with lurched slightly and caught himself. He said something, and Silka laughed. Grant paused. Her laughter was like her dancing, sultry and dangerous. She laughed again and took the man's arm. He pulled her close, his hand sliding down over her ass before leading her farther up the block. Something like jealousy knotted in Grant's stomach.

Grant followed, frowning, as Silka let the drunken man fondle her as they walked the half-block it took to reach a cheap-looking, dirty motel. Grant ducked into a shadowed doorway across from them and watched.

The man laughed and pulled Silka against him, his hands disappearing underneath her light jacket. She laughed again and stepped back, shaking her head. She pointed to the lobby and made shooing motions with her hands. The man reached for her again, but she neatly sidestepped out of his reach. He shrugged, laughing, and entered the cracked-glass door as Silka moved out of the flickering light of the buzzing neon to wait.

Grant waited with her, hidden in the alcove across the street. He swallowed back bitter bile as he thought of that man's hands touching her body. *Stop it,* he told himself. *She's just a dancer. She's just the movement you want for your music. She's nothing to you beyond that.*

When the man emerged from the lobby, dangling a room key, Grant decided it was time to go home. And yet he waited, watching as they crossed the parking lot and entered a room. Finally he stepped out of the alcove, but instead of retracing his steps to the club and his car, he crossed the street and stared at the door they had entered. *Room 3.*

Without meaning to, telling himself he was crazy and would end up in jail if caught, he slipped into the weedy alley that ran behind the room they had entered. Their room was easy to find; it was the only one with lights on. He called himself a fool and told himself to go home, even as he knelt beside the window and peered inside. He was surprised to find that he could see the entire room.

The man wasn't in sight. Grant assumed he was in the bathroom. Silka had taken off her jacket. She wore a long-sleeved blouse with poet's sleeves. As Grant watched, she pulled something out of her small purse—a cassette player—and set it on the table. She dropped her purse beside it.

Grant heard the toilet flush and the man stepped into the room, wearing a smile, socks, and an erection. Silka smiled and pressed the button on the small tape-player. Grant recognized the lead-in to the Eagles' song, "Desperado."

"C'mere, baby-doll," the man slurred, reaching for Silka. "Lemme help you outa all them clothes."

"I'm a dancer," Silka said, her voice deep and husky. She lightly pushed the man back until he sat on the edge of the bed. "Let me dance for you first." She swayed as she backed away from him, her fingers playing with the buttons on her shirt. The man started to push himself off the bed, but something—a look from Silka, perhaps?—stopped him. He stared at her as she moved before him, slowly stripping her shirt off her shoulders. Grant grinned in sympathetic understanding as the man began stroking his engorged cock.

Grant was as drawn to Silka's dance here in this seedy motel room as he had been in the club. His own cock stirred with the first twinges of desire. He glanced at the man, expecting to see the same rapt fascination mirrored on his face.

He didn't expect to see an expression of terror.

Grant glanced at Silka, and then the man again. She had stopped dancing and was moving toward the man. He sat, motionless, staring, eyes wide with fear, as Silka approached. Her white poet's blouse hung from the waistband of her jeans.

As Silka leaned toward the man, his mouth opened as if he wanted to scream, but no sound came forth. Silka placed one hand on his shoulder and one on the side of his head, tilting it to the side and back. The man's hands twitched in his lap, clenching around his swollen cock.

Silka's head dipped toward the man's neck, her mouth open to reveal long, sharp canines. A primal, visceral spasm of dread raced through Grant's veins as he stared at Silka's fangs. He tensed, wanting to pull away, wanting to run and run and run. But he couldn't. As Silka's teeth punctured the naked man's neck, strains of sweet, eerie music, his music, wormed into Grant's head. The man jerked once and ejaculated, his come spurting onto his stomach, mixing with the blood that ran from his neck.

Grant watched, horrified, mesmerized, fascinated, as Silka fed. And as he watched, music, a new composition, built within his mind.

Grant crouched beside the window, his head full of the notes and slides of Silka's music as he witnessed her cool and deliberate murder of a drunken man. Several times she stepped back from the man—eyes half-closed and a rapt smile on her bloodied lips—and danced, slowly and seductively, her hands running lightly over her breasts and ribs and the tight hips and thighs of her jeans. Then she would feed some more.

Despite his terror, Grant felt himself hardening, savored the tight pull of desire in his groin. And still, alien and beautiful music poured into him. His hands itched for paper on which to capture the notes, his fingers flexed, straining for the keys of his piano, wanting to bring this beauty and fear into form. Instead he rubbed himself, increasing the sharp pangs of desire and strengthening the lines of his music.

One last time, Silka lowered her mouth to the gashes in the man's neck and drank. The man was gray now, and limp, his eyes open, blindly staring. Gently, Silka lowered him to the bed and kissed his brow as his chest convulsed with his last gasping breath.

As she stood looking down on the man, Grant noticed the flush of color in Silka's white skin. She danced slowly to the strains of Carole King's "Will You Still Love Me Tomorrow?" as she pulled her shirt back up and buttoned it, never taking her eyes from the dead man. Grant could see her lips moving to the words of the song.

Suddenly, Silka turned toward the window where Grant crouched. Her eyes—black in her flushed face—met his. Run! his mind shouted to his body, but he couldn't move. Cold sweat beaded on his forehead and his heart felt as if it would explode in his chest. He couldn't breathe! And still, Silka's song played in his head.

Silka licked the last of the blood from her red lips and smiled at Grant. It was a horrifyingly understanding smile. A chill of dread fingered Grant's spine as he recognized his own death in that smile. He pushed himself away from the window with a gasp of indrawn breath, the cold air searing his lungs. Run! He scrambled to his feet and ran. He ran without direction or reason, shoving late-night walkers out of his way and dodging cars as he careened across streets and through intersections.

And the music Silka had inspired played on and on and on.

Somehow, he found himself back at the parking lot behind the dance club. His side pinched painfully with every sobbing breath as he fumbled for his car keys. Every sound jerked him around, wide eyed, staring into the shadows. Finally he got the car door open and threw himself inside, closing and locking the doors.

The dark interior of his Firebird wrapped him in an embrace of safety and security. He leaned back against the headrest and closed his eyes, willing his breathing to slow, his heart to stop its pounding, his body to stop its shuddering.

Music screamed in his mind, scales and chords he would have thought impossible before tonight.

As the first lemon-stained hints of morning streaked the sky, Grant started his car and drove home. He was eager to reach his piano, desperate to record the music that swirled and raged like a caged beast inside him. He would write, and then, then he would sleep.

*And tonight,* he told himself, *tonight I'll look for a new dancer, someone to dance to "Vampire's Rhapsody,"* Silka's song.


Grant stood for a long time outside before entering the nightclub where Silka danced. He selected a table in the front, near the hallway leading backstage. In his shirt pocket, a cassette tape pressed against his chest. He could hear its twisted threnodies and convoluted chordings even over the loud blare of the club's speakers. A glass of scotch and melting ice sat on the table before him.

He hadn't slept, hadn't eaten, and the small amount of scotch he sipped burned in his stomach. His body vibrated with exhaustion, exhilaration, and fear.

He knew he was crazy for coming, but nothing, nothing could have kept him away. Not when the music burned in his veins and his heart yearned to have it brought to life. Nothing, not even dying, could stop him from sharing this newest composition with her. This was the moment he had lived for. He knew without question that this was the finest music he had ever written, would ever write.

A shiver of anticipation raced through him as the lights on the stage dimmed and he felt the low double-thump of a heartbeat bass. A dark, robe-swathed figure appeared in the darkness and was gradually lighted in dim, pulsing red.

Silka saw him the first time she turned toward the audience; Grant could feel the power and heat in her gaze. The music in his soul played louder, drowning out all other sound. Silka's eyes sought his whenever her dance allowed. Grant's breath rasped in his chest, hot and heavy with fear and need. Finally the lights dimmed and her dance ended.

A waitress came up to his table and handed him a folded piece of paper. He held it, his hands shaking, almost afraid to open it. As the latest dancer on stage made love to an invisible lover, Grant unfolded the note.

*Meet me at the stage door. Five minutes,* the note read in Silka's familiar scrawl. The signature was a stylized *S.*

Grant refolded the note and slid it into his pocket next to the cassette tape. He finished his drink. Silence filled his mind. He tried to find the quiet terror that had been his constant companion for the last twenty-four hours. He tried to summon the music that was his reason for being here. Nothing.

He pushed away from the table and stood. It was time. He waded through the press of people, blindly seeking the exit. Once outside, he rounded the corner toward the backstage door.

Silka stood under the street lamp, waiting for him. She wore jeans again, and boots, and a loose turquoise sweater that hid the supple curves of her body. Her hair was pulled back and held by a fuzzy turquoise band. Grant was struck suddenly by how young she looked.

"You are either very brave, or a fool," she said as he approached. Her voice was like the rest of her: deep and supple. Grant stopped and shrugged.

"A fool, perhaps," he said. His heart thumped in his chest. "Or a genius."

"You saw me last night. You know what I am." It wasn't a question. Grant nodded and suppressed a tremor of fear. "I should have killed you, you know." She shook her head and stared at him. "I don't know why I let you run."

Grant reached into his pocket and withdrew the tape he had made.

"This is why," he said, holding the tape out to her. He tried to keep his hand from shaking as she took it from him. Her touch was icy; it burned his hand.

"You want me to dance for you." She stared into his eyes. He thought he could see a flicker of red—like flames—within the black. "You know what happens when I dance for a man."

"I know." Grant couldn't take his eyes from hers. "Will you dance for me?"

Silka smiled and looked away. "Take me somewhere."

Grant led her to his car, a part of him curiously calm, another part gibbering and howling in mindless terror. He drove to his home, neither of them willing to break the silence between them. Grant glanced at her occasionally, but Silka kept her face averted, staring out the window at the passing buildings. He parked the car and opened her door. She followed him up the flight of stairs to his apartment, brushing against him like a freezing wind as he held the door open for her to enter.

Grant's apartment was an open studio, wood-floored, sparsely furnished. His piano sat silent in the corner, waiting.

Silka looked around as Grant flipped a switch. Soft white light illuminated the center of the room. She walked slowly toward the light, her heels clicking against the wood floor.

"I could make you like me, you know," Silka said as she pulled the band from her hair and shook it loose. She turned to face him. "I could do that instead of killing you. That's what you want, isn't it? That's why you brought me here."

Grant nodded. "But will you?" he asked.

"If I like your music," she said, pulling her sweater off and tossing it into shadows. "If I like it enough to want more." She bent and pulled off her boots, sent them sliding after her sweater.

"You'll like it. I promise."

"You would be better off wishing I don't like it too much," she said, smiling that chilling smile she had given him the night before. "You should hope I don't lose myself in it and forget you aren't supposed to die."

Grant shivered at her words as he crossed to the high-tech recording equipment that rested beside the piano. There was no going back now. He took a breath and hit the Play button.

"I'll take that chance," he said.

His composition, written for Silka's ears and his eyes, swelled and filled every corner of the room. She turned toward him, her eyes wide with pleasure as the music wrapped itself around her.

"This is mine," she whispered, her feet already moving to the subtle sub-themes hidden in the music.

"Dance for me, Silka," Grant whispered, unbuttoning his shirt and exposing his neck, already half-hypnotized by her movements. "Dance to my Rhapsody."

# THE SCRIPTORIUM

# VAMPING THE MUSE

*Jane Yolen*

My muse lay snoozing atop the kitchen counter, as always, her long legs tucked up beneath her. She looked a bit like a superannuated kitten, with her striped ash-blonde hair and long pink nails. She was a great snoozer, that one. It put me behind on a lot of my projects.

I knew that only a bit of blood would rouse her, so I got one of the pet-store mice out of the fridge. I keep them there to make them sluggish and slow and besides, I don't want to add a new gene strain of mouse to the population under the floorboards. The pet-store people think I collect big snakes. I encourage that fiction. It's a small lie, but a necessary one. My muse needs regular feedings.

"Here, E," I said, waggling the droopy white mouse under her nose. "Time to get to work."

She sniffed, her classic aquiline nose moving slightly. Then she stretched her wings, one at a time, and put her right hand out, cupped. I dropped the mouse in and turned away.

When E had first become my muse, I used to watch, fascinated, as she bit each mouse on the back of the neck, as precisely as an owl with its prey. The mouse would go limp immediately, and she would proceed to suck its blood with such a sensuous display, I found it quite arousing. I sometimes had a hard time forcing myself to work. At night I had long, languid dreams about her feeding. Of course she's not much bigger than the mouse, so nothing much could come of it. But the time I went away for the weekend with a girlfriend and came home to find E finishing up a neighbor's white cat ended the pleasure I got from watching her eat. From then on, E and me—it's been strictly business.

I went upstairs to my workroom, knowing that she would fly up once she had drained the beastie. My workroom. Actually, it's the attic, with a bit of baffle on the ceiling and heavy-duty mover's quilts on the walls to keep out the street sounds. My last girlfriend but one called it my "own private padded cell." I suppose it is. But the jingles I beat out on my keyboard do pay the rent—and then some. I'm not big time by any means. But I hoped that, with E as my muse, I might actually get there. I've already moved up from a Tascam four-track to a reel-to-reel, after all.

All the jingle writers I know have muses. They're imported from Greece. But not all of them have a work ethic that meshes with the American market, and only a few of them are really talented. Most jingle writers go through a half-dozen muses before they get one they like. Or else they quit and go into something that doesn't need a muse. Like stockbroking, editing, or being a book critic.

E is my very first muse and I went into deep debt to get her. All her genetic markers are good. In fact, on paper, she's sensational. Her mother-lines have spikes into both poetry and music: Erato *and* Terpsichore. But this far down, those lines tend to run a bit thin. That's probably why she needs to drink blood. The older muses all eat ferns and lotuses, and they drink pure water.

Still, jingles ain't real poetry and they ain't fine music. They just pay better than both!

Since E arrived, I have done several so-so jingles for the Glow-Over Lipstick folks and one memorable ad for Merry Markets. Do you remember the "Very Merry Berry Fairy"? That's mine. Text *and* tune. It's a local market, of course. But you have to start somewhere. And in fact, it's the new Merry Markets jingle that I am really behind on. They want something just as good as the VMBF—as we call it. With the promise of the whole account. But I just haven't been able to come up with the right thing yet. I was going to have to really push E this session. Or think about getting a new muse. Only the running-in time on a new muse is a bitch and I *am* rather fond of the little thing. And it's pathetic what they do to trade-ins. She might end up as one of a dozen muses linked into a musak composer.

I heard the small sound of her wings and waited for her to perch on my shoulder. She works better when we are physically close. Some muses prefer sitting on the keyboard or behind a screen. One jingle writer I know lets his muse sit on his fingers, but I don't like the weight. And when she settled in, breathing her short, warm exhalations into my ear, I knew we were ready to begin.

"Think 'Very Merry Berry Fairy,' " I whispered. Loud sounds at this point startle her and are counterproductive. "Like and not like. Think bouncy. Think amusing. Think vegetable or fruit."

"Blood," she whispered. "Think blood."

"No," I said. "Merry Markets has no meat counter."

"Too hard." She sighed warmly into my ear.

I said a Greek swear at her, one of three I had learned from the manual.

It means *masturbator*. Actually it means: *you do it with one hand.* She hates the sound of it, though I don't think muses actually have a concept of *masturbation.*

She licked my ear. It tickled but I was careful not to move. When she gets to the licking part, we are more than halfway there.

"Very Hairy Berry Fairy," she said.

"No. Too ugly."

"Very Merry Berry Peri," she said.

"What's a peri?"

She sighed hotly into my ear. "A Persian fairy, you yutz."

"You mean *putz.*"

"Whatever." She glanced down at her nails.

"No. Too exotic."

She stood up and paced on my shoulder, up to the neck and back again. "Not merry?" she asked. "Not fairy?"

I nodded vigorously, dislodging her. She fluttered her wings and lifted off my shoulder about an inch, something she'd never done before.

"Listen, E," I said, "this one's the big one. I have to show them I am not just a flash in the pan. A one-night stand. I need a big follow-up or I am through and you go to the musak meister."

She landed heavily back on my shoulder. "Blood," she whispered loudly.

"You'll get another mouse when we are done."

"You want mouse ideas, I give you mouse ideas," she said. "Very Hairy Berry Peri."

I turned my head to really look at her, which made me kind of crosseyed and her kind of blurred. She was smiling. I didn't like her smile.

"Another Fairy idea costs. Putz." She licked her lips, which were a rosy color, what Glow-Over calls Perfectly Pink.

And then I remembered. The original Fairy idea had come after she had drained the neighbor's cat. I shuddered. "Look, I can't go rounding up the neighborhood pets for you . . ."

She smiled again.

"Or buying anything larger than a mouse at the pet store. Someone might notice."

She was smiling even more broadly now, her little fangs sharp as needles.

The jingle was due tomorrow. In a manner of speaking, my life was already on the line.

"Does it hurt?" I asked. "Will you take much?"

"Not much," she said in a voice full of promises. "After all, it's not like this is really art."

# THIRTEEN LINES

## Don Webb

Before I encountered the unfinished sonnet of Henry Salt, I would have said that there was nothing in the world that was worth my life. Everything has changed by my reading the thirteen lines. I now know Love and Terror.

My door into the place of damnation was (appropriately enough) the love of money. I work as a research assistant at the Harry Ransom Center at the University of Texas. We've got quite a collection, including a fine copy of Bram Stoker's *Dracula*; you should stop by some time. My job is to aid those scholars and seekers after the mysteries who visit our air-conditioned halls. Sometimes the work is both hard and exhilarating; sometimes there is nothing to do. Being the thrifty sort that I am, I use my free time to produce little gems of independent scholarship that I sell for small recompense. My real name does not matter, but perhaps you know my pseudonym of John Kincaid, who writes lots of articles on the paranormal or just plain weird.

I had an idea for a honey of an article on strange manuscripts and cursed books. I figured I'd cover four or five texts, plus some pictures, and I'd have a feature. Maybe if I played my cards right Omni or Playboy could be tempted. My formula for success in paranormal writing—what the heck, I can give it to you now that I'm leaving the field—was to cover the same old ground for 75 to 80 percent of the article, and then add one truly new item. This would make my article hot and quotable and ensure that I could sell my next piece.

Very, very few people are aware that I am John Kincaid. It would probably make most researchers uncomfortable. Would you want your research assistant to be the man who wrote "Was Lincoln's Father Bigfoot?" No, I didn't think so.

My article on mysterious texts covered the magical papyri of Thebes, the Voynich manuscript, and Dr. John Dee's "Enochian" cipher. All well-researched and well-known texts for the occult crowd. I was browsing through the on-line catalog for occult curiosities when I came across *Blood*

*Loss and Poetry: An Account of the Inanna Sonnet* by Austin O. Emme, London, Dawglish & Son, 1925. " 'An account of the so-called vampire sonnet, its translators since the Middle Ages, and the discovery of the original text in Sumerian, with especial emphasis on the life of Henry Salt, Esq.' Private edition of 333 copies. LOST."

The last word dashed my hopes as much as all the others had raised them. LOST meant that the book had been part of one of the rare book collections, and that most likely it had walked away with some visiting scholar. Our current security system prevents any such thefts, but in a more trusting age—say, thirty years ago—such a stringent system wasn't in place, and the occasional visitor overcome by bibliophilic lust took a book or two. I decided to post queries on a couple of electronic librarian's lists looking for either *Blood Loss and Poetry* or any information on Henry Salt.

Then I went out to lunch.

It was a couple of days before I got a response. A couple of postings revealed that Henry Salt had been an undistinguished curator of Egyptian and Mesopotamian antiquities at the Sallust Museum. A third indicated that he had died during a scandal of 1898, and the fourth proved most interesting.

We too have lost our copy of Austin Emme's book, but one of our grad students in the sixties had begun a study of "Scarlet Woman Motifs in Ecstatic Poetry" and provides a copy of the vampire sonnet:

> *Look into the heart of wind on storm night*
> *and find a sudden black rainbow.*

Just as I read the first couplet I heard a sudden metallic noise, like a huge wreck, and I ran to my window. Below on Guadalupe Street what had been a small Japanese car and a large four-wheeled Jeep were now one. Three or four other vehicles had hit each other or parked cars in an effort not to smash into the central pair. Students, homeless beggars, street entrepreneurs were pointing and yelling. Amidst the crowd stood the oldest and ugliest woman I had ever seen. She was dressed head to toe in black, Iranian somehow. Sirens sounded, and I could hear my co-workers going to their windows.

I went back to my terminal, but the screen was blank. Goddammit! Had I hit the delete key or otherwise screwed up? I spent several minutes trying

to retrieve the missing message, and wound up sending a note to the
computer center asking if they could help me.

I worked till dusk. I had gone through a painful divorce a couple of years
ago, and one of my best defenses against loneliness is overwork.

It was a beautiful warm Texas night and I didn't want to hurry home. I
walked through campus. UT has a beautiful campus, full of Spanish buildings and fountains. I sat on the edge of one of them, where hippocampi
sported in the backlit foam. Very pretty, and the white noise filled my ears
as spray soaked my tired face . . .

And I found myself dancing in an old palace, all soft stone and candlelight. My partner wore a black veil that shimmered like moonlight on a lake
and we danced by vast windows which looked upon a world in perpetual
night where the ground outside was white as snow, but I knew it wasn't
covered with snow, then my head plopped back and I woke up.

I had fallen asleep by the fountain. I felt dizzy and confused, and very
embarrassed. I'm sure I looked drunk or drugged. I stood up, a little bit
staggered by my experience. Someone laughed behind my back.

I didn't feel like driving home, so I decided to return to my office. I was
there several minutes before it occurred to me that I might need medical
attention. I was frankly hoping to fall asleep again and regain the sweet
feeling of the dream.

As my orientation returned I decided to check my e-mail. Two more
messages on Salt. One was from a college in Denver; after pleasantries he
got to the point:

> We have the Emme book. Henry Salt went from respected "Orientalist"
> (as they said in those days) to a kind of street person. He had acquired a
> clay tablet bearing a hymn to Inanna, which he translated and then
> discovered that it matched a medieval French poem. At first he pub-
> lished this as a historical finding—evidence of a poetic tradition going
> back to the Euphrates. Then he went through a period of trying to form
> a "Cult of Insubstantiability," which got him fired from the Sallust.
> Then he had a change of heart and spent all of his money buying every
> copy of his articles on the hymn. He even snuck into the Sallust and
> hammered the tablet to bits. He apparently died in front of the museum
> a few days later, some said of blood loss. To my surprise I discovered that
> we've never made a microfilm copy of the book. As soon as we have one
> made up, I'll send it to you. Thanks for the interesting read.

The other was from the Oriental Institute in Chicago. Its message was
more to the point.

Leave the "Unfinished Hymn to Inanna" SM 10188 alone. It claims a scholar every couple of decades. Stick with something safe like crack cocaine.

Needless to say I was more intrigued than ever. All commercial dreams had vanished. I wanted something that I could know—some Mystery that was for me and me alone. There is nothing that can be possessed as fully as something within one's mind.

I waited daily for the microfilm from Denver, and I continued to have my little dreams. I remembered little of them, save for the slow lovely dance with the veiled woman and the delicious sense of swooning that accompanied each dance. I wanted to have her, take her, but even more than that I wanted to speak with her, to know her thoughts and being.

I don't recall ever being so much in love.

Certainly not in my marriage to Beth, certainly not in college or high school romances. Never in fiction or movies or fantasy.

My boss called me in and asked what was wrong with me.

How did she mean?

She said that I had been getting really sloppy about finishing assignments. The other day I had been speaking with a man from Utah and I had just wandered away from him in mid-sentence.

I sort of remembered this, but shrugged it off with a bad joke about Mormons.

She also asked about my health, saying that I was looking pale and wan.

I asked if she was worried about expenses for our health plan. It was all in all very unpleasant.

I knew that I could stop, but I wanted to let things go on for a little while at least. I needed a better picture of things, and besides, I felt so dreamy.

The microfilm arrived. I'll quote from relevant sections.

Dr. Salt's initial paper on the clay tablet from Persepolis stressed that it was not a fragment—that the poem was actually incomplete. He speculated that this was perhaps the first poem to be written *first*, before being recited—and that the unnamed scribe simply couldn't think of an ending before the clay dried. (pg. 14)

Salt never revealed his sources for discovering the medieval French, ancient Greek, or seventeenth-century English versions of the hymn; although the existence of some (but not all) of these translations has been verified. His published remarks merely say that these were brought to his attention in a "mysterious manner." This probably marks the beginning of his death as a scholar. (pg. 23)

Little is known of the Church of the Yellow Light. Salt took in members from all races and classes. When I tracked down members some twenty-five years later, most could recall nothing. A few had vague impressions of meeting in a drafty cheap hall that Salt had rented, and watching some sort of magic lantern projections. Fewer still had been so stirred by their experiences to try their hands at Theosophy or various occult practices—but for the most part their whole involvement with the Church had been a particularly obscure dream in their dreary dreamlike existence. (pg. 48)

Salt gave many alternative translations for the "Hymn to Inanna." Some alternate opening couplets include:

> *She is Thunder, the Perfect Mind*
> *Adversity and Advantage is her Name.*

> *Sweeter than my own thoughts is she*
> *She, who invented thinking for me*

> *What cost red blood for golden nectar?*
> *What cost the world for splendor?*

> *Suddenly a black rainbow in the blue night*
> *and in that other world living gold.*

Clearly these cannot be objective translations from the Sumerian. Salt's own explanation for the variations (he apparently produced 418 of them!) was that the original had been written in "an unknown tongue." (pg. 52)

The last meeting of the Church of the Yellow Light occurred on October 16, 1898. Salt had been giving one of his lectures on the insubstantial, when he abruptly seemed to change his views. He began shouting, "No! She's mine! Mine alone!" and chasing people from the hall. The rumor that he later set the hall on fire is unsubstantiated; perhaps this was the work of a disillusioned follower or maybe a random vagrant. (pg. 101)

One of the most ingenious theories was that the poem tried to define the undefinable, or as Salt put it, "to make the Unknown Known." Most of the poets or translators had tried to add a word to the poem, some even attempted a whole line. According to Salt, it was the *strain* of extending the poem that caused the blood loss. The Sumerian version was a mere eight lines long. Salt had located an English-language version of 1814 consisting of twelve full lines and the beginning of a thirteenth. Salt's final version of the poem was cast in the form of an unfinished sonnet awaiting its fourteenth line. I have published the verse as Appendix B to this volume. Although I find the supposed occult or "vampiric" nature of the sonnet to be utter rubbish, I must admit I find the lines a bit too fascinating. This no doubt speaks of the suggestibility of the human mind, and perhaps lends support to the theories of Dr. Freud. (pg. 135)

Although Salt's death was rumored to have been caused by anemia, no autopsy was performed nor medical report of any kind made. The sheriff attributed the death to exposure. The body was to have been buried in the family vault, but was stolen by person or persons unknown and no doubt performed its last civil service for aspiring medical students. (pg. 167)

The microfilm broke before I could read the thirteen lines of Henry Salt. I had to wait and get help to repair the machine, because I didn't want to risk gumming up the microfilm reader and possibly losing my chance to read the microfilm for several days.

While I was waiting for the technician to come to fix the microfilm, my boss sent for me.

She told me that my clothes were dirty. She told me that I *smelled*. She told me that I needed a shave.

She said my eyes looked sunken. Was I *on* something?

She told me to go home.

"But I'm waiting for some film to be fixed."

"It's five o'clock. You can look at it tomorrow—when you come in clean and shaved. Get some sleep. Take a vitamin pill, for Christ's sake."

"But this is a very important project. I've been working on it since the day of the big wreck."

"What wreck?"

I began to understand. I went home. I would have to make the decision whether or not to read the poem, because I began to see what the implications were.


The woman came to me in a dream that night.

As I had expected.

I found myself in the vast stone hall whose windows looked upon miles and miles of ground as white as snow. I could see the land clearly now; it was covered in bones. The soft glow inside the hall, which I had attributed to candlelight in all my dreamy dreams of love, had no source. It came from everywhere and cast no shadows. As I pondered this, a voice came from behind me—a voice so sweet that I could feel it make my sleeping body shiver.

"The light is the force of mind. Ultimately it is the only light we have in this darkling universe. It is my light."

I turned to face her. She had removed her veil. I took her in my arms and we began to waltz to silent music. How can I describe her face, a face that has the beauty of a thousand moonlit nights? Or the eyes of a blue not of your earth, for it is such a blue that can only be imagined? Or her hyacinthine black hair, whose luster suggests another spectrum—an anti-light whose unknown colors could be spread only by a prism whose angles are unknown to man?

All of this and so much more was she.

"None of this is real, is it?" I asked.

"No. Not in the way you mean real," she said. "This is imagination alone. This is the insubstantial. Yet alter anything here, and those things in that other world which are symbols of here are altered proportionally."

We waltzed and waltzed, and stone wall and dark windows spun.

"I am the goddess of this place. I am the source and the form of all dream lovers. I am real as long as I am loved."

"You are Inanna?"

"I have any name you want to give me."

"And how long would you keep that name? How long would you be faithful?"

"I would be faithful as long as you lived, devoted to you absolutely. My love and lust would be as absolute as could be imagined by anyone, anywhere. For I am the form of the dream lover."

"And when I died?"

"I would spirit your body here, to lie in the endless lands of insubstantiality. Your bones would join the millions, and I would become the old woman wandering the Earth till another was chosen. One who could see me and my illusions."

"Would you remember me, out of your millions of lovers?"

"No," she said, and I could feel my sleeping twitch with agony, but I did not awaken. She continued, "No, but while we loved, the rain of inspiration would fall upon your race. While you struggled to add another line to my poem, a thousand poets would be born. While your blood itself boiled away, the idea of Love would become more perfect."

I awoke and I thought of her. I pictured myself crazed and bloodless, trying to live one more day so that I could dream one more night.

I could put it aside. I could throw away the microfilm and delete my computer files. I hadn't taken a vacation in a couple of years. I could go to Vegas, blow some of that money I'd socked away since my divorce. I could get drunk and go to a cathouse. I could . . .

I wasn't even fooling myself. Tomorrow I'd shave and bathe, and put on a clean suit. I'd get up early so I could catch breakfast at a restaurant downtown, where I'd have beefsteak and eggs Florentine to build up my blood.

And I would read Henry Salt's unfinished sonnet and start to work on the fourteenth line.

*(For Lilith)*

# SING HEAVENLY MUSE

## M. Turville-Heitz

On a fine August day, in the year accounted by the Christians as 1637, a vessel passed into my notice as it traveled from the mouth of Dee toward Anglesey and beyond, perchance making for Dublin. The winds were calm, and as night fell they abated to a bare whisper rare to this tumultuous sea. I slipped aboard the vessel with a silent skill that never failed me in the thousand years and sixty since Arderyd. In the matter of perhaps an hour, I had drunk my fill of the passengers, stove in the hull, and left her to founder as I had the many ships before. Of the offspring of the Roman Church I drank, I their Judgment. The thirst for vengeance does not sate in centuries, or a millennium. It consumes.

Among them, I learned later, was a man of no great account, a young clergyman, recently of Christ's College, named Edward King. I do not know which of them he might have been. Which of those begging for my mercy, whether he was the one who tasted sweet as if he had fed upon honeycomb all his days, or the bitter one who had feasted instead upon sage and acorn flour. They were young and old on that ship. I can be certain the older ones were not Edward King, nor the women whose sweet breasts bore the sour milk of Christianity. Even shown a likeness, I doubt I would know him. In sixteen centuries I have seen much of this world.

One more foundered ship might have been of little note among the hundreds upon which I meted vengeance—and sweet taste the young— but some time later, I took note of a bard who had written an ode to this Edward King. I always listened for voices of reason among the clamor of righteousness in this land gone Roman. This bard sang so sweetly, but what pastoral claptrap he had penned! Within it smacked the better part of wisdom, and perhaps that pastoral nonsense was part of the irony he sought. Not only did he slash the almighty Roman Church with his two-handed sword, striking through the jugular, but he did so with relish, in the end deifying young Edward King as a poet, as a shepherd better than the corrupt clergy he walked among. And this creature I had drunk deeply of, the bard memorialized in a syrupy ode, "Lycidas."

I knew I must find this John Milton, the bard.

Of little interest, I am sure, will you find the years of my search. Know only that through correspondence I located him in Horton in Buckhamshire, England, only to learn he had left on an extended holiday to Italy and France. It was several years after first I had read "Lycidas" before I learned he had returned home at the news of civil war. He had taken up rooms in London and there, first, I came to find him.

Moonlight does not trouble me. Cold like my skin has become. White like my features have grown without true life to feed them. Deep shadows like my eyes, which have witnessed so many Roman-bred evils. So it was I selected a moonlit night to visit the bard who had in so brief an instant touched me. When one has an eternity, such pursuits smack of high adventure.

A creature of habit, Milton had retired early, I lurking in the garden shadows beside his window until I felt certain he slept deeply. Only from a distance had I marked him, a man of middle stature and pale skin—like, almost, unto mine own—and auburn hair. He struck a fine figure of health, a man in his thirties, and quite capable with the sword he wore at his side on those rare occasions he troubled himself to go out. His journeys were marked with strong will and politic and in later years, with relish, I watched him bait those Roman-loving clergy and flaunt his views. Such a waste, this vigor, without reason.

I hefted myself upon his sill. The moonlight fell on his fair face, and translucent eyelids that hid dark gray eyes. Look upon him! I could mold from him greatness. He sought a Muse! I had come.

I spoke first in angelic voice, that of a patroness, an illicit love, like the Muse he imagined. Too easily did my words slip into him so like a sponge, twisted and sweetened with the ancient arts I sipped from that Cauldron so long ago upon the Isle of Mona, now Anglesey, when the Romans annihilated the bards and their magic and I alone survived. I could see the route we would take as I held beneath his nose the herbs of ancient lore, reviled by a Church this man eschewed. A bard, true, like those of old lurked somewhere within him, awaiting freedom. Too young he was yet. Too unwizened by the world. Too distracted. When the lift of breath in him came more softly, when his heartbeat in my ears throbbed ever so slow, I bent to his ear.

"I am the Muse," I whispered into his dreams with the high tones of a woman such as he would dream. "Inspiration I am, knowledge, kin to wisdom. I am what you seek." I let my lips brush his neck, sensual as a lover, my cool flesh to the heat of life. He turned onto his side. "Remember, supreme are the words of the bard. Ancient are the tales that guide us on the true road. Lost is the greatness of the past, the dragons restless beneath the land. Only by overcoming the evil that took from us will we regain that which we lost." I could sense the pulse of blood in him, the life, the spirit of a bard, alive, like none I had known since the tragedy of Mona, and the betrayal of Taliesin so many years later.

I needed him. I could not rip his blood from him as I had from my victims in the past. How many ships had I slipped aboard in the dark nights as they wandered the coast from the mouth of the Dee to Anglesey? Certainly reefs grew in the deeps there, ships staves piled upon mast and hull, the spirits of those dead cresting each wave, mourning for the folly of their deeds. The blood of those who wronged me tastes sweet in my throat. I hear the dragons mutter their approval with each sip I take. But not this time. I could not leave marks John Milton might note and question. Yet I must drink of him, to taste the sweetness of inspiration, illumination. Gently, from the soft flesh at the back of his neck, I drew as deeply of his life's blood as I dared, then treated that spot with a mash of herbs I knew would speed the healing.

For a long time I regarded him, casting a moonshadow across his sleeping figure, unsated, needing more to still the hunger in me, needing more to recall the luminosity of inspiration I had once known when the world yet felt fresh and young. Had I not known how the future would treat us, foretold how to inter the two dragons, the red and the white, that gave life to the land and strength to the High King? Not since Mona have I known life. Not since Arderyd have I felt inspiration.

Arderyd. Since Arderyd did the madness fill me, when the practitioners of the Christian cult killed my dear Gwendoleu. Fair Gwendoleu! A leader as fine as any Briton since, great among warriors, forgotten in song because no prince would hear me after Arderyd. So long ago, yet like last eve, I see the battlefield. I, but a mere bard whose stature grows only with legend, with no weapon but lore and staff, stood beside him, weeping, as he leaned his last breath into the spear of Rhydderch Hael. I could only take the blooded sword from his grip, and drive it deep into the dragon's back, and proclaim my oath.

How these followers of Rome tore up the spirit and bruised the dragons who fed and protected our land! So many corpses rotting on the shores of that isle now named Anglesey in the first years, and in the five hundred to follow. So much blood spread wasteful upon the dragons' backs, sinking into the leaf mold beneath Kelyddon's eaves. After Arderyd I could hear the world groan, the very heart rock weep, the dragons gone still as the waste of blood sank through them. Since the battle of Arderyd, I lost all feeling but the hope for revenge. Since the battle of Arderyd, I thought of nothing but the blood that had washed that battlefield.

Even my dear friend Taliesin claimed me insane and swiftly threw his lot in with Uryen and his get Elffin, and the followers of Rhydderch. A true bard gone Christian! A true bard—

Like the promise in this John Milton. Life came too easily to this Milton. To inspire him, he must be brought to his knees. To see, he must be blind. To love, he must be hated. He must cry out in longing for the Muse, a longing born of heartbreak. He must lose all that he loves to know all that he has. He must know pain in his life to find his fulfillment. Well that I had heard him.

That next morning, I later learned, he proclaimed a Muse had come to him. He would write a great drama, he declared, of paradise lost. The words he penned that morn, a few verses he would later weave into that epic work, were not those I would have chosen for him. When I came upon them in his study that next night, I saw in them promise, even if they told a story slightly different than that I sought to tell.

My work had only just begun.

I took that first taste in 1640, when he remained strong, and his gray eyes were sharp. He became a name in the politics of his day, and in his evenings he sang for friends, his voice melodious. Surely some blood of ancient bard reared up in this long-descended son.

Nightly, I caressed him with gentle inspiration and drank from the light within him, so delicately that he barely knew what life I drew from him, how unsated I departed, unfulfilled but leaving behind enough inspiration to take him through another day as I sought others to slake my thirst. But he made little progress on the great work I had commissioned of him. His father came to live with him. Then nephews. Then the sons of notables who saw in this great bard a teacher. Then he took a wife.

Enough! Distractions. Joy. Never would he know what he must know if he kept such counsel, such pleasure. Too many troubles took up his time. The man refused to write in winter, and with a gaggle of children and students about, and the nagging of wife and family—

I took his father first.

None doubted John Senior would live only a short time longer. Thus, none questioned the morn the man woke no more, though I felt sated that night for the first time in many nocturnal visits to this house.

Mary Powell Milton, his wife, deserved my sentence more than most to whom I meted it out. How she dallied with him! For better than two years she hid away on her parents' estate, biding her time to see if the Royalists would win. When it looked its worst for the Royalist cause, when Cromwell had marched through her father's holdings, then she begged Milton's mercy. How she fawned over him and coyly came to his bed, she who had yet to grace it in months of marriage! She was a shrewish girl, petty, raised to too much privilege. I let her stay, hoping her nature would drive Milton to seek solace in his work, to pine for peace. Not long after her return, she bore those simpering offspring whose loveliness and devotion to their father alone did I permit for his pleasure. Seven years I bided my time, waiting for Mary's nature to at last torture him into his transcendence. Eternity is a long time and I barely noted those years as they passed, but to lament how seldom I tasted the greatness of the bard I had commissioned.

Milton had not suffered yet. He had not made his sacrifices to greatness. One night, when Mary was thick with child and confined in separate rooms, I caught Milton alone in his bed after a long absence. I drank more deeply from the light within him than ever before. That morning, he woke, eyes bleary with a malady from which he never recovered. Months passed in which blindness stalked him. The aches in his joints, the pain in his waking, he named the gout. Better that he name his troubles for the Muse who inspired him while he slept. He remained of cheerful disposition. A bard who could not see. Could he not help but find this tragic? Yet each day he woke to his routine, counting on those around him to read when he could not, and write down the words he could not pen. He sang; he laughed. He must yet suffer.

His son John was a tiny morsel, sweet. The infant cooed at me. I have met many infants. They inspire nothing in me, small and unformed in intellect as they are. Milton's sorrow deepened, but the fire I inspired still smoldered only. Mary mourned, too loudly, drawing the master from his writing. This in summer, when his writing vein flowed its sweetest! It became intolerable.

Of Mary I drank deeply. I did not care that veins collapsed, that heart and lung labored, that her body tremored, that a child inside her insisted on what little life I left, so it could ensure another child would be born to trouble Milton, to perhaps be taken from him. For there is no room for children in the life of a bard, a master. Sacrifice Mary must be, perhaps the child, in the name of the greatness I had commissioned. That she survived childbirth a few days stunned me. Soon Mary, too, had gone to dust.

One must suffer to be great, as an honor to one's people. Did that not fit the legends of my people, the lore of our lands as we wandered in search of our place in the world? Is that not what is presaged by the dragons' eternal standoff? Is it not in our constant search for the peace of the Otherworld? John Milton claimed himself a servant to the public good of England. John

Milton must suffer as I had. He must lose all. From within that Hell, he would see the truth of this world. I would show it to him. And he would be great.

I realized one day that Milton was aging. Thirteen years had passed since first I read "Lycidas," and eleven since I first tasted his greatness, his potential, each night leaving a morsel in his ear. It was not enough. In that time he had gotten himself three surviving daughters to trouble his life, the eldest a sickly thing with infirm mind. Perhaps I drank too deep of Mary when that child was first forming from the chaos of Mary's womb.

Milton remained affable, sweet. Nothing troubled him. He fired off political rebuttals, becoming too involved in the politics of the world to remember that it was the Church he must battle, the Church he must slay with the two-handed sword he had glorified in "Lycidas."

Still, each night, I came to him.

"Man is like the apple tree of Avalon," I whispered into him one night. "Mind and body a replica, a microcosm of nature. Like the tree's roots set deep into the heart of the dragon, the knowledge, with the branches reaching skyward to the god of the sun, and through the middle runs the heart-sap, the link."

The following morning he asked his nephew to write for him of Adam and Eve and a Tree of Knowledge. There were times I wondered if he truly heard the Muse who troubled him each night. In a young boy's script, the nephew penned some claptrap about the fall of man due to an evil serpent. At first I thought to rage at Milton in his dreams, to call him the true fool he sounded spouting such Christian tropes. Then I saw the kernel of that seed I'd sown, running through his tale of some fallen angel who had somehow authored, through pride, all evil in the world, had orchestrated the tragedy of Man. That fallen angel, whom he named Satan, confessed in pride that not only had he challenged the Christian gods, but in doing so created Hell. An inner Hell. As I created in John Milton his inner Hell.

That night I drank most deeply.

"Myself am Hell," Milton muttered the next day, squinting for some glimpse of pen and page. He attributed the line to Satan. Sometimes I find John amusing.

His sight failed him completely. Still he would not settle in his ways. He needed me more than ever. I could taste the genius within him, the sweet flavor of revenge, the words of truth. He advertised for an amanuensis who might do more than take dictation, but also read in the many languages in which John had an interest. I could not have asked for better opportunity if I had whispered it in his ear. Of course, I had.

At last I came openly into his life, an amanuensis fit to order. I named myself Merrill. Each morning before dawn I arrived to read him his Bible in Hebrew for half an hour, not without a great measure of revulsion. Long before cock's crow he would send me away while he took his breakfast. I dared not slip out into the growing light of day, but would retire to his darkened study. There, through the morning to midday I would write his words. With far older face he might have seen me, could he, and more masculine of feature than the Muse who dropped words into his ear. But he could not see. Each day as Merrill I recorded for him the verses I had inspired in my visit as his patroness the night previous. In deepest night, I was his heavenly muse, immortalized in the words I penned for him.

"Sing Heav'nly Muse," he implored in the opening verses of his great epic.

I sang for him. Indeed.

Mornings he awoke, verses in his heart, a weariness he blamed on the gout, and often even open sores that still leaked a trace of blood, a measure of his light I dared not tap. He awaited me impatiently as I hugged shadows in the early morns of summer, me a creature of the night forced to embolden day. If late come from finding the blood to sate me when I could not take my fill of him, he would lament his need to be *milked*, mewling and plaintive like the she-cow to which he compared himself with his gentle humor. He did not know that it was at night that his Muse milked him.

In this manner, John and I penned many a verse for his epic tale. Ever did he try to twist my meanings, ever did I try to spin them back into the sphere of their intent. His Satan becomes serpent, dragon, wyrm. Red Dragon, White Dragon in the great Cauldron beneath the land, battling ever to hold the forces of evil at bay—these he names serpents. Name is nothing. Intent is all. He claimed a survival of sacred history in the legends . . . my past. Pagan, he called my beliefs, claiming that even the Titans, who took serpent forms in the battle with the gods of light on Olympus, proved a revolt of angels. It proved only that the dragon slumbers beneath all the lands. He said of this Satan, that within him is Hell. Like unto my dragons?

"You chose a tragic hero in this Satan, and made him Hell," I stated once, seeing it with a wonderment I let escape aloud. His sightless eyes gazed at me. It is not unlike that fate I have chosen for him, this inner Hell. "Here, the angel Abdiel rejects Satan, our hero, and proclaims his brave obedience to Adam and God. Was it not rather foolish disobedience to his nature for Abdiel to reject the leader who fostered him, a leader who espoused a belief in the free will necessary for worshipping your god?"

John could always justify his musings, making me cite biblical passages to support his twisted beliefs, even one in which free will was important. Except for angels. Sometimes his thinking came so close to where I led him, yet the Christian poison in him steered him so far from the mark. Like his claim that the material world is what his god made, and the Romans' miracles were only so much superstition, clouding truth. He could see this wisely, yet would not accept the miracles, the magic, in nature—the very thing he called god-made.

"You should seek truth in the beliefs of the ancients of this land," I told him once. "See? In nature is the perfection of your beliefs. You claim that. In your epic you grant glory to all these great pagan gods, showing by example how they demonstrate free will in following the way of the dragon, Satan."

"You try to twist my words to support paganism," John laughed, then as swiftly his mouth turned sour. "I want no doubt here. They are symbols that Pride—that Pride so crucial to the Fall—brought them from their perch. Dispersed in air, earth, water, and under earth, it is the pagan gods' constant rebellion against the laws of God that the heathens mistakenly honored, thinking it nature. This is the heart of Chaos."

He ordered me to pen the words claiming that Saturn fled to the Celtic land and was imprisoned on the Isle of Anglesey.

"Near to where Edward King's ship foundered?" I aimed my knife surely. The sweet man never took it amiss but merely nodded, and prodded me continue.

Vengeance is not always so easily won.

I sang to him in his sleep some nights, sitting in his dark room, the scent of euphoria-inducing, narcotic herbs thick on the night breeze, his breaths slow and measured in a silent house where all slept with the power of my skills in their lungs. Even if standing in the doorway of his moon-washed room, no one but Milton would hear my angelic song so softly sung.

"The beginning is music," he told me one morning. "The songs of angels created the world. So doth the Muse sing to me of the beginning I seek."

"As the bards are wont to sing?" I prodded, hoping he would remember the roots of his inspiration.

"If I knew no better, Merrill, I would think you a pagan. I am a man of science."

How I laughed at that. "You called upon a Muse, a pagan tradition."

"Figurative—"

"Powerful to seek the aid of pagan inspiration, John."

He laughed then, that high pleasantness that I could not yet purge from him, though I had made waste his body.

"Write this," he said to me, ordering me to pen that his Muse is a Celestial Patroness, who "deigns her nightly visitation unimplor'd, and dictates to me slumb'ring, or inspires easy my unpremeditated verse." Certainly he knew his source!

"Urania, you claim your Muse here, this pagan cosmic creature," I counter, gesturing at a verse he could not see. "The Urania of understanding? Sister of wisdom? Is this the fruit of the Tree of Knowledge?" Did the first words I had ever spoken to him still twist into an unfamiliar shape inside him?

"No, no. That Shepherd who first taught the Chosen Seed," he countered, ordering me to pen his inspired verses. "In the beginning, how the Heavens and Earth rose out of Chaos. I call that Muse Light."

"As in Beli?" I return. "As in the god of death who is the celebration of the light of the Otherworld? Or perhaps you think of Don his wife, goddess-mother?"

"You and your mythos, Merrill. Perhaps I refer to the light to illuminate my world, so I needn't rely on an impertinent—"

"You beg of the Celestial Light to 'shine inward, and the mind through all her powers irradiate, there plant eyes—' Do you thus claim a divine illumination? You who claim there are no miracles, that dreams cannot be prophecy?"

"Oh, Merrill, you are becoming foolish."

With that he dismissed me yet again.

That night I spoke into his ear of light, of the sun god, of the gods of the Otherworld, of the fires of Beltaine. Fiery light. He turned it into his Empyrean light of the heavens and tried to distinguish it from hellish fires. How tragic the way his Catholic upbringing wormed its way into his subconscious, subverted the wisdom all knew to be true.

"Who are these Belial, Mammon and Beelzebub," I asked as I sought proper spellings one morn.

"Tropes," John explained. "Readers expect them. All because of Tasso and his popularity."

"Are there not other names for the other devils in Satan's assembly than those names of the pagan guides readers would not expect to be named among the devils?" I looked over the list of pagans he had named, even my own mythos, as among the evils gathering against his god.

Again he laughed. From where did he find this wellspring of humor? I sought it, and drank deeply of him each night, slipping in like a dream, departing a nightmare, a silent shadow on his windowsill, his bedside. The gout worsened. He needed to suffer, to see through his blindness.

Years passed.

His daughters grew restive, forced to read to him when day glimmered through windows and I must retire. He took another wife, Katherine, who, thankfully, kept separate rooms.

I drained her slowly, and she failed this world in childbed. Though this time the sweet morsel went to dust with her. John had enough children and this second wife was no less shrewish than Mary, taking his attention from that which he must do, his commission, his role. I felt no remorse and though John mourned, he overcame it quickly.

As fond as I had grown of his daughters, they too became trouble. Anne, comely but slow, I shopped out as a seamstress. Deborah could read French, Italian, Latin, and Greek passably well. She replaced me too easily. The Muse left behind a hint and soon we married her off to Dublin. And Mary, that girl was too like her mother to last long in any house I had come to run. I sent her away as I had Anne.

I had John to myself.

At one point I moved him into the country, with claim that the plague might be a threat to him, though I knew well I could protect him from it, as all who knew the dragons' prophecy could. It took him from all those friends plying him for favors and wisdom. I could make a more comfortable home, dark, with no one about to open shutters. I could illuminate his mind night and day, feed to my heart's content, plant the seeds of greatness. Oh that those heady days could have lasted!

We did not always write. There were times when debate with John almost warmed me, almost gave me the sense that perhaps blood once again flowed in my veins, that the Cauldron from which I had drunk on Anglesey might be unmade with the fire of another bard's wit and lifeblood. John advocated liberty against tyranny. He hated the monarchy. With such poison pen could he slap the monarchists!

"You Welsh, still praying your High King will come?" John laughed at me once. I don't think he knew how that assault stung. "And in his dictatorial might will you find better than a tyrant?"

"As your One God?" I returned, letting just a hint of my power, my scorn, leak through my words, slap him back against his dark. How he recoiled! "Oh, pardon, there are saints and angels are there not? Would they be Parliament?"

"Humility is virtue," John said quietly. "Remember your role, Merrill. Your arrogance forgets whom you serve."

"You claim humility a basic tenet of your faith," I returned. "Which you exceed. You think to proclaim the word of your god!" I held up the sheaf of papers that would one day become his *Christian Doctrine*. He knew to what I gestured. Yet he would not rise to the bait.

He wanted to dedicate his life to some public good. A virtue, perhaps, even the virtue in the man that made me love him so. The poem we crafted together, I thought that a thing for the public good. Thinly veiled beneath each pious line the dragons called. He could not see. He would never see. And when I read back to him each verse, he heard not the deception, so well had I hidden it in inflection and double entendre. Oh Arderyd!

Once, in a quiet moment when winter and the gout could not bring him from his bed, he asked me in his soft humor why I clung so hard to the myths of the past.

"Sweet appletree who grows in the clearing," I sang softly, a lay I had written in those evil times. "The lords of Rhydderch's court do not see you although they trample the ground at your feet . . . I am hateful to the followers of Rhydderch. After Gwendoleu, no prince honors me. I have neither joy nor visits from my beloved. At the battle of Arderyd I wore a gold torc but now I am despised by the swan-white woman."

"Now you quote Taliesin at me, you rogue," John laughed with pleasure at my cleverness.

"That is Myrddin, not Taliesin."

"Myrddin, Merlin, was but Taliesin's pseudonym. A myth given life. Taliesin served the Christian King Uryen—"

"And Myrddin sought the death of Uryen in revenge for the murder of Gwendoleu, for the loss of the kingdom. Taliesin, a traitor—"

I went cold, as cold as the deeps of the Irish Sea, at his derisive laughter. I think *he* was the Adam of whom he wrote. The pride in him! The sureness that his was the doctrine in which to believe!

He had married again. Elizabeth. As if the man had no mission to pursue! But we wrote now in earnest and I allowed him this small pleasure to warm his dark bed at night. I drank little of him these days anyway, so little he had to spare. Elizabeth kept me sated and she smelled sweet when I caressed her warm skin, like the memory of my humanity.

The drama he once envisioned became an epic poem of such magnitude it took my breath from me, me who had breathed so many breaths. Thirty years after I dined upon Edward King, we published *Paradise Lost. A Poem Written in Ten Books.* So desperate he felt, that death was soon upon him, it went to press not quite finished.

So uncanny how his mind worked, taking his Muse's inspiration, refining, crystallizing each thought. He countered his Roman Trinity with an unholy trinity: Satan, Sin, and Death. I saw in them the whispers of late nights when I crept into his herb-scented room, singing my spells: Satan the twin dragons that gave life to our land and protected us from ill; Sin the will of our people, the strength to hold true in the face of the usurpers from Rome; and Death, promise of wonders in the Otherworld where goddesses awaited, the ghosts of the Isle of Mona watching the wheel of stars overhead as the vengeance is played out, paid out.

Not quite finished. Not quite done, we reworked and polished, and created the perfect balance, a work of music in words. I gave him small breaths of life, then stole from him in those same breaths, illuminating his soul, illuminating his being with the Truth of the land he stood upon.

At last, thirty-three years after that first taste I'd taken of him, the final draft of the masterpiece went to press, the final draft of my ultimate vengeance. For in a treatise to his Christian gods did I craft a bard's heroic song. For beneath each word did I illuminate the truth, the folly, of this usurping god.

John turned his attention to *On Christian Doctrine*, his claim of Christianity, his treatise that a book translated in the words of the Roman Church could somehow espouse Truth.

I could not let his doctrine negate all the work I had done. I needed the scholars to question his intent, to remember that he had claimed the clergy corrupt and had been maligned for blasphemy. This doctrine confirmed his belief that he celebrated *his* god, not mine! I needed this final act of revenge, to take at last, and most finally, from one I had loved most deeply, to again, through this sacrifice, transcend my existence as I had when I touched my lips to the dark liquid in the Cauldron. My end, certainly, was not come. I might yet find Vivian in the Forest of Broceliande, if such place lives beyond the legends made of me, and let that creature of Fairie lead me on the paths of the Otherworld for a time, to rest from the trials of vengeance and vow.

One night when the humors had sent Elizabeth to her own room and left John in his own darkness, alone, I came without my herbs. Though at first I sang in the angelic voice he had always known—his eyes peering up at me in wide wonder, though they could certainly not see me silhouetted in the moonlight washing his bed—I slowly let my voice sink down into its natural tenor, the voice he had known all these years as Merrill.

"You claim that the paradise lost is the power to know good without knowing evil," I said to him. "The Fortunate Fall, as you yourself know, John, is not fortunate at all. It is a fall into arrogance and pride, into the belief that you must usurp all other beliefs. And in your sin of pride, in your failure to see, you perpetuate that evil. As myth you decry Truth. As Truth you claim myth."

"What blasphemy comes from a mere amanuensis hired to take my dictation and read my tomes!" His rare anger kindled. It warmed me in a

way that felt ancient and unfamiliar. The hunger in me licked up from
within. So long had I waited to be sated.

"You choose of your own will to confuse good and evil," I went on. "You
accept as divine the thoughts you hear in your sleep, to mold the wrong-
ness. It is the nature, as you said once, that is the closest to the maker and
spirit. Not you, little man. You worship pride—"

"And you are the expert in this!"

"Since the battle of Arderyd I had lost all feeling even were the sky to
fall and the sea to overflow," I chanted softly, the words I penned so long
ago. "I thought to find a bard who might again see through to the Truth.
The twin dragons grow restive."

"What foolishness, Merrill, are you spouting at this late hour?"

I went on with a dialogue I once recorded between myself and Taliesin,
cited now in tomes I knew John had read. "It was Maelgwn whom I saw
fight, his warriors roared in the heart of battle. The army of Maelgwn will
hurtle forward striking men with death in the bloody plain. At the battle of
Arderyd, when the moment comes it will be they who lead the hero to
victory . . . Seven score generous warriors have gone to the shadows. In
the forst of Kelyddon they found death." I felt his blood, heard its movement, rapid. Then sudden, slow. Fear. Faltering heart. Tremoring limbs.
"You know not what you scorn, what oldest of Truths you have set aside
with a wave of your hand and a laugh, John Milton."

"Merrill—"

"That is not my name! In the end, when all was lost, you gave us the
reconciliation of Adam and Eve, the symbolic triumph over ignorance. You
must show us, too, the reconciliation with Truth. John, we must be one. I
can give you eternity as a bard of worthy stature, one like me to sow in the
dreams of the great, wisdom—"

"You are Satan!"

"No, I am Hell. Yours. Living, breathing, within you, drawing from you.
The internal Hell you created, John." I drew nearer his bed. His empty eyes
sought the source of whatever furtive sounds I made, recoiled from the feel
of me leaning across his bed.

"I refuse. I will not be a tool of Satan!"

"Then, like Adam and Eve, be cast out of your garden, John. I give you
now Truth."

More gently did I drink from him than my hunger would want. But we
had been long together, crafting this journey of vengeance. So deep I
drank, of illumination, of all. His breath gasped in my ear as he clutched at
his blankets, fell back slowly, sagged against me with his auburn-grayed
head tilted to one side, giving me room to draw the last, last, last light

from within him. An Empyreal light he would call it, like something heavenly and God-made. He knew not the Truth even then.

Before his family could find him, his breath a shallow rattle as only but a tiny gathering of lifeblood trickled through him, I hid his blasphemous tract. His fool friend, Skinner, found a draft before I could consign it. What foolish sins have lived on in his *Christian Doctrine*, scholars refuting the words I built with such painstaking precision as they point to his *true* meaning as set out in his doctrine.

One last breath he took. His blind eyes, gray eyes, looked upon me, saw, knew me.

Beneath the land the dragons wept.

# NOTES FROM THE BRIDGE

### Richard Parks

February was a bleak month for Tom Obrien at the best of times, but this particular February had gone too far.

Tom couldn't say just what settled the matter. Maybe it was the latest publisher's rejection letter with its vaguely dismissive wording, or maybe it was the simple act of rereading his latest novel manuscript, now cold in his memory. Either way, on this particular February evening he was moved to write one more page—just a short note, really—tape it to the computer screen, and find the open walkway on Armview's tallest bridge.

"I never really thought I'd fail," he said softly.

It was the first time he'd even used the words. Twenty years of trying: books, plays, short stories . . . and all he had to show for it was a file cabinet full of rejections and a few small press magazines that had clearly been short on filler that particular month. Tom looked at the cold, dark stream wandering along far below, losing itself in the evening shadows. He tried to describe it out of habit, and all he could come up with was that it was probably deep enough . . .

Someone was crying. Tom looked up from the void and saw a young woman standing by the rail about ten feet away from him. She looked out over the distance, occasionally dabbing at a tear with a white lace handkerchief. Her hair was long and black. She wore a long white coat that might have been leather or cloth—he couldn't quite focus on it because her face had taken all the attention he had. She was the most perfect, the most heartbreakingly beautiful woman he had ever seen.

She didn't have the commodity looks of this year's starlet or model; Tom felt almost nothing of the attraction such a woman would normally hold for him. This was beauty in the sense of a Botticelli painting or a Michelangelo sculpture.

It occured to Tom that perhaps she was here for the same reason he was. Yet it was hard for him to imagine what could be so wrong in such a person's life, try as he might.

*Only the one who bears the trouble can judge its weight.*

Tom blinked. Where had that come from? The thought seemed alien, as if it didn't even belong to him.

"Are you all right, miss?"

She looked at him. Her expression didn't change. "It's just very sad, that's all. This is always sad." There was a trace of an accent in her voice, something suggesting time and distance and melancholy. Hearing her voice, Tom didn't feel sad at all.

He didn't know what to say, not knowing what "this" was, but he very much wanted to say something. Anything. He wanted her to speak again. "I'll get better, I'm sure. It just doesn't seem like it now."

"Is that really the best you can do, Tom?"

Tom sighed. His personal gloom settled back over him, stronger than before. "I guess so," he said. His best wasn't good enough, never had been. He looked back out over the water and thought of—very briefly—flying.

"If you're going to speak to me, then look at me," she said.

Tom looked, and for another long moment he forgot about the bridge, about everything. One thing he did know—she wasn't here to kill herself. "Why were you crying?"

"Grief. It will pass."

"I'm sorry. Did you lose someone close to you?"

She shook her head. "Not yet. Soon."

"I'm sorry to hear that, miss . . . ?"

She looked at Tom and the sorrow in her eyes made his heart want to break. "Lana," she said.

"Lana," Tom savored the name. "Who are you crying for?"

"You, Tom," she said. "It's you."

That was twice she'd called him by name. Tom knew there was something strange about that but for the life of him he couldn't bring himself to care. He was enthralled. It was not simple lust, or even mystique or fascination. He'd known all of those before, with different women over the years, and there was no doubt in his mind—this was different. She said she grieved for him and the only thing he felt was relief that it was him and no one else who called that much emotion from her now. Just him, even though he did not understand it at all.

"I'm not dead," he said. Tom wanted her to know that. It seemed important.

"Then why did you come here?" she asked.

"I—" Tom's excuse died on his lips. Truth was needed here. Truth was all that would serve. "I was going to kill myself. I changed my mind."

She smiled. "Remember that, Tom. I'll be in touch."

There was a sudden murmur of voices off to Tom's right, a boy and a girl arm in arm coming up the walkway. When Tom turned back, the woman was gone.

Tom lingered on the bridge for a long time, not really hoping that the woman would return because he knew she would not. He looked out over the rail, trying to recapture the proper mood for suicide, but it just would not come. It needed despair to work, and for some reason he was fresh out. He finally gave up and walked the streets downtown to his apartment.

The note was still taped to the computer screen where he'd left it. Tom stared at the outpouring of his wounded soul for as long as he could stand it.

"This really sucks," Tom said, honestly surprised.

The note was full of cheap despair and excuses and a sort of maudlin self-examination that was worse than embarrassing: it was badly done.

Oh, the prose was fine as far as it went. The sentences were tightly constructed and grammatical. The scenes were rendered with a vivid, active voice for the most part. But it never quite worked, never produced that moment of connection or clarity that could move a reader to share his grief, his anger, his pain. Without that connection, what was the point? What did it matter how well the piece was written? It was like an elegant building in which no one could live.

*Twenty years of trying, dead-end jobs, writing day and night, and this is the best I can do?*

Tom crumpled the note and threw it in the general direction of his overflowing wastebasket. He had the computer turned on before the wad finished bouncing off the pile and onto the carpet. Since he'd met Lana on the bridge, everything had changed but nothing had changed. Tomorrow he might be on the bridge again. Probably would be. And Tom would be damned if he'd let his last cry of despair be less than perfect. Tom started his word processor and typed the first line without even slowing to think about it. The truth. Simple and brutal as a punch in the gut.

"I never thought I'd fail."

He kept typing without a break until the page was done. He didn't stop; he wasn't finished. There was more. Much more. Six months later, his suicide note was a five-hundred-page autobiographical novel titled *Notes from the Bridge*. Six months after that it was a Wesson Press hardcover with a more than decent advance for a first novel and an even better print run.

The reviews were glowing.

                              *   *   *

Tom met Kathy on his second book tour when she picked him up at the Atlanta airport.

"You don't enjoy this, do you?" she asked by way of introduction.

"Huh?"

She smiled and held out her hand. "Sorry. I recognized you from your jacket photo. I'm Kathy Land, from the Wesson Press publicity department. I've been assigned to drive you to the Tate & Matthews signing." She eyed his carry-on bag suspiciously. "Is that all?"

"Hmm? Oh sure. I don't need much." Tom felt about two steps behind her already. Kathy was a small, freckled redhead who moved with the quick energy of a minnow.

She shrugged. "Whatever. Follow me."

"I'm trying . . . what did you mean back there, about me not enjoying this?"

She grinned back at him. "I can tell. Most first-time authors would kill for the kind of publicity push you're getting. You look like you'd rather be somewhere else."

"I'm not ungrateful," Tom said.

"I didn't say you were. I just don't think it's that important to you."

Tom reddened slightly. "I've been working for this for twenty years, Miss Land."

Kathy's expression didn't change. She indicated the terminal with a sweep of her arm that at once indicated the crowds and the noise and even the confusion with one expressive gesture. "For this?" she asked mildly.

Tom understood, and he couldn't help smiling. "No. Not for this."

The attention had been pleasant enough at first, but none of it compared to holding his first book in his arms, seeing his name on the cover, seeing strangers in a dentist's office or on the plane reading it and smiling or getting misty-eyed or frowning, or reacting in any one of a hundred ways to the emotional connection it made with them. That was what he'd worked for. Not, as Kathy Land had indicated, "this."

"You're a very perceptive young lady," Tom said.

She smiled. "Yes. But they don't pay extra for that."


It had been a good signing. The Tate & Matthews clerks were attentive, the crowd of a good size and very appreciative; there were few obvious crazies and even those well behaved. Kathy appeared near the entrance and smiled at him. It was almost time to go. He signed the last of the stock and turned to greet Kathy when he noticed the envelope on his author's table.

*I'd swear that wasn't there a moment ago.*

Tom picked up the envelope, admiring the flowing, elegant script. His name was written on the envelope, but that was all.

"You have an admirer, I think," Kathy said. "Quite a lady."

"You saw her?" Tom asked.

"Sure. Long, lean, and drop-dead gorgeous. Hair like a Spanish señorita, smile like a shark. I'd kill for those legs, frankly," Kathy said. She frowned. "Don't tell me you didn't notice. She was standing right by the table when you waved to me."

Tom felt a sudden chill. It was rather pleasant. He just shook his head and slit the envelope with his penknife and pulled out a piece of creamy vellum notepaper. Tom read what was written there in the same flowing script. It didn't take long.

> Tom:
>     You've done well, and you're almost ready. Soon. Be patient. Remember me.
>
>                                                   —Lhiannan S.

That was all. Tom put the note back into its envelope and tucked it away. He had no doubt that the note had come from Lana. Even the odd spelling of her name—her proper name, he realized—attested to that. It was no great surprise. He'd suspected what Lana was all along, and now he was sure. She'd as much as told him. It didn't matter. He owed her everything, and whatever she wanted of him he would give when the time came.

Kathy was frowning again. "Are we still on for coffee? I mean, if you're busy I'll understand."

"Hmm? Oh, no, nothing like that. I'd love to have coffee with you," Tom said, though for the life of him he couldn't remember making the date. That didn't matter, either.

The diner was heavy on atmosphere and service and the conversation hadn't been nearly as awkward as Tom had expected. Their second cup was nearly gone but now Kathy was looking more and more distracted.

"There hasn't been time for hobbies since *Notes* was published," Tom said. "But I have a few outside interests. Folklore, for one. Discovered that when I was doing research for my first novel. A real dog, I'm afraid—damn . . . I'm boring you. I'm sorry."

Kathy shook her head. "Not a bit. It's just that it's way past time for a confession."

"About the coffee date?" Tom asked, trying not to smile.

Kathy looked a little chastened. "I wondered if you'd figure it out."

"I'm smarter than I look," Tom said. "Well, a little anyway."

Kathy leaned back in her chair. Tom decided she was rather cute.

"It's not that," she said. "I've just been around writers often enough to recognize that out-to-lunch stare you get sometimes. You need someone to deal with the real world for you when you get like that. Otherwise people could take advantage. Like me."

Tom raised his cup. "Here's to advantage."

Kathy smiled. "You're sweet. So. Was she your girlfriend? Or want to be?"

"Oh, you mean the one who left the note? No. Just someone I met once. She saved my life," Tom said, realizing what he'd said only after it was said. He hadn't meant to reveal so much, but Kathy was easy to talk to. Besides, it was the simple truth.

"Remind me to thank her if we ever meet," Kathy said. Then she fixed Tom with a look that reminded him uncomfortably of Lana. "I'm too forward. Say so. It won't hurt my feelings."

"It's all right."

"Then would you mind telling me just how she saved your life?"

"I was depressed when my previous books weren't publishable. I was going to jump off a bridge."

Kathy's eyes widened. "I knew it! She's Elaine!"

That was the name Tom had given Lana in *Notes from the Bridge*. "Well . . . she inspired Elaine." What he didn't say was that she had inspired the whole thing.

Kathy glanced at her watch. "You have a plane to catch. I'm going to be in Armfield next week on business. Would you like to get together then?"

Everything that happened to Tom since that day on the bridge was all about possibilities. He didn't know how many there would be, or how much time there was to explore them. He saw no good reason to pass any of them by. "Yes," he said. "I'd like that very much."

The next letter arrived in the mail in the usual way, some three months later on the same day that Kathy's plane was due in from Atlanta. Tom didn't tell her about it when he met her at the airport; there was no point in worrying her until he was certain, and he didn't know how to explain it anyway. That evening Tom sat down to write the first book he'd attempted since *Notes.*

This book began with Kathy Land, but it didn't get very far. In the old days he'd have just pressed on, blissfully ignorant that what he put down was shallow at best and not very interesting at worst. No low points. No high points. Well-written, but not special. Tom knew his work would be that way from now on, and after *Notes from the Bridge* he knew he could never settle for anything less than special ever again.

The envelope with his name so carefully written on the outside now sat folded in his pocket like the weight of the world. A reminder. Tom had known that what Lana had written was true, knew what was required of him now, but out of fairness to Kathy and his own stubbornness he had to prove it. Now he had.

"Damn."

Tom gave up and turned the computer off. He peered into the bedroom to make sure Kathy was still sleeping peacefully as he'd left her some hours before. The curtains were open; soft light from the nearly full moon shining through framed her like a portrait. Not Venus, perhaps, but strong and loving and real. The last few months had been—if not exactly peaceful, that wasn't Kathy's forte—good. Yes, very good. Tom could even honestly say that he was happy.

And that it didn't make a damn bit of difference.

*Happiness is a fine thing, Kathy. I've enjoyed it. But I never asked for it, and that's never been what mattered to me. I'm sorry.*

The time he'd had after the book, and the time with Kathy had been a gift, that was all. He was grateful, but more important than any of it was that one brush with the divine that had allowed him, just once, to get it right. And for all that *Notes from the Bridge* was Tom's heart and soul given form, they did not belong to him. The book, yes. That was his forever, perhaps literally. But not heart nor soul. There was only one each of those to a customer, and his coin was spent.

*Can't have your cake . . .*

Tom grinned, thinking that the real trouble with clichés is that they're simple truth, simply told. That's how they got to be clichés.

Tom went back into his office and handwrote all this in a letter to Kathy. It wasn't a book this time or even the start of one, but he made it good enough so that, if Kathy had to see it, at least he would have no reason to be ashamed. Regret was another matter, and he did want her to understand. Tom crept back into the bedroom and kissed Kathy very softly on the forehead, careful not to wake her. Then he dressed quietly and quickly and stepped out into the bright moonlight.

Tom knew where to go. He kept to the most direct route, cutting through alleys and darkened street corners with barely a thought. There was no danger of meeting anyone, of finding any interference at all. He recognized the dim figure waiting for him on the bridge long before he was close enough to see her face.

*She's still the most beautiful woman I've ever seen.*

It seemed strange to think so, especially now. Tom may have had regrets, but meeting Lana was not one of them.

"You're prompt. I like that," she said. "Do you know why you're here?"

"I know what you are, Lana; how could I not know the rest?"

"You do? Then tell me—what am I?"

"There are several names for it, but what they all distill down to is a kind of muse. With teeth."

Lana showed those teeth, flashing white in the moonlight. "All muses have teeth, and the best ones have the sharpest of all. I am the best, Tom, and for a while, so were you. Now I will have my due. Would you deny me?"

He shook his head. "Never."

Lana looked a little wistful. "You called me, you know. That first day on the bridge. Whether you understood or not, you did ask for this."

Tom recognized the kindness Lana offered him, but he didn't need it. His death stood before him but that wasn't what he saw. Nor, as before, a woman. Nor even a creature pretending to be, with all the names such had worn over the centuries: vampire, succubus, *lhiannan shee*. No. It was the idea of beauty itself given form and voice by a thousand generations of poets and writers and painters and singers. More, Tom knew that—in common with all of them—he had been privileged to touch that divine ideal, and bring back a shadow of it to the world; a world now just a little less threadbare. That was more than simply enough—it was everything.

Tom's smile was pure devotion. "I know. I love you."

"Of course," she said and began to feed.

# DRAMATURGE

*Susan Shwartz*

Rain sluiced down from the cliffs of Elsinore, mingling with the froth of waves dashed onto the rocks. Even with his keen night-sight, the Player King could scarcely distinguish rain from spray. Neither was as bad as running water, much less water that had been blessed; but the water made him faintly giddy the way he'd felt, centuries ago, when he drank too much ale.

Thunder pealed out, vying with the cannon's roar as the new king caroused with full Danish ceremony. Melodramatic and wasteful, thought the Player King. He had to get his company—what was left of it—into some safe haven.

The remaining tragedians edged cautiously along the winding road in a storm that outroared even their finest rants. As their horse stumbled, an actor unharnessed it. Taking its place, he and the Player King drew their last battered wagon up the twisting road to the palace.

"Put not thy trust in princes," murmured the Player King. These days, he answered to the name of Gonzago. That had been the name of one of his greatest successes until its last performance brought them closer to the stake—through the heart or surrounded by fire—than they'd been for decades.

"What's that?" grunted Lucianus. He was younger than the Player King, both in birth years and in life after death, and skilled at saving his strength. Now he was hungry. If they could not find some drunk or stage-mad collegian on whom to feed, they might be glad of a live horse before long.

Gonzago paused, letting the traces slip from his shoulders. "Long ago, I used to hear the priests say 'Put not thy trust in princes.' And then I would go out and play Noah or Herod or Pilate. At the church door at first, and later upon pageant wagons."

Lucianus listened, despite his exhaustion. Gonzago didn't often deign to talk about his centuries of life, and knowledge was survival. "Mind you," the Player King went on, "my lines were not nearly as good as the priest's, but I also earned the crowd's cheers and a guild's thanks. And its silver and the occasional pieces of gold, which were much more to the point."

"There haven't been pageant wagons for years."

"Longer than that." Gonzago set shoulder to the wheel, this time, and pushed upslope. "Unsanctified, the priests decided we actors were. Unworthy to be buried in Christian burial. So *our* numbers rose."

He had had a longer run than most players. Much longer. Was it coming to an end now? Last season, they had been the rage: the tragedians of the city, favored by the prince, absent though he was in Germany.

Lesser companies played in the afternoon in open theaters; they played at night, lit by candles or torches. Hardly authentic, said the Grecians, who quoted Aristotle rather too often, but quite brilliantly eccentric. Admission to performances was highly prized—and highly priced, as well. Now Gonzago would be surprised if there wasn't a price upon their heads.

"He that plays the king shall be welcome."

Most gratifying, Gonzago had been sure. Cocksure. He remembered the invitation that fool chamberlain had carried from the prince, back from Wittenberg for the king's funeral. Gonzago remembered the man from at least a generation back. He had spent time grubbed from his lectures sniffing about theaters, whether after boys or secrets Gonzago never cared to guess. Worse yet, he had pressed into Gonzago's hands the worst piece of bombast in blank verse—his own composition, God save us all—Gonzago had ever read and urged him to stage it. Tragical-comical-historical-pastoral, indeed. Gonzago shuddered as if from the elevation of the Host.

Old Polonius's rheumy eyes had bleared and squinted, then finally blanked even as he greeted them. Gonzago need not have grown his beard. It grew hard for the likes of him to change his appearance as the centuries crept by. Those very centuries had refined his art, his caution, and his presence—which drew admirers as honey lures flies.

The chamberlain had scurried off on his thin hams, determined to intrude upon his prince with the good news. At least, it should have been good news had it come from anyone else. He always had been long-winded. If he rose again, like Gonzago and his company, and walked the nights, he would talk his victims to death, not bleed them dry.

Lucianus and Clown, who doubled on secondary roles, pressed their shoulders against the wheel of the wagon that was now their sole daytime refuge. This close to winter, the days were shorter: less time unconscious and at risk.

Who would have thought *The Murder of Gonzago* had blood enough in its argument to bring down a royal house? In the riot after King Claudius and Queen Gertrude had fled the play, drunken louts—otherwise known as courtiers—torched two of his company's wagons. At least that was at night, so they lost only some spare costumes. Worse luck yet were the imbeciles who stayed drunk long enough to heave a third wagon over the battlements. Two of the company, the boy and a musician, had sought protection from the sun in that one; and their bodies were dashed upon the rocks, past hope of rising once again.

The first guardpost was near. *You do not see us,* Gonzago whispered in his mind, exerting his will to cloud their vision, turn their faces away. They passed the cave he had scouted out the night before. He gestured to Clown to draw horse and wagon deep within. He, at least, would find sanctuary at dawn.

Gonzago and Lucianus slipped past the guards and into the palace grounds, toward the main building. Torchlight so bright that the feasting hall looked as if it were on fire leapt up to assault them. The lives within drew them like desirable fire. The new king, Norway's heir, young Fortinbras, stood before the throne, holding aloft an ancient drinking horn. Any archer could have picked him off. The kettledrums rumbled, the horns blared, and, as the great cannon fired at the clouds, the warrior prince drank the horn dry, and hurled it into the fire, to shouts of *"Vivat! Vivat!"*

There was blood in that man, and strength. Blood and fear prickled in the air, making the Player King's nostrils flare with longing. To feed *now* . . . if a guard had emerged right now, Gonzago would have drained him, and never mind the risks, bruiting the king's rouse. Some grave-ale indeed.

"You think *he* looks like a patron of the arts?" asked Lucianus. "Give him an axe and a bearskin, and it's 'from the fury of the Norsemen, God deliver us.' The lilt of Erse in his voice was very strong tonight. When he had been a stage-mad student, his name had been something like Lucius O'—no, Gonzago did not wish to remember that far back.

"Not he," said Gonzago. He pointed at the two men who sat close together, uncomfortably close to the young king should he take a mind to turn on them. Tributaries. Skeletons at the feast. "The English ambassadors. At some point, they'll have to go back home and report what's happened. And everyone knows they dearly love a good play in London. They're civilized. That's why they lost the war."

Lucianus nodded. "So we go to the ambassadors and say, 'Excuse me, your excellencies, but we're a cry of players with this little problem—we can't bear the light of day. But we'd like to go to London, please will you take us?' " His supple voice oozed sarcasm. "You've written better."

"Don't overact," Gonzago ordered. "It just needs the right actor."

Again, the new young king drank. The ambassadors tried for their lives' sake not to look mortally bored. They had brought news and tribute to Denmark; their lives depended on the new king's welcome. They would be very glad to return home as soon as possible.

A young man in a worn scholar's robe, a mourning band about his arm, bowed toward the throne, then slipped out of the room under cover of horn and kettledrum. Alone of those in the hall, his face bore the scars of genuine grief. Men in slashed and puffed finery that could be termed mourning only because it was black glanced daggers at his back. One whispered—from a safe distance—in Fortinbra's ear. The young king shrugged.

"Who do you suggest?" asked Lucianus. "You?"

Gonzago chuckled. A bolt of lightning seared down, almost purple, and the ground trembled with more than the buffeting of the sea far, far below. For an instant, neither of the men could see, not even with their augmented night-sight. "Our ambassador to the English ambassadors shall not," he said grandly, "be a player king, but a true prince."

He gestured toward where the lighting landed, on the grassy slopes below the palace. "Did I not always say that our prince had the soul of an actor? With his sins, do you really think he'll be welcome up in—" The word almost slipped from Gonzago's mouth. He gagged, and a trail of blood trickled down his chin, washed quickly away by the rain.

"So now what?" asked Lucianus.

"Now we find him and, somewhat prematurely, trade him The Resurrection for his old Mousetrap."

Lucianus began to laugh. His voice rose in the insane laughter that could rob the undead of their control. Gonzago should have slapped him. But the cannon that celebrated Fortinbras's crown and his capacity for ale boomed out, overpowering the terrible laughter of the two vampires.

As if their laughter had frightened the storm away, the clouds parted. Far, far overhead, the pitiless stars shone, inadequate rivals to the torches burning within the palace.

"Now what?" asked Lucianus.

"Now we find him. It shouldn't be hard."

"We've had enough rain to wash away the spoor," Lucianus protested. The rain was hard on him.

"It'll take more than rain to wash away the traces of death by violence, death by treachery. Blood's the least of it, though not for us. Follow me." He turned, sodden cape trying to swirl from his shoulders, toward the chapel.

Lucianus hung back.

"You call going into a chapel, standing before the—" even Lucianus's superbly modulated voice caught at the thought of crucifixes, the odor of sanctity, perhaps a priest chanting words that would pierce the ears of such creatures as they were.

"There has to be belief," Gonzago declared, "for there to be pain."

"You claim not to believe? You, who performed in . . . in . . ."

"These others," Gonzago said. "How strong do you think their faith is? Strong enough to turn it against us? Now, come on, if you have any hopes of making it back to the wagon before dawn."

They flitted across the courtyard, toward the battlements where once, as they had heard, the ghost of the old king had walked. No ghosts walked tonight: King Hamlet's murder had been avenged in blood—his brother, his wife, his son, and what seemed like half the court—and like the Norwegian, his enemy's son, who kinged it in the hall, his thirst was slaked.

"They brought him to lie here in state," said Gonzago. " 'Let four captains bear Hamlet like a soldier to the stage,' the new king said." He knelt as if in homage to the prince who was dead. His preternaturally long fingers scraped along the flagstones.

"They've moved him. I can sense it." Without needing to be pressed, Lucianus turned and strode resolutely to the chapel.

Whispering came from opened double doors, whispering and the clean faint light of candles. Gonzago and Lucianus, who had not flinched at the brilliance of torches in the hall, recoiled from the branches of candles, the red votive lights that burned within the church. Summoning his courage, Gonzago peered bravely within the chapel.

"He's been here, too," he whispered. "But I can tell you what isn't. The incense; all the images—the new learning's come and stripped the chapel almost bare. Careful now . . ." he ventured into the great cave of the chapel's mouth and started down the central aisle, expecting to find the prince's bier laid out in the crossing or before the high altar itself.

No candles flickered at the head and feet of the man who lay prostrate before the altar. No candles were needed, for the man was not dead. His shoulders shook, and Gonzago could hear him sobbing. Horatio, who had left King Fortinbras's grave-ale for the prince they sought. A good man, Gonzago thought. He shadowed the prince, but you'd never mistake him for a courtier. And now he grieved not the loss of a place or some danger to his own life, but the death of a friend. Gonzago took a step forward to comfort him—his first involuntary move in how many years?

*What are you thinking of? Approach an* altar? *Comfort a man you may have to kill?* He made himself stop. Mad vampires, like princes feigning madness, might be the stuff of drama, but they didn't survive for long.

Silent though Gonzago was, Horatio heard him. He rose without haste or shame.

"Lord Horatio," began Gonzago, but the scholar shook his head. Hollow of eye and cheek, it looked more like a death's head than those of the vampires. His own eyes ached in this sanctified space, and he felt himself starting to shake.

"No lord at all, except by *his* courtesy," said the scholar. The life in him seemed to glow about him and wake Gonzago's hunger. *To drain his throat in the church* . . . If a guard wandered by, he would be a dead man. "I am glad to see that you have come back to mourn him. He loved your plays."

Gonzago bent his head. Make it look like sorrow, not a reluctance to meet Horatio's eyes. *You'd be doing him a favor,* a devil's voice whispered in his ears.

"I wish this last one had worked out better," he murmured. The prince who was dead had lounged before the thrones of King Claudius and his mother, his head in the lap of a young girl who kept her back straight, though her voice quivered and her eyes shone enormous with tears. Surely he had drunk too much that night to speak to an innocent girl that way. But could anyone at the court truly be termed innocent?

The man who stood before him certainly was.

"It brought out the truth," said Horatio. " 'What is truth?' asked Pilate. No less than everything. But after what else happened, what else my poor prince did, I don't suppose he could have gone on . . ."

*Maybe it was for the best* quivered on the edge of sound, but was ruthlessly suppressed. The prince had forbidden *his* suicide, had commanded him to go on living.

"You're looking for him? They buried him, buried all of them, as quickly as they could."

Damn! Gonzago could understand why they'd shovel the king and queen and even that quenched firebrand of a Laertes underground as fast as possible. But Prince Hamlet had died a hero and a king. Why couldn't he have lain in state before the altar just one more day? Now they would have to play resurrection-man indeed and break open the tomb.

"The poison, you know. They were afraid the bodies wouldn't keep."

"Where does he lie?" Gonzago tensed. If it were in the crypt of this church, he was defeated before he began.

"In the old graveyard." He gestured rather vaguely in the direction of outside. "It was my idea. It's peaceful out there—not all this gloom. And it lets *him* pretend the murders never happened."

A rash man, this Horatio, to speak thus to a cry of players. But he thought he spoke to his prince's clients. His other clients.

"I'd take you to him myself, but there's been some trouble." A quiver in Horatio's voice, imperceptible except to a trained ear, brought Gonzago to heightened alertness.

In the storm of rumors following King Hamlet's death and Prince Hamlet's madness, he had heard that the old king walked and that guards, now said to have retired to the country (where no one had seen them either), had led Horatio to see him, and he had told the prince.

What now walked the night? Would Gonzago have to fight it? Perhaps he should send Lucianus back to fetch Clown, so there would be three of them.

Clearly, Horatio thought Gonzago's hesitation was a disappointment. "The . . . the *king* has given orders that no one go out there except under guard. Better wait till dawn if you want to pay your respects."

They didn't *have* till dawn, but they could hardly say so. If they picked up a guard at a checkpoint, there'd be another man found dead, that was for certain.

"We must be gone before break of day," said the Player King. "But I thank you for your good counsel." He bowed more deeply than a scholar merited.

Manners—and safety—called for some words about God's mercy about now. He knew he could not force them from a throat that tightened in the presence of so many holy objects. A sweat was forming on his cold brow, and he feared it was tinged with blood he could ill spare.

He bowed again and backed away, too weakened even to swirl his cloak correctly. He could feel Horatio's living human eyes upon his back, draining him further. If the night did not strengthen him, he would have to seek out a guard for sustenance or he would never be able to open the prince's tomb.

"I wish you good fortune," vampire and mourner said, in ludicrous, accidental unison, then shook their heads at the impossibility.

Gonzago escaped the church. Again, he glanced up at the night sky. The wind scudded wisps of clouds past the remote stars and the terribly sharp moon.

"This way," he mouthed at Lucianus, trusting the actor's inhuman eyes to see it. Then he sagged.

The younger vampire bore him away, one arm draped over his shoulder. When they had lived, there might have been comfort in body holding body close, braced against the death they mourned; but there was no warmth in this, only a stubborn refusal to lie down and let the sun consume them. Once away from the church, the terrible lassitude induced by holiness and honest grief faded.

Gonzago straightened up and looked alertly about. "The gravediggers have to store their tools somewhere. 'A pickaxe and a spade . . . a spade . . .'"

"Follow your nose," Lucianus told him. "Never mind seeking out the blood trace. You can smell the ale on them a mile off."

Their tools still crusted with dried earth and tossed into a corner, the gravediggers lay asleep, one face down upon a rickety table, the elder by the fire, his belly rising and falling ridiculously as he snored. The vampires stared at each other, then at the drunken men.

"We'd be too drunk to dig," said Lucianus.

Maybe afterward, when they came back. The ale would have worn off by then, but not the stupor. The prince would hunger, would have to be shown, like an orphaned colt, how to feed.

They seized the tools they'd come for and approached Prince Hamlet's tomb.

"Pitiful," Gonzago sniffed. This new king Fortinbras could have spared the man he succeeded a better burial, not this headstone that looked like the best the sculptors had lying about—a pale block adorned with little in the way of heraldry or portentous Latin. *Resurgam*, for example, would have been nice and, in this case, no more than the truth. Horatio had been right. Lock them away in the earth fast. Out of sight, out of mind.

The earth around it looked freshly turned.

"You think someone's been here before us?" asked Lucianus.

The Player King knelt. If he had lived to be old, his knees would have ached from the dampness of the earth. Now only hunger or holiness—or a blow to head or spine—could cause him pain. He bent lower, lowering himself to sniff at the stone. Something had been here, had pushed hard against the tomb. He smelled blood on the foundation, faint, attenuated, as if one of his own people . . .

"Let's put our backs into it, lad," he ordered Lucianus. "Once the stone's off, we still have digging to do."

The second vampire knelt, braced himself against the heavy marker, his nostrils flaring at the spoor that Gonzago had noticed. They heaved with the preternatural strength of vampires needing to be fed. Once. Again. The white stone toppled. Gonzago and Lucianus rose, dusting off their hosen, and reached for pickaxe and shovel.

"'A pickaxe and a spade, a spade . . . For and a shrouding sheet . . .'" Lucianus sang as they dug. "'O, a pit of clay for to be made . . .'"

"Quiet!" Gonzago hissed at him. Already the hunting hounds in the palace kennels had begun to howl. Vampires left a blood spoor. They could be torn apart by hounds. He glanced up at the sky. Some hours left till dawn.

The earth was soft. It turned easily. Finally, Gonzago's spade clanked on metal. It was the work of minutes for creatures of their strength to clear a trench beside the coffin, then heave it out to lie beside the overturned stone. It was heavy, wrapped in lead against corruption. Three blows from the spade shattered its hinges. Gonzago lifted the lid.

The prince, their former patron, lay as if he slept. Death had erased the agony induced by grief and the poisoned wound from his features. They bore, in fact, the bloom of life. He had been a handsome man, with the bearing of a king, if not an actor. Richly garbed in black, he was wrapped in a heavy cape of sables. Moonlight winked off the gems that had been buried with him. Enough there to wake the greed of any resurrection-man —except those who had sought him, not his treasure.

"Thank . . ." Lucianus let out his breath in a superstitious little puff.

"Thank *me*," said Gonzago. "I don't know how much he's going to need to wake him to our life." He bent his head and his fangs extended, sank into his wrist, until a watery reddish serum rose from the wound. Blood followed, as if reluctant to leave the body that so needed it. Holding his wrist over Prince Hamlet's mouth, Gonzago let the blood drop into the slightly parted lips.

He could feel himself weaken, paling in the moonlight. Lucianus stepped close to brace his shoulders. The moon shifted in its course across the sky. A faint dimness showed at the horizon.

"This isn't going to work," Lucianus muttered. "Let's put him back in and take him to the wagon. We can try again tomorrow night, after we've fed."

Gonzago stopped himself, palm to the desecrated earth, as he slipped sideways. The blood trickled into Prince Hamlet's mouth. "I don't think I could carry him that far," he whispered. "Wait . . . ahhhhhhh." He sank back upon his heels, sagging in relief as he sucked at the gash he had inflicted on himself.

The prince opened his eyes. For an instant, starlight, and not sense, shone in them. Then, the intelligence that had made him such a delight to perform for blazed back into the restored consciousness.

As he tried to rise, Lucianus and Gonzago leaned forward to catch him.

He raised his hand to sign himself in the old way, then dropped it as if his fingers burnt. "Oh my—" His voice choked off. He raised his hand to look at it and the rings—a prince's ransom—that gleamed on it.

"The rest is silence," he whispered. "I feared what dreams might come, but nothing . . . nothing at all . . ."

He looked around in mounting horror. "This is a *tomb*. I *died*, from that poison Laertes rubbed on his sword. I could feel myself dying . . . I did not even dream as I feared; and now I wake. Am I a ghost like the king, my father?"

He glanced up at the two, pale with dread and exhaustion, who knelt beside him.

"You woke me." It was an accusation. "Why did you wake me? How?"

Gonzago smiled at him, allowing his fangs to descend once more. "You went to Wittenberg. You traveled to the East. You know what we are."

"But that was against the Turks and long ago. In a Christian land, a civilized country . . ."

Lucianus chuckled.

"Am I your . . . prey?" asked Prince Hamlet.

Gonzago rose and made his courtliest bow. "As you have always been, Highness, you are our patron and our prince. And now you are our brother by blood."

"Those that die by violence often rise," Lucianus cut in. "We but eased your way, Your Highness."

"To your life in death? I'll die first . . . die *again* . . ."

"Think about it," urged Gonzago. "I could offer you the role of a life-time—"

"Lifetime? My life is spent. No, I know what you made me. I will not have it, do you hear? Take it away from me and let me sleep."

Gonzago bowed, this time in mock apology. "Highness, the blood is in you now, and you have risen. For you to die the final death, the spine must be severed, the head crushed . . ."

"Or the body burned, is that not so?" the prince demanded. "I have but to wait for dawn and . . ."

"He's maddened," Gonzago mouthed to his companion. "We can take him. On the count of three . . . one . . . two . . . three—" They lunged forward.

"What? You lay hands upon your prince? By . . . by hell, I'll make a ghost of him that lets me!" Hamlet snarled.

A cloud brushed across the face of the moon, darkening the sky. They might have time to take him. Or the sun might rise, turning them first to cinders, then to dust.

"Back! Away from that grave!" the voice that also assailed them sounded strained almost past the admitted limits of human endurance. Twin lights flashed, one more terrible than the other. Player King and Lucianus flinched as Horatio advanced, carrying a silver cross he must have taken from the church.

"I crossed a royal ghost's path. I'll cross *you* though you blast me," he said. He followed the words with a volley of Latin—the ancient, horrific words of exorcism. Lucianus and Gonzago dropped the prince's arms, hiding their faces from the terrible twin flames of torch and cross.

The scholar raised the torch yet higher. "You," he said, his voice chill with disgust. "I saw you flinch from the Presence. I saw the blood dew form upon your brow. And I thought, 'Perhaps I am wrong, perhaps I have run mad.' But men have been found dead, their throats ripped; and so I prepared myself and came here."

He spat. "Bad enough you rose from your graves yourselves. I prayed for flights of angels to sing my prince to his rest, not the howls of damned beasts to raise him."

"Horatio." Just a breath of sound from Hamlet, but it mastered the scholar wholly. He dropped to his knees before the risen prince, jamming the torch into the earth and tucking the deadly cross away.

"I told you before. There are more things in heaven and earth, Horatio . . ."

The living man sobbed. Tears untinged with blood gleamed on his face. "You helped me die once before. Help me now."

Horatio rose, arms extended as if to embrace his friend. Hamlet stepped back in horror. ("He scents the life in him," Gonzago murmured, "and he fears his own appetites. Excellent, excellent . . .")

"How can you ask me to kill you?" Horatio demanded. "My prince, do you know *how* vampires must die?"

"I do not ask you to drive a stake through my heart or cut my head from off my shoulders. But drive these actors hence and wait with me. Pray with me until the dawn comes to free me."

Horatio's hands rose to cover his face. He does not want to see the prince die again, Gonzago thought. The actor in him noted the gestures. The vampire observed that, with the cross hidden, the torch out of reach, they had but to kill him and seize the prince . . . aye, and forget any hope they ever had of winning him for an ally.

"Let the man live," Gonzago hissed. "Take him!"

Lucianus seized Prince Hamlet's arm again.

"No!" he cried.

"Why do you hurt my love? Give him to me—ee—ee . . ." A slurred voice rose up into a wail, and from a wail into the shriek of a bat in mortal anguish.

The wind had blown the clouds from the moon, which silvered the figure that approached them. It was slight, clutching about barely budded breasts the tatters of a kirtle that had once been white. A wreath of long-dead flowers tangled with a sodden veil above a rat's nest of long braids. Her eyes glowed hungrily like those of a cat caught in torchlight, but they held no sense at all.

Even as hideously changed as she was, Gonzago recognized the young girl who had answered the prince with such desperate poise the night of his disastrous performance. She had run mad and died, he remembered hearing. Drowned herself and been buried, by intervention of the sentimental Queen, not at a crossroads with all the usual, deadly precautions, but in the wedding dress she had never had a chance to wear when alive.

"The fair Ophelia," Hamlet whispered.

She was not fair now. Her long nails were caked with earth, her fingers blackened. One or two were bent back. She must have clawed her way out of her own grave, lingered, attacking guards and late-night mourners . . . until she saw Prince Hamlet buried. So that was why the stone marker bore the spoor of vampire sweet. She had determined to join him after death as they could not be joined in life—and been too weak to reach him.

No wonder Elsinore had suffered from hauntings and night slayings. A vampire without cunning or even what passed for sanity among the undead. God have mercy, if God took pity on vampires. But there wasn't that much pity in heaven or earth, much less in hell.

"Before my God," Horatio murmured, "I might not this believe without the sensible and true avouch of mine own eyes." He had ceased to weep, and his eyes blazed with the scholar's lust for knowledge, avid as any vampire's blood hunger.

"The king, my father, is at peace. But she! Horatio, I trusted you to care for her . . ."

"She ran from me and drowned, my prince. Forgive me."

Hamlet shook his head. "I am beyond all mercy."

"Call her, lord," Lucianus murmured, His voice purred with the seduction that made him play villains' parts so well.

He glanced at Gonzago for permission. At the Player King's nod, he snapped the handle of the pickaxe he bore from the metal, producing a jagged wooden stake. Let the poor maid run forward and impale herself upon it, and her suffering, at least, would be over.

"No!" Hamlet said, and held out his arms.

Ophelia ran to them, seeking shelter. A moment he held her off. "My uncle's dog, though he had bit me, should have had better." He swung his cloak from about his shoulders and draped it to hide her dirt and bridal tatters. She reeked of earth and carrion, but he folded her gently against his heart and rocked her.

His cheek against her hair, he crooned to her as if he had never treated her love as if it were an old toy, humiliated her in open court, or slain her father by mischance. Gonzago thought he could hear her singing faintly, "At his head a grass-green turf, at his heels a stone."

"I saw them lay her in the earth," he said. "My lady mother gave them a wedding dress for her to wear, and they strewed violets over her. She looked more like an angel than of earth—and now . . ."

"She *rose*," Gonzago told him. "And she rose as she was. Mad."

She raised her hands with their hideous strong nails, as if she would touch her lover's cheek. Hamlet took the filthy hand and kissed it.

"We both will wait for dawn," he declared. "The fire will cleanse her. Leave us. Horatio, you too. Pray for us both."

"She is mad," Gonzago repeated. "When dawn comes, will she have your courage and your will? Or will she plead with you as the sun rises and shriek as she burns?"

Hamlet had plucked the sodden veil and wreaths from off her hair and laid his face upon it.

"Let me take her away," Horatio pleaded. "This time, I swear to keep her safe."

Ophelia turned toward the human voice. Her mad eyes focused, and she started to pull away from the prince toward a living source of blood.

Hamlet laughed, his voice rising in the true vampire's pitch. A hound, hearing its master's voice, began a frantic yelping. Someone in the kennels shouted and threw something. The prince drew a breath he had no use for and fought for self-control.

"Horatio, my dearest friend, my living friend, of all of us here tonight, you alone have a chance for salvation. You are not safe. You could not control her while she lived, and now you would swiftly become her prey. I would not see you rise too."

If they kept up like this, Gonzago thought, they would all be vampires. This was worthy of a play, if the groundlings did not burn any theater in which it might appear. He could feel dawn approaching, reaching for his life-in-death with her deadly fingers.

Gonzago thought faster than he ever had in an agile life and an even more agile undeath. "My lord, when you ran mad and killed this lady's father, they determined to send you to England, did they not?"

Hamlet chuckled. "He shall recover his wits there, or if he do not, 'tis no great matter," he said as if repeating words he had heard once and relished.

"There the men are as mad as he," Horatio took up the joke.

"My lord," Gonzago forced sincerity into his voice, "we ask nothing more than to go to England ourselves. They dearly love a good play there, we have heard. The English ambassadors will be going home, their errands done, to inform their ruler of the new king. We could travel with them."

"And how do you expect me to win their permission? Work magic? The ambassadors all saw me buried."

"They do not know about us. Teach us how we should approach them, what to say. Give them a letter . . . a letter from you, back-dated, promising us your patronage," Gonzago ventured, greatly daring.

"After all, while you lived," Horatio said, "it was no more than the truth."

"You support this . . . this damned charade?" Hamlet turned on him. "You, of all men?"

Horatio bowed his head. "My prince, truly I cannot bear to see you die again. Least of all burnt as a witch or heretic, and the lady with you."

"England," mused the Prince. "They thought it would heal me." He held Ophelia at arms' length from him. She looked up into his face with a child's trust. Her gaze focused now, instead of seeming to reflect light as shattered glass reflects it. It focused on her prince.

"You think she might recover her wits?" the prince demanded.

"With you to tend her?" Gonzago shrugged. "I have seen stranger things in all my years."

"That I cannot believe," Hamlet retorted.

"Oh no? Stay with us. Work with us as fellow in a cry of players. Should your lady come around, I presume that she can sing or sew?" Ophelia turned toward the wheedling voice and smiled.

"Take us on trial. And at the end of a century tell me if you wish to go on or no. And then, if you do, travel down the generations with us." It was a good bargain Gonzago offered. No need for his eyes to well with blood-washed tears.

"What would *you* do?" the prince asked Horatio.

He shook his head. "Do not make me watch you die again," he begged again.

"Would you come with us?"

Horatio recoiled. "No, but I will vow my silence. Aye, and come to see you next time you are in this city."

"That might be some years," Lucianus commented. "At least, I hope so."

"And better thus," the scholar said. "I shall stand among the groundlings, and perhaps you will see the old stooped man watching you, remembering you as you were once, in the sun."

He raised his head and sniffed, not as if he wept but as if the wind had changed. The sky was paling now toward dawn.

"We must go now," Gonzago warned. "Come quickly!" He tugged at his once and future patron's splendid sleeve.

A reddish light smouldered in the east. The cock crowed.

"One thing further," Hamlet called to Horatio.

"Anything, my prince. What is it?"

"Adieu . . . adieu . . . remember me."

Horatio sank to his knees. His tears were as hot as the scent of his blood.

The cock crowed a second time. Lucianus was already halfway down the slope, racing past the guards, who only now rose from ale-drenched sleep. Hamlet swept Ophelia into his arms and ran: vampiric strength, as he would learn. The sky's pallor reached out to scorch their backs as they reached the safety of the cart and the caskets stored within. Gonzago opened one and gestured: down. Lie down. He slammed the lid down and sought his own refuge.

By the time the cock crowed thrice, Gonzago too lay safe. The last image he took with him into the day's oblivion was how the mad girl lay beside her prince, head against his heart. Perhaps she would heal, given time and patience and love. Even a vampire might be pardoned for thinking so. Gonzago took the thought down with him into the day's oblivion as the fierce sun rose.

# SPECIAL EXHIBITS

# BLIND FAITH

*Susan L. Williams*

My Master did his work only at night. So I had been told, but the why of it had not been explained to me. I was only an apprentice, and a new one at that. Boys such as I did as we were told and did not ask questions of our betters. What the Master or his journeymen chose to tell me I would know; nothing else was my concern. That had been made clear to me from the moment I entered his house.

I had never met the Master. The negotiations with my father had been conducted by Jerome, the most trusted of his journeymen, said to be second only to the Master in his skill. My father had paid dearly for the apprenticeship. Rafael was acknowledged as the finest worker in stained glass in all of Europe. To be his apprentice was to be assured of a prosperous career.

Yet Rafael himself did not profit from his artistry. He would accept no payment from the Church, nor ever had, it was said. He was not poor. His house was large, his clothing of the most costly fabrics, and his apprentices and journeymen lived well. Where he got his wealth, none knew, but many speculated. My mother said he was a nobleman from a distant land, but my father scoffed at the idea, though he had no explanation of his own.

On my first night of work, the Master was overseeing the installation of a small window in the transept. Begun when my great-grandfather was a boy, the construction of the cathedral was nearing completion. As yet, only a few of Rafael's windows were in place, but their beauty was already famous. None could match the richness of Rafael's colors or the grace and majesty of his figures. The thought that I would someday know how this magnificence was achieved made me dizzy.

Jerome had instructed me to present myself directly to Rafael, saying I would know him by his silver hair. Entering the transept, I caught sight of him immediately. He stood atop a scaffolding, working right alongside the other men. He was clad as they in plain, drab wool, yet I knew him, for he was taller than any there, and in the torchlight his hair gleamed like the purest silver. I hesitated to disturb him, but I did not wish to begin my apprenticeship by idling. I approached the scaffolding timidly, clearing my throat.

"Master?"

He turned his head. "Yes? Ah."

Excusing himself to the workers, Rafael stepped to the edge of the scaffolding and jumped off. The fall was one of a dozen feet or more, yet Rafael landed lightly and took no hurt. He smiled at my astonishment.

"You must be Michael. Jerome tells me there is hope for you. You should be flattered; he doesn't say that of many."

I didn't know what to say, so said nothing. I could not stop staring. Rafael's smile widened.

"Is something wrong?"

"You're—you're young," I blurted. Realizing what a fool I sounded, I blushed and hung my head. "Forgive me, Master."

Rafael laughed. "I'm not so young as I look. Still, I thank God for these gray hairs of mine. Without them, I'm sure I should never be taken seriously."

He spoke truth. Rafael's face was that of a young man. Had I not known he had been twenty years laboring for the Church, I should have thought him scarcely older than Jerome. He was handsome, with teeth strong and white, and eyes of a paler gray than the stone of the cathedral, nearly a match for his silver hair. His skin was very fair, almost the milk-white one heard of in songs. Though I had never before seen anyone whose skin approached that hue, I thought perhaps it was due to his habit of working always at night. Certainly, he was not unhealthy. The sleeves of his linen shirt were pushed up, revealing muscular arms.

Rafael took me by the shoulder. "Come, Michael. Climb up, and I shall introduce you to the intricacies of window installation."

I did as I was bidden, the Master climbing behind me. The window to be installed was in the shape of a many-petaled flower, done in subtle variations of red and gold, the colors clear and bright even at night. By day, they would blaze into brilliance.

"There will be some dozen of these," Rafael told me. "Normally, this would be done in the day, but as the shape is so unusual I was anxious to see the first correctly set. Watch carefully, Michael. You will serve as Jerome's advisor when the others are installed."

I, advise the journeyman? This so alarmed me that I determined to pay the closest attention, dreading lest I miss some tiny adjustment. Rafael seemed pleased by my concentration. Whether he knew the panic his statement had caused in me I cannot say.

Contrary to what I had been led to expect, Rafael explained everything that was done, both the how and the why, patiently repeating what I did not at first understand. When the installation was complete, he dismissed the workmen but did not himself leave the cathedral. Instead, he took me to the nave and there knelt to pray. Though the choir was empty—the entire cathedral was empty save for my Master and me—Rafael remained in the nave and made no attempt to approach the altar. This humility impressed me even more than his patience, and as I knelt beside him I knew my father had chosen well for me: this would be a Master like no other.

His prayer done, Rafael crossed himself and rose, gazing at the distant altar for a moment before shepherding me from the nave. He took me through the choir, transept, apse, and chapels, even through the crypt below, though he had no work there, and as we went he pointed out places where the windows would go, one hundred eighty in total, and he master over all the other glaziers. It was an important post, yet he did not brag of it or think himself better than other men. He spoke only of the windows and the beauty he would create for the glory of God. Hearing him, my heart swelled with pride that I would assist in this undertaking. It was a sin, but I am not sorry for it.

We returned to the house, my Master guiding me through the midnight streets without fear. Four journeymen and five other apprentices lived in the house with Rafael. All were abed except Jerome, who waited to make certain the Master arrived home safely. Rafael scolded him, but I could see that he was not really angry. Jerome took himself off to bed, and the Master led me to the workshop.

Once the main hall of the house, the workshop was vast, with room and equipment enough for five master glaziers, their journeymen and apprentices. There were great cauldrons of molten glass, kilns to bake the painted pieces, stacks of lead cames, shelves crammed with jars of pigment and stain, brushes, grozers, and pontils. Barrels of sand and ash lined the walls, and a dozen tables held sheets of glass, cuttings, and half-finished windows. Near each table, a cartoon hung on the wall, depicting a window as it would be when finished. During the day, I had found the workshop uncomfortably hot, though Jerome said I would grow accustomed to the heat. Now, with Rafael and myself its only occupants, the hall was pleasantly warm.

Since I was too new to be trusted with any task more complex than fetching jars of pigment, brushes, or water, Rafael gave me few orders. He allowed me to watch his work, talking the while of what he did. A sheet of glass blue as the autumn sky lay on the table before him, set atop a pattern. Taking an iron rod heated red-hot, Rafael drew it along the glass, following the pattern. Where the rod touched, the glass cracked. Returning the rod to the fire, the Master took up a knapping hammer and gently tapped the glass, achieving a clean break along the lines of the pattern. He took up a grozer and sat down to smooth the edges of the glass. His every movement was quick and sure, his touch with the cut glass delicate. When the glass was smoothed to his satisfaction, he fitted it into place in the mosaic of glass that would become the finished window when joined with the lead cames. It was to show the Annunciation. The blue was for the Virgin's robe, and for feathers in the angel's many-colored wings. Green hills rolled behind them to a sky of pale blue, and white lilies framed the scene, their leaves and petals gracefully curved. I had never seen anything so beautiful, and I told Rafael as much. He smiled.

"I'm glad it pleases you," he said, as though my opinion mattered.

"It would please anyone, Master."

"Even God, do you think?"

"Of course," I said, wondering why the Master should ask me such a question.

He stopped working then, and looked at me. "You sound very certain."

"I am, Master. How could He fail to be pleased by such beauty?"

"Perhaps the artist will displease Him."

"How can that be? You are the best in the world."

"You flatter me, Michael." His brief smile faded. "Does God judge the skill or the man?"

"I don't know, Master. You should ask a priest."

"Yes." Rafael ran a finger lightly over the blue glass. "I was to have been a priest. My father wanted it. And so did I."

"What happened?"

"I became—ill."

"But you are well now."

"Oh no, Michael, I am not. The illness has left me with certain— needs."

Rafael fixed me with a sad silver gaze. Reaching out, he put a hand to my neck, drawing me closer to him. His fingers were gentle, like my mother's. They slid just under my shirt, circling my throat, and touched the narrow gold chain around my neck. He tugged on the chain, pulling the small gold cross out of my shirt. Holding the cross in his hand, he smiled more sadly still.

"There is fine work in this, Michael."

"It was my mother's," I said. "She gave it to me when I left."

"Is she unhappy that you've come here?"

"Not here. Just that I'm not at home."

"Tell me," he said. "Why do you want to be a glazier?"

"To be like you, Master," I answered truthfully. "To honor God by filling His house with light and beauty."

"Do you love God, Michael?"

"Yes, Master." Encouraged by his interest, I boldly said, "My mother thought that I might be a priest. But I would rather serve God by making windows for His house."

"Do you believe that God loves you?"

"As He loves us all, Master."

"But God does not love us all, Michael. There are some whom God despises, some sins He cannot forgive."

He was speaking of himself, I knew, but I could not understand why. "If God loves any of us, Master, He must surely love those who create beauty in His name."

"I should like to think so, Michael," he said.

I knew I had not convinced him, and I was sorry for it. His hand was still at my neck. I patted it awkwardly, and he embraced me. One hand smoothed my hair, brushing it away from my neck. His head bent toward me slowly, and I thought he would kiss my cheek, but he drew back suddenly and kissed the top of my head as my father had done when I left. I was so moved that I dared to return his embrace. He allowed it for a moment, then gently pushed me away, holding me at arm's length.

"You would have made a good priest," he said softly. "Go to your bed now. Jerome will have work for you tomorrow."

I did not want to leave him, so sad and alone. But he was my Master, and I could not disobey. Bidding him goodnight, I sought my bed.


For six years I learned from him. For six years I learned, and worked, and grew. He taught me all there was to know of the glazier's art. Apprentices became journeymen, journeymen masters, and the newly made masters moved on. Jerome stayed as one of the glaziers under the Master's command, but he no longer lived in Rafael's house. I progressed from apprentice to journeyman, and looked forward to being a master glazier someday, yet I had no wish to leave Rafael.

Since that first night, I had worked more often with the Master than anyone else. Two nights of three I would be with him, helping him with his glorious work. On the third night, another of the apprentices or one of the journeymen would assist him, and on those nights I was not allowed to enter the workshop. He never told me why, and I never dared ask, but I was

284                                    *Blind Faith*

jealous of the nights he gave to the others, though they had as much right to his time as I. I confessed my jealousy, and regularly did penance for it, but it would not go away even as I grew older. I comforted myself by believing that he did not talk to the others as he did to me.

Every night when I was with him, we talked. He did not confine himself to instruction any more than he had on the first night, but spoke to me of the world and man's place in it, of philosophy and science and a thousand other subjects. His store of knowledge was vast, and he shared it all with me not in lectures but in discussions, as though I were his equal in intellectual matters.

One subject only was forbidden, and that was himself. He would tell me nothing of his family or childhood, or even where he had been born. His illness was never mentioned again, and I saw no evidence that it had left any mark upon him as he said it had. I questioned Jerome about it once, and was told to mind my own business or be put out onto the street. Jerome had none of the Master's patience. None of the other journeymen or apprentices would speak of it either, but I developed the feeling—for which I had no proof—that they all knew something of the Master that I did not. However, as I was certain that I knew a great many things that *they* did not, I did not pursue the answer as I might have. I was content to be the Master's favorite, and did not wish to lose my place.

With so many craftsmen under Rafael's command, the work went quickly. By my eighteenth birthday, all was completed save the great rose window above the main door and the five windows in the apse that looked down upon the altar. The design for the rose window was Rafael's, but he left its construction to the other glaziers, Jerome chief among them. Every day, more sections were put into place, glaziers and stonemasons working together to fit thousands of gem-bright pieces of glass into a glorious whole. I went often to see it, and joyed to stand bathed in its myriad hues when the afternoon sun poured down through the frame.

Rafael had never seen it so. In all his life, he had never seen any of his windows as they were meant to be seen, with the sun behind them to show us what the light of Heaven must be like. That he should be so deprived was a source of grief to me. He never spoke of it, nor gave any open indication that he felt a lack. He seemed able to visualize exactly how each window would appear at any moment of the day, and to take his joy from that.

He had not much joy else. The state of his soul troubled him always. He prayed daily, yet never attended mass. He proclaimed himself a sinner, yet would not go to confession. When I asked him why, he said only, "God knows my sins." I could not imagine what dreadful sin he could have committed. I never saw him less than kind, never knew him other than gentle. He spoke no ill of anyone, nor ever lost his temper. He gave his art to God, asking for no reward, yet he was convinced that God despised him. It was that, I was sure, which kept him closeted during the day, that which held him from ever seeing his work as it should be seen. And I did not know why.

The windows for the apse were Rafael's final work on the cathedral, and he had chosen to do all five himself, with only my assistance. Tall and narrow, each window would hold a single figure: in the center, Christ risen to Heaven; and flanking him, the archangels Gabriel, Uriel, Raphael, and Michael. Our Lord was robed in white and crimson, bright blood on His poor pierced hands and feet. Crimson roses framed Him, and around His head was an aureole of gold to shame the sun. The archangels were also robed in white, but their wings were made of every hue that Rafael could produce, each feather subtly different from that next it, sweeping grace-fully in a shimmering rainbow. White roses bordered their windows, and each had an aureole of a different design.

Jesus was completed first, yet Rafael would not have the window in-stalled until all were done. The image of our Lord stood in the workshop while Rafael made the archangels, and he did them all together. First the wings were pieced together, a long process that took many nights. Next the robes were made, and the borders, then the backgrounds, and finally their arms and feet, leaving only the heads. With those, I was not allowed to help. Rafael did all himself, from mixing the sand and ash to piecing the cut glass together, and as the work drew near completion, I saw the reason why. The face of each archangel was a portrait. Uriel was the bishop, a well-favored man made more handsome by Rafael's art. Gabriel was given Jerome's features and his golden hair. To my embarrassment, Michael's face was my own. And for Raphael, the Master intended to use the features of a wealthy donor to the cathedral.

I could not dissuade Rafael from making me the archangel for whom I had been named. Since I could not, I enlisted Jerome's help in persuading the Master to allow me the privilege of completing the fourth archangel. He was loath to do it, but could not stand against us both. Thus, the archangel Raphael acquired the silver hair and noble features of the master glazier Rafael.

Rafael was shocked. I had thought he would expect it, but he had not, nor was he pleased. He thought it a terrible vanity for the Master glazier to be so portrayed. Jerome and I argued that as he had not made the portrait, there could be no vanity, but he would not hear us. We appealed to the bishop. The bishop was greatly pleased by all the windows, and would not hear of any changes. After all, what would be vanity in Rafael would be vanity in the bishop as well. Therefore, it was not vanity.

Though it distressed the Master, the bishop's decision was final. Rafael and I worked with the stonemasons to install the windows. For three nights we worked, and at last the installation was complete. The rose window had been finished the previous day. The Master's work on the cathedral was done.

As was his custom, Rafael dismissed the workmen and remained in the cathedral to pray. As always, I knelt beside him in the nave, but that night I could not pray. I was consumed by the thought that the years of Rafael's labor were done and he would not see the results. The injustice gnawed at me until I could think of nothing else. It was not right that he should be barred from witnessing the full magnificence of his creation. It was not right, and I could not believe that God meant it to be so. The Lord Jesus Christ had died that our sins might be forgiven. Surely, no matter what he had done, the Lord had forgiven Rafael. I had only to make him believe it.

"Master," I said. "Wait with me until dawn and see the rising sun fill the windows."

"Michael, you know that's not possible."

"Why?" I demanded. "Why, Master? What sin have you committed that God would deny you the light of day?"

"A sin too great for you to know."

"I don't believe that." I swept my arm around the cathedral. "You have made all this for God's glory. Whatever you've done, He has forgiven you."

Rafael shook his head.

"He has! He must have! If God despised you, would He accept your work? Would He have allowed the bishop to hire you, to make you Master of glaziers?"

Doubt crept into his expression. "I don't know."

"Would God hire devils to build His church?"

"No. Neither does He employ saints as His stonemasons."

"Rafael, listen to me!" I shouted. "Do you repent your sins?"

"Yes!" he cried. "But I cannot stop them!"

"Which of us can? We're all sinners, Master. All of us. And God forgives us. He forgives us all, and He forgives you. I'll prove it to you. Stay here with me. Watch the sun shine through your windows."

"Michael—"

"Stay. Nothing will hurt you. God won't strike you down. You made these windows for Him. He won't let anything happen to you."

A whisper. "You sound very certain."

"I am, Master. Stay with me. Stay, and see."

Rafael turned away from me, gazing to the east, where the Son of God and the archangels graced the wall beyond the altar. The longing on his face was painful to me. When at last he answered, I rejoiced.

"Very well, Michael. I will stay with you."

Dawn came slowly. Rafael prayed the night through on his knees in the cold nave, and I prayed beside him, prayed that he would be assured at last of the Lord's forgiveness when he was rewarded with the sight of the wonder he had created in God's name. I was certain he would be, certain I was right.

The first gray light seeped in among the stones, and Rafael began to shiver. I had never known him to be cold before. Removing my cloak, I gave it to my Master, and he wrapped himself in it, pulling the hood up over his head. I pushed myself to my feet, rubbing my aching knees. While I walked back and forth, the light grew.

Rafael did not move until I pulled him to his feet. Keeping hold of his arm as though he were an invalid, I shepherded him through the nave, past the stairs to the crypt, and into the choir. We approached the altar, his steps hesitant not from any ache in his legs. He was more pale than I had ever seen him, but if he prayed then he did so only in his thoughts.

Six feet before the altar, we stopped. The windows filled the east wall, waiting for the sun to display their glory. Rafael's head was bent, his eyes shadowed by the hood. He remained so while I watched for the sun.

A pale glow touched the roses on the bottom of the windows. Rafael lifted his head, gazing at sunlit crimson and white. The glow crept upward, illuminating flesh and folds of cloth, climbing roses and rainbow-hued wings. In moments, the faces of the archangels and of our Lord blossomed with light. Aureoles blazed with the rays of the risen sun. Rafael stood motionless, transfixed by the beauty he had made. Tears streamed from his eyes.

"Michael," he began.

I do not know what he would have said. Crimson light touched his face, cast by the strengthening sun, and he screamed. His arms flew to his face, covering his eyes, and he stumbled away from the altar, still screaming. He fell, writhing on the floor, and I dropped to my knees beside him in terror.

"Master, what is it? What's wrong?"

"The light!" he cried. "Michael!"

He screamed again. God help me. I had done this to him. I was responsible. I had to help him, had to take him from the light. The crypt! Pulling Rafael to his feet, I led him toward the staircase, struggling under his weight. The stairs were narrow, curving downward, disappearing into darkness. I descended as quickly as I could, Rafael's screams becoming moans as we left the light behind. I could not see the bottom, and I was forced to slow our steps lest we fall.

The stairs ended, leaving us in total darkness. We moved some way into the crypt, our only guide the wall at my left hand. When my hand touched air, we nearly fell into a room. I dared go no farther. Lowering Rafael to the floor, I knelt once more beside him. In the dark, his hand clutched at my arm.

"Michael," he whispered. "Help me. The pain—"

"How, Master?" I cried. "What can I do?"

"One thing," he said. "One thing I have—never asked of you."

"Anything, Master! Oh God, I'm so sorry, I'll do anything!"

Rafael's hand found my neck, his fingers sliding over the chain of the cross that I still wore. He drew me down to him. I felt his breath on my neck, and I thought he would speak again. But no more words passed his lips. His mouth opened, and I felt the pain of damnation as his teeth plunged into my throat.


Fifty years have passed since that last morning. I am a master glazier. I travel Europe seeking employment, and I have found it in several places. Many windows in many churches and cathedrals—even in private homes, now—are of my making. By some, I am accounted the best in Europe, though I know that is not true. They do not seem to mind that I work only at night.

I have had to change my name twice to avoid suspicion, but that is easy enough to do. What is not so easy is arranging to travel at night or, failing that, to be safely enclosed during the day. The danger of the sun is not something I shall ever forget.

Rafael does not blame me. He says he wanted it as much as I, that it was his own fault. But the fault was not his. He is still gentle and kind, still handsome and strong. His work is as brilliant as ever, though he cannot see it now by night or by day. The silver eyes are white where the sun burned them. For my sin, I gave all the blood in my body, but they would not heal. When he knew that they would not, he might simply have let me die, but he did not blame me even then. Rather than avenge himself, he gave me to drink of his blood, and I was reborn.

I am not as forgiving as he. For a very long time, the guilt did not go away. I thought that I deserved to die, but Rafael would not let me. He taught me how to live in the night, and I helped him learn to live in darkness. I no longer wear the cross my mother gave me. We know that God has no forgiveness for us; I know that I have none for Him. When we do work for the Church, we are paid handsomely for it, as we deserve. We are content.

# NIGHTWEAVER

*L. S. Silverthorne*

The shuttle whispered across the woollen warp strands, green as ever-greens, and wefted crimson fibers into the cloth that poked at Muriel's belly. The scent of dry wool clung to her face like a mask as she smoothed the heavy fabric with an aching hand. Two generations intertwined the green and red serpent's knot. It was nearly finished after all this time. She glanced back at Himself, quilts pulled tight across him, skin pale, thinning black waves showing above the patchwork roses. Wind ached around the walls of the cottage, rustling the thatched roof and copper pans hanging over the hearth as it moaned on its way across the moors.

The amber candlelight flickered with every pass of the shuttle, beams and pedals squeaking as she raised and lowered the warp. This cloth had begun with her mother, the knotted design born on a lonely winter moor night when the heather frosted and the stones turned to hunks of gray ice. Tonight, she felt in the company of the weavers who had gone before her, weaving life on this loom. The company was welcome; it was a long, lonely stretch until dawn. She sighed at the vanishing skein of crimson flax. She needed more madder dye for the pattern. Himself needed her to finish, otherwise it would be another long winter.

Muriel laid down the shuttle and shuffled over to the wooden bed. Leaning down, she patted Himself on the shoulder and kissed his cheek. "I'll be back before dawn," she spoke as she slid into a black cloak, thin white fingers thrust into the sleeves.

After pulling her traveling satchel from beneath the cupboard, she flicked her flaxen hair into the hood and went out into the night.

Something howled across the moors tonight as her boots crunched through the long grasses. She glanced around at the swaying trees, the darkness thick like wool. Perhaps a lone hellhound fearing the icy air and the roar of the winds? Cold enough to choke the life from the fieriest demon. Many shades of undead walked these moors at night, especially with the longest night approaching. She wrapped the cloak tighter about her middle and pulled a small bundle of sheepskin from her pocket. Quickly, she wrapped her sore fingers in the soft skin, the night mist frosty and ashen. Even the wind smelled of ice and soon-coming snow. Himself needed her to finish tonight.

The hard path wound through a clearing. That's when the rustle began, soft like a rabbit's scamper. Muriel's pace quickened. She slid her right hand out of the sheepskin and felt for the wooden stake wedged into her other pocket. Her tired fingers wrapped around it. Abruptly, the howl strangled in mid-bay and fell silent. She shivered. Even hellhounds feared the undead.

A mournful wail reverberated across the moors, the lap of water touching her ears. The sound rolled up into layers like whispers in a crypt and dissipated into the frost. She clutched the stake, the scrape of branches puncturing the lament. It sounded closer now. It was then that she heard the echo of footsteps on the path behind her. A bird screeched. She paused. Breath frosted in icy puffs. The boot-sounds stopped, matching her step. She glanced behind, the heaviness of the cold against her pale cheeks. No one. Ahead, the silvery moon illuminated the path away from the moors, toward the plains and one of the stone circles. When brush crackled, she ran toward the path.

It was too late in the season for most of the Druidic rituals, the moors too stark and the moon too cold. Except for their vigil on the longest night of darkness. That would come soon, but not tonight. The circle of stones would be empty. Again, the dull thunk of boots touched her ears and she fled down the path until the shadows pooled like the simmering elder bark she used for black dye. The indigo sky was crisp and nearly starless as the ancient forest finally receded from the plains ahead and the circle's power. Mist hung like mourners' veils across the plains that stretched an eternity's length to the circle. She had to reach it.

Brush snapped. A bird took flight. Mist rippled closer. Muriel drew an icy breath and dashed toward the stones. As she stepped into the center of the circle, she saw the sacrificial stones splotched ruddy brown. It had been some time since the Druids had been here.

No one approached, but a flock of birds clattered out of the trees and fluttered low overhead. With a hand still on the stake, she glanced around, watching for the approach of something she felt only in the sudden evening stillness. Slowly, she set down her satchel, watching the plains from all sides. Off to her right, the mist billowed and began to coalesce. From it stepped a brown-haired young man. He moved toward her, the trees at his back.

His long, angular face, pale as the winter moon, hungered, frost-blue eyes leering. He moved like a nobleman, his steps steady and sure. She stood motionless as he approached. As he drew closer, she saw his light brown hair soft and smooth against his forehead. As he reached the outermost stone, she saw the hint of fangs at his mouth and backed away until she felt the sacrificial stone at her back, chilling her through her cloak.

"Shouldn't you be home in bed?" said the man, his voice like ebony silk. His smile leered at her again.

She gazed into the light eyes, the fangs white as a child's headstone, and smiled. "I needed more madder for my weaving," she answered in a husky voice, her breath misting.

"Stone circles are even more dangerous than the moors, dear young lady."

She took a step forward. "Yes, there is danger here."

"Especially for maidens unfortunate enough to visit them at night."

He moved closer, a bony hand reaching out to her. He took her gently by the shoulders. She closed her eyes, feeling his warmth through the cloak as it radiated across her skin. He had just fed on something, she thought, or someone. She smelled the metallic, warm scent of blood mix with the wool of his cloak. His eyes waxed with pleasure as his hands slid down her arms and beneath her cloak. His lips pressed against hers and she felt his need. It ached through him until she felt it tremble through her own body. She thrust her head back and gasped as he kissed across her chin and down her neck. His lips parted to embrace her neck, fangs visible, and she leaned in to him, the sheepskin falling away from her hands as they slid to her side.

Even when she plunged the stake through his back and into his heart, she embraced him, feeling the warm blood of his body against hers until she felt his aching need ebb. She heard his gurgled hiss as he struggled to pull away, but she thrust the stake harder until she felt his strength fade to weakness. His knees buckled and he sank to her feet. Finally, the life force receded and he fell motionless against the ground. Releasing his arm, she reached into her satchel and removed her milk jar.

It was only about two hours before dawn when Muriel returned home. She hung her cloak on the wall near the hearth and plucked the skeins of ivory flax from the wall. She dipped them lovingly into her blood-filled milk jar until the skeins sparkled crimson and left them to dry beside the hearth. With a yawn, she returned to her loom, feeling her fellow weavers close as the shuttle fit into her palm. Wind swept across the cottage as she finished off the remaining strand of crimson. Once again, she heard something wail in the moors, but she let the sound slip away as she studied the intertwining knot pattern that twisted and swerved across the evergreen background. Interconnected as was the lifeblood of her ancestors. She would try to finish again tomorrow night, now that she had more crimson flax.

Rising from the chair, she went to Himself and sat down on the bed beside him. She straightened the quilt and then turned it down. A russet hole encircled with dried blood gaped in his faded white shirt. The hole revealed a puncture in the powdery, blue-white skin, so near his heart. Thank the moors that the villager's stake had missed its target. She had dyed her first skein of flax with that man's blood—only out of spite, for a mortal's blood was nothing more than coloring for the pattern. It would take much undead blood to complete the Pattern of Life upon Himself's shroud to restore him, but she would finish what her mother had started. Mother had taught her the intricacies of the pattern as well as the art of weaving, and she would finish the serpent's knot shroud for her father. Himself would be pleased.

She smiled at him, feeling her fangs press softly against her lips. Smudging a bit of dried blood from the corner of her mouth, she rose, the lament of the wind rushing across the shutters. It was a comforting sound. When the cloth was finished, the Pattern would restore him. Until then, there were many undead walking the moors. The nights were long and the Druidic circles were close enough to shroud her again. She would have more than enough dye before the madder bloomed in the spring.

# THE HAND INSIDE

### Adam-Troy Castro

I am nothing without him. Not a man, nor a parody of a man; not a living thing, nor the corpse of something that once lived. I am merely a thing, beholden unto him, damned to his service, given this distant semblance of life only because that is all he requires of me.

I hate him. I despise being his slave, hate my dependence upon him, loathe the things he makes me say and do.

I need him. I am helpless without him. I cannot move, cannot act, cannot speak, cannot even truly think.

I love him. I ache for those moments when he takes me from this place and holds me and feeds me life through the soft place at the base of my spine. It is not much of an existence, even then: it is still his will that controls me, still his words that he forces me to speak. But for the hour or so I must endure his arm inside me, pulling my levers, moving my mouth, making me caper and jape like a wisecracking clown. I taste his soul inside me too—and while it may be a tiny, desperate thing, rendered bitter by the constant struggle for the success that he is only now beginning to realize will never be his, it is still a soul that has experienced the world directly, and I savor the taste as best I can, taking just enough nourishment from that to sustain me during my next long imprisonment in darkness.

It is not enough. If for just one instant I possessed a voice of my own, I would beg him to hurl me into an open flame. But I have no voice other than his. And so I lie in my black cramped place, with my boneless arms and legs folded across my chest, and my hinged mouth agape, in the expression that should be a scream but . . . damnably . . . remains only a goofy, bucktoothed grin. Waiting again for the touch of his hand, and the taste of his soul.

# BLOOD AND LIMESTONE

Richard Lee Byers

Raoul paced through the chilly expanse of the cathedral, newly completed despite all, drinking in its beauty and grandeur, the darkness little hindrance to his unhuman sight. Slender columns rose past the aisles and triforia to the high, vaulted ceiling. The stained-glass windows, scenes from the Bible and the lives of the saints, along with depictions of all the laborers, stonecutters, mortar makers, plasterers, blacksmiths, and even bakers and farmers who'd helped in one way or another to raise the edifice, shone with the moonlight. Not as they'd shine with the sun behind them, he thought with a pang of sadness, but still, brightly enough to tell their tales to a creature like himself. Alabaster statues of apostles and kings watched him from the shadows, still smelling, like the murals, of fresh paint.

And all the loveliness was gradually destroying him. His head throbbed, twinges stabbed through his joints, and his silent heart ached in his breast. The site had been poisonous to his kind since the bishop—not the current ass but wise old Etienne, dead these sixty years—had blessed the first foundation stone, and every bit of work completed thereafter had made the place deadlier still. It was high time Raoul took himself elsewhere, but he was having difficulty tearing himself away. Because he knew that after tomorrow morning, when the bishop would lead a procession into the cathedral, consecrate the structure, and place the sacred relics in the receptacles prepared for them, the building would become so lethal that he could never return.

At last his discomfort waxed too great to ignore. He turned in a circle, taking a final look, and then, somewhat dizzy, trudged into the south transept, melted his substance into shadow, and tried to slip through the crack between the door and its frame.

Agony, not the dull aches and nausea he'd been experiencing but a sharp, sudden pain, as if someone had thrust a dagger into him, hurled him backward. Solid once more, he sprawled on the floor.

From past experience, he understood what was wrong. Some pious mortal, perhaps employing holy water, or the Host, had sealed the exit against him. Given time, Raoul *might* be able to breach the barrier, but it would be considerably easier to escape via another route if he could find one that hadn't yet received the same treatment. He scrambled to his feet and hurried back into the nave.

A woman's voice spoke. He could tell that she wasn't truly shouting, and yet to him the sound seemed excruciatingly loud, jabbing knives of pain into his ears. But despite the apparent volume, he couldn't comprehend the words. She must be reciting a passage from the Scriptures, or a prayer.

Raoul lurched around, to see his tormentor advancing up the center of the nave. He wondered fleetingly how she'd gotten the front door unlocked. She was young, surely no older than seventeen, painfully thin, with a pinched, prim face that was nonetheless rather pretty, although she seemed to care nothing about her comeliness. She wore a drab, coarse, shapeless gown, and her long blond hair needed combing. A feverish light glowed in her pale gray eyes, and she was clutching a rosary. To his sight, the beads blazed with blue fire, radiating a more potent version of the poison that pervaded the cathedral itself.

Raoul struggled to mask his distress, smile, and bring his supernatural powers of influence to bear. Evidently she'd come here hunting vampires, but that didn't necessarily mean that he couldn't beguile her into believing him mortal. The ploy had worked before. "Good evening," he said.

She sneered at him, then continued her exorcism.

Though his anguished body wanted to recoil from her, he forced himself to move forward instead. It would be impossible to impel himself within arm's reach of the rosary, but perhaps he could make it appear as if he could. "I'm one of the painters," he said. It was difficult to speak in a normal tone. He felt as if he needed to bellow to make himself heard above the din of her voice. "I'm allowed in here, but I don't believe you are, not until tomorrow."

"Liar!" she cried. Probably she'd actually raised her voice, though to him, it seemed to have grown considerably softer. To his disappointment, however, despite the cessation of her litany, the rosary glowed as dazzlingly as before. "I know what you are! Christ showed me your face in a vision! He guided me here to destroy you!"

So much, Raoul thought grimly, for his hypnotic talents. Either his current malaise had wiped them away, or a strong will rendered her immune. He wheeled and ran toward the sacristy. There was an exit there.

The girl laughed. "There's no way out, monster! I barred every door!"

When mortals lied, he could hear it in their voices, and she was telling the truth. Then, abruptly, he realized that unless she could fly, she couldn't possibly have sealed all the potential exits above the ground floor. Perhaps he could leap from the tower!

He pivoted and ran toward the stairs, but his dizziness and weakness slowed him to a hobble. Perceiving his intent, the girl dashed around him and blocked his path.

Raoul stumbled to a halt. Panting, she peered at him and then suddenly lunged forward, brandishing the rosary as if she meant to wrap it around his neck and strangle him.

He made his eyes burn red, his teeth sprout into jagged fangs, and his nails grow into yellow claws. At least he could still manifest his bestial face and weaponry, even if he did feel too sick to injure a gnat. Goggling, the girl lurched to a stop a few feet away.

Raoul shrank his fangs back into puny human teeth. Otherwise, he wouldn't have been able to speak. "Run away," he snarled. "Run or die, and become like me." He hoped that if she did bolt, she'd leave a door open behind her.

The girl set her jaw in resolution. "No," she said. "God sent me to slay you, and I will. To cleanse this sacred place."

If the cathedral awed her, then perhaps, Raoul thought desperately, he could persuade her to abandon her purpose. He extinguished the crimson fire in his eyes, and surreptitiously eased his taloned hands behind his back. "I *built* this sacred place," he told her.

Her mouth twisted. "Liar."

"I wasn't always as I am now," said Raoul. A lance of pain stabbed through his belly. He grunted, and went rigid. "Once upon a time, I was a living human being. My name is Raoul de Cormont, and I was the first master builder here. The one who drew the plans for the cathedral."

"I don't believe you," she said, but he sensed that she did or at least was uncertain what to believe. Perhaps she could hear the ring of truth in people's voices herself. "Why should I? Your master is the Father of Lies."

His legs quivered, and he sidled to one of the columns and set his back against it for support. The touch of the sculpted limestone made his skin burn and itch, even through his mantle and jerkin. "I thought I knew everyone living hereabouts," he said, "but I don't recognize you. Who are you?"

She hesitated.

"Are you afraid to tell me?" he asked, arching an eyebrow. "It's a bit late to worry about evading my notice at this point."

She scowled. "I'm not afraid of you! My faith will protect me." He reflected glumly that she was all too right about that, at least inside these walls. "My name is Genevieve. People call me Genevieve of Amiens."

He nodded. "I've heard of you." Given to fasting, self-flagellation, and visionary trances from an early age, she'd recently taken up preaching and sending admonitory letters to bishops, secular lords, and even the Pope. Some people considered her a saint. "And surely such a learned maiden has heard that the undead begin existence as mortals, then change after perishing from another vampire's attentions. So it was with me. A lamia attacked me on the road that runs from the cathedral into town." He smiled wryly. "Well, perhaps *attacked* is the wrong word. She was lovely, and I thought she was human. When she offered herself to me, I was eager enough to sample her charms. At any rate, she drained me white. I rose from my grave three nights after my friends—the chapter, the quarriers, the masons, the carpenters, and all the others—laid me to rest."

For a moment, he imagined that her expression had softened slightly, as if interest in his tale had taken the edge off her self-righteous loathing. Then she scowled even more ferociously than before, as if now angry with both him and herself. "It doesn't matter who you *were*," she said. "Now you're an abomination." Clutching the rosary, she drew a breath.

Hastily he cried, "How can you kill me when I've done so much good? *Since* I became what I am! How could a just God desire that?"

Genevieve glared at him. "Oh, I've heard about your good works! The townspeople tell stories about the fiend who kills in the night!"

Raoul was grateful that he'd managed to divert her from a resumption of her exorcism. Evidently, saint or no, she was too enamored of her own rhetorical prowess to resist an invitation to argue. Or perhaps she could tell that his strength was failing. That the power radiating from his own creative efforts would annihilate him soon enough, even if she didn't augment it with her invocation.

"I've never killed anyone intentionally," he said. "And I regret the accidental deaths. But I can no more forego drinking blood than a mortal can survive without water." He wouldn't mention the ecstasy that feeding brought him, even during his first months as a vampire, when he'd struggled to resist it. "And in payment for my predation, I gave the town the cathedral." He glanced around at the arches, the colored glass, the carved wood and stone, and even now, with his very existence in jeopardy, felt a swell of exaltation. "Don't you think it's a fair trade?"

"I think you share your king Lucifer's pride," Genevieve answered. "For aught I know, you did draw the plans for the church, but you certainly didn't build it. Generations of Christian men did, toiling in the light of God's sun, while you were hiding in your lair."

The bottoms of Raoul's feet began to sting. The power of the cathedral was seeping up from the floor through the soles of his shoes. "I don't disparage the efforts of those good men," he said. "I consider them my friends, for all that none of them remembers ever having met me. But I still say that without me, the cathedral would never have been completed."

He shifted his shoulders in a futile effort to ease the grinding ache in his bones. "After I changed," he continued, "I was tempted to relocate to another town, where no one knew me. My existence would have been easier, and far less lonely, in a place where I could pass for mortal. But I lingered to see the cathedral rise, and it was well that I did. Jehan, the builder the chapter hired to replace me, had a good heart, but didn't deserve his reputation. He lacked any deep understanding of wood and stone, and he didn't know how to talk to the craftsmen. I had to take him in hand."

Genevieve glared at the vampire. "I think you mean that you possessed and enslaved him."

Raoul shrugged. "I taught him the skills a builder needs. He took no harm from it, quite the contrary. Without me, he never could have managed here. And in later years, I kept money coming in, and no great monument can be raised without it."

"So now you're claiming credit for the generosity of all the pious souls who donated to the chapter," Genevieve sneered.

"People are generous when times are good," he replied, "but for the last forty years or so, that hasn't been the case." Though she supposedly preached vehemently against the evils of her age, he wondered if anyone so young, who'd known only the world devastated by the Black Death and the endless war against the English, could appreciate just what a bleak century this was. "How many towns have you heard of that have begun building a new cathedral? Not many, I'll wager. And how many where such an effort has been abandoned for want of cash? When the money hereabouts dried up, *someone* had to prevail upon the rich to open their purses again."

"So you enslaved them too."

"I did only what was necessary. Over the years, we builders here have had more than our share of accidents and misfortunes. A quarryman crushed. Two wrights fallen from the roof. When lightning struck the tower, people began to whisper that the cathedral was cursed, that their God didn't *want* it finished. Some even advocated razing what already stood! None of the lords and merchants felt inclined to give any more money, nor did many laborers find the courage to work here, until I gave certain influential people a nudge." He sighed. "Even afterwards, things were difficult."

"Perhaps the church truly *is* cursed," said Genevieve. "Cursed by your presence."

"Look around you," said Raoul, nodding at the vast, imposing space in which they stood, at the organ, intricately wrought screens, richly embroidered cloth hangings, and all the other splendors. "Does it *seem* cursed, or does it seem like a holy place?" He smiled crookedly. "Rest assured, *I* can feel your deity's presence even if you can't."

She grimaced. "I do sense Jesus hovering near," she said grudgingly. "And I've heard tales of saints who compelled devils to build churches and bridges, so perhaps the cathedral isn't tainted. But I'm sure those holy men didn't let the unclean spirits run free when their task was done. They must have driven the demons back to Hell, and that's what Christ has told me to do to you!"

"Are you listening to me?" Raoul demanded, squinting. As his remaining strength faded, her rosary seemed to blaze brighter, until he could barely make out her features beyond the glare. "No priest or magician forced me to shepherd this work to its completion. *I wanted to.* Because I don't like being as I am! I still cherish your god, for all that I can't partake of the sacraments, speak his name, or pray in the usual way. Don't you see, the *cathedral* is my prayer, and my plea for deliverance!" Fleetingly he remembered the sacred imagery he'd sketched for the craftsmen to create from wood, stone, metal, paint, and glass, and the way his hands had ached for hours afterward.

"I don't believe you," said Genevieve. "I hear the gloating in your voice when you speak of this place. You had to see it built out of *pride!* As a monument to your own cleverness!"

Raoul sighed. "That was part of it, too," he admitted. Hot spots of pain began to smolder on his face and hands. He suspected that the malignancy emanating from the stonework and her beads was blistering his skin like sunlight. "This is the grandest thing I ever thought to build, and I yearned to see it live. But that doesn't mean that it wasn't a work of devotion as well. Even mortals rarely have absolutely pristine motives. You preach because you think your god wants you to, but don't you also *enjoy* it? Take pride in your oratory? Don't you relish spinning finely phrased arguments and exhortations as much as I did raising this magnificent structure?"

Genevieve's gray eyes narrowed.

"I suspect you do," Raoul persisted. "I think that in that respect, at least, we're two of a kind, and so I beg you, as one craftsman to another, spare me. If your god bade you rid the town of me, fine, I'll go far away and never return." He meant it; he had no reason to linger now that his task was done. Only the gargoyle that he'd prompted one of the sculptors to carve in a parody of his own fanged image would remain, crouching on the roof.

She gazed at him for a moment, then gave her head a violent shake. "Your powers are strong," she said. "For a moment, they almost had me sympathizing with you. But my Lord is stronger, and it's time I finished His work." Chanting her deafening, incomprehensible recitation, thrusting out the shining rosary, she marched toward him.

His head pounding in time with her words, he reeled backwards. He hated himself for trying to talk to her. He should have found a way to fight her, or tried to force his way through one of the sealed doors, while he had a little strength left. Now it was too late.

He stumbled past a pillar and into the aisle. As he blundered against one of the pungent, freshly painted murals, a depiction of the martyrdom of St. Stephen, he trod on something that cracked beneath his foot.

Looking downward, he saw that he'd stepped on a clay mortar and pestle. One of the painters must have left them behind. And Raoul realized that there might be a way to strike at his nemesis even if the agonizing radiance of her rosary did keep him beyond arm's reach. He stooped, snatched up the biggest piece of the shattered mortar, and threw it.

He wanted to hit Genevieve between the eyes. Instead, the shard glanced off her temple, but that was enough to stagger her. Her exorcism faltered, and, its glare dying abruptly, the rosary slipped from her fingers.

Raoul launched himself forward and slammed into her, knocked her down and fell on top of her. Thrashing, she struggled to scramble out from underneath him. At the moment, her merely mortal strength was more than a match for his own.

But he had his claws, and he started ripping at her, shredding her gown and the pasty, dirty, sour-smelling skin beneath. His attacks flung spatters of blood through the air. Despite her frenzied efforts to shield herself, in another moment he'd rip out her throat.

And then, his fury and desperation notwithstanding, he imagined the possible consequences.

He hoped that if she was no longer alive to hinder him, he could escape via the spire. But if he did, he wouldn't be able to return, nor could he haul her corpse up the stairs with him. He was simply too weak.

And many of the townspeople were still afraid that the church was haunted or accursed. How much more terrified would they be tomorrow if they entered and found a butchered saint on the floor? Would they still consecrate the cathedral, or might they abandon or even demolish it after all?

As he hesitated, she thrust her arm out and just barely managed to grab her rosary. The beads shone with azure fire as she lashed them against his head.

The worst pain yet blasted through his skull. He collapsed, and she dragged herself from beneath him, already gasping out the words of the exorcism again.

Wracked by convulsions, he tried to crawl after her and claw her, but succeeded only in flopping over onto his back. His body crackled, blackened, and shriveled. The ribbed vault in the section of ceiling above him seemed to rush down like a set of terrible jaws.

# PRESERVER

*Tim Waggoner*

"That has to be the worst piece of crap I've seen in some time."

Benjamin Moulton looked away from what could only charitably be called a sculpture, startled to hear his thoughts echoed so precisely. The speaker was a petite woman, not much over five feet. She wore her blonde hair short, the cut too ragged to be called a pageboy, although that's what it put him in mind of. He expected her to be dressed in black—after all, well over half of the people milling through the gallery were. But she wore a maroon jacket that was a little too large for her and far too light for late January in Ohio, and a simple pair of jeans, not even designer as far as he could tell. In Benjamin's estimation, that gave her more real taste than ninety-nine-point-nine percent of the people in the place, himself probably included.

He smiled. "Don't hold back; tell me how you really feel."

She chuckled, the sound more mature, more knowing than someone of her apparent years should have been capable of making. She seemed to be in her early twenties, at most. "I could go on, but why bother? That . . . object isn't worth the time it would take."

Benjamin looked at the sculpture again. It was by an artist he'd never heard of, someone named Kopinski. The piece was a hunk of wood, nothing more than a small upright log, really, that had been scored numerous times with a sharp object, the deep cuts crisscrossing and zigzagging in random, senseless patterns. The hand-lettered placard on the wall said it was called *Orpheus Screams*, and that the artist was willing to part with this masterpiece for the paltry sum of $365.

He turned back to his newfound fellow critic. "Come now, surely you can see what a bold statement the artist is making," he said with a smirk.

She grinned. "The only statement I see is 'I'm a no-talent hack desperately hoping to find someone gullible enough to pay a few hundred dollars for damaged firewood.'"

Benjamin laughed. "Now, now, they say art is in the eye of the beholder."

The woman was suddenly sober. "They're wrong. Art exists all by itself." She reached out and placed a pale, slender hand atop the chunk of wood. "Kopinski's got a whole pile of these behind his house. It took him ten minutes to score the wood, and that only because he paused to go get a beer."

"You know the artist?"

"*Artist* is far too kind a word, but no, I do not know him."

"Then how . . . ?"

She removed her hand, smiled, and gave a little shrug. "Just speculating."

"I wouldn't be surprised if you were pretty damn close to the truth." And that seemed to be all there was to say about Kopinski and his log, for suddenly a silence descended between them. The woman seemed undisturbed by it, merely looked at him and continued to smile, and Benjamin realized how attractive she was. Not that she was pretty, not really, was more on the plain side actually, her complexion washed out, hints of dark circles beneath her eyes, her nose a touch too long, her lips a smidge too thin. But those eyes . . .

Her eyes were large and bluish green, with little flecks of color in them that seemed to change from moment to moment, first gold, then red, then black, then back to gold again. The pupils were dark and deep and wide, and it felt as if they were pulling at him somehow, as if they might suck him in and devour him whole if he wasn't careful.

Benjamin suddenly felt self-conscious. He had never been an especially attractive man, and at forty-seven, whatever looks he did possess were on the verge of deserting him forever. His rusty-brown hair was thinning on top and too long in the back, and he hadn't shaved in two days. He wore a gray trench coat that was probably as old, if not older, than the woman standing before him, and that was a decade overdue for dry-cleaning. His brown slacks were rumpled and sported several stains—some old, some fresh—and his tennis shoes, which had once been white, were now sooty gray-black.

He was old enough to be her father, too old for her to be looking at him like she was, too old to be liking it this much.

He knew the smart thing would be to say goodbye and get out of there before he embarrassed himself. Instead, he said, "So what besides the opportunity to indulge in razor-tongued criticism has brought you out to the galleries on such a cold night?"

"You, Benjamin Moulton. I'm a great admirer of your work."

Of all the possible responses she might have made, that was the last he expected. "How—?"

"Do I know you?" she finished. "I frequent the galleries; I've seen you around."

He smiled ruefully. "I didn't think I had any admirers. Most people don't understand my stuff."

She made a dismissive gesture. "Most people lack vision."

"But not you?"

"Not me," she agreed. No hint of pride, just a simple statement of fact.

Benjamin was a collage artist, but instead of paper or cloth, he used everyday household items to create his art. He took all manner of odds and ends, bits and pieces, and fitted them together with glue, solder, wire, and string to create his collages, to make his statements. Statements no one ever seemed to understand.

"Prove it," he challenged.

"All right. But you don't have any pieces on display here. We'll have to go to the Plaid Pony." And before Benjamin could respond, she turned and began threading her way through the crowd and toward the door, leaving him hurrying to catch up.

Outside on the sidewalk, Benjamin coughed explosively as the cold night air filled his lungs and he wished desperately to light up a cigarette, but he hadn't had enough money to buy a pack of Camels for the last four days. He briefly considered asking his new acquaintance if she smoked, and if so, could she spare a cigarette, but he decided against it. So many people were anti-smoking these days, and he didn't want to turn her off before he had a proper chance to turn her on.

The streets of the Old Brewery District were covered with a light dusting of snow, and tiny, almost imperceptible flakes were still drifting down, but they were few and far between.

"They look so small and lonely, don't they?" she said.

"What?" he asked, startled.

"The snowflakes."

"Ah, yes, they do." That was exactly what he had been thinking. He felt a sudden chill that had nothing to do with the winter air and he stuffed his hands deep into his coat pockets and wished he had a shot of whiskey to warm himself up, or at least a pair of gloves or a scarf. But the problem with the cliché of the starving artist was that it was a cliché for a very good reason.

They trudged along the sidewalk, slowed by the crowds who'd flocked from all over town to attend the first gallery hop of the year. Fifteen years ago the Old Brewery District was a pesthole of rundown and abandoned buildings, the only residents rats, drug addicts, and other assorted vermin. But a wave of urban renewal had gone through the city, thanks to flocks of yuppies with money to burn, and the Old Brewery District slowly became reborn as a haven for artsy-craftsy types, and where once bars and twenty-four-hour porn emporiums had stood were now art galleries and coffee shops. And once a month the yuppies—no longer so young but still well monied, thank you—came down, along with a mixture of college students and a sprinkling of curious middle-class types, to wander from gallery to gallery, sometimes buying, more often just looking and feeling virtuously intellectual for taking a few minutes to stare at what was mostly hackwork in between cups of cappuccino and cheap burgundy.

Benjamin hated it. But he came every month. It was a good way to make connections with gallery owners and, better yet, potential customers. He might have been an artist, but that didn't mean he was above prostituting himself. The only problem was finding someone who wanted him to spread his legs.

Benjamin breathed as shallowly as he could to keep from coughing, the air curling slowly out of his mouth like miniature fog. He looked at his companion and noticed that her breath, unlike his, wasn't misting in the frigid air. He shrugged mentally. Some people just handled cold weather better than others, he guessed. After all, she had on that light jacket, right? She probably sweltered in the summertime.

Before long they came to the Plaid Pony and went inside. The Pony wasn't as crowded as the last gallery had been, but then it was a small place with only a few works displayed. The girl brushed past the scattering of browsers and headed straight for his piece, the only one of his displayed in the Pony. For that matter, the only one displayed anywhere right now.

The collage hung on the wall, a conglomeration of household junk glued to a piece of plywood. Screws, bolts, and clock springs, doll parts and matchbook covers, playing cards and Legos, unopened condoms and small plastic dinosaurs, a riot of the mundane, an explosion of triviality.

The collage wasn't titled; none of his work was. The placard on the wall announced it simply as Number 142 and said he was asking $145.

*Dream on, Ben,* he thought. *Dream on.*

He turned to his companion and gestured toward his piece. "All right, Ms. Visionary—go to it."

Her eyes narrowed and she took a step back. Her fingers came to her chin and stroked it lightly as she examined every inch of the collage.

Benjamin found himself growing uncomfortable. He was used to people glancing at his work and moving on, not giving it this kind of concentrated scrutiny. This woman wasn't just looking at his collage; she was truly *seeing* it.

She studied Number 142 for a full five minutes before speaking. "On the surface, it appears to be about AIDS. The screws and bolts represent sex. The clock springs time, which is running out. Unopened condoms, which the ignorant and foolish refuse to use. They'd rather take chances, as evidenced by the playing cards. The matchbooks are empty, their fire gone, standing for those who have died. The Legos, oh, they're lost innocence, I suppose. And the dinosaurs represent the ultimate and final extinction of a species, which might happen to humanity if it doesn't wise up.

"Of course, beneath the particulars of the imagery is the heart of the work, the deep sense of isolation and futility in the face of death."

Benjamin didn't notice his mouth was hanging open, and if he had, he wouldn't have cared. "You . . . understand."

"Of course. It's rather obvious, really. Not that I'm criticizing, mind. It's quite good. Perhaps not up to the level of your best pieces, but still far better than anything else in town."

Benjamin didn't know how to respond. After all these years of waiting for someone to actually get what he was trying to say, now that someone had, he had no idea what to think, how to feel.

"What's your name?" he finally asked, resorting to simple social custom.

"Seina," she replied with a smile. "Would you like to get some coffee?"

Benjamin smiled back. "I'd love to."


Seina passed by several popular coffee shops before finally stopping at Java Hut, a hole-in-the-wall joint that Benjamin had never visited before. "It may not look like much . . ." she began.

"And ten dollars says that in this case, looks are definitely not deceiving," he finished.

She grinned and led him inside.

Sure enough, it was small, cramped, dingy, and dirty, with only a handful of tables and even fewer customers. Seina led him to a table in the back and they sat.

The only employee in sight, a pimply faced college kid behind the counter, looked sullenly in their direction, his lethargic gaze saying, *You don't really want to order anything, do you?*

Benjamin looked at Seina. "What would you like?" Ordinarily in this situation he would've added *My treat,* but all he had in his pockets at the moment was lint.

"Nothing, really. I just wanted to go someplace where we could talk."

Benjamin turned toward the kid behind the counter and shook his head. The kid nodded once, relieved that he wouldn't have to exert himself, and went back to staring into space.

"So tell me, how did you get to be such a fan of mine?" Benjamin asked.

"I follow the arts. Your work stood out. It's as simple as that."

"Not that I'm fishing for compliments—ah, hell, of course I'm fishing for compliments—but what makes my work stand out?"

She answered without hesitation. "The subtlety. The playful irony. Although it's gotten less playful and more biting over the years."

*Years?* "How long have you been following my work?"

"Oh, for a while now."

Benjamin didn't know what to make of that. She hardly seemed old enough to have taken a serious interest in art for very long. Months, perhaps, but *years?*

She smiled a private smile. "I'm older than I look."

"You did it again."

"What?"

"Responded to something I was thinking."

"Coincidence." But there was something about the way she said the word that made it clear she didn't expect to be believed. "Tell me something, Benjamin. Do you like being an artist?"

Benjamin started to answer, but before he could speak, he was seized by a fit of phlegmy coughing. It took him almost a full minute to get it under control and regain his breath. "Sorry," he wheezed.

Seina acted as if it hadn't happened. She just sat patiently, waiting for him to respond.

"It's a mixed bag," he said. "Sometimes it's great, like when an idea takes hold of me. I start hunting for objects. And not just any old objects will do; they have to be the right ones. I can spend days—sometimes weeks —searching for the appropriate materials. And then when I finally have them, I can start putting them together. At random at first, or at least that's the way it feels. But before long a pattern begins to emerge, a pattern that was there all along. It just takes me a while to see it. After that, the actual assembly goes fairly quickly. And then, when the collage is finished, I can see how close to my original idea I got." He smiled. "Or didn't get, as the case may be."

"But sometimes it's not so great. There's the dry period between ideas, when it feels like you'll never have another again. And of course, there's the money, or rather the lack thereof. If I was a painter, at least I might be able to get some commercial work, you know? But there's not much call for a commercial collage artist. I end up working a lot of odd jobs. I've done everything from painting houses to driving cabs."

"And what does it feel like to know you're past your prime?"

"I'm only forty-seven," he said stiffly.

"I wasn't talking about age; I was talking about your creative prime."

"What do you mean?"

"Come now, Benjamin. I said I've been following your work for some time, and I meant it. I've seen you grow from an immature artist with little skill and even less to say to a seasoned master of his craft. But lately your work has been . . . lacking. Like your collage in the Painted Pony. It's still an accomplished piece of work, but nothing like what you used to produce."

Benjamin wanted to be angry, wanted to defend Number 142. But he couldn't. He knew she was right. "Maybe I'm just in a slump." He didn't sound convincing, even to himself.

"Perhaps. But there comes a time in every artist's life when he begins the downward slide to mediocrity. It's as inevitable as the approach of the grave."

"Now isn't that a cheery thought."

Seina leaned forward then, her remarkable eyes shining. "But it doesn't have to be like that, Benjamin. Not if you don't want it to be."

"I don't understand."

She leaned even closer, her voice low and intense. "I know a way to keep your talents and skills at their peak, as fresh and vital as they ever were— for all time."

Benjamin chuckled. "Sounds like you're about to launch into some kind of religious spiel."

Seina smiled, displaying sharp incisors. "Hardly."


Seina's home was the top floor of a condemned building not too far from the Brewery District. There was some furniture—a bed, couch, kitchen table, a few other pieces—but mostly her place was filled with creativity. There were paintings and sculptures in all styles, from the minimalist to the gaudily bizarre. A piano rested in one corner, and next to it, on a table, were a saxophone and a flute, along with a stack of sheet music, some of which was pre-printed but most of which was handwritten. Quilts hung on the walls, next to framed poems—original, Benjamin presumed—rendered in ornate calligraphy. Origami animals of all colors were scattered throughout the rooms wherever there was space. Mobiles and wind chimes hung from the ceiling, stirring in the icy breeze wafting from the open windows.

He shivered.

"My kind doesn't need heat," Seina said.

Benjamin knew he shouldn't take her remark seriously. Vampire fixations were not uncommon among artsy folk. Some of them would go to any lengths to indulge their fantasies, including purchasing a pair of quite realistic-looking fangs. Still, there was something about Seina, a sense of age, a feeling of restrained power. And those eyes . . .

"I am what I say I am, Benjamin. How else could I know what you're thinking?"

"Maybe you're just a good guesser."

"Maybe." She closed the windows then led him over to the couch. Not quite sure what else to do, he followed and they sat.

"Have you ever wondered what it's like to live for eternity, Benjamin? It's wonderful for the first century or two, but before long, much sooner than you'd think, it grows dull. Each night is like the one before it, and the next night, and the next . . . Some of my kind take their own lives rather than endure any more of the numbing sameness. Some go mad. But some of us find ways to fill the emptiness, take up pursuits to keep us amused."

Benjamin told himself that he was humoring her, that he really didn't believe. "And so you collect art?"

If she truly was what she claimed to be and caught his thought about humoring her, she gave no sign. "In a manner of speaking. You see, I've always been attracted to the arts, but I lack talent. And since I have no talent of my own, I preserve the talent of others. Preserve it forever."

Stories flashed through Benjamin's mind, novels he'd read, movies he'd seen. Immortality—the vampire's most seductive promise. For him? He couldn't bring himself to believe it. "Why me? Why here? Why aren't you in New York or Paris, searching out real artists?"

"Because, Benjamin, those artists have opportunities to be noticed, opportunities for their own sort of immortality, a place in a museum, a niche in a canon of Artists with a capital A. But there are other artists in other places who don't have such opportunities, artists of great talent and skill who are equally deserving, but who are destined to remained unnoticed. Artists like you, Benjamin."

She laid a hand on his. It was ice-cold.

He jerked his hand away. "So just like that, I'm chosen to become immortal, like I'm some sort of supernatural sweepstakes winner?"

"Not at all. I said I've been following your work for years, Benjamin, and I have. I frequent the galleries, the museums, the university art shows, concerts, and plays, always searching for another artist whose gift I can preserve. I first became aware of your work fourteen years ago. I remember the piece. It was your Number Eleven, a eulogy for the death of sixties' idealism."

Benjamin remembered that particular collage. It contained peace signs, Beatles memorabilia and reproductions of draft cards, all covered by dollar bills stained red.

"It was a simple piece," Seina continued, "but even then your talent shone through and I knew you were an artist to watch. And watch I did for nearly a decade and a half. Until I noticed your work begin to decline in quality, even if only slightly." She held up a hand as he opened his mouth to speak. "No need to protest or make excuses, Benjamin. We both know it's true."

"Yes." It was a soft, painful admission.

"And the decline will continue, slowly but surely. The ideas will come harder, and those that do come will be common, pedestrian. You'll stop searching so hard for just the right objects to create your collages and start using whatever's at hand, because it's easier. You'll find that you complete fewer and fewer pieces, and those you do finish will be further and further away from your original vision.

"But it doesn't have to be like that, Benjamin." Seina reached for his hand again, then stopped as if thinking better of it. "I can end this dissipation of your powers, even reverse the degradation which has already taken place. I can ensure that your talent will never die, Benjamin. Never."

Benjamin knew he should stop playing along with Seina's fantasy, that he should get up and leave right now. But he stayed where he was. If it wasn't a fantasy, if it was true . . .

"What do you have to look forward to for the rest of your life, Benjamin? You have no family, no real friends. You smoke and drink too much. I can hear your lungs laboring to draw breath, your flabby heart struggling to pump blood. You'll be lucky to live another ten years. Ten years of working odd jobs and watching helplessly as your artistic abilities slowly but surely desert you. Is that what you want, Benjamin?"

It sounded like a worse hell than any Bosch had ever depicted. "No, it isn't."

She did take his hand this time, and this time he didn't pull away. "Then allow me to help you. Give yourself to me, Benjamin."

Benjamin looked into her eyes, and what he saw there finally convinced him she was what she said she was, and that she could do what she said she could.

He uttered a single, final word. "Yes."

And then Seina embraced him and her mouth found his throat. There was pain, then warmth, then a coldness which began to seep into his limbs.

As he listened to the sucking sounds, he began to feel that more than his blood was being drained. It was as if Seina was taking something else as well, something even more vital than blood.

And then he realized the true meaning of what she had said. *Your talent will never die.* She'd said nothing about *him.*

He tried to pull away, but by this time he was far too weak. Finally, as he sank into the darkness, he was comforted by one thought: at least the best part of himself would live on. In the end, wasn't that every artist's dream?


Seina wiped her mouth and watched as the dried husk that had been Benjamin began to crumble and decay. Within an hour it would be nothing more than dust, easily disposed of. She felt his abilities settling within her, alongside the countless others she had preserved over the years.

Her first collage should be something special. Something . . . and then an idea popped into her head. She would create a memorial to Benjamin. Yes, he'd like that.

She stood and flexed her hands. They felt alive and eager to get to work, ready to help her stave off the boredom of eternity for yet another night.

# MAN OF THE DEAD

*Billie Sue Mosiman*

Every half century or so I feel compelled to speak the truth. I pick my confidant carefully, but more often than not the result is unfortunate and . . . blood is spilled. The reason I keep talking about these things despite the dozens of failures is because the pygmy part of my soul that still clings to its humanity longs to make honest contact with another. It's possible that in the distant future the part of me which desires human understanding and warmth will be eradicated. Even now, before it happens, I mourn that day. This compulsion is all that keeps me from being unholy.

It has been twenty years longer than usual this time since last I indulged my need. If I've kept a good record in my head, it has been seventy-eight years since the choosing of my last confidant.

I am Tian Hou, resident of Nanchang, China, for this past half century. Nanchang, during the Uprising in 1927, was a city I emigrated to because, frankly, there were war dead. The streets were littered with them. I was able to feast to my heart's desire, with no one the wiser, upon those who lay mortally wounded, seconds from their oblivion.

I've been happy here, though soon I will have to move on. Longer than fifty years is too long for a Man of the Dead to remain stationary.

The day when I found the one person trustworthy enough to hear my confessions, I was walking along the river Gan while working out in my mind an intricate design for a gold-and-jade ring commissioned by a customer. I keep a shop in whatever city I make home. Before I was taken and made prisoner of life everlasting, I was a lowly artisan of the craft of jewelry-making, but fortunate enough, after my . . . change . . . to be taken under the wing of a master who taught me the real joy of handling gold and silver. "It is as sacred as praying to your god to lay in the precious and semiprecious stones," he said. "This is just not your vocation—a way to feed your belly. To excel at anything, you must bring your soul to bear on the work. Let your hands and your mind find freedom in creation."

I've now had centuries to perfect my art so that I am sought out by people who wish to own a beautiful piece that might one day become an heirloom. It was not until I had lived hundreds of years on the earth that I discovered my supernatural powers could be instilled within a gemstone. It happened one night when I worked late, feverish to be done with the pouring of an ingot of gold. I was hungry, starving, trembling with wild need. I was new to Nanchang and hadn't yet even found a hunting ground.

With my thoughts elsewhere, I mishandled the liquid metal and it splashed over my shoes. I cursed and put away my tools. I was about to ruin everything if I didn't feed first.

I went on the prowl in the city night. I didn't notice how the moon glanced from the golden streaks and spots that shimmered on my shoes. I came upon an old man about to drown himself in the river Gan. He was very old and shriveled, and entering his mind, I sensed his weariness of living. I was about to call to him to stop his plunge when he turned as if he'd heard my approach—but that was impossible. No one knows when I come. His gaze drifted from my countenance to the ground where I stood. "Look at me," I commanded. I could call him into my arms if he would only look at me. He continued to stare spellbound at my feet.

I glanced down and saw the gold dancing about on the shoe leather as if it had a life of its own. It should have cooled and frozen in place, but it was as alive as when it first splashed there. Then it came to me what must have happened. My fury at my own incompetence and impatience had in some way been imbued in the metal I'd been working with. It was a part of my soul, as my mentor had so wisely tried to teach me. It carried within its basic elements my lust for blood, my urgent longing, my pure scorching need.

The elderly man was in an enchantment. The part of me he would have feared most lay within the golden sparkles shining from my shoes.

I stepped to him and whispered against his ear, "This will be easier than a death by water." And then I proceeded to relieve him of the life he found unbearable while the gold liquid metal ran like mercury from me onto the old man, slithering up his leg, his chest, and circling tightly as a band around his throat just below where I set my teeth.

From that time forward I gave myself—my *self*—to my creations. I made necklaces that caused the wearer to return to me when near death, impelled by my will imbued in the precious metals and stones. Not for everyone did I make these special pieces. Only for those in their last prime, those with fewer years left than they ever thought possible.

As I walked along the river, my hands behind my back, contemplating what sort of gold filigree to cast over the cool chunk of jade I had carved into the semblance of a tiger, I saw a young woman standing at the crumbling riverbank, staring out across the slow moving muddy waters. She stood approximately in the spot where that night long ago I found the suicidal man who taught me something even a master craftsman had been unable to impart. Her hair was braided down her back the way some of our peasant women wore their hair, but she was not Chinese and her hair was like a gold rope shining in the evening sun. A tourist to our city? An adventurer, perhaps? We saw so few, most Westerners content to visit Shanghai or Hong Kong.

I wondered at her thoughts enough to project myself into them. I hardly do this anymore except to further enhance my jewelry pieces so they match the picture my customers have in mind. I hardly do it otherwise because I've discovered a salient point about most of mankind. They do little but worry about petty concerns. That is all they do. Rarely do they dream and seldom do they actually plot their futures. The minds of men have become somewhat alien to me over the long years. I find their thoughts sadly lacking in maturity or any gleam of intelligence.

So my stumbling upon the girl along Gan Jiang and entering her mind was an unusual departure. The second I ventured there, inside her head, I halted and was taken aback. I had intruded mid-thought.

. . . *lived forever, if I lived forever, I would sit beside this old river and watch it until it either went bone-dry or spread its banks to flood the land.*

Startled that she was thinking of what she would do if she lived forever, I strolled over to her and introduced myself.

Speaking English, I said, "Hello. I am Tian Hou and I see that you seem to enjoy the view from our river. Are you English?" I didn't guess Scandinavian or German or some other nationality because in her thoughts she used English.

"American," she said, extending her hand. "My name's Vivian Lancaster. Do I look English?"

I smiled. "I was just guessing. Your hair is so blond. You are from California?"

She laughed, tilting her head back slightly to expose a creamy white throat that pulsed with what I knew to be rich red blood. I stilled my heart and by so doing, dampened the craving. I tried never to take blood from one who had life ahead of him. I feasted on the fatally diseased and dying, the old and weary. It was the only way to live in a city for as long as fifty or seventy years without being detected. And it was the only way I could live with my affliction without wishing to lie down on the earth and press my face into the soil, remaining there immobile until I starved.

Her laughter was abrupt and pure. As it died down, she said, "No, I've never been in California. I'm from Wyoming."

"Ah, the cowboys and steers. The mountains." This too amused her.
"Would you like to join me for tea? I walk along the river at sundown and
then I stop for tea before going back to my shop."

"Sure, I'd like tea." She turned to walk with me along the path that led
back into the midst of commerce. "What kind of shop do you have?"

"A humble one."

She glanced over at me to see if I was playing a game.

"A humble one where I make original jeweled pieces for my customers."

"I'd like to see it some day. Where's it located?"

I saw she wore no jewelry, but one such as she needed no adornment to
distract from her native beauty. She was kind to show interest in my work.
"After tea, I could show you if you like."

She agreed that would be nice. *Nice.* Americans always talked this way,
I'd noticed, as if that was how human interaction was made more tolera-
ble. Everything was nice. Have a nice day. Wasn't that a nice tournament?
China had a nice atmosphere. The porcelain possessed a nice glow. And in
the end, hadn't it been a nice life?

We sat inside the smoky dim tea parlor and shared a pot. I poured for
her and saw she didn't ruin the flavor with sugar lumps or cream or lemon
the way the British were prone to do. I found out she was a scholar interested in geology, that her parents were wealthy, that she was taking a
leisurely tour around the world. She didn't seem in the least spoiled, however, or smug in her good fortune. On the other hand, she didn't pretend
to a guilt that would make her appear foolish just because fate had be-
stowed upon her money while others scraped by in poverty. There was
much of it in evidence in Nanchang, so much I'm sure it didn't go beneath
her notice.

What *did* go beneath her notice was that I poured just one small cup of
the tea for myself and when I brought it to my lips, I did not drink. One of
my major regrets of being a Man of the Dead is the loss of a palate. I can
eat and drink man's meat and drink, though I'll vomit it later, but it tastes
so bland, like stale rainwater on the tongue. I don't take in anything that's
unnecessary to a pleasant conversation with the mortals.

I made up stories for Miss Vivian Lancaster about my life, and tossed in
a few true stories of the city I'd witnessed the past half century or so. She
sat with her chin resting on her palm, watching me, complimenting me on
my command of the English language, delighting in my small tales of
making a vulgar pendant for a rich lady from the nearby town of
Jingdezhen (which I imbued with my craving for her blood when she
feared she would live no more) and of creating a diamond solitaire of
extraordinary beauty for a young groom-to-be who came from the north

country (which I did not penetrate with a lure, as I would be gone from Nanchang before ever someone so young would face death).

"I've never seen anyone actually make a piece of jewelry," she said, intrigued.

I rose slowly from the table. "Come, then, and I'll show you how it's done."

In my shop, with the lamps blazing and my jeweler's loupe attached to my head, I put the finishing touches on the tiger jade, connecting the gold filigree like fine threads over the animal's hind and front quarters to hold it in place. She sat on a stool nearby, watching silently.

I found it pleasant to have an audience, one so willing to be as immersed as I was in the creative process. I ended my work with a flourish, holding out the ring for her appraisal. "Do you like it?"

"It's beautiful," she said. Her eyes did not lie, but I moved like a wraith into her thoughts to be sure. Yes. Yes, she liked it very much, she thought it *grand*. That was so much better than *nice*.

My stomach rumbled and I raised my eyebrows in embarrassment. It was late, time to feed, and I must be rid of her soon.

She smiled at me, neglecting to mention the noise my stomach made. She rose and took up her shoulder purse. "I need to be going. Maybe I'll drop by again sometime while I'm in the city. Thanks for the tea. And the chance to watch you work."

"You're welcome, Vivian Lancaster," I said formally, bowing my head. "I would like you to come back very much."

I watched her leave the shop, the little brass bell tingling as she closed the door behind her. The hunger drove me to drop my tools and to find my keys to lock up. My brain swirled with images of blood and my mouth watered. After I had locked the door, I put away the key and stood at the back of the shop near the little cocked-open window. My cloak fell from my shoulders and my bones liquefied, my body shifted and drew inward, my being changing into the black, fluttery sharp-toothed bat of the night.

I flew out the window and into the fragrant wind that drifted above the city buildings. I found the hospital and flew gently to roost on the window sill of a room of one dying. I listened for a while to the mild susurration of a breathing machine attached to the near-dead body. I scanned the room to be sure it was empty of prying eyes.

And then I swooped inside, transformed into myself again, and bent over the poor old soul who waited so patiently for death to take it away from the suffering field of pain it walked on this earth.

* * *

Vivian came regularly. She had booked passage on a ship to the Philippines, but turned in her ticket, explaining that she was captured by the old oriental charm of Nanchang. I think, craven and egotistical as it might sound, that she did not stay because of the city. She stayed because of me. We talked while I worked, shaping gold and two large diamond-shaped one-carat rubies into a bodice pin. We talked at the tea shop and while walking along the river Gan.

I took her to see a traveling Chinese dance troupe, to a pagoda, and to shop for needed supplies in the open-air market. She spoke of a wildness in her she was unable to suppress. "I can't be still," she said. "Nowhere seems like home. I feel as if I have to stay loose and free; I'm not tethered to a place like other people are. I mean, my parents have lived in the same town in Wyoming all their lives! My friends went off to college and came back to settle in."

"That's why you've taken this trip around the world?"

She nodded, dismayed it seemed that she couldn't control her own urges. "I don't know what I should do with my life because I can't stand still long enough to have any sort of life. I'm not happy unless I'm on the move."

I thought of my own incredibly long life and how so many times I had yearned to call somewhere home. I had no home and could never have one. A Man of the Dead could not afford to stay put long enough to be found out. What would she say if I told her travel and homelessness could be taxing? What would she say if I confided to her . . . what I was?

I was very lonely. The days with Vivian were days of blue luminous joy, a welcome release from the prison of my self-imposed solitude. Gloom had lifted its head and looked elsewhere for a time. I needed to talk of things, to be seen for what and who I am. To be accepted and understood. I would have to make her a chain, to bind her to me, and insist that she take and wear it. Only one bound could be my confidant. The chain would let me know if she ever revealed my secrets.

"I would like to make something for you," I said, "A small gift of friendship."

"You don't have to do that. I don't wear jewelry really."

"But do you like it? If it was something special, a gift? You could not refuse a gift, could you?" I had never been turned down.

She smiled sweetly and I loved her then. "No, I guess I couldn't refuse. I'd like to pay, though . . ."

I dismissed the idea with a wave of my hand. "No. I'll accept nothing.

When next you come to visit—in a few days? I will have something for you."

She came again in three days. I'd worked late every day on the special chain, putting aside the ruby brooch I'd been commissioned to make. As I worked, I stared into the depth of the silver I'd chosen, and with each link I forced the elements to listen to me, to obey me, to be part of my hands and eyes and ears, to take a wisp of my soul into it. Call to me, I commanded the chain as I formed it, call to me if the throat you encircle ever tries to speak my secrets.

I handed her the completed chain. It was eighteen inches, the links an eighth-inch thick, with a claw clasp. It shone like starlight on a pond.

"Wow, this is gorgeous. You won't let me pay you for it?"

"Absolutely not. Here, let me fasten it for you."

She held up her braid from her slim neck and I cinched the chain in place. She was mine now. If ever she betrayed me, I would know. If she tried to unfasten the clasp, she'd find the task impossible. She'd never be able to break the links. She might as well have taken an iron collar to wear. One tethered to my cerebrum.

"Vivian," I said later, while she sat on the high stool quietly watching me work one of the rubies into place in the brooch, "has anyone ever told you a secret?" My compulsion to speak of the unspeakable was upon me. It had been building ever since I met her, and with the security of the chain around her fair neck, I was free now to confess.

"Sure. Why? Do you have a secret, Tian?" She was teasing me lightly, so I smiled.

"And if you swore not to tell, would you keep your promise?"

Her gaze penetrated me, her expression serious now. "I think I would."

"First, I must preface my confession with a warning . . ."

"Yes?"

"I'm sure you've seen movies and read books in your country about the . . . vampire. Those are fictions. They are not altogether true."

She was about to laugh at me, but my scowl prevented it. She swallowed and I saw her neck work. "Not *altogether* true? You're a vampire? That's what you want to confess? The secret?"

I looked down at the ruby reflecting glints of red light from the points of its many facets. It was a gorgeous jewel, one of my favorites. Red like blood. Rich and red and warm, like blood. Asian rubies were too orange, so I never used them. These I'd had imported and they were truly scarlet. Turned a certain way, the ruby could be a droplet that had leaked from the vein of a healthy specimen. I would bind these gems to me, too, and when the woman who wore it fell ill, she would come to me. Rubies and silver both were the best materials for the creation of psychic bonds.

I suddenly smelled Vivian's fear dragging my thoughts away from the rubies. That fear was as palatable as had been her previous exultation when she first held the two perfect rubies in the palm of her hand.

"Don't be afraid," I said softly.

"You really mean it," she said. "You really believe it. You believe you're a vampire."

"I'd never harm you." This was a necessary lie. I would not hurt her if I wasn't forced to it, but I couldn't say that.

"Tian . . . I don't know what to say. I know those vampire stories are fictions and I don't really be—"

"Believe," I finished for her. And then I put down the brooch, though the carefully positioned ruby would roll out and have to be redone. I stood, dropping the cloak I always wore to keep me warm. I reached out with both hands and wrapped them fully around Vivian's throat. She gasped and jerked away, but I held her. Not too hard, my fingers just above the silver chain. I didn't mean to do more than show her there was no warmth in my flesh, no blood flowing in my veins. She was still, her eyes wide and more alarmed than ever.

"You see how cold I am?"

She nodded once and blinked. I took my hands from her throat and took one of her hands to press hard against my diaphragm. "You see my heart does not beat?"

I moved her hand from my chest to the jugular in my throat and back again to my chest. I waited for the dawning of understanding to come into her eyes. She stared open-mouthed at me with a look I had seen countless times on my chosen confidants. It made me melancholy that the expressions never vary. They never wanted to believe. And when forced to it, they usually lost their minds for just a little while. I saw her slipping, saw her sanity waver and fade in the blue thready depths of her irises. "Don't," I commanded. "Stay fast and be whole."

"You're dead," she whispered.

"Yes."

"You're a vampire. You . . . you drink blood."

"Yes. But not of the brave, the young, the innocent. I take only those hovering over the precipice of their deaths."

"I can't . . . I don't . . ."

She still didn't believe, dismissal camped in her eyes at the rim of madness.

My shoulders fell and the change came on rapidly. Transforming before her eyes was a man, cold with chilled blood in his veins, who now shifted into a black-winged, red-eyed beast of the night. I swooped around her head as she screamed, sorry the display was called for, but knowing there was no other way to confirm my claim.

I perched on the back of the chair I'd vacated at my jeweler's table and again changed, appearing before her as Tian Hue, the human monster.

"I have been thus cursed for more than a thousand years," I said, baring the usually hidden fangs that helped me feed.

She sank onto the stool and covered her face with her hands. "What can I do to help you?" she asked.

I was heartened to see she had returned to a saner self. "If you'll only listen to my troubles, I would be most appreciative. Vivian? Can you?"

She took away her hands and tears stood ready to overflow the lower lids of her eyes. "I'll listen," she said, trembling.

"And you won't tell anyone? It will be our secret?"

There was a momentary flash in her eyes that made me stiffen, but then it was gone, replaced with pity. "It will be our secret."


I told her of the beginning, when I was a middle-aged peasant living on land outside of Lhasa, the Forbidden City. I had a wife and five children. "We scratched out a living, though I was being taught to work as a jewel-crafter and we had hopes of having a better life. One day on the way to the city, I was waylaid by a Buddhist monk who stopped me on the road. I had not spoken before to a monk and instinctively feared doing so this time, for I was not worthy. He came to me silently and took my face in his hands, much as I took your throat in mine just now. He was cold on a warm day, his hands slabs of ice. His eyes were full of misery and pain. I didn't know what was wrong with him, so I inquired.

" 'I have been bitten,' he said. He went on, in stumbling language, to explain what had happened to him a fortnight before while he prayed alone in the temple. 'And I am hungry,' he said, 'so I must feed on you.' At first I didn't understand what he meant. Certainly I didn't think he would mean to make a meal at the expense of my soul, but that is what he did. He latched onto my head with one hand that was strong as the talon of a great bird, and put his cold, cold mouth against my neck . . . here." I put my hand against the old wound. "I think he meant to devour me, to murder me, but something at the last stopped him—perhaps his religious background—and he halted seconds before I left this world for the next. He was too young a vampire to know that by stopping, he was condemning my soul to wander the earth the same as he. He knew only he must stop, that to continue taking from me my lifeblood meant my death. He didn't want to kill. It was his morals that condemned me.

"He laid his curse on me. When I woke from where he'd dropped me beside the path, I was a Man of the Dead. I had to flee and leave behind my family, never to see them again. I had to make my way in the world the best I knew how. Unlike the monk, I swore not to make more like me. I would kill, but I would never leave a body lingering at the door to heaven so that he could come back to haunt mankind."

I watched Vivian and saw her sorrow. Soon after the confession was when my confidants lost control completely, going to the authorities. Or they tried to go to the authorities. None yet had made it. The silver always spoke, like hisses from the grave, of their betrayal.

"You kill to live?" she asked when I was quiet for a while.

"I go to the hospitals for the terminal and seek out the dying in their homes. I haunt war-torn areas. I fly through the night across vast distances and search only for those who have no hope of living until sunrise. It's only those I drain. It's the compromise I have been able to live with all these terrible long, lonely years." I failed to tell her of the customers I linked to return to me when it was their time. I could not, after all, tell her everything.

"That's horrible. That's worse than death," she said, clearly sickened.

I picked up the loose ruby and rolled it around in my palm, watching lamplight glitter from its fire. "I cannot love or procreate. I know my family lived and died and are no more. They are dust. I watch the planet turn and countries rise and fall. I know no end."

"Will you never die?" she asked. "Is there a God if there are people like you walking the earth?"

"Die?" I turned back to her. "I've tried to die, submitted to several different executions in various forms, and none of them take away the shambling hunger that drives me. Nothing stills my brain or destroys my body. I'm not quite—human—now. I'm supernatural. A beast of the night. As for God, well, I have never met with God and do not know if He exists or not, but I must be truthful—I don't think there is such a supreme being, for I've called on Him without answer. If there is a God or a race of gods or a knowing intelligence anywhere in the universe, none of it is interested in anything that happens on this watery ball swirling through endless space." I had spoken too much. But I couldn't stop my tongue from wagging. This was the time for truth.

She looked worn and dispirited, her whole body sagging and her lips drooping like a woeful child's.

"I hope you understand," I said. "I get to a point every so many years where I can't keep this to myself any longer. When I saw you, I knew I had to tell you."

"You've told this before, then."

"Many times."

"And did it help?"

"Sometimes. When my confidants didn't fail me."

She glanced away into the shop's shadows. "You kill those who tell, don't you?"

"Yes. Yes, I do, Vivian. I'll never lie to you."

"But you already have."

"How is that?"

She looked directly into my eyes. "You said you didn't kill the innocent. You took life only from the dying. But you lied."


I stepped back from the bed that was washed in moonlight and stood in shadow, weeping blood tears the way I always did when this had to happen. Vivian lay quiet and still on the covers, her eyes open in frozen terror.

Throughout the hotel I could hear every sound, every whisper. Lovers in their coupling, the bartender mixing a drink at the bar downstairs, the cook plucking the feathers from a chicken in the kitchen, guests conversing on the patio, a bellboy being berated by his captain in the manager's office, a fat man snoring in his bedroom.

Outside the hotel I heard the rustle of a ragman's cart down the street, the beeps of horns and roaring of cars, the clatter of feet as they slapped pavement and sidewalk, the laughter of children, the cries of caged birds in the square.

I could smell the one drop of blood on the pillow that had escaped my lips as I suckled at Vivian's throat. I could smell her body already decaying, enzymes breaking down, gases mingling in the cavities.

"I'm sorry, Vivian Lancaster," I said to the body. I stepped closer and reached out for the chain lying in the hollow of her throat. I gently pulled at it and the clasp let go. The silver links puddled in my hand. I slipped the chain in my pocket, then pulled the sheet up over the rictus of Vivian's face.

She had kept her promise for longer than most managed to do. She stayed on in Nanchang another two weeks, dropping by my shop now and then, asking unanswerable questions, peering at me with distress plainly written on her features. I knew the day she bought the airplane tickets for America. The neckchain I'd made her called to me and whispered in solemn tones that the heart it hung above had turned grave and cowardly. I knew the moment she stepped, trembling like a reed in rushing waters, into the Nanchang police station, looking around wildly, her heart steeped in apprehension. The chain then clamored at my ears like brass gongs beaten by a dozen wild hands.

I stood from my desk, dropped my cloak, and locked the front door. I took wing from the small window and flew into the second-story window of a closet at the station. I hurried down the stairs and found her just as she waited to be shown into the interrogation room. "Come with me," I said, gripping her upper arm and showing her a glimpse of my unsheathed fangs.

She came with me peacefully, but her feet stuttered down the steps and to the street. "Don't," she pleaded. "I won't tell."

"You would have, had I not come."

"How did you know?" Her voice was high and piping, teetering on the brink of utter madness.

"I told you some of my powers, Vivian. I didn't tell you all, but I warned you fairly."

"But how did you know?"

I halted in an alleyway and reached out toward her neck. She shrank back, but I held her still with a glance. I reached out again and stroked the silver chain. "I am an artist," I said. "I make things that last, things that shine and bring pride, but I also make things from the inner core of my heart and those I give to my confidants."

"The chain . . . ?"

"It is I, Vivian. I gave you a piece of myself when I gave you the truth and when I gave you the necklace."

She arched her neck in recoil at my lingering touch, horrified, I'm sure, that what I said must be true. "I won't tell," she repeated. "I promise. Please let me go."

I led her to her hotel and her room. I talked to her for a long time, giving her the wisdom I'd gained over many lifetimes. I assured her there was probably a God and an afterlife, I had been wrong, I was surely wrong. I told her to have faith and if she had none, to borrow it from whatever system she wished as I explained several to her.

I gave her time.

I restrained her only by having the silver chain tighten against her windpipe whenever she lost control and started to make a sound for help.

I took her life only when she was ready.

I turned to the open window, a breeze riffling the thin curtains, and flew into the chilly midnight sky.

Now I pack my tools, my packets of jewels, my gold and silver. I am on my way to find another city, another life where I can work, make my beautiful pieces for sale, and hope I can last another half century or more before I feel compelled to speak the truth again.

For a time I will grieve for Vivian. But only for a while. Time is all I have and too much of it. More than enough time to contemplate my sins until they are so great and burdensome I will be hopeful of a new confidant to hear the confession from my monstrous lips, a confession from a wandering, homeless, forsaken Man of the Dead.

# BEAT SURRENDER

### Cynthia L. Ward

On the J Church tracks, a windowless wall fresh-painted white: a blank canvas *calling* me, man! And I'm *burning*, the Krylon cans streaming, the spray flowing out of my hands like my life—art flowing out of me like the blood out of Jesus' nail holes! The bright colors are climbing to the stars, a cross ascending from a mob. Christ twists on the cross; he is a muy guapo Anglo, a black-bearded beauty dying at the hands of brown and black and white dudes and chicas in jeans and T-shirts and hightops: a party crowd, celebrating a second Crucifixion.

I'm standing at a bend in the Muni Metro track, on a hill between high buildings, the city spread below me in a million white knifepoint lights on black, looking like the stars above, and reflected in San Francisco Bay; it's like I'm standing in the middle of the universe, empty except for me and the stars and the great white wall. At any moment, one of those ridiculous little Metro trains might come around the bend, the J Church, electric, silent, and smear me across my work like red paint flung out of a gallon can. In the morning, the owner of the building will cover my work with whitewash.

Nothing lasts, man. *Nothing.*

Christ on the cross ain't nothing you see in the guerilla art of the Mission or Hunters Point. I'm the hottest dopest baddest bomber ever to pick up a can. I'm King of the Murals!

It's a warm night for December, in the fifties, and my Skatenigs T-shirt's sticking like a second skin. But black clouds are rolling over the sky, the stars are gone, and a cold breeze is up, chilling my sweat, making me start to shake; and I'm feeling like something is *watching* me, man. Not someone—some*thing.*

I'm going faster now, finishing up, sculpting martyr's pain and pleasure under Christ's crown of thorns, and I'm just about to tag my mural when something *slams* me! I'm knocked clean out of the narrow Muni alley, tumbling dick over nose down the street; the train's smashed me and any minute now the pain's gonna take my breath away and send me choking blood down to death, and my only thought is regret I didn't get to sign my name. *Satan.*

Then I realize there's a weight on me, some fucking heavy dude in a big open coat flapping around us like black wings, and behind the wings the Muni train's rolling past.

"I should have realized you would never notice anything except your canvas," says the man in a low, deep voice, rising up. His back's to me, he's dusting his hands on his trenchcoat, but it's obvious this short stocky dude is all muscle.

I leap up, ignoring my new bruises. "Why the fuck you *jump* me, man? I would've had a *great* finish!" I'm angry, even though what I'm saying isn't true; my name wouldn't've been on the mural above my body.

"I prefer it when you paint something I can look at without burning my eyes," the man says, turning around, and knocks the breath out of my body again by looking at me with a white face like an angel's and black eyes like the stars in some weird reverse-negative universe. My imagination must be all fucked up on adrenaline, 'cause those eyes look like they've looked into Heaven and Hell and seen everything; and he turned his back on Heaven.

Then I register what he said—*I prefer it when you paint something I can look at*—and I'm pissed again, and yelling: "You been *watching* me? You a cop or a pervert?"

"I've seen all your work," the Anglo says, which is hard to believe; it always gets slapped over fast with a coat of paint. "I am an admirer of great art."

"You're a pretentious, condescending yuppie asshole!" I yell, and walk away—or try to. Turning away from this man is the toughest thing I've ever done. I'm shaking like leaves in a windstorm by the time I get my back to him.

Then I go and look at him again because he speaks in Spanish: "Brother, I am far too old to be a yuppie."

Even an Anglo can't possibly think I'll believe such a blatant lie; but I don't feel like laughing. I feel like something ancient and inhuman is looking out of that young face.

"We shouldn't stand talking in the middle of the street," he says. "Let me buy you a drink."

I don't want to go anywhere with him. "I'm underage, man." Sixteen.

"That will not be a problem."

And it isn't; the doorman lets us pass like he doesn't see I'm underage and underdressed, doesn't smell my sweat or the lingering whiff of paint; like he doesn't even *see* us, man.

I'm getting all creeped out, and then the Anglo touches my shoulder and says, "Order anything you want," and we're sitting in a booth with water-beaded bottles in front of us. I realize I left my Krylons and sketchbook at the J Church track, and didn't tag my mural. I didn't even notice how we got to the bar—whether we walked, or came in his car, or took a cab—because I was so astonished that this Anglo was talking about graffiti like it meant something. Talking about my murals like they meant more than a slap in the face of my family and world and the Church.

I gulp my beer in one long swallow, and the Anglo glances at the bar and the bartender brings me another Pacifico so fast I think my head's gonna spin right off, but the man who's buying hasn't even touched his beer; he just sits there looking at me with those weird black eyes, and I almost chug my second bottle too. Christ, am I afraid of some guy who's such a big spender the bartender and doorman treat him right? A man who understands my art—who understands *me* like no one ever has?

I look around. The bar's dim but fancy, dark wood and polished brass, "tasteful." It's full but not crowded; and I realize, despite the darkness, that there's nothing but men in here. And only now, slower than a fucking moron, do I realize the Anglo's brought me to the Castro. And I realize he knows me even better than I thought, *far* better: he instantly saw what I've *always* kept hidden.

I never come to the Castro, but not because I'm worried someone from the Mission might see me. Because I got no use for a fucking yuppie haven for diseased Anglo maricónes.

I jump up, enraged. "Pervert, bringing me *here*—!"

His voice is quiet, but when he interrupts I can't keep talking, I've got to hear that smooth soft voice like a black jaguar's pelt; and he says, "Satan, no one here will solicit you. Including me. I brought you here so we can have a drink and quiet conversation."

"Okay," I say, but it isn't okay. My pito's been hard as a crowbar since I first saw his face.

He says, "You are a religious artist, Satan, after your fashion. But I wondered about your lamb-eyed brown Christ in chains, the robe torn off his back, which streams blood as he is flogged by caricatures of Reagan and Clinton and the Pope. For one of your works, it seemed unusually sympathetic to Jesus—"

"I was showing how presidents and priests use religion to oppress the people!" I'm shouting, I can't help it. My parents were born in the U.S., but they're no better off than illegals, and it doesn't have to be that way— but they bought the whole nine yards of Catholic bullshit. I'm falling into memory, of being hungry all the time; of ten, twelve, fourteen kids and two adults living in two rooms. Of sitting in church, nine years old, choking on incense and summer heat, as the priest described how all people like me burn in Hell for being what God made them.

The angel-faced man says, "Do you believe in God?"

"There is no God," I say. "There is no Devil. Jesus was a fraud, the priests are charlatans."

He puts his white hands together, propping his chin on his fingertips. "I have sometimes imagined how you might paint the walls of Mission Dolores."

"Fuck, I can't imagine a more public canvas! I don't need no more jail time, man."

"It is regrettable," the Anglo says. "It would have been an exquisitely suitable canvas for your portrait of the Pope sodomizing the sombreroed Mexican peasant stereotype. I do wish John Paul could have seen it."

"You're lucky *you* saw it. It was painted over at *dawn*, man. Nothing lasts."

"Not so."

"Even the Catholic Church will turn to dust some day!"

"You should paint on canvas, Satan—"

" 'Ey, man, I'm a bomber, not a fucking *artiste!*"

"Spray your visions on vast canvases, and I will show them in my gallery—"

"So I can be Flavor of the Month for rich, bored Anglos?"

"No," he says. "Paint on canvas so your work will live longer than a night. Your art is important, Satan. It should be seen. It should live forever. *You* should live forever."

"Nice fantasy, dude. More likely I'll die tomorrow."

"You need never worry about death again. You need never worry about a drive-by shooting, or AIDS, or any disease, even if you have it now." He leans forward. "You may live forever, if you choose."

I ought to be howling my ass off over this crazy bullshit, but I got to *make* myself laugh. "That is one *desperate* come-on, puto. Nobody lives forever!"

But I know he's not desperate, not someone so impossibly handsome. Not someone so deadly *serious*. His face is intent as the Angel of Death; his black eyes are like the stars of Hell, burning me so I shiver with cold.

"Nobody?" he asks softly. "I remember the raising of Mission Dolores. I remember the Inquisition. I remember the Christians and the lions."

I want to laugh, but my throat is, like, sealed with ice.

"So few of this generation know history." His eyes pin me like a spike through the chest. "But I see you understand, cholo. I am ancient. I am immortal. I am a vampire."

You can't steal spraycans that're locked up by law, so a bomber in California needs money; more money than I make at the video store. But it's easy to score a quick twenty or fifty if you know the right places to go; and one time I met this dude who said he was a vampire, scraping his blunt teeth on my neck to get himself off. Lots of fucked-up fetishes out there; blood-sucking is hardly the weirdest, man.

But the angel-faced man isn't a fetishist.

He says, "I offer you life eternal."

Nothing lasts forever. Except the eternal nothing of death. But to live longer than threescore years and ten . . . maybe *much* longer . . .

If he's been alive so fucking long, why hasn't everyone in the world been turned into vampires by now? Blood-sucking alone must not turn somebody into a vampire. Maybe he's lying so he can drain me dead without a struggle. Well, I'm a fag, a hustler, a dropout, a bomber, a kid who wasn't down with the neighborhood gang, a street kid for a few months. Mi vida loca! I never expected to make it to sixteen.

Vampires are supernatural. If a supernatural creature's real, maybe God exists. And El Diablo . . . A vampire stays alive—undead—for centuries, but nothing in this world lasts forever, and the vampires are the Devil's creatures, they're *damned;* when a vampire's destroyed, his soul goes down to Hell and the fires of eternal torment!

Shit, I can't believe what I'm thinking! The Catholic Church sinks its superstitious claws so fucking deep. There's no God. And if there is, *fuck* Him, I've been Hell-bound since conception.

The vampire says, "Will you accept my gift of immortality?"

"Yes!"


I've been with a lot of guys; but I never been to bed with someone. But he lays me back on his wide bed, on sleek, fine sheets, and his hands are so smooth and sure I know I'm going off like a skyrocket in about two seconds. Only suddenly he clamps his thumb and finger in a way that stops me. "I adore a hot-blooded lover," he says, smiling. His eyeteeth are sharp, I never saw how sharp, and they're growing longer.

And he closes his mouth on my cock and sinks his fangs into my flesh.


The draining seemed to go on for hours, and the pleasure only grew and grew, impossibly, until I couldn't stop screaming.

And when it's over, I never felt so exhausted, so *weak*, I just want to sleep for a week, a year, forever—but he's grabbing my head and shoving my lips against his wrist and saying, "Drink! Damn you, Satan, *drink* or you're dead!"

My lips are wet. Suddenly I've never been so thirsty in my life, and I'm drinking, gulping his blood like beer. Christ, this is disgusting! And I can't stop.

"Enough!" he says, and pulls me away, and I'm sated and so alive—

"Wake up, Satan."

My eyes open to darkness, no lights, heavy curtains over the windows, but I can see fine. And I see him standing beside his bed. *Our* bed. He's wearing his trenchcoat, jeans, boots; he never took them off. He throws my clothes on top of me, stinking of last night's sweat, and says, "Night has returned. We must feed. Get up."

I want to pull him down on me and feel what I felt last night, and make him feel the same way, but I get out of bed. I'm freezing cold, dressing as fast as I can, but I'm slower than a dying snail; I can barely even stand. I never had enough to eat when I was growing up, but I've never been *this* all-consuming hungry!

No—*thirsty*.

"When do we drink?" I whisper.

"Soon," he says.

I'm asking to drink blood? Christ, I *am* a vampire, condemned by God to Hell—

Oh, *right!* There's no God. But there are vampires, and I've become a vampire. I'm going to live forever!

He starts talking out of left field: "Satan, I know you're not a reader." I don't want him thinking I'm stupid, I want to tell him I've read tons of Anglo novels; nobody else in my family liked to read and for sure wouldn't try to read anything in English, and that was the only privacy I had when I was growing up. But I don't say anything; getting my jeans on is taking all my strength, and he's still talking in that beautiful dark voice. "However, I am sure you've seen many trashy horror movies and picked up many foolish ideas about coffins and garlic and stakes through the heart. Most of what you've heard is utter nonsense. But there *are* two things which will kill a vampire." My head jerks up. "Vampires must drink blood every night and sleep every day. Sunlight and unsatisfied thirst destroy us utterly, with no hope of revival."

I can deal with that, for such a tremendous gain.

"You've given me eternal life, man, and I don't even know your name."
He says, "You will call me Master."

What! I try to tell him *I'm not into S&M*, I try to tell him *I never had a lover before, I don't want to play bullshit hustler games with my lover*, but I hear myself saying, "Yes, Master."

"I made you a vampire. You are my slave." He turns away. "Follow me."

I try to yell *No!* but I say, "Yes, Master," and follow him out of the bedroom.

In the dark hallway I see two people, a black woman and a white man, both young and beautiful—and they both got fangs. They're glaring at me with angry, jealous eyes. And I hate them, because I know he made them vampires, years or centuries before I was born, and for all that time he's been giving them the inhuman ecstasy he gave me last night.

"These are two of my slaves," he tells me. How many slaves has he made over the years? The *centuries?* "Therese, Clausius, this is Satan. Do not touch him or harm him in any manner."

"No, Master," they say in unison.

He gives me the same command about them, and orders me to follow him out of his house. It's a fancy Victorian near Duboce Park—I never noticed last night. Somewhere down the hill a car stereo's blasting; distance and the bass boom should make it mush, but I recognize the song, The Jam's "Beat Surrender," something I haven't heard since I was a niño mas pequeño and my oldest brother worked at Tower. Fucking incredible, I hear every note like I'm wearing the best Walkman headphones in the world.

We're crossing the park under the winter stars; they're bright as the sun to me now. I'm never going to see the sun again. I worked afternoons at the store and nights at my art, I didn't give a shit about the sun—but suddenly I miss it terribly. Because I will never see it again. I'm trapped in darkness. I'm a slave. I'm screaming.

The people at the N Judah Metro station glance at me and look away, just like I would've yesterday. This is the city. Strange shit happens all the time. Shit that ain't any of your business, so you better ignore it. Otherwise it might kill you.

"Silence!" Master says, and I shut up mid-scream and follow him across the lightrail tracks, staggering with hunger. I can smell every one of the passengers waiting for the Metro, smell all the flavors of sweat, cologne, tobacco smoke—I smell their *blood*. I want to leap on that plump Asian prettyboy and rip him open with my teeth and drink like a borracho who's been in the dry tank for months and just found a bottle of Night Train.

I follow Master, and when we're alone he speaks. "There is no need to stalk prey, no need to take humans against their will. That way lies discovery, and destruction. In all the centuries I have been alive, it has always been possible to find people who will let you drink their blood under the guise of sex, if you don't take from the neck—everyone *knows* vampires have to drink from the jugular vein. Usually your prey will not even notice you're taking blood, because they've never experienced pleasure as intense as you are giving them."

I want to speak and I can't. So I put one hand on my cojones and the other on his.

He knocks my hand off. "Don't touch me unless I tell you to! Vampires don't come. It's not possible for the undead."

I want to howl with rage, but I'm bound to silence. I want to knock him down and tear him to shreds, but I can't touch him. I try to prove Master a liar, but no matter how I touch myself or what I think about, I'm dead meat. Just like when I woke up. Why didn't I realize what that meant? I always wake up hard. The vampire's taken away the only pleasure I ever had outside of art, and never told me I'd lose it.

What else didn't he tell me?

Why didn't I ask?

And now I can't speak, and anyway, it's too late for questions. Far too late.


"Never let anyone know where you live," Master commanded, so it's in the leather bar he's brought me to that I learn to feed. When my fangs enter his groin, my prey thinks I'm going to bite off his cock and yells, *"Don't!"* But instantly I'm drinking his blood with the full strength of my terrible hunger, and instantly he stops complaining and starts coming. He's lost in the same impossible pleasure I knew last night, for the first and last time.

There's pleasure in feeding. Heat spreads through me like lava; my hunger's getting satisfied, and it never felt so good. But it's the pleasure of arousal, not release.

Master's nowhere near me, but I hear his voice clear: "Stop, Satan!" I stop and the guy collapses, groaning, against the padded wall of the back room. But it's not enough. I feed several more times, and Master stops me every time. He says I must learn self-control. To keep me from draining my prey dead, and revealing our existence to the world.


The bar has closed and we're walking through the darkness to Master's house when he says, "Satan, your canvases await."

"Master?" I say uncertainly.

"Your art must live," Master says. "I have filled my house with blank canvas and every tint of spraypaint my slaves could find. You must re-create your lost art for the ages. The world needs your vision!"

My vision—what kind of vision is it to throw up murals I've already done? I've finished them; I've spoken; and they're gone. Nothing lasts. Nothing is *meant* to last forever.

But he has spoken; I have no choice. "Yes, Master."

"You will re-create all your paintings—save one. Do not paint last night's mural. The crucifixion. The cross would burn your fingers, and your sight."

I suddenly remember him saying, *I prefer it when you paint something I can look at without burning my eyes.* O God, You *are* real! And I am damned—

Master's watching me expectantly. I must respond. "I understand, Master."

"Is something wrong, Satan?"

"I'm just wondering, Master." I force my voice to keep steady. "What should I paint first?"

"I don't care what you paint first. You're the artist. Do what you must."

"Yes, Master."


This is the last hour of darkness, and when the sun rises, Master said, sleep comes. And I've lost a lot of time because the spraycans all had wack stock tips, most of 'em useless and the rest I had to cut just to be able to draw a line; and the slaves didn't think to buy me markers or paint sticks. At least Master listened when I said I couldn't work if I knew anyone was watching me, and let me shut the door of my room.

The room assigned to me. I am to sleep alone.

But finally I'm done fixing tips, and I pull back the heavy black drape. Half the sky's a washed-out blue; sunrise is near. I slip out of my room and close the door and sneak downstairs, wary as a kitten in a room full of pitbulls. I see no one. The house screams money, and age. It feels like a museum: empty, full of paintings and sculpture from a jumble of ages, ancient Greece, the Renaissance, twentieth century—Christ, is that an original El Greco? What else does he—

I can't stay! The front door opens without a sound, and I'm running. Running to the Mission.

I keep glancing back, but see no pursuit. Still, I run as fast as I can. I pass cars speeding to beat a red light. I'm flush with blood and energy; my strength's more than I'd ever imagined. I'm carrying this huge armload of spraycans and I'm running farther than I ever liked to *walk*, and I'm not even winded when I see my destination.

Of course not. I don't breathe anymore.

I feel so fucking *alive*, but I'm not. Can an undead man create? Master is sure I can; but he's no creator. He feeds off other people's art like he does their bodies. Is it because the undead can't create? Did my art die when I did?

I'm stupid enough to glance up, and the rooftop crosses scorch my eyes. I shove the cans into one arm and rub my eyes and blink till I'm not blind anymore. I wipe my hand on my T-shirt. My fingers leave red streaks.

I run across the street, and my chosen canvas is before me. The Mission Dolores.

The Sixteenth Street wall, over half the size of the block. Huge and blank and scary. But suddenly the lines are flowing out of me, forming the image that's suddenly burning my mind—I'm dead, yeah, but I'm still an artist!

I hear honking horns and angry shouts that fade fast when the cars are past; I hear the disbelieving curses and quick prayers of people walking by. Dawn's an ungodly hour, but San Francisco never sleeps; and the morning commute's in full effect.

In the city, people mind their own business; but graffiti on Mission Dolores is *blasphemy* in this superheavy Catholic neighborhood. But so far nobody's tried to stop me. They should thank God they haven't. I won't be stopped. I *can't* be stopped. Not by anything human.

I've always done murals, so I've always painted characters: cartoon characters and powerful people turned into cartoons. This time there can be no caricature.

I paint faster than I ever did before. Superhuman speed. But can I finish before sunrise?

I know la policia are being called, from some cellular phone, or an apartment overlooking my canvas. I hate cops—pigs, always hassling street kids, arresting them, beating them, raping them. Goddamn scum of the earth! But they'll investigate. They won't ignore a brazen bastard spray-painting the wall of Mission Dolores. They won't ignore an accusation this fucking dramatic.

I never threw up old-school graffiti pieces, but now I make big fat bubble letters, writing fast and furious. I don't know his name, but I'm writing TORTURER and MURDERER and SERIAL KILLER, and his address, under my lifesize, realist portrait of Master.

He'll be asleep by the time the cops arrive. I imagine the cops breaking in and dragging him out into the light of day, screaming in terror as the sun blasts him to dust. Madre de Dios, I wish I could see it!

According to this novel I read once, when a vampire master's destroyed, his slaves are freed. But there's no guarantee I've caused Master's destruction. He's probably already realized that the directions he gave me—*You're the artist. Do what you must*—were too vague. Maybe he's already out of the house, racing the sun to track me down with his sharp vampire nose.

Only one more thing, and my portrait will be done!

Suddenly my energy's flowing out of me like the sweat used to. I fall against the wall, my arms dropping like lead weights. I'm in shadow, but the sun's come over the horizon. My body *knows*.

I drag my hand up and sign my name, a big bold tag. It looks like *his* name. *Satan*.

"*Judas!*" The harsh screech fills my ears as he collides with me. My knees smash into the wall, but I don't feel pain. I'm imprisoned in his arms, thrashing weakly, helplessly, and Master's running west through shadow, holding me up like it's an effort, but not too great; you live for centuries, you learn to deal with the exhaustion of dawn. His face is wrapped in a scarf and shades, but I feel his eyes burning me from behind the black lenses. "I give you eternal life and you repay me with betrayal! You are *dead!*"

I was dead the moment I decided to come to Mission Dolores and paint his portrait under the dawn sky. But oh God, I've failed to destroy him! He's seen what I've done, he's going to get out of the city, get *away!*

He wouldn't've come after me now if he didn't have boltholes all over the city. He's taking me to some dark safe space. Sadistic bastard, he'll tie me up and watch the thirst kill me! I fight as hard as I can, but I'm a feeb. I can't escape his grip. I'll die, and he won't.

I draw up my legs and smash my feet into the wall.

Master goes spinning into the street. We land on the hood of a car and the sunlight falls across us, and my arms and the hair on my head burst into flames.

"*No!*" Master screams, struggling to get away. But I'm on top of him, and I got my arms around him now, and I keep him pinned. My fangs tear off the scarf and glasses, exposing his face to the sun.

Undead flesh doesn't feel pain—but the flames are *agony!* We scream like babies. I can hardly see for the smoke pouring off his flesh, and the sun's stolen all my strength, but nothing can stop me from holding Master in the sunlight. Giving him a foretaste of eternal Hellfire.

I never believed in God, and I was wrong. But I was damned before I ever became a vampire.

Master falls silent. His head's a pile of ash, his body flat under mine. Destroyed *at last!*

My arms fall to pieces. My head's on fire. Soon I join Master in death. He didn't listen. He didn't understand. Nothing lasts.

Except Hell.

F Blo B

Blood muse